GJS II

by

Shawn Stewart Ruff

JEWELLS

1

The whiff of baby poo looks bad for me. I crack open the car window hoping Stepmom won't notice before we get to the mall that I fuckin' forgot to put Alyssa's Pamper on. I can picture the plastic thing sitting on my dresser, right next to my Civics book where I left it, and my little baby step-sis' pootie how I left it, baby-powdered and velcroed in pee-proof Dr. Seuss shorts.

So I'm like, "Dad must've told you Coach McGlad said he's gonna let me play first string this season?"

She goes, "He didn't, but you know how your father is."

So I go, "Well, he should have, it's a big deal."

Then she's like, "He meant to, I'm sure, you know your father means well. If he doesn't mention it tonight, I'll prod him. Of course, it'll be redundant, since you're about to tell me all about it, but it'll make the point that he's not exactly present."

What? I know the Pamper has got me all paranoid and shit, but she speaks in this annoying way like she's reading from a teleprompter, with this say-cheese smile on her face, which I guess is like a habit from her old job as the host of *Today In Cincinnati*, which she was just before she hooked up with my dad.

So then she goes, "And . . . why's it a big deal?"

"It means that I'm top quarterback on the team, so one of the top quarterbacks citywide. And the funny thing is, I didn't even try out for quarterback . . . I tried out for running back, and that's why I was third string and sat on the bench all last year."

"I see this as yet another example of how you underestimate yourself."

"Yeah, okay." But I'm really like, what the fuck is she talkin' about?

Then she goes, "Why didn't you try out for quarterback?"

"I dunno. I guess I only saw myself at the receiving end … and I'm kind of tall for a quarterback."

"Be grateful. It's been proven that being tall and attractive will pay off in your earnings potential."

And I'm like, "Yeah, okay, Mom," but I'm thinking, I can't stand talking to her. Her sunglasses are as big as fuckin' knee guards, so it's more difficult to figure out my next move. I'm staring at her hands on the steering wheel when all of a sudden this light beam from her diamond wedding ring scans me like a barcode for bullshit. Now I'm worried on top of being paranoid as hell. I mean, should I just bring up the Pamper screwup and deal with the fallout? I can already hear her bitch: "Jewells, this is really an impossible situation. What, if anything, were you thinking?" Cleaning up baby poo is like fuckin' gross, so I always leave the room when the Pamper comes off. And it's not just the smell, the baby private parts totally weird me out too — it's like the pootie's making faces at me, like it wants to say, "Jewells, what a loser you are to be cleaning up baby poo."

And Stepmom knows I hate baby poo, and hate even more the runny baby poo Pamper. I'm thinking the only reason she made me change Alyssa in the first place was to trip me up. See, I'm this fuckin' close to finishing driver's ed, but the fact that she won't ever let me drive doesn't bother me at all. I mean, normally I don't need her for anything, only now I do need her, 'cause Dad's stuck in Chicago and my scrimmage is tomorrow. It was supposed to be just me and him hanging out today for my pre-birthday, and I would've gotten cleats and whatever else I wanted, but as usual he like fuckin' punks out on me. I'm like, never mind that I don't get why he had to go on a one-day trip to Chicago, when he's only in town with us for like five fuckin' days, and when we haven't seen him in like seven fuckin' weeks. He says he came home to celebrate my birthday, but it's not 'til Wednesday. Which is like two days from now, but watch, shit'll happen and he'll have to rush back to D.C., where he lives most of the time now. So fuckin' typical. I'm like, it's cool though, 'cause he promised me these bad-ass sneakers that I've been wanting like forever, ever since I saw them last week, and that's all

I care about anyway. I'm counting on styling in them later tonight, 'cause some of my boys at school are taking me out for my pre-birthday. Except now Stepmom's in the way, running interference. Dad said she will buy me what I want, but now, 'cause of the Pamper crap, maybe not. Yeah, it's my fault. Like, I fucked up, I know it. I gave her ammo to take me down. Like, I was totally hip to her trying to trip me up and muck up my plans, but then my girl Sophie called and started talking about the tonguing she was gonna give me later, so I was thinking about her pootie, not baby sis', and so, here we are . . .

So I crack the window a little wider, letting in toxic interstate air, then I turn to see poopie Alyssa and her doppelganger behind me, slobbering on pacifiers and fast asleep in their car seats. I'm like, how can she sleep in shit? Maybe she just has bad gas. Maybe it's not her stinking, maybe it's one of my stepbrothers. It's hard to know which one. It's like crazy, because since the girls were born, my brothers are identical-twin-wannabes, like synchronized swimmers or some shit. One is six and the other's like almost five I think, and they look nothing alike — one chocolate like Dad and me, the other light like Stepmom and the girls. They're riding in the cargo hold of the Suburban, playing games or something. 'Cause of all the screaming and hollering, it's usually like fuckin' insane riding with all of them, so I avoid it like the baby poo. But now I wish one of them would like hit or throw something at the other, just so I wouldn't have to deal with Stepmom.

Shazam, the carphone rings!

"Mr. Saunders," Stepmom goes, talking to the windshield.

"Mrs. Saunders," Dad goes, through the car speakers. "What's the plan?"

"We're all here, all but Mutti, she didn't make it back in time, she'll meet us at the Greenages. The traffic's not bad on 71, and we're only maybe ten minutes from Parisienne Mall."

"Jewells, too?"

"Yes, of course. He's sitting right next to me."

"Driving, I hope?"

"No, not driving. I'm driving."

"Why isn't he driving, Margeaux? I asked you to —"

"We're on speaker, Griffin."

"Jewells, Jewells," his voice calls out to me.

"Dad?" I shout.

"Hey son, listen, my good friend over in Erlanger got some box seats for the game against the Cardinals on Saturday coming. How's that for a birthday present?"

"Sure, Dad. That'd be great. But I thought you were leaving on Thursday?"

"I've changed my mind. I'm gonna stay."

"Wow, I can't wait then."

"I'll see you at home a little later. My flight's at seven, so hopefully by nine or ten."

"Sure, Dad."

"Margeaux, take me off speaker, please."

She goes, "Griffin, that would be distracting since I'm obviously driving. I'll call you when we get to the mall."

"It's just a button, Margeaux. Just push the button and —"

"And then I'll have to hold the handset. I don't have the earpiece in, and it pinches my ear. I'll have to remove my earring, I'm wearing the Bulgari nuggets."

"Well . . ."

He totally chumps out, like he always does, like he's afraid of her, like she'll crack or something if anything upsets her, and I watch her finger trace along the line of her lip like it's sharpening steel, while the stink of baby poo circles my way, and hers too, 'cause she looks up at the rear view mirror, her nose pugged.

"Mr. Saunders, this isn't a good time," she goes. Dad switches to playback mode, repeating himself, "Hopefully I won't be too late tonight, dear."

"Fine, dear, we'll go over things when you get home . . . whenever that is, hopefully not too late." She disconnects him, pausing to press the hair down around her temples, before saying to me, "Sorry."

But I'm like, she totally isn't sorry — she's pissed, I can feel it. I'm thinking, like if this was a scene from *South Park*, right now the car would go into a 360 tailspin and roll over a couple times, then double-flip, explode, and like we'd all be spurting cartoon blood, but none of us would actually be hurt, in our cartoon bandages only for a hot few seconds, and Stepmom would by some miracle be a better person, and so not hold the Pamper debacle against me, until something else pisses her off, then it's game-on with the same shit all over again.

It's all real though, too real for words — like the stink of baby poo.

Straight ahead and just over the hill, I can see the Parisienne Mall. Thank God. As my Meemaw used to say, "Praise be," 'cause in a minute I'll be out of this fuckin' car and away from Stepmom and the baby goon squad. I can picture myself lacing up the sneakers I'm getting, and I pray to God that they'll be on my feet. I'm interrupted when Stepmom's scary sunglasses glance my way, and then she goes, "Jewells, let's not be at odds with each other. I'm really not as hard on you as you think I am."

I'm like, "Oh, okay . . . well, like, from my perspective, it, uh, feels like you are, but that's just my interpretation, obviously."

She goes, "It's just that you seem to delight in trying our patience. Your father and I are worried about you. We really are."

"I don't know about delight . . . Lock, Mom, I know this is about school, right? You want me to do better, I know that. I mean, like Coach McGlad even said I have to pull up my grades, like you've been saying all along. I will, you'll see."

"I hope so, Jewells." Then, in her best teleprompted voice she goes, "I truly truly do. Your future is at stake. Both your father and I feel that your education is the most important thing, and there's no excuse for barely passing given all the resources you have at your disposal. I had extracurriculars too, just like you — beauty pageants, modeling, what have you. And your father was a ballplayer in undergrad and even worked a job through business school, as you know —"

I'm like, okay, let's get it right: "And, maybe you didn't know, but the job he had was really about paying my expenses when he left me with Meemaw —"

"Well, that was part of his school expenses. The point is, we all have busy lives, and there's no reason you can't get through your homework after throwing a football all day. What kind of example are you setting for your brothers and the girls?"

"I know, Mom . . ." Right now, I like totally fuckin' hate calling her Mom — it kills me to call her that — but it would be so much worse for me if I didn't. " . . . but school is just hard for me."

"Because you don't apply yourself."

"I do."

She goes, "Let's get back to the subject at hand, let's talk about your birthday. Your father and I are at an impasse. He inconveniences and tests me by asking me to buy sneakers for you, and he also puts me in an awkward position because I don't believe in it."

I'm like, "What's there to believe in sneakers?"

And she goes, "This isn't as harsh as it seems, but there will be no sneakers. Punishment is punishment, and you're still on yours. And the only reason we're going to the mall now is because you need the cleats by tomorrow, and your sisters and the boys have a birthday party and playdate in Indian Hill with Astrid's twins; and yes, that's Astrid Marcson of *Sunday in Cincinnati*. Otherwise you'd get a cake, candles, ice cream, a gift of our choosing, not yours, and the *Happy Birthday* song, just like the other children."

"But Mom, Dad promised you would get me the sneakers too."

"He also said I should let you drive us around."

"Hey, it's called a learner's permit for a reason."

"It's your best accomplishment so far, but I believe in rewarding good behavior, not indulging a...."

"A what?"

Yeah, I know she wants to say something else, but being the fake person she is she would never. She rubs her lips together, and then turns toward the wing mirror, but I can see her jaw muscles bench-pressing with nerve.

"A what? You don't believe in indulging a . . . what?"

"I was going to say, I don't believe in indulging bad

behavior."

"But Dad said . . ."

And she goes, "Lower your voice, please." She looks at herself in the rearview mirror, smushes her lips together, then slides the sunglasses down again, and goes, "Take that up with your father."

"What do you mean?"

"Jewells, I can't bear this ugliness from you."

"What's ugly about trying to understand —"

"I won't indulge you in a pair of $325 sneakers, period."

"Mom, it's my pre-birthday and I'm going out tonight, Dad said I could."

"I'm not too happy about you going out either." Sniffing like a cat, she like zeroes in on the twins. One of them makes faces. "Did Mommy's girls make a poopie?"

"Like what am I supposed to wear?"

"One of the twenty pairs of sneakers you already have should do just fine."

"Mom!" It's Fletcher shouting from the back. "Why do we have to go to the mall when we're supposed to go to Chelsey's birthday party?"

"Your father's had a scheduling difficulty, and the mall's on our way. Your brother's got a football game tomorrow . . . remember? I told you that."

"Are we almost there?" shouts the other one. I turn around just in time to see Percy stick his tongue out at me.

"Soon enough." And then, glancing toward me, her big ugly sunglasses like something cyborg, she goes, "Jewells, you know, there's more to life than sneakers. A nice pair of loafers, for instance."

"Mom, I have to tinkle," Fletcher shouts.

"Hold it, honey, we'll be there soon, it's just a few minutes away."

"I have to go now. I'm gonna tinkle on myself."

I so hate them all. For real, the boys, more than the baby girls, get on my fuckin' last nerve. The whole make-Jewells-change-baby-diapers bullshit began with them, them with their peepees like little squirt guns. Some shrink told Stepmom and Dad that wiping baby ass would help me bond . . . I mean, if that isn't the most whacked thing I ever heard! I mean, like the only thing worse than baby pooties is baby peepees, and I bet both of my stepbrothers are gonna grow up to be little weird dickheads and my sisters little cunts.

The Parisienne Mall looms like a strip mall-styled Oz at the end of the expressway ramp, and then it's all up in my face as Stepmom navigates to the Saks Fifth Avenue side. I turn around and I can see the growing wet baby poo stain around Alyssa's pootie. Soon as Stepmom parks, I fuckin' jump out the car, and before slamming the door I tell her I'll go and pick out the cleats and I'll come right back, and then she can go in with her credit card. I want to say that none of this would be necessary if she hadn't persuaded Dad to freeze my credit card, but I don't. She's like "Wait," but I'm playing defense like I'm being chased by tackles.

And I'm like halfway across the parking lot when she screams "JEWELLS, YOU LET ALYSSA COME OUT WITH NO PAMPER ON."

Fuckkkkkkkkk! I pretend I don't hear and keep stepping.

Serves her right.

But I'm sooo screwed.

I hope she calms down by the time I'm done, but then like the phone starts ringing and then it dings for an incoming text message: JEWELLS!!

Fuck, I'm standing in front of the mall entrance, staring at the danish spackled with icing on display at the Cinnabon shop just on the other side of the double doors, and I'm thinking about how good it would taste when the memory of baby poo makes me want to vomit. I know sure as shit, Stepmom will be pissed off 'til hell freezes over.

I don't look back.

Now I'm heading to the Feet First store but get stopped before I put a foot in the entrance by a dirty-blond babe in tennis short-shorts.

She goes, "Aren't you Jewells Saunders? You quarterback for Roger Bacon, right?"

I'm like, "Yeah," and I'm totally loving the flirt in her gray eyes.

"Blaine Kaufmann," she goes, reaching for my hand. "Erny Kaufmann's my twin."

"Oh wow, like y'all favor. Guess that's why I'm thinking we met before?"

"No," she giggles. "I go to Ursuline Academy. But I've seen you play, and you're like awesome."

"Tite."

"Erny didn't say you were coming to our pool party tonight, but I hope you will."

"Erny didn't say his sister was all that."

"Erny wouldn't."

"Erny's a dick." I do a quick recon. "Yo, sorry, Blaine. I'll check you out later, but I gotta run now."

"Serious?"

"For real."

"You know where we live?"

"Wyoming, right?"

"Just off Compton Road. Dude, promise you'll come." She seals it with an air kiss of glossy lips that says "cum on me." Tite!

"Yeah, I'll be there."

Watching her walk away, I'm like fuck the cleats — for real, there's nothing wrong with my old cleats! I'll get the shoes, and Dad can buy the cleats, since he's the one that fucked everything up. I've got like two hundred in my pocket, and Stepmom can charge the rest.

But the baby poo, the Pamper — it's like so over, I know it. I go in the Feet First thinking I'll get nothing.

The sneakers I want are Nike but then I notice the new Air Jordans on display. Silver leather with this chrome-like detailing going on. After me and the salesman dude go "Wassup," I have him bring me out a size fourteen just to see. This salesman calls out the fact that they are like ridiculous, plus they're twice the cost of the Nikes, but I'm like fuck that, nothing comes close to the sneakers of my dreams. Like wearing Lamborghinis on your feet, versus the Corvette — apples and oranges. But when they are side by side, my feet are kickin and saying all the right words, so now I want both. No, I should just get the Air Jordans — like, not every homie can afford them, and that's also why I gotta have 'em. So I sit down to tie these bad boys up, checking them out — I even pull my pant legs up but that's like too punk — and then notice the salesman go in the backroom. First he pokes his head in, shouts some shit at someone, and then he just disappears like I'm not there. And no one is around, just me, the Air Jordans and the bad boy Nikes I dream about. I could walk right out of the store, right this fuckin' minute, and touchdown. So I'm staring at the entrance, wondering if it's wired with sirens and cams. But right when I'm about to make my move, the salesman comes back — I don't know this scrawny dude but if I did, maybe we could like work something out. Fuck it, I tell him my mom will be in right behind me to charge them. He's like "cool," when I ask him to box the sneakers up so she can't see.

So then I run outside, and I'm standing there feeling lost in the black hole of the parking lot. I wander over to where she parked, but I don't see the car anywhere. The Suburban is so visible, it's pretty cool. It's got blackened windows, short antennas and a cryptic license plate, the inside is like fuckin' Madonna's ride — and it's definitely gone.

Fuck me. I stare at the phone. The first message from Stepmom growls: "Jewells, I'm very upset and disappointed right now. I don't *believe* you deliberately let Alyssa come out here without a Pamper on—"

I delete without hearing the rest.

Dad doesn't answer his phone — and never does when you need him. So I leave a long message telling him about the cleats, the Pamper and baby poo, that he'll have to get the cleats for me — fuck it, I deploy "Stepmom" very carefully, like only when I want him to know that I'm like so fuckin' done, and he gets it, just as I get it when he says "Mar-go" like he's about to lose it — if only he would, just once, not for me but for his own damn self-respect. Then I go back inside to tell the sales dude to hold them for me, feeling like a total loser.

So I'm like, who can I call? Uncle Chief? Yeah, and he'll be giving me a birthday present anyway. But then Dad will be really pissed if I tell Uncle Chief what's up, and shit will really hit the fan then, spraying baby poo from East Walnut Hills to D.C. and back. I made that mistake once before, when the beauty queen talked Dad into putting me in juvie for a day.

Situation All Totally Fucked Up!

'Cause of Uncle Chief working for the Clinton White House, reporters sometimes hit Dad and Stepmom up, and I'm not supposed to say anything if one comes up to me. If only one would right now, man, I would so like to comment.

2

The back of LoQuan's ride is like five to ten inches shorter it's been jacked up so many times. Fuck me, exhaust fumes screw into my head and I can't breathe without it stinging, plus pretty boy LoQuan is wearing some kind of cologne that smells like room deodorizer. I've got the window wide open, and we shout to hear each other over the beats of DMX. But soon as we stop, it's toxic again. I'm like, bad as I want to drive, get my license and my own car, ain't nothing happening with his piece-a-shit Ford Escort.

LoQuan goes, "Jewells, man, I wish I had your $300 to give you back. Things be squeezed up my way. They ain't called me at the golf course yet, so I ain't got a summer job and no doe-re-me either."

He laughs like something's funny, flips his Aviators up, showing off paperclip eyes and an upper lip like a shrimp roll. Add the cocoa-brown-black skin and long down-to-his-butt wavy hair all the chicks envy, and you get a real exotic foreigner-looking dude alright, like somebody from someplace that only a couple dudes know about, like Bora Bora. But at the same time, he's all Lockland ghetto— and way too pretty for the golf course, and I wanna tell him that only Republican, all American-looking dudes need apply for caddy. Even better if they're black, the golf course doesn't discriminate in that way.

Then he goes, "Yo, Jewells, man, I gotta say, shit be pretty fucked up when you asking a broke-ass nigga like me for money. Yo, I should be hitting you up for money, you and your rich-ass family."

"Man, you been owing me the $300 for going on six months now, and I'm not asking."

"Yo, I know, but like you know how it is."

"Things are . . . be difficult my way, too."

"Meaning for you?"

LoQuan laughs like I'm full of shit. That's the problem with lame homies like him, they think they the only ones it's fucked up for.

And I'm like, "Yeah. Punishment. Stepmom ordered my dad to take my credit card away and cut my phone time down to 200 minutes and 300 text messages. Like what'em I gonna do with fuckin' 200 minutes and 300 text messages? That's like a day for me."

"Jewells, what you done did this time?"

"Nothing. No juvie stuff, I swear. It's school. The only thing I like is animation."

"That like cartoons?"

"Yeah, but I'm talking video games."

"You know how to do that shit?"

"Yeah. I mean like what you expect? Every year my school sends dudes to the Big Ten and the Ivy Leagues, or that's what the brochure says."

"That's deep."

It's not deep, but I'm like, "Fuck me, I wanna go to a dumb-ass school like yours."

And he goes, "All school's a fuckin' waste of time. Man, why don't they make a course like Beats 101? Or Advanced Rhyming? Or the Art of Blunt Rolling?"

"Right. I could pass that!"

"You still be getting D's!"

"C minuses."

"And like you'd be valedictorian of your class. Nigga, what you gonna say to inspire your class of graduates?"

"Fuck y'all, all y'all."

And we crack up, and I forget how pissed I am.

Then he goes, "Jewells, man, I can't believe none of your rich-ass friends got three hundred dollars to give you?"

"No doubt."

"You embarrassed, nigga, that's what's up!"

Fuck me! I *am* embarrassed. And as usual LoQuan hits the nail, it's fuckin' freaky how his broke-ass knows me like a book. I mean, I really do listen to him, literally — like what I know of homie talk I picked up from rap and hiphop videos but mostly from him. We met at juvie last year, and it's the one thing Stepmom did for me that turned out cool. Like, it was fucked up, 'cause what happened was me and a couple of other underage dudes on the tennis team got busted drinking at Tuesdays. Fuck me, it was just our luck to be there when there was some sting operation going on. We all look eighteen, but I had just turned fourteen.

Me and LoQuan hit it off big. When we met, LoQuan was like, "I didn't know they let white boys in here." At first I didn't get that he was talking about me, and when I figured it out it was cool 'cause he's cool, even though there were white boys, three I think, around. And you might think I would have been offended, but instead I was like, what the fuck, this Chinese-eyed, Bora Bora-looking black dude talking like a homie is right, and just then I didn't want to be me, no more the white-black boy, I wanted to be a real homie, not a fake one. I mean, like when I was a kid and lived with Meemaw, all the homies would be laughing calling me white boy or Saltine or Private School, and I was like so offended to where I wouldn't even go out of the fuckin' house. So I'm like, no more white black boy, I'm a homie.

Dad is always telling me to just be true to myself, but this is my true self. He's a hypocrite, 'cause he lets Stepmom harass me . . . and it *is* fuckin' harassment. Like I don't hang with LoQuan all the time, and it's not 'cause he was at juvie for assault. No, I don't know shit about that, just what he told me: "These boys up the way tried to rob me, but yo, I might be a pretty nigga but I was ready for'em, nobody takes my shit." Man, the crap he's seen and been through.

No, I don't hang with him 'cause I don't have my own wheels and my folks would freak if they ever saw us together. Stepmom and Dad divide people into good influences and bad, so LoQuan's just not their kind of people. For real, I like LoQuan that much more 'cause I know how much it would piss them the fuck off.

I'm like, "You know, LoQuan, man, I can't stand home . . . I don't fuckin' wanna be there at all. I'll just get yelled at like I'm fuckin' five . . . man, sometimes I feel like I could just go off on her, she makes me sick."

"I hear that . . . I gotta get my own crib. Just one more year, then I'm eighteen and I'll be out on my own."

"I don't know if I can last that long."

"Man, least wait 'til you got some wheels."

"That's another thing. She's got my old man thinking that I'm too irresponsible to have a car. You believe that? I'll get my driver's license in like a week, and I'll be the only dude

I know that's my age that ain't got wheels."

"Get your own car then."

"How?"

"Work, nigga. You know, job . . . get a job."

"Job, shit, you kidding me? That's for lame niggas like you."

We laugh, but now nothing is funny to me.

"Yo, you got a credit card, so that mean you got credit?" LoQuan says. "You can get a loan."

"How?"

"Just get a credit report. I mean, they'll practically give you a car just because you live in fuckin' Hyde Park."

"Dude, for the tenth time, I don't live in Hyde Park. I live in East Walnut Hills, right on the border with Hyde Park."

"Niggas live in Walnut Hills, ain't none except y'all where you live, and there ain't none in Hyde Park but rich ones like y'all. So you live in Hyde Park to me, and it fuckin' sounds rich."

"Word!" I gotta give my homie props.

"Word."

We crack up, and then he goes on about credit reports again. I've seen ads on TV, but it's real ghetto, seems to me. But it's kinda cool if you can get a fuckin' car out of it.

Then he goes, "Home ain't no happy place. But at least your mom is a babe. Man, she's the finest mom I've ever fuckin' heard of. Like a supermodel, man!"

And I'm like, "LoQuan, that's Stepmom, she ain't
my real mom." My head hurts, and I stick my face out the
car. "And dude, she was not a supermodel, she just did the
catwalk when she was in college, and yeah, she was called an
up-and-coming star in like *Vogue* and *Glamour* magazines. Her
big deal was *Today in Cincinnati*. She was co-host — not even a
weather girl, which I could respect. So get over your Victoria's
Secret panty dreams of her."

"You just jealous, nigga. Your dad . . . man, he's doin it
at the fuckin' top."

"Yeah, at the top! She's mind-fuckin' him . . . that's
what's up. You know what the scheming Miss *Today in
Cincinnati* did? She told my dad that I was a liability for his
career prospects, that he should send me off to military school
before it's too late. She thought I was over in my place —"

"Nigga, you got your own place?"

"Yeah man, it's a little apartment over the carriage-
house garage, which is behind the main house."

"Tite."

"Fuck yeah . . . so, like I was saying, she thought I was
I was in the kitchen but I was in my place, and I heard her on
the phone. She even named the Army and Navy Academy,
like she'd been planning to enlist me there all fuckin' along
and was just waiting for Dad to sign on the dotted line. I
googled that shit. It's in fuckin' sunny San Diego!"

"Wow, that shit's deep. What's career prospects?"

"You know, like, potential."

"What kind of career prospects?"

"Fuck if I know." I did know but I figured it didn't help me none to say my dad's maybe gonna be mayor of this city someday. "And it don't matter none anyway, 'cause nothing I do is right far as she's concerned."

"Man, like you ain't alone, 'cause everybody be wantin' to fuckin' get rid of me too."

"Like I would go to sunny San Diego just to get the fuck away from her and the baby squad!"

"I hear that, Jewells, man. But the military . . . hell naw!"

"You got that shit right."

"Cruel."

I'm so done I can't talk about it.

"Thanks for picking me up," I go, and like curl into the seat, head hurting, wishing he could stay with me in the carriage house. A part of me knows that I should just go home right now and deal with Stepmom and the rest. At least Dad's in town, or will soon be, so he's got my back — but you never know how long he'll be around, or like when he'll wimp out. It didn't used be like that, when it was just me and him, and now it's like all messed up. Everything is fuckin' messed up. I mean, I think about the shoes I won't get, and the party I won't go to, and the pussy I'll be missing tonight, while LoQuan and me like chitty-chitty-bang-bang through the construction maze along the Norwood Lateral intersection.

Fuck me!

And then we like swerve to the Reading Road exit, heading where I don't the fuck know. I'm about to ask, when LoQuan like pulls into this ghetto-looking auto repair and dealer parking lot — Otis' Used Cars is the name of the place — late model Mazdas, Escorts, Celicas.

I'm like, "What we doin here?"

"I wanna show you the ride I'm gettin."

"With what, nigga? You ain't got no job, with your broke ass. Fuck, I don't wanna look at cars."

"Too late, we're here."

"There's no sign that says they take foodstamps."

It's so ghetto too — like thirty cars, dirty looking, and the "t" in the Otis sign stutters, about to go out. We laugh and walk toward the middle of the lot, and he's all wow over this black Miata with a hardtop.

He goes, "Man, I'd kill for this."

"Tite," I go, but it looks like something a chick or a queer would drive, you ask me.

So we get in, LoQuan behind the wheel. My head is like not far from the roof, and my knees are on the dashboard practically, but there's room behind me to let the seat back. LoQuan, like he's in heaven, a pig in shit — he tools the rearview mirror around to make sure that he looks as good as the car.

"Mi-a-ta, Mi-a-ta. Makes my dick hard."

"It's tite."

"Ain't it? Fuck, man, I want this car so bad. My cousin Xenobia works there in credit. And she's like helping me. Soon as I get a job, it's mine."

"What, they holding it for you?"

"Yeah, somethin' like that. I got to get a down payment. We should buy it together, you know, co-own it."

"LoQuan, dude, remember, I don't have money either."

"But you got credit. Xenobia says all I need is some credit and I could get it even without a job."

"I don't have credit."

"See, you do, nigga. Like I said before, you got a credit card, even if it's you daddy's name, it's still your credit. And your credit is backed up by your daddy's, and your daddy's got perfect credit, we know that — the house in Hyde Park, your daddy's Jaguar in the driveway, the Suburban for the supermodel and y'all kids. So all you got to do is give Xenobia your Social Security number, and then we got us a Miata that's mines and yours."

I'm like tite, but then I'm like, what? How we gonna share a car when we live in two different parts of town? This nigga's been owing me $300 for almost as long as I've known him, so he must think I'm completely retard.

He goes, "Man, we'll work out a schedule. And then, in a couple months, we'll get our own crib. Tite?"

"Tite." It's not a real "tite" but a mousy "tite" — and the

nigga knows the difference, but it means beans to him in his Miata daze.

The office is a double-wide trailer, and we go inside. Diet Coke-swilling Xenobia is perched at her desk like a voodoo doll in an Ikea display. Xenobia confirms that I do have credit 'cause I have a credit card, and she takes down my Social Security number to see what else I got. Afterward, she says to us both, "If it's not perfect, and if you can't get a co-signer, no Miata . . . unless you've got cash. You'all maybe do better getting the cash."

Fuck me. Fuck him. Fuck us!

Back in the piece-a-shit Ford Escort, LoQuan says. "How bad you wanna make some money?"

I'm like, I don't answer. My immediate problem is the sneakers, fuck the punk Miata.

"Nigga, I know you heard me."

Sometimes I can't think of the right homie-ism quick enough. When in doubt, add 'fuck' and 'nigga.' "Fuckyeah nigga!"

"I know how we can earn some quick, but . . ."

"No drug dealing or shit that's gonna get me in more trouble again."

"Shit, nigga, you crazy? I'm in foster care because my daddy is dead over some sorry fuckin' crack, well, and some other shit too, so I don't play that."

"Well, what then, nigga?"

"There's this dude lives right up there in Finneytown, off Reagan Highway."

"Okay."

"See, he likes to see a nigga play with his dick."

"Huh?"

"You know. He's a homo. He just likes to watch."

"How you know?"

"I let him look, and he pays me."

"You do what?"

"I let him look and he pays me. I ain't be doing that shit for free. I usually step over there when the money's tight. Once a month, maybe. He pays like fifty."

"I dunno…."

"You got a big piece?"

"No doubt."

"Show me with your fingers."

I do.

"Nice. Mine big too, and uncut. He likes that."

I'm like, this is so sick, but I go, "That's nice," trying not to laugh, complimenting a dude's dick.

"He's always telling me to bring somebody over, but man, most of the niggas around Lockland, they'd go over and rob this dude, and I ain't trying to ruin my gig — that little bit of money is all I got, and it's like timely, you know what I'm saying?"

"LoQuan, man, I dunno."

"If I get him to pay us $200, what you gonna say then?"

"I dunno."

"Nigga, I'll give it all to you . . . for your fuckin' birthday shoes."

"Ask him first."

So LoQuan gets on the cell phone . . . "Yeah, nine inches. Yeah, he big and he's chocolate, he's black mufucka. Yeah, we'll do it for two hundred . . . Okay, one-fifty. Cool. We gotta make a stop first, and then we're on our way. About an hour."

LoQuan looks at me like he's gonna light into me, and then he goes, "He's down. You down?"

I'm like, "You for real, LoQuan, I mean . . . that's all we gotta do?"

"Yeah, just like I said. I been knowing this white mufucka for a long time, since I was in middle school, and he just likes looking at black dick."

"But you a Bora Boran or Uzghur Chinese or something?"

"Nigga, I'm more nigga than you'll ever be."

"And you got the rap sheet to prove it!"

And we're like cracking up. We both high-five, even though I feel bad for him. I got it made compared to him.

"Two hundred ain't one-fifty."

"But it's one-fifty more than you got."

"You for real, he'll pay that much just to watch us?"

"Like I said, he's for real."

"I dunno."

"It's easy money."

"I dunno."

"First of all, you've never been in juvie shit 'cause of me, so let's be clear, nigga. Your white boys the ones corrupting you."

"Check."

"Checkmate, nigga."

"LoQuan, you a faggot or something?" I go, laughing again.

"Not. Just trying to make a buck," he grins. "And you know, a nigga always got to be playing with his dick."

"Tite."

3

Like, I don't know Wyoming, but I know dudes from there. They aren't like dudes I hang with. Most of the dudes I hang with live in Hyde Park, Amberly Village, Finneytown or Kenwood. A couple dudes from Indian Hill, they live in big houses, their folks way richer than mine. I'm talking ridiculous — like, thirty-five rooms, with the maids and the works. The Havenstads' even has a fuckin' stable and like ten horses. Horses, the fuckin' Kentucky Derby could run around their backyard. And this dude on my team I hang with sometimes, Barton Steuffens — the Steuffenses have a driveway that like climbs all the way up a fuckin' mountain. I exaggerate, there ain't any fuckin' mountains in or around Mason, but let's just say they own a big-ass hill and at the bottom of it is the Little Miami River, and the driveway just goes round and up and up and its kinda scary like a horror movie, especially in the summertime when the woods are thick with creepy-crawlies and you can't see shit. But man, scary or not, when Barton's folks go on vacation in July, it's a fuckin' blast. Last year, about three hundred kids showed up from all over. The sheriff showed up too, just before the ambulance, after some fucked-up dude ran his Mustang into the trees. Some a-holes got busted with Crystal and a few other old-school pharmaceuticals like cocaine and heroin. Barton's folks were not pleased about it, but they made it all go away — like poof!

I didn't know LoQuan then, and I'm thinking LoQuan would have loved that last party. My friends say I'm a badass, the way I talk now and the stance — rapping, the Gumby walk to keep my pants up, and grabbin my dick all the time, you know. I know my friends would dig LoQuan, maybe even more than they dig me — I do, so why wouldn't they?

I've never been to LoQuan's, and we turn in this fucked-up neighborhood with drug pimps thugging their corners, and he goes, "Welcome to Mount Hood," but he isn't laughing, swinging the Escort to the curb, the look on his face says, "Yeah, Nigga, this what it be like." And I'm like, wow, that's awful, and right then I decide I will definitely invite him to the next big party, and I mean I don't give a fuck where it is or who's throwing it, because this is so fuckin' depressing. I now get it why his "realness" is so authentic. I mean like he's a classy pretty nigga in his way, and deserves better. And I guess he can see I'm shocked. It's a row house and it's like the color of a black-and-white photo of my great grandma and grandpa in fuckin' 1932. The inside too, it's dark and there's no air. Big dusty chairs and a couch with a raggedy cover over it, and it's like if you touch it you'll be attacked by fleas. And old-ass wallpaper with greasy-looking dead flowers, and this smell, and I'm like man what the fuck — old cheese, old feet! In one of the chairs is his foster mom, Mrs. Illinois, looking like a mummy.

She goes, "Boy, that you?"

"Yes, Ma'am, this here is my friend Jewells."

Mrs. Illinois nods like she's got a stiff neck, and then LoQuan steps behind a curtain that is behind the sofa, and gets some clothes or something. Then he goes into the bathroom, showers, and the plumbing squeaks and bangs. I sit on the sofa 'cause Mrs. Illinois just waves me over but she's cleaning a window, and the skinny bitch Vanna on *Wheel of Fortune* turns over letters.

"Heavens wonders of . . . " Mrs. Illinois mumbles.

I'm like, I got the puzzle and say, "Seven wonders of the world."

"That's righ," she goes, and then I'm trying to remember who the wonders of the world are . . . the Beatles, Tupac, Michael Jackson? . . . She's still smiling like she's finally found her *Wheel of Fortune* partner, but I'm like don't get it twisted.

And she goes, "You live 'round here?"

"No, ma'am. I live in East . . . in Hyde Park."

"Don't know it. That in K'tucky?"

"No ma'am, it's next to Walnut Hills."

I hear a train coming, and I'm like, this is so weird.

"Yes, I believe I know Hyde Park. White peoples living

there. What you doing there?"

"I live there."

"That righ? Some white family foster you?

"That's right. They done turned me into a slave."

"Lotta peoples abuse the foster chilrun, ba'cause they just in it for the money, you see, and I done heard some turrble things just about break your heart, and I always tell the chilrun what come to me, you gotta stand up and don't take no mess — why, the rapin' and beatin', it's just turrble."

Fuck me!

Finally LoQuan's ass comes out of the bathroom saying I should go in and like clean up. So I'm like finger-brushing my teeth when I hear the train horns again, and the house begins to tremble. The trembling turns into shaking, and when the shaking starts getting worse like the house is about to explode, I run the fuck out of the bathroom yelling, "LoQuan, man, it's an earthquake, a fuckin' earthquake."

He goes, "Nigga, it's the train. It's the train."

"The train?"

"The train, nigga," he shouts, stooped over laughing.

Mrs. Illinois goes, "Boy, I done told you, don't be using that word in my house."

And the train horn screams three or four times, and the house is like shaking even more, but it's nothing to the pterodactyl scream and in-the-teeth clacking of the steel wheels — so fuckin' loud I now can't hear anything else. I like go to the back door, and I swear it's like a million tons of steel speeding down two skinny tracks, with its headlight staring down at us like a fuckin' cyclops. It's almost right up on us, and I'm scared, but I don't run. I can see that the tracks curve away from the house and are like thirty-five feet from the back porch, and I just stand there like I can't move, the sparks flying, the dust parting as the cyclops scares a path through the air. And then the engine train passes, and I'm staring at the names GE, Union Pacific, and CSX, and the sparklers from the friction of steel on steel, until the dust kicked up is so intense I can't breathe.

WHAT THE FUCK!

LoQuan shouts: "Close the door, fool."

I do, but the noise is inside the house with us. The train is endless, and I'm like, how can they be used to this shit? Mrs. Illinois is struggling with a new round of Vanna clues. LoQuan is brushing his long hair, and it is all like slick and wet, and it seems like the mirror's shaking doesn't faze him one fuckin' bit as he braids. I guess he knows how to focus, and maybe he just likes what he sees and that's all there fuckin' is to keep yourself from going crazy when a fuckin' speeding freight train is like right outside the window. Some chicks at juvie were like whispering about how fine he is, how pretty his babies would be, with all that pretty hair, but now I'm sorry for him, he's all of that and then some but this is where he lives . . . it's fuckin' sad, and I'm thinking he should be with me, we could be in the carriage house.

Finally, LoQuan is grabbing his backpack.

"See you later, Mom," he goes, with close-quote fingers.

"Boy, I'm all outta starch. You stop and git me some Argo."

Outside, I go, "Boy, what's Argo?"

"Cornstarch. She eats that shit."

"Is it good?"

"Yeah, if you like baby powder 'cause that's what it looks like."

I'm like, that's wacked, and start laughing.

"What's fuckin' funny?"

"Nothing."

"Damn right. Nothin is fuckin'fuckin' funny, nigga. And don't call me boy."

He turns the music up, like loud. I think to apologize, but don't. I want to say that I wasn't laughing at the cornstarch, or at Mrs. Illinois, but at him for calling her "Mom," 'cause it's like me having to call Stepmom "Mom" — a big fuckin' lie, and I'm laughing 'cause if I did the close-quote fingers, she would know.

How am I supposed to know what he's pissed off about?

I don't know where we're going, but LoQuan is flying up Galbraith Road, heading toward Ronald Reagan Highway, the chitty-chitty-bang-bang getting louder and louder. It seems like forever, in slow motion, with the fumes and the fucked-up muffler and 2 Live Crew slinging hiphop and all, and I'm almost outta my fuckin' mind. Wherever the fuck we are, it's like a stretch of trees along the turns in the road, with driveways and little mailboxes, but that's all. Finally he slows down and turns into this gravelly driveway that looks like a service road for utility trucks and city vehicles. I'm thinking he's lost and we've passed our place and I expect him to make a U-turn, but we like drop below the road and putter along it to the other side of the trees. After a couple of sharp turns, we arrive at this house that kinda seems like it's slid down the hill, that's how deep down it is in this ravine, and all I see is hills and it's like we're in the ground. I'm so glad to get out of LoQuan's death-mobile that I don't at first notice the house is like tite. It's got a roof like butterfly wings, like the two sides of it could flap up and down and carry the whole fuckin' house away. It's like the color of the woods too, so you don't really see it all that well till you like drive up on it. There's a carport, and then it's like a small cliff right behind it, like maybe fifteen or twenty feet high. I could see being fucked up and driving off the cliff, and I'm like fuck me.

"Tite, right?"

"Tite."

LoQuan is smiling at me like we've passed through a black hole in the universe and we've just entered a new planetary system that I don't know shit about.

He goes, "The dude's name is Mr. Fritz."

"Mr. Fritz. What does Mr. Fritz do?"

"Nigga, I dunno and don't wanna know. He's cool, don't say much, but this ain't the social hour either. So like don't do or say anything fuckin' embarrassing. In fact, don't say anything, nigga, let me do the talking."

I'm like, "Cool," but I'm thinking, dude, you're the one from the fuckin' hood, I'm the one in private school, I'm the one whose dad is like Donald Trump, whose dad ain't dead from a crack-related shoot out, and I'm the one whose uncle is in the Clinton Administration, and fuck me, I'm the one whose stepmom is a TV celebrity.

"Just do what I tell you, and ack like you really into it. I mean, you ain't gotta go crazy, but act like you really gotta bust one. You beat your meat all the time, and this ain't no different. He's got dope and shit, and some porn video shit, and before you know it, man, you'll forget he's even there and be dropping a load."

I'm like, "I hope so."

"And nigga, if none of that keeps your dick hard, just think about the money and you'll be fine. Keep it tite."

"My shit's always tite."

I'm thinking the theme of this place must be Japanese, because the doorbell sounds like a gong, but it's not like samurai warriors are gonna bust through the door any minute, but more like dinner is served, like Benihana's steak house.

"Hey boys," we hear through the intercom, and the

door opens and we go in. Mr. Fritz isn't as cool as his house. His face is lumpy and shiny from old acne and his teeth are ground down like he's been gnawing on wood. He's wearing just a T-shirt, shorts and flipflops, his red toes as big as thumbs. For some reason he reminds me of the soccer coach at school, so I'm not too weirded out at all. That dude used to watch us in the showers.

He goes, "Glad you could come by."

"This is Junior," LoQuan says to Mr. Fritz, as we walk into the room. We're kinda on a balcony, and the whole wall behind the balcony is glass and the view is of the curve of the hillside and sky. It's fuckin' sweet, like being in the middle of a giant fuckin' wave of green. I'm thinking if I look at it long enough, I'll see dudes whizzing by on surfboards.

Mr. Fritz is saying to me, "Well, Junior. Nice to have you aboard."

I'm like, "Cool house."

"I toldya," goes LoQuan. "Mr. Fritz is the man."

Seems like Mr. Fritz ignores LoQuan, but he nods at me like I've guessed the right answer.

We follow him to stairs that look like planks of wood on this big metal frame so you can see all the way down. There are twisted sculptures and weird paintings, but we're going fast so it's hard to make anything out. At the bottom of the stairs and I guess the house, I can hear the "ohh, aah, ohh" of chicks getting banged. The room is dark. I'm thinking the glass wall must be behind the curtains, 'cause there's light hanging around the curtain edges.

Now I see there's this ginormous TV screen where the porn bitches are getting nailed and it's like they're all black bitches and I'm like where are the blonde babes? And I'm like shazam, one of the black chicks has a blonde wig on and I'm like, best of both worlds, tite. A pitcher of vodka lemonade is already out on the table, plus other stuff like pretzels and peanuts, and me and LoQuan guzzle and chew, while Mr. Fritz just watches us from the sofa.

Mr. Fritz is like, "You boys have everything you need?"

LoQuan is like, "Yeah man," and Mr. Fritz turns the music up a little — it's Jay-Z, but I'm into the blonde porn ho with the pink cunt that this Latin-looking nigga with this fuckin' baseball bat dick is beating up. Then I see a light flash.

What the fuck, I'm like, "LoQuan, anybody else here?"

He's like, "Naw, just us and him."

Him, definitely — like Mr. Fritz's T-shirt is off and he's rubbing his chest and flat nipples, but it's kinda dark and I can't really see him all that well in the TV light, and I still feel like somebody else is here too.

So LoQuan pulls his clothes off like down to his underwear and like when I've done the same, he hands me this little bottle that he's just sniffed. I sniff it too — and suddenly my heart rockets into my eardrums and, shazam, my dick goes boing, sticking straight out of my boxer shorts.

What the fuck!

LoQuan is like, "Yeah man." He looks, smiles and winks. I focus on him as he slides his underwear down and grabs his dick and begins stretching it across his thigh, then up his stomach, like it's some kinda workout routine like chin-ups. I do the same, and now I'm like watching the chicks on the TV more than I am him, 'cause I don't want him to get the wrong idea.

Mr. Fritz is like, "Now make out."

I go, "What? I ain't making out with nobody."

LoQuan is like, "How much you paying?"

"Three hundred."

"Three hundred!" LoQuan looks at me, and I'm like, "Nigga, you crazy."

"What you want us to do?"

"Kiss. Jerk each other off."

What the fuck, I'm like standing there, shaking my head, my dick done like fainted.

LoQuan goes, "Jewells be a little nervous. This is his first time."

"Ahhhh, well, I like that," goes Mr. Fritz. "That's hot. Real hot. We straight boys."

LoQuan winks and mumbles to me, "Jewells, you just stand there, and let me . . ."

I go, "I'm not nervous," and I'm thinking I should leave, get the fuck out, but not without the money, we've come this far, wherever the fuck we are — and LoQuan will be so pissed, even though his lying ass is to blame. If only I had my own wheels, I would leave. Mr. Fritz there, looking like a big marshmallow, glides his tongue over his lips and his fingers makes squiggles on his nipples.

LoQuan goes, "Earthquake," and I'm like what the fuck, and then he goes, "Nigga, you just stand there." Then he turns around, and his V-shaped back is facing me, the braid is hanging down the middle of it like a rope.

And then he's like, "Unplait my hair."

It is black and like slippery and shit, and as I unplait it it spreads out into long, thick wads down his back.

"Run your hands through it. Play with it, baby."

I'm like, what the fuck, but I run my fingers through it, and when he turns around, his piece like brushes against my thigh and wets it with dick juice. I'm like looking into his eyes, and I'm thinking he's one pretty nigga, and then I'm like I really do get it now, and then I get a hard-on again, too, and he grins like we're about to get the big prize, and with one hand he takes my dick and with the other clamps onto my neck and then he like pulls my face into his. Our mouths crash into each other, and I'm sure there's blood from his sucking my lip, mauling it. Next I know, his tongue slides along my chest, circling my nipples. He turns his back to me, pushes his body into mine, then turns again. Lips to mine. Fuck. As we grip and grab, his hair swirls around me like a curtain and when we pull apart it's like this show is live and we like shoot all over the plastic on the floor rug. Damn!

Mr. Fritz shouts, "Man, that's so hottttt!" and cleans the squirt off his chest and goes, "So fucking hot!" and we wipe ourselves off, and I'm like, wow. Minutes later, we're following Mr. Fritz's beat-up feet squeaking in flipflops, and he's totalling thanking us, he'll be in touch, and shows us out.

LoQuan goes, "See that was easy, man," and slams the car door.

I'm like, "Yeah, considering all we have to do is just stand there, right?"

"Nigga, if Mickey D's was paying three hundred an hour, I'd be like hey, but they ain't."

"Starbuck's neither."

"Three hundred just to let some fruit watch you beat your meat for 10 minutes, that's the deal. I mean, I'm always thinking about my girl or money, so it's like whatever."

I'm like, "Yeah," and I'm watching a long string drifting around to my face. It's his hair, a long black thread that like curls all the way down across my chest, tying me to him. And fuck me, I realize I wasn't thinking about any of my girls or even the money. I was thinking about him. I let my tongue circle the burn and bruises on my lip, and it still tastes like his wintergreen breath mint.

He goes, "It's cool, right?"

I go, "Yeah, it's cool."

"Man, we could get us a ride and a crib, do this just a few times a week, and we're set. Tite, right?"

"Tite."

"We could depend on ourselves, man, nobody else. I got your back, you got mines."

"Yeah." He's fuckin' right. I'm thinking about my dad, and it's not if but when he'll leave town. I'll be lucky if I can get my license at all, and then Stepmom, running defense and always trying to block me.

He goes, "Nobody else, just me and you, Jewells, man."

And I'm like, "Okay, like, I'm not saying I'm in . . . but you know, anybody else paying?"

"Maybe I do. Maybe I don't. I'll let you know. But I know one thing, man, you can't be acting all disgusted, and be dissing people and shit. I mean, a little scared is cool, a little thug color is cool . . . he ate that shit up, right? But it's gotta look for real, gotta look cool, like you into it. We just straight-up niggas doing our thang, that's what we givin'. You got that? I mean, you laughed at my foster mom, and you know, like, you disrespected her, and like, nigga, not everybody got platinum credit cards and livin' in mufuckin' Hyde Park."

Fuck me, I knew he would come back to that. So I'm like, "LoQuan, I'm sorry," but he ignores me and I feel bad that I've hurt him, even if he has misunderstood. And maybe I was laughing at her too, but just a little, not a lot, which would have been rude.

His hair spills out of the red Cougars' baseball cap, and he looks at me and I'm like God you are a pretty nigga. He cocks the cap at an angle, like he knows that's what I'm thinking, and I look at the profile of his lips, how the top shelves over the bottom, and with the wintergreen taste of him in my mouth still, the feel of him on my dick, I know I could come again, right now . . . all over myself. I put my hands over my stuff, and he goes, "You dig what I'm saying, Jewells?" and I'm like, "Cool."

Reality check comes with jamming 2 Live Crew and ten messages from Stepmom. But I'm not wasting my minutes on her, even if they are free. Fuck me, I'll get plenty of her bullshit in the morning, so I ignore them.

Like, he pulls up at Parisienne Mall, and I get the sneakers at a twenty-five percent discount for signing up for a store credit card, and when he drops me off in the real Hyde Park, I hang at my dude Chase's place and play video games, and I'm thinking I will never do any freaky stuff like the Fritz saga again, like no matter how much we get paid. Red-headed and freckled Chase is like, "Dude you got hickeys all over your neck, it musta been good pussy," and I'm like fuck me.

Later, we hook up with some of our teammates. They're all like, "Dude, your sneakers is tite."

I know I got swag. "Y'all niggas playing with me." All of 'em love it when I call them niggas.

No shit.

4

Butterflies like to chill on my window screen like it's a nightclub. One time I had some ridiculous dope from Maui — Maui Wowie — and I was like these butterflies have wings with big eyes peeping me. Fuck, I know I was trippin' — but I ran up to the window and smacked the screen and they all flew away. The next day they came back, and I'm like what the fuck, why are they peeping me? Then I'm like, yo, I'll peep them. And then I'm like, wow, they're peeping each other or the garden for food. They line up in this pattern that makes me think of a chessboard, moving their wings like they stoned too, or tired, and it's like the wing-eyes are flirting. They'd been doing this for a week, since it turned really hot, and mostly now they show up before sundown. And I'm like, wow, it's an orgy — that's what's going on. Hopping on and off each other's backs, chasing each other through the air, and then most times they come right back to the chess game, sometimes not. This fuckin' humongous tree vine has like these python roots on the side of the garage, and the thick trunk stretches up about fifteen feet and spreads out into these purple flowers that hang like dining room table lights. The flowers come in the spring, and seems like that's when the butterflies first start showing up. Seems like they circle the purple flowers till they're dizzy, and then they like jump on the one they want the most. I peep and at first it seems like the butterflies are horsing around, with their curling tongues, and their wings wagging with the peeping eyes, like they're all excited, like they're sexed up, and then they get full of nectar or whatever they're eating, and then they fuck a little, snooze and then move on. The purple fancy flowers have been gone since before spring break ended, and maybe that's why the butterflies chill out on the window screen playing butterfly chess and screwing, like they're waiting for the flowers to come back. For fun, sometimes I'm like y'all got to go, and thump the screen and they all scatter, but they come right back a little later, so I let them chill, just leave them alone . . . and now I like them there hanging out all summer. What a chill life they've got . . . fuck me, exactly the kind of life I would want. But sometimes it seems like they're some kind of calendar saying that vacation begins and, then like fuck you, Jewells — now it's over and it's back to the hard life of school again.

Like, I'm buzzed right now but I don't think that's why the butterflies seem like homos and my window screen is like a fag bar. And I'm like, wow. And then I'm like, whoa! I think of LoQuan — and I like put my hand in my shorts, yeah! I can almost smell and feel his hair in my hands pulling at me, and I'm like wow this is ridiculous weird. Glad I like pussy so much, 'cause I'd be worried. Not that there's anything wrong with being a freak.

Fuck me, there was another time a dude got under my skin, but it was like so different. Russell Mueller, our star quarterback, was my competition. Rusty had a great throw and he's solid like a fuckin' tree stump and could rush like a torpedo downfield, usually with a big-ass tackle and two defensive backs hanging off him before taking him down. And like, my long pass was better than his, Coach McGlad said, but his hustle was better. I think Rusty's jealous of me, like I was of him, and there's this thing in me that makes me want to fight him. In the showers, I'd watch him, and he watched me. He's got this big red ass and one time it was just me and him in there, and he like took his washcloth and started rubbing circles up his fireplug thigh and over his ass until he was all lathered up. And like then he was rinsing, he pulled his ass apart and bent over so the soap would wash out of his crack. I don't remember what I was pissed about, but I kinda got a hard-on thinking I how much I wanted to ram my dick up his ass, the nasty muthafucka. Now I don't mind him, the punk doesn't even register, but at the time, and for a long time after that, I dreamed of him pulling his red butt cheeks apart. I'd wake and jerk off — imagine shooting on his face. I wanted to humiliate him, but never had to actually do it, he managed to do that himself. The team got its ass kicked by Withrow, a fuckin' mediocre public school, 'cause of him and two of his bad passes that were intercepted. On top of it,

Rusty got a concussion that sent him to the hospital and had him like dizzy and throwing up for a month and made him forget fuckin' everything — no more football for Rusty, and now every time I see him I think loser! And he looks at me the same way, like I'm the one busted up. Like, on his AOL profile, he's trying to come off as the All-Star hero, in every picture he's wearing his shoulder pads or knee guards or helmet or uniform, but we all know the score: 36–7.

Thanks, Rusty.

Right now I'm like fuckin' starved. Normally Oma will buy cereal, milk and Fritos and Funyuns for me for my place, but fuck me, Dad and Stepmom don't like it; so Oma does it on the sly. Oma is Stepmom's mom, and her name means grandmother in German, and she lived in that country till she was eight. She isn't giving me love these days, or she's too busy trying to keep up with the twins, now that they're running around all over the place — 'cause there is nothing to eat here. Which makes me get it together and go to the main house. The playroom is next to the kitchen, at the back of the house, looking out on the garden and the ski slope view down to the river. I'm on my way to the refrigerator, and the hall smells like Oma's lemons and oatmeal. The rooms are far enough apart that she probably doesn't see or hear me, and I'm like glad since I'm still shaky — too much smoke and somebody had some blow last night, which was tite. I mean, I love me some blow but man was I fucked up! It made my birthday special, even though we didn't do different shit, 'cause we like got carded in Clifton and turned away and ended up at my dude's pool party in Wyoming, which was like so fuckin' lame 'cause they had chaperones, like we were a bunch of children, a bunch of children high on blow! I'm like hey, it's my fuckin' birthday, give a nigga a break! But it's like, when you see a detour sign, go around it and have a blast any damn way, and just deal with the hangover.

I flip the video intercom on and with my cereal I watch the lame sitcom starring my step-siblings and Oma.

Oma is like a baby magnet, part Labrador and Big Bird and giant sponge, and sounds like a bedtime story. My twin baby stepsisters, in matching yellow sundresses, wobble near her knees, and one of the twin-wannabes crashes cars just past her feet while the other is drawing, looking like little gargoyles in identical blue sweaters. I like . . . no, I love Oma too. She's always nice to me, always offering me homemade granola bars and cheese and a hug and kiss. Sometimes I'm like all jealous and shit when my stepbrothers run from the school bus calling her name — not so much now but when I was a kid, man, I was like crazy at the sight of them. First I was jealous of Percy, the older one, but then I was even more jealous of Fletcher. And like, I knew it was jealousy, I didn't need a fuckin' psychologist to tell me either, but I guess they did . . . they meaning Stepmom and Dad. Some kids complain about being the only child, but not me. Stepmom the baby factory never really gave a fuck about me since I'm not blood and didn't travel down her baby-drop chute.

Oma has been with us like since Fletcher was born, so she's never been all mine. She used to live in Kenwood, but then her house burned down. I'm like, Stepmom probably rigged the gas leak just to fire the nanny and the housekeeper to get Oma to move in to take care of everybody and everything, freeing her to run around being her beauty queen self. The only thing Stepmom loves more than my step-siblings is shopping and beauty, which she spends a lot of her time doing. Oma, poor ole gal, does all the work. So, I have no food in my refrigerator, 'cause Oma, old and fat and out of shape, is like worn out, beat down.

In all her puffiness, it's hard to see Oma was nice looking once upon a time, but she was . . . okay, not as pretty as Stepmom, but she was kinda pretty, like President Clinton's wife, Mrs. Hillary Clinton, and her family heritage is actually Polish, she says. I never knew Grandpa Chenault, 'cause he like died when Stepmom was a kid, but from photographs Stepmom looks like him. I mean, she got all of Oma's pretty European features — the things that make a white chick not a black chick — but she's got his height and golden coloring and eyes that are like brown and blue together. Grandad Chenault was a light-skinned black man and he must've been handsome. My Dad says Oma was a brave woman marrying him back in the Sixties, when it was all about hating on black people … we're talking murders, lynchings and shootings, right here in Cincinnati. Like, now homies be killing each other all the time, but that's totally different. Yet and still, it's hard to see the soldier in her. I mean, I'd love Oma anyway, 'cause she always good to me, but her sitting there being a jungle gym and talking like the Old Woman Who Lives in a Shoe doesn't seem so brave to me.

I had to do a school project on family history. Dad asked me to ask her what it was like when she and Grandpa were dating. At first she didn't want to talk about it, to bring up all the bad feelings, but then she changed her mind. "I tell you because I think it will help you a little when you think about your own life. We have a word for it in my language — *Schadenfreude* — it means bad joy, and it basically describes how you feel a little better about your own situation when you hear how badly someone else has it. Very different times than now, much much worse. Your grandpa and I were Romeo and Juliet. Our families were dead set against us, so it wasn't easy, but we were in love since we were in junior high school. You could say that things were kind of set in the stars for us. Sometimes you just have to stand for what you know to be right. His family came around to accepting me, well before he died. But not mine. And they never would."

I'm like okay, but how did you deal with them?

"I don't like to talk about this at all, but I will — and not for your paper but for you to know. My father was a

Klansman. He first came to America from Germany when he was 14 years old, and he learned to speak perfect, unaccented English and nobody knowed or cared to know he was from the enemy country they fought the war to defeat — and that's because many of their own ancestors came from Ireland, England, Italy and Sweden a long time ago and it just didn't matter. All they really cared about was that he was willing to take up their cause to keep the blacks out. He was a grand wizard or something like that, a little monster behind the big machine meant to keep blacks from coming near Price Hill, and his gang did things to terrorize them, like setting cars on fire, beating people up. My mother was just as bad as my father was. I didn't speak to them after they threw me out of the house. They have never even seen your mother, never even asked to see her, not even when she was a little girl. They are dead now. I say good!"

"Wow." Hard to picture anybody ignoring Stepmom. It makes me hate her a little less and understand a little more why she's always looking for the spotlight. "Oma, I don't want to make you sad, but you think about your folks?"

"No, honey, I don't . . . I did, when I was young, because I couldn't understand why they hated your grandfather so much. When they threw me out, they told me I was no daughter of theirs. So, no, I never think about them. Just because you share blood doesn't give them any right to mistreat and harm you. I don't look back. Now, that's all I have to say about all of that bad business."

I don't know about the bad joy shit, but I admire her for that. Maybe that's what I'll do too — go away and never look back. I keep this to myself. Now whenever Dad gives me history lectures on all that civil rights shit, just so he can say I am lucky kid to live where I live and have what I got, I think about Oma. She calls a spade a spade.

I used to think Dad meant me good, but I don't anymore. Dad's mom mostly raised me. Meemaw took me in after my real mom left. My real mom took off when I was a little baby, or that's the story I've been told. Not that anybody's trying to turn her into a villain, but they kind of did just by never talking about her. I don't know when it happened, but I started to think of her as somebody who had been handed off, like I was. Dad left me with Meemaw so he could go to business school for three fuckin' years — I probably saw him six times while he was living in Chicago. I sometimes wonder who my mom was handed off to, or how she was discarded like for the garbage can. The difference between me and her is she never came back.

Meemaw was good to me, but now Meemaw is dead too — and she really fucked me up. I still see her like the last few minutes she was alive, and it's like I can hear her breath sputtering. I was playing basketball in the driveway of our first house, which was in Hyde Park, and the ball took a hard bounce and broke the garage window. And she came running out to see what was wrong, really to see if I was alright. "JewELLSSSSSSSSSSS," she screamed my name out. I like had this feeling and I turned just as she grabbed her breast and fell down the fuckin' porch steps. It happened so fast, so fuckin' fast, and I'm like, shit, what the fuck! Instead of holding and kissing me like she always did, I was holding her, crying like a helpless fuckin' retard. Her face was all bloody and an arm bone sticking out the skin, the bone was all sharp and splintered with a blob of muscle and white stuff around it, and her dentures got like twisted in her mouth, and it was like an alien coming out of her mouth when the teeth on the brace slid loose and hit the sidewalk — fuckin' CLACK — I can't get the picture out of my mind, or that sound. My basketball playing ended for-fuckin-ever at that moment.

Fast and like fuckin' fatal — a massive stroke is what killed her, the doctors said. Like they were not saying it was my fault for just sitting there crying with her head in my lap — I mean, the blood, the slobber, her eyes rolling back in her head, her mouth open, the gums, the fuckin' dentures . . . but I know what's up, if I had called the ambulance she'd be alive now, I know that.

I think that's why I don't give a fuck. Like, I'm not blaming Meemaw for making me feel guilty like this, and I'm not saying she died on purpose, but damn . . . Sometimes, though, like when I see Oma, I really miss Meemaw something bad. She used to always say I was her one and only, and she always wanted me to be right next to her, so she could hug and kiss me. Must be a grandma thing, but Oma is always hugging and kissing too, and it reminds me of Meemaw — plus the big chest, like a rolled-up sleeping bag. The problem is, Oma is on Stepmom's side, and I'm not a little kid, so I tiptoe around the booby traps Stepmom has hidden like everywhere to trip me up. I'm smarter than Oma, and Stepmom too, for that matter. I know what's up, and they the fuck don't, Oma 'cause she always running after my snotty siblings, and Stepmom 'cause she's like brain-damaged from a radioactive cloud of perfume, skin cream and makeup.

So now I turn the volume of the intercom's little video player up. The kitchen speakers crackle out their conversation, and like I hear one of the twin wannabes talking about some dumb shit involving cards. Then, they like start talking about me. It's Percy saying, "I don't know why you have to let Jewells sign the card."

"Because it's a wish for Daddy to feel better," Fletcher says back. "So he will get out of the hospital before they perform an operation."

"There's no operation, Fletcher," says Oma. "He is just not feeling well. Our card is a wish for good health. It's from all of us. And that includes Jewells."

"Mom says Jewells has his head on backwards," says Fletcher. "That's what Mom says. Doesn't she, Oma?"

"She does say that. You know it hurts to have your head

on backwards."

"Maybe he should get an operation?" says Fletcher.

"Owls can make their heads turn backwards. Jewells' head doesn't look backwards to me, it's sideways," says Percy.

"Percy, it just means that he isn't thinking clearly."

"About what?"

"Nothing in particular. It's his age — boys his age don't think clearly. You boys will experience all that your brother is going through too when you turn into teenagers."

I have to laugh cuz, like, Stepmom's got it all wrong, just the fuckin' opposite is true — and my little creepy stepbrothers, well, I know they're just kids, but it's like so obvious they will be against me, like everybody is against me in this family.

"He's almost sixteen. In two days," goes Fletcher.

"Oma, do you like Jewells?" goes Percy

"Yes, I like Jewells," she goes. "I love Jewells."

"I don't. He's tacky."

"Don't say that, dear."

"Mom says she doesn't like Jewells all the time, but she always loves him. I love him and I like him too," goes Fletcher.

"Is that what you mean, Percy?"

"Mom says he's tacky because of his hiphop pants and baseball caps."

"It's his style."

"I think he should wear Hugo Boss."

Little punk! "That's nice, dear," says Oma, and I'm like with her when she goes, "But then why don't you want him to sign the card?"

"Because, because . . . he doesn't like us or love us . . . he's, he's . . ."

Fletcher goes, "Jewells is confused."

Oma goes, "It's hormones. Hormones give him pimples and make his voice deeper and he's getting bigger and bigger. The deep voice in his head tells him to be bad, to dress like the cool guys in the rap videos. There's another voice telling him to be good, and then there's another voice that's always talking about girls."

"All the voices, that's why his priorities are mixed up," goes Percy. "Who's that talking? It's confusing. I feel like that at recess sometimes. I *don't* wanna go outside, I wanna stay inside and make dresses for Mommy, but the teacher says I have too. And me and Salena . . ."

"Yes," goes Oma. "But you listen to the teacher?"

"Yes, I do. I won't listen to harmones when I'm sixteen," goes Percy. "I'm not tacky."

"You'll have stylish hor-mones."

"Yes. Chic ones."

And then the little creep Percy, who every day is more and more like Stepmom, is like, "I think that Jewells has to remember his memory more, then he wouldn't be confused by the voices and he wouldn't get in trouble. Then he could listen to the right voice."

"Maybe. Percy — and you too Fletcher — it's always good to remember your memory, and to mind your Mommy and Daddy, and your Oma too. Now, let's get Jewells to sign the card and he can take it to the hospital when he visits your father."

"Yes, Oma," both boys go.

Hospital! And I'm like, fuck me! I like stare at the little monitor on the wall, push the speaker button, and then I'm like, "Hospital? Dad's in the hospital?"

"Jewells dear . . . oh dear! I can't believe that infernal machine is spying on us again. Jewells?"

"Yes, what's wrong with Dad? Why's he in the hospital?"

"He's alright. He just wasn't feeling well. Now please come and speak to us directly."

"What's wrong?"

"You need to speak to your mother!"

"Is he gonna die, just tell me that?"

"Jewells, darling, no. He's fine, there's nothing wrong, now call you mother, please."

I'm feeling kinda gross myself, but I'm like I wouldn't check into a hospital, but then Dad's like old and outta shape, I'm not. I'm pushing chocolate chip cookies into my mouth and I grab a banana and head for the playroom.

Then Percy cuts me off in the hall.

"Here's a string for you. I made it."

"What for?"

"It's a memory string. It's color coordinated."

"What's it for?"

"To help you remember. Mr. Stewart at day camp — he says that a string tied on your finger is good. It will help us remember to put our toys and drawings away when we're done."

"Okay?"

"Maybe it'll help you remember to put the Pamper on, so next time Alyssa won't poopie in the car again—" goes Fletcher, coming down the hall, laughing.

"It was disgusting," goes Percy.

"— and Mommy won't get mad at you."

"Thanks," I go, "but I always make poopie as far as Mommy is concerned."

"Huh?" goes Percy.

"Everything I touch turns to tacky poopie."

Percy reels back as I like raise poopie-covered hands to smear him with, and I go, "Including little brothers who think they're twins when they're not. I'm gonna touch both of you at the same time and you'll be identical turds, twin poopies, how's that!"

Now he's like screaming and I'm chasing him, and then like Fletcher starts screaming and I grab him, hoist him onto my hip and we like gun for Percy. I horse around with them.

I should record this shit. Fuck, Dad and Stepmom paid the psychiatrist and the psychologist a lot of money for him to say that I'm like jealous of the boys and the babies 'cause I'm no longer the center of my dad's attention. And you know, I figured out a long time ago that that's like bullshit 'cause I was like never the center of my dad's attention — it was always work or school . . . that's probably why my real mom disappeared and who knows where the fuck she went. And like, I don't really hate my stepbrothers at all, really. . . no, I love them . . . and then there are times I don't. And like I don't know why either — why I don't like just feel one way about them all the time, like it's supposed to be, but then I don't feel one way about anything, so why should it be different about them? Usually it's like when Stepmom is around that I can't stand any of them. She's usually out shopping or like playing tennis or getting massages or her hair done or going to cocktail parties. I also figured out she's not the center of Dad's attention either. Fuck, none of us are, really. One time, Stepmom yelled at Dad that Uncle Chief gets more attention than anybody does, and I'm like wow, it's true. But, fuck me, I don't mind Uncle Chief, he's like so cool.

After I sign the stupid "get well" card, the phone rings and even before Oma calls me, I know who it is when this cold, Dracula feeling like comes over.

"Dad, he's . . . "

"He's fine," Stepmom goes, and I don't understand the

rest about a panic attack and a Holt heart monitor. She says Dad wants to see me like now, and I hang up, scared. Since Meemaw died, anything to do with the heart or brain like worries the living shit outta me. I go, "Sure, I'll be right there."

I could get one of my boys to drive me down to the hospital to Dad, but that's what car service is for. We're not that far from University Hospital, so I'm there quick, almost too quick. I'm wearing Fletcher's pink memory string — maybe it'll also ward off Stepmom evil.

I never met my dad's and Uncle Chief's dad, but Dad and Uncle Chief look like brothers in the face and eyes, even though Uncle Chief is gold-colored and comparatively short and Dad is dark and tall like me. My Dad favors Meemaw a lot, in the shape of his face and like in the way he is — she was a church lady. Dad used to be a deacon when I was a kid, I think. She was a big woman and he is a big man — I mean, he used to to play center for the University of Cincinnati Bearcats — and to me it seems like the hospital bed is too short, and even the room is too small, like if he stretches out his whole body the fuckin' walls will come down. Now they've got him turned longways on the hospital bed, and one of his legs is hanging off the side like an oar. His fingers lift the phone to his ear like a little construction crane, but he isn't talking but listening, and shaking his head, not like he's pissed but like he's real disgusted. Stepmom is sitting on the edge of the bed when I walk in, her phone fixed to her ear too. My phone goes beep.

Stepmom is like, "Speaking of the devil," and she claps the phone closed and stands up. "Don't bother answering, Jewells. It's just me."

"Hey, hey Dad," I go, not even looking at her, just at him. He points a long critical finger at me, then switches his phone off.

"Come here," he goes.

And I'm like scared again, and I don't respond at first. Then I just go over and hug him. I try not to show him I'm scared, I'm not as cool as I let him think I am. I would be more scared if it were just me and him and I like found him unconscious and it was up to me to save him. I feel the tears coming.

"Dad, you okay?"

"Fine, the Lord willing, don't worry about it," he goes. "And you?"

"I'm okay, too, Dad."

He hugs me again, hard, and I feel her hatin' on me. She is all shiny lips and eyes flashing warnings and grudges, with the ugly eyewear on her head like a secret alien weapon. She is wearing one of her designer sweat suits that shows off her Nautilus shape; and her arms are crossed at the elbows like she's pissed. And these nurses are standing outside the room, and I guess they're like starstruck over the *Today in Cincinnati* bitch, who pretends like she doesn't notice them and then goes over and closes the door in their faces.

"What's up, Dad? Watcha doing here?"

"I'm alright, son. It's just for observation. They want to make sure the ticker is working."

"Your heart? What's wrong?"

"Don't worry, I'm alright." He like reaches his hand to my face, and I bend down to kiss his cheek, seeing a tear of mine splash into the pit of a deep pore. "I wasn't feeling so good, but I'm fine."

And Stepmom is like, "Stress is your father's problem. Some of it caused by an out-of-control son."

"Margeaux, please," Dad goes. He like waves her words away with thick fingers. "Where've you been, Jewells? We've been worried. We've not been able to find you for the last twenty hours. Where have you been?"

"Okay, like, I know what I did."

"Your father asked where have you been . . . we all know what you did."

I'm looking straight at Stepmom for what I'm about to say, but I'm really talking to him. "I was having fun celebrating my birthday — please recall that I was given permission to hang with my friends!"

Dad nods and Stepmom is about to start but I interrupt her.

"Please, so . . . Mom was mad at me . . ."

" . . . still is mad . . ."

" . . . and after I listened to your first message laying into me, Mom, I figured like it was more of the same."

"*More of the same!* This is beyond outrageous . . ."

"Margeaux, please. Jewells . . . so you were out all night, Jewells?"

"I crashed at Nick's — you know Nick, his folks own the potato chip company."

And like, I only get so many brownie points for name-dropping, because Stepmom associates my friends with their parents' careers, but she is like so fuckin' sarcastic. She goes, "I see, you were out all night eating chips!"

"No."

"But you weren't home, which is the point, Jewells."

Dad goes, "Your mother's right, Jewells."

"Yeah, I know she is."

And like I want to say to her that I can tell fuckin' time, but I know this situation will go from bad to worse if I match her sarcasm point for point.

So I'm like, cut to the chase, and then I go, "I'm sorry for the Pamper . . . and . . . I'm sorry for not calling back . . . and . . . I'm sorry like for everything . . . sorry, sorry, sorry."

"Jewells, your father is exhausted, and the last thing he needs is to be worried about you."

"Alright, I've heard enough," Dad goes. "I'd like to save these intense discussions for home, please." Then he adds, "It'll give me something to look forward to."

Dad has this way of looking at me with his eyes a little squinted. It's like he can't actually see the basketball and is waiting for it to come into play, but like he really doesn't know what the fuck is going on. I once read these old articles about Dad's basketball days at UC, and he wasn't a very good ballplayer, and I think it's 'cause of his weird squinting. At me, though, usually he's smiling too. But now he looks away, squinting, and like when his eyes come back to me I'm like thinking he's angry. At first I think it's me, but then I see it ain't me — what's he got to be mad at me for? He's the one that fucked up my birthday, and he's probably gonna fuck up my driver's license test too. I know Stepmom isn't going to take me down to the DMV for it. Mr. and Mrs. Griffin Jewells Saunders II are so fuckin' inconsiderate.

"Hopefully I'll be out of here in a few hours," Dad goes. "I've got some test results due in. Jewells, your old man is just out of shape. Too much fat on the heart. Wasn't that long ago when I was as fit as you."

"Back in the day when you were a b-baller," I say. "Too bad you don't have time, Dad, we could work out together, you know. Remember when we used to play tennis?"

"Yes, you could have been a star. Like Pete Sampras."

"I don't think I was any good, Dad."

"I think you're wrong. I think tennis was more your game."

"I like football more."

"Son, you're a born athlete. You could be great at anything you set your mind to."

Stepmom goes, "I say we set our minds on getting you well, sweetheart." She's smiling a little — like she must have done on *Today in Cincinnati* when she was disgusted by a guest but couldn't show it. "Your father needs a new diet. He needs a new agenda to go with it, and a workout buddy he can trust. A summer in Washington would do you good too, Jewells. Wouldn't you like that?"

Like, I know what's up. But I want to be gotten rid of. I go, "D.C. is tite!"

And then she's like, "What does 'tite' mean anyway?"

"On point, cool, fine, all that and then some."

And then Dad goes, "Like tight end, right, son?" and he laughs a little, but like it hurts. "If I can't trust and rely on my own son, there's no one, right?"

"I wanna come with you, Dad."

"What about football?"

"I'll play next year."

"No, that's not fair. And you know, Jewells, I'm going to Eastern Europe with your Uncle Chief in about ten days. It'll be for two weeks, and then I'm going to Buenos Aires at the end of the month, that's another week."

I'm like, here we go, and so I say "whatever" but under my breath, and then I say "That's great, Dad. Uncle Chief is like so the man."

"It depends on your health, sweetheart. You work hard for us, and we appreciate it, don't we Jewells?"

"Yes, Mom."

"But you've got to take better care of your health."

"We have to strike while the iron's hot," Dad goes. Looking at me. "Your Uncle Chief's tite. The golden boy. You know, it's about being in the right place at the right time. I coulda —"

"You'll only be in Croatia two weeks," Stepmom cuts him off. "And you can take Jewells with you to Argentina."

"That's true." Dad's teeth like overtake his face when he smiles, and it makes me think cameras are around — sometimes he's a performer just like she is. "Jewells, son, I didn't move you all to Washington with me in the first place because I didn't want to interrupt your schooling here, but I think I should have."

"Yeah, I hate it here . . . without you." I almost look at Stepmom. "It's not the same without you, Dad."

"It'll be really good having your son with you," Stepmom goes, slipping her phone into her purse.

"It's a win-win." He nods and then is like, "Soften my image a little, keep me grounded."

I'm guessing he is speaking more to her. Like, I don't know or care what he means, or what she means for that fuckin' matter, but I do want to go with him. D.C. may turn out to fuckin' suck, but it's not like here, and like she won't be there, so I go, "I'm ready, Dad. I just need to get my driver's license on Wednesday, and then I'm like totally ready. You say when."

He nods, and for whatever reason he looks down at my feet, at my birthday sneakers, and his eyes squint as he bites down, his jaws muscles like fists, like he's in pain.

"Those are the sneakers at the store that I didn't buy," goes Stepmom.

"Margeaux, please . . . " Dad holds his hand up to stop her. "Jewells, sounds like a deal, son. Now I know you have practice today. Is the scrimmage this weekend?"

"Yeah, Dad."

"I'm proud of you, son."

But he doesn't sound proud, just sad. On my way out, Stepmom snarls, "Jewells, the only thing that's changed is your curfew. So after practice today, you're expected home."

What-the-fuck-ever!

5

Coach McGlad is like psycho for punctuality, and I know the second I hit the field that I'm on his shit list, even with a legit excuse. I called Coach ahead to say I'd be there at 10 a.m., and it's now only twenty after, so what's the big fuckin' deal?

But he's like, "Saunders!" with his finger picking the air.

Heinz and Mason, my best dudes on the team and best all-around niggas otherwise, use the knife-edge of a finger to slit their throats. Both of them are red-faced and dirty-looking in the bright sun, because they were like hanging with us for my birthday too, so I know they're just as fucked up as I am. Then my dude Chase, who is a real nigga — that is, a black dude — sticks out his tongue and I'm like fuck you.

"Your beauty appointment run a little late?" goes McGlad, while the animals snicker.

"My dad's in the hospital. I left you a message."

McGlad, with his Beavis face sprinkled with like old zits and craters, goes, "Come here. The rest of you fellas, I want ten laps around the perimeter."

And then the animals are like a flock of geese whooping and winding up to get airborne.

"Sorry, I haven't listened to my phone messages. I'm up on the technology, you can text me. Your father alright?"

"I don't know," I like exaggerate the distress. "Stress . . . that's what he told me. They're like keeping him there for observation. He's ready to leave now, but they're gonna make him stay another night. Attached to a Holt monitor."

Like, something is fuckin' wrong with me. Coach's voice can sound like a born-again's, so when he puts his arm around me and says, "You alright, son?" I immediately start wiping my eyes. It's fuckin' embarrassing.

"Yeah," I go.

"You know, when I was your age my pop was gone all the time too. It was hard on me. I know how you feel."

I rub my eyes again, wondering if anybody really knows how I feel.

And he's like, "But, Jewells, I'm the coach," and he grabs my shoulder. "I need you to be one-hundred-fifty percent. Unless you really want to play hard here today, I think you should be with your family. I don't think your mind is on football."

"My mind is on football. I don't wanna go home."

"Then you're gonna run, and you're gonna run some more. And after that, you gonna do push-ups and sit-ups. And then you're gonna watch the others play from the bench."

"The bench?" — what the fuck!

"You're a talented young fella, and I know you'll make

us proud. But it's like I told you before, the next time you're late, it's the bench. It's not about today, and not even about yesterday, when you were five minutes late, it's about your attitude. If you keep it up, the season will be over for you."

"Whaaaa?"

"You're part of a team, and the team abides by the rules. That's how it is, no matter what's going on. Discipline is how you win, Jewells, and that applies to everything in life, big or small."

I wipe my eyes again. Fuck me, like no way am I spending my last hours of freedom sitting on the fuckin' bench! I watch my team members run their raggedy formation around the field, and I want to be with them, but . . .

"Okay, I know the rules. I'mma go. I'll be here on time tomorrow."

"Good." He pats me on the back, his teeth like yellow sugar cubes. "Tomorrow morning then, bright and early, on time. Right?"

I can see my dudes waving at me as I leave the field like I'm never coming back. I give them the middle finger and like take it across my own neck, and then make the universal symbol of blow job. I know how much my dad gives this fuckin' school, so I'm not too worried. McGlad will be McSorry. Sometimes it's cool having a dad that can throw his weight around. Don't fuck with Mr. Griffin Jewells Saunders II.

Stepmom may or may not be at the house. It's like three

hours before I'm expected to restart my punishment. I know it's all my fault that I'm on punishment, but she pushes my buttons and I know I'd be a whole lot fuckin' better if I didn't always like have her fingers jabbing me in the head.

I'm about to call LoQuan, when a text from him dings. He like called me a couple times last night, but I didn't listen to his messages. His text reads "Ready, nigga?" He lives closer to my school than to me.

"Yo, Jewells, what's up? Cain't call a nigga back?"

"Sorry, some family shit. What's up with you?"

"Just chillin' at the moment. Where you at?"

"School. Football. I'm just leaving practice."

"I was going up to the putt-putt course for a few games, but my dude Morris bailed on me."

"Putt-putt, what the hell is that?"

"Miniature golf, nigga. You know how to golf? I thought all you Hyde Park boys played golf?"

"I can golf, but I don't do kiddy golf, and even if I did, I can't. I gotta go home, too. Capital punishment."

"Whaaaaaat, they turning on the juice?"

"Yeah, at six. That's when I'm supposed to be home."

"Man, they should just pull the switch, put your black ass outta misery."

We laugh like fools. I feel like so cool with him; like, his homies ridiculed the way I talk, called me a nigga-lite from Hyde Park. Not LoQuan though, I get respect from LoQuan.

"Six, huh? Yo, that means you got a couple hours."

"I didn't know you could tell time, nigga . . ."

"I can do a lotta shit you don't know about . . . I'm comin to get you."

"No, don't."

Plan A is LoQuan's scheme, which probably won't work out, whatever the fuck it is. Plan B is about getting Stepmom and Dad to lay off. I'm thinking I should just go to the library to check out the summer reading list, maybe get a head start, before I fall too far behind.

I'm like, "I'm gonna be grounded till I'm eighteen if I don't get the evil Fashionista off my back."

"Fuck her," he goes. "You don't need her, and pretty soon you won't have to deal with the pretty bitch at all. I got us another hookup."

"You do?"

"That's why I was calling your black ass last night." He hollers the "black ass" bit. "It's the dude we met, and five of his friends. It's the same scene, pay and we play, and they payin' *mucho mas*."

"How much?"

"Half a 'g'."

"Five hundred?"

"That's what I said. He wanna pay us the same like before, but I told him each of them fairy mufuckas had to pay a hundred bucks. I told him we're in summer school and you're in driver's ed, and he ate that shit up, so it's five hundred. That's right, right?"

"How many of them you say?"

"A few of his friends, so like five."

"I don't know."

"Nigga, what you mean you don't know? I thought you was down? I set this shit up, and now you going pussy on me."

"Well . . . I don't know, man . . . You don't know these people."

"Nigga, you kiddin' me? I know Mr. Fritz. And they all just like him, they all got jobs — this dude with the house we going to is a doctor — and some of them be married, too, that's what Mr. Fritz say."

"I don't know . . ."

"Look, nigga, they got more to lose than us. I mean like, we'll give 'em up to the police. We're minors and they know it, so I don't think we have to worry about them doing shit to us. So, you down?"

"Man, I don't know. And my dad . . . I have to cancel my driver's test till he comes back."

"What's that got to do with shit, huh?"

"Dude . . ." I'm like what the fuck, he doesn't have a Dad, so he doesn't get the pressure!

"Jewells, man, I tell you what, you do this for me, and I'll like get us a fuckin' car from Avis and we can get your license. You down with that?"

"I have to have my dad's signature."

"Naw you don't. You can get one of them driver's training dudes to go with you and sign for it, if I can't myself. Cool?"

"LoQuan, I don't know. My dad really wants to do it, and I'll let you know about the other thing."

"You sound like a little bitch. Fuck you, Jewells!"

"Are you for real?"

"Am I for real? A course, I'm for real, nigga."

"I don't know."

"Man, you shouldna said you would."

Fuck! What should I do?

"Okay, just this once. When?"

"It's Saturday night. You got five days to get it together."

"I'm on punishment, remember," I say, my voice trailing off to a whisper.

"Now I know you ain't hanging with your supermodel stepmom 'cause she don't even like your ass."

"And it's mutual."

" . . . so slip yo ass right out yo little carriage house and we'll like meet on Madison Road or you go down to the high school or something and wait. Sound like a plan?"

I'm like silent.

"Dude, you better not bitch out on me, I'm countin' on you."

"I won't. Later."

Fuck me, I hang up, and I'm like thinking the five days will give me time to see how it plays out with Dad. If he stays in town for my birthday, I'll bail on LoQuan. Dad will give me anything I want, so I don't need to do no dick show for money. I'll offer LoQuan to sleep over at my place sometimes, if he comes late at night when everybody's asleep. And like fuck, I'd even be down with messing around again, hell yeah.

I call my girl Sophie, and like ten minutes later she picks me up from the Kwik on Vine Street, because she's like totally jealous and thinks I'm tite with my girl Luna, which I am. Luna's family is from Ecuador and lives in Kenwood, but Sophie lives just down the road from us, and me and her been fuckin' since like thirteen, and she's like wild, which is like wack 'cause she's a sophomore at Ursuline Academy for Girls. I mean, Luna is all that, Jennifer Lopez ass and all. Except she is like God this, God that, so boring — but there are other considerations, like the instant gratification of a blowjob. Unlike me and Luna, Sophie's already got her driver's license and wheels, a little yellow convertible Fiat that used to be her mom's. Plus Sophie is pretty fuckin' hot. I mean she looks like one of those blonde, thonged-out beach chicks you see on *Baywatch*, and you can just picture the Santa Monica boardwalk with a yellow cherry sun dangling over the Pacific Ocean.

It's not long before Sophie pulls up, all coppery from driving with the top down, her blonde hair in the jaws of a hairclip.

She goes, "What's up, Jewells?" and flips her sunglasses to the top of her head, with a look in her hi-def blues that says I should know what's coming next.

I'm like, "It's all about you, Sophie" and slide over to kiss citrus-flavored lips that sparkle and shine.

She goes, "Jewells, you are like just the biggest liar."

"I'm not. It is all about you. I'm like in fuckin' jail starting at six o'clock, and it's like you are the last happiness I will know . . . like my last meal, a last fuckin' rite."

"Dude, please tell me you didn't steal those sneakers?" she goes, looking down at my feet.

I laugh. I laugh 'cause like she knows me well enough to know just how much I wanted the Nikes. I laugh 'cause I want to tell her that I kissed and jacked off a dude in front of some freakin marshmallow pervert. I laugh 'cause maybe I shouldn't want anything that much because it's like toxic to want so much you'll do anything for it. I mean, fuck me, people might get the wrong idea.

"'Cuz you know I got them for you," she says, pouting. "Size fourteen."

She like points to the familiar box, sitting on the back seat. I reach behind me and lift the lid, and like there they are, in gold, and I'm like the Tin Man seeing his new heart for the first time. Now I've got silver and gold. Tite!

What the fuck, I tell her my troubles, and she like tells

me hers, that her parents don't want her to spend the fall in France. They want to host a French student in Cincinnati instead.

She's like, "It's some girl whose dad works with my father. I mean, like, the whole point is for me to be independent. Situation all fucked up!"

"Like, you need to be chaperoning some 'brie baguette' around."

"Right? How lame is that? I mean, I wouldn't mind if she was like cool, but she's like totally a dork. She wants to study spiders. She is chic — I love her scarves and eyeshadow — but she's not even pretty. I thought all French girls were pretty."

Sophie guns the engine shifting between second and third gears. I like the Fiat, except it's like so fuckin' noisy, but at least it doesn't have fumes like LoQuan's piece-a-shit. Too bad I can't learn how to drive a stick by Wednesday, then my license dilemma would be solved. I wonder what she knows about credit reports, but I might as well be asking her about the first-draft NBA picks.

Why is nothing ever like fuckin' simple anymore?

In Devou Park, I'm sad about curfew in an hour, so we like cheer each other up as best we can. We agree she will text me to let me know when she can like sneak into the carriage house in the middle of night for a real thank you, but for now my fingers are like sticky with pussy after she blows me — like nobody sucks dick better!

6

Stepmom is on the warpath. She calls to make sure
I'm at home at the start of my curfew. I show up for dinner
and listen to the munchkins, but I keep cool and clear of her.
At one point, I try a little reverse psychology, throwing her
a compliment about how she's kept Dad's spirits up. She
ignores me, which is like cold-blooded. Munchkins turn on
me too. Like, I don't know if she's put up to it by Stepmom,
but Alyssa gets revenge for the Pamper debacle by hitting me
in the neck with a cracker. She's got a good arm, I'll give her
that, and I'm not mad 'cause I know not to style around them.
Babies are fuckin' nasty.

Back in my space, I chill with my video games. It's
eleven p.m., and I start dozing. A text comes from Heinz,
which I like ignore, but then when he calls, I pick up. Heinz
goes, "Dude, it's part two of your birthday. We'll be by to get
you at midnight." I'm like, "Dude, I'm on punishment."

"So, what else is new?"

"But I'm so fuckin' tired."

He's like, "Get a power nap, and meet us at the usual."

I'm like a power nap is for the middle of the day, not at
bedtime, but what the fuck.

The usual is Madison Road, which is not far from my house, and it's the only part of my after-hours life that is like dangerous. I've been stopped before, but the private security cops know I live here and Dad has flipped a switch on them, and then on me, when they've dropped me off past my 10 P.M. curfew. Like when I was in eighth grade, I took up running, and a few times I'd take off in my track gear at midnight, and I'd run right up to the police car deliberately just so they wouldn't fuck with me. One night I tried slipping out in like jeans and T-shirt and my favorite jimmies, and fuck me if they didn't scoop me right up. Dad made a big deal about suing the city for racial profiling, so now like when they see me they go, "Hey Jewells, have a good run!" even though I'm like decked out in my dress jimmies and my Tommy's and a cool T-shirt.

Heinz's father and mother are in the fuckin' Azores, and Heinz has the BMW all to himself. It's the 730i, a big black muthafucka of a sedan, and the license plate says doctorike — he's like a brain surgeon or something, and has this massive sci-fi head. Heinz didn't get the alien head or the massive brain but instead is a ginger with freckles and a massive appetite for smoke equal to his linebacker build. Contrary to the image of the footballer, the dude is famous in his own right as a hacker; he's a Gray Hat, not some evil dude trying to break into people's checking accounts and or the telephone company records; his moniker is Hyptic. I've never seen him not buzzed — but he's always cool, calm, collected, always tite, so his folks are not on his case. They left him the BMW, or left the car keys so he could take it — which is the same difference in my book. Even if my dad entrusted me with the keys, I'd be driving a lame-ass Jaguar. Dad says the Jaguar is just right for driving around where he has property, the BMW is too fancy. I haven't seen my dad's properties before, but I have been to Over-the-Rhine, Avondale and Evanston, and I'm like what Dad means is he doesn't want the folks in the hood to think he's a drug dealer, even though he looks like a businessman or a lawyer or a funeral director, 'cause the players are the ones with BMWs and Benzes and Esplanades, and the players keep lawyers and funeral directors busy. The Jaguar only suggests Dad's a serious, if second-tier, dealer of tax-paying shit.

Heinz texts that he's turning on Madison now. So I slip out of the carriage house through the back and cross our yard. There are only like four houses between ours and Madison Road, and there's no sidewalk, so I walk right down the middle of my street. If private security cops come, I'm like out in the open, not fuckin' slinking along the bushes or running through yards, but right there for anybody up at this hour to see me. Two of our neighbors have pretty big yards, and I think one of them, the Erkenbachers', has a motion detector or a video camera that's like aimed at the street. That's what Mr. Erkenbacher told Dad, and he said it was 'cause of the robberies, even though the robberies are never like happening here. Fuck me, I'm thinking maybe they have us under special surveillance, so I always wave when I pass the Erkenbachers', just in case.

Luckily I'm home free, and Heinz's BMW is sitting there all official-looking, like the KGB or Interpol waiting to pick up a fugitive. It's kinda cool, and I spring into the backseat feeling like I've made it to safety.

Heinz is like, "What's up?"

"Not much, where's Mueller?"

"He got busted. He just phoned me not to come, and he'll meet up with us late, if he can."

"Dude, you should have said. I'm like beat."

"He didn't text me till I was like turning onto your street."

"Where we going?"

"Your birthday, dude — surprise!"

"Tite."

"Fuck, Jewells, I thought maybe you got busted too, with your old man home."

"Right, but no, he's still like in the hospital."

"Oh shit. Dude, you didn't say he was in the hospital. That's what was going on at the field with you and Coach yesterday?"

"Yeah, Coach was still like giving me grief."

"Man, wow. Well, hopefully your dad'll be alright."

"Yeah, it was a panic attack . . . that's what my dad said it was."

"Cool, I mean, like panic attacks are not like cancer or anything like that."

"Yeah, well, it was probably 'cause he just realized he married a fuckin' asshole."

"Dude, my dad was always flipping out on my real mom, but him and my stepmom, it's funny, but they are like right for each other."

"Like how you know that?"

Then he goes, "They talk stuff out and I have never heard them fight. It's hard for me to be mad at her since she like totally makes him happy."

Boring!

"Jewells, dude, would you like be pissed off if I said I was gay?"

"Oh wow, like, what? You?"

"Yeah, me."

"Wow . . . no, why would I?"

"I figured you'd be cool. I mean, like you came out as black."

"What?"

"I mean, like, you were black, but now you really are black . . . you know, black black dude."

"My nigga, I guess we both came out."

We laugh and I'm like this close to telling him about

LoQuan, when he goes: "So, I was thinking I'd give you a blowjob for your birthday."

"What?"

"Just kiddin'."

"Dude!" Now I'm like totally confused. "No really, dude, I mean, it's cool if you are. . . no to the blowjob, but gay is cool. What do I care? Live and let live."

"Jewells, dude, you I think I'm a homo or something?"

We laugh, but I'm like too exhausted to appreciate the joke. The night is young and old in a flash.

7

Like, I've barely got the sleep snot out my eyes when I see Stepmom standing at the foot of the bed, her sunglasses giving off cyborg scariness. She's in her tennis clothes — the tight stretchy outfit with the short skirt that rides the top of her thighs and the tank top that crisscrosses at the back of her bony shoulders. I'm like sprawled across the bed, and my friend inside my boxer shorts is excited as always in the morning, flagpoling out the pee-hole. I pull more of the lime green sheet over me, and turn my back toward her.

"Jewells," she says, "your father is being released in an hour. I was going to pick him up, but he wants you."

"Sure."

"Please get out of the bed . . . now."

"Why?"

"I just want to make sure you get up."

"I'm up."

"If I leave, you'll just go back to sleep, and your father will not be happy to be left sitting there waiting for you."

I spring to my feet and let the sheet drop to the bed. She turns away, but she looked! I know she did even behind those scary glasses, I can tell. And it's not like looking at a baby squirt gun, 'cause I'm a man, in case there was any doubt — a big man. That's what's up. Tite!

"I'll call a cab," she says, heading toward the door. "Bring your learner's permit. You'll need it to drive his car back."

"Huh?" I like turn back toward the bed, and she stays at the entrance, her back still to me.

"Your father's car's already at the hospital. He drove himself to the hospital when all this happened — you know how your father is."

"Wow, I didn't know that."

"He was on the highway when he got sick . . . I think he was on his way to see you at football practice."

"He was coming to see me? Wow, like wow."

"Jewells, sometimes you act as if you are unloved." She says this with her "what a loser you are" tone. The nerve! And, like I see a pattern in the way Dad and everybody else talks to me. I could be wrong, but it seems like the only way anybody can talk to me about me is like through comparison with others. And I'm like, Hey, I'm not like her, so fuck you . . . and her.

"There's nothing your father wouldn't do for you. You're almost sixteen years old and you should know that by now."

"I do know that I'm almost sixteen years old." I grin to myself; Stepmom's easily fucked with. "I'm really clear about that."

"Jewells, I'm talking about your father's . . . never mind."

"Mom, you might not know it, because I don't often show it, but like, I'm glad that I have you to remind me that I'm not unloved. Like, because the problem isn't his unlove, it's yours. You don't love me. You unlove me."

"Of course I do . . . love you." She like pivots toward me. "You're unlovable at times, but I love you . . . it hasn't been easy between us, but we've come a long way."

"We have, yeah," but I say it like to challenge her. Stepmom's gotta have the last word, and I half-expect her to spin around, her anger blazing at me over the Pamper. But she doesn't move from the door, and it's like she's waiting to figure out if she should or shouldn't.

"Just bring your temporary permit. You're always wanting to drive, now's your chance."

"You know what the problem is" — and I say it like yeah, I know you can't walk away from this — "the problem is he trusts me and you don't."

"Let me count the ways." She's talking to the door, but I hear her clearly. And just like I knew she would, she turns, flips the sunglasses back and stands there, shifting her weight from one foot to the other like she's expecting my hard serve. "At this point, Jewells, there's not much you could do to make me trust you. If you're talking about driving, you haven't done a lot to earn my trust, and the thought of you driving the children around doesn't make me feel comfortable at all."

"I guess it's just bad chemistry between us," I say.

"Chemistry? If you mean, we disagree about indulging you just so you have your way so you can stay out of mine, you're wrong."

"That's not what I'm talking about!" I like give her the pregnant pause, then, "You know what I mean!" I almost said bitch.

She slams the door on her way out.

Right, like I know what I am, and I know what's up. I drop the sheet, palm my nuts, grab my dick and want to stick it into something — first Sophie's warm and wet mouth comes up for me, and then like I'm thinking about Luna, beautiful

Luna's pussy sandwich I love tonguing and nicking with my teeth, and then the chick I met in the parking lot just after Stepmom's screech about the Pamper, and then him.

Like, I'm showering when I hear car tires kicking the gravel, which can only mean that a car has like backed into the gravel safety areas by the garage. What the fuck, she's probably on the phone with Dad complaining about me. So!

I shower, throw my clothes on and ten minutes later, I'm like on my way, like Rocky about to take the championship. I TKO'ed Stepmom, and she'll leave me the fuck alone now. Dad will make sure of it, he better.

I actually hate car service. It's like so old-people, like I need a ride from the fuckin' nursing home to have my stool analyzed. I used to go to the doctor's with Meemaw — and she'd have her stool in a nice little envelope sprayed with Lysol and all taped up and in her vinyl pocketbook — and Dad would always send us by car service if he didn't have time. He never had time, and still doesn't, only now I'm taking the service over to get him like he's an oldy like Meemaw. It makes me nostalgic. Should I shit in an envelope for old times' sake? Meemaw had a humongous behind and I always wondered how she like aimed it just right to shit on a little square the size of a matchbook. One time I went through her medicine cabinet in the bathroom and I like found stool sample instructions about using a knife or spatula. It like totally cracked me up picturing her squatting over a bread plate, then with a butter knife smearing a little poop on the square like fuckin' jam on a cracker.

I really don't like hospitals. After I make a right turn down the hall like the nurse told me to, my stomach says *hell no!* It's that smell — I don't know what stinks, but it's like sanitized baby poo — and I just want to hurl. I don't though, and when I come into Dad's room I'm like thinking fuck me. But then I feel better, 'cause Dad doesn't look sick at all. I mean, he's on his way to play golf, with his pink polo shirt and Rolex. Tite!

"Wow, Dad, it's cool they finally letting you out. Everything working properly?"

"Wasn't but a holiday, son. Nothing but R&R with a checkup."

"You got a tan too — that purple shine like eggplant, or like them really black people from Senegal. Been at the pool?"

"Yeah, a cove in the Cayman Islands . . . in my dreams!"

"You swim . . . in your dreams?"

"Something like that. Did I ever tell you I was born here in this hospital? Your Meemaw too. Isn't that something?"

"Wow, Dad."

"It's nothing like it was then. Now it's all high tech, but then it wasn't the place where you wanted to go if you were sick — but back when Meemaw was born, just before the Depression, it was one of the few places you could go if you were black. 'No Coloreds' signs were posted at the entrance, but everybody knew it wasn't enforced. Hard to picture, huh? It wasn't a world for you, nothing like the way you live now."

He says this like he knows anything about my life. It makes me mad for a minute, but then I think I should cut him some slack, him being here in the hospital and all.

"Did you pass the garden when you came up?"

"I don't know."

"Well, there's where I got my tan," he says. "The delphiniums are in bloom. Delphiniums were Meemaw's favorite flower. You probably don't remember the tall white flowers next to her garage?"

"I remember. The dolphin flowers, that's what she called them. I never could see the dolphins. We looked and she couldn't either."

"It's good that you remember things about your Meemaw."

"Like, why wouldn't I, Dad? I like lived with her. Remember, you went to business school and left me with her? Three years I lived with Meemaw." I don't mean for it to come off a criticism, but it does come out that way. It comes out that way all by itself, like just mentioning anything about him leaving me with Meemaw makes it a criticism. I was like five and he left me. Like he never says I wasn't wanted, I was a mistake, but I wasn't wanted and I know it 'cause my real mom ran off from the get-go and he left me. Fuck me, he wasn't wanted by his real dad either, and I guess that's why it was cool for him to leave like that. I like cried all the time, and fuck, me and Dad have that in common — that we were abandoned — but, you know, it really annoys the fuck out of me that he's always trying to imply that me and him are alike, 'cause like *he left me*. Yeah, he went away to better himself so I could have a good life, I believe that. He could have gone to school right in Cincinnati, he could have taken me to University of Chicago with him. But he didn't, *he fuckin' left me*. I mean, like he'll never ever say the truth, 'cause to say it means to admit that he ain't the hero — the Mr. Sacrifice for the family he likes to think he is. Like, yeah, yeah, yeah . . . blah, blah, blah!

So here we go, for the thousandth time, he is going to say he worked like a dog through business school 'cause he loves me and wanted to set an example. He's going to say he's temporarily moved to Washington for better opportunities for me and now my siblings too, so that I don't have to struggle the way he did. Sure, like Uncle Chief and him might share a famous father, but their father was like a shit to my dad. Next comes how his father never acknowledged him or even lifted a finger to find out anything about him. How instead Uncle Chief like got the silver spoon in his mouth — like silver is impressive! — and had all the opportunity, while nothing was given to him except what *he* himself made. Uncle Chief went to the best schools and had a first-class ticket thanks to their father, the same father who didn't do shit for *him*. *He* killed it in college and business school at the top of his class, and he like did it not 'cause he had something to prove to his father. He did it 'cause he learned the lessons taught by Meemaw, who was always there for him. His and Uncle Chief's father, who was probably basically a decent, good man, was proof that good men don't always do the right thing, or do right by their responsibilities.

"See, Jewells, your Meemaw willed me to be successful. Jewells, she was smart, and would have finished college if she hadn't gone to New York and gotten hooked up with my father. She put all her hopes and wishes into me. She practically stood looking over my shoulder 'cause she wanted to make sure I did everything I could 'cause learning was the key to a better life. And Meemaw loved you. That paddle with your name on it, you know, I keep it in my office. There's one with my name on it, right next to it. If she were alive, she'd take that paddle to your behind for all the trouble you've been in. And then she'd whip my behind for letting it happen."

"Yeah, Dad."

"You think it was easy for me? It wasn't. Jewells, to tell you the God's honest truth, I felt rebellious just like you. She suffocated me, but I knew I had to do right anyway."

"Yeah," I go, so not interested. "Meemaw had a swing… did she play ping-pong when she was a girl?"

"No, she played my behind. Meemaw perfected her swing on me. That's why I went to grad school in Chicago, so

I wouldn't get paddled."

"Dad, let's say we just keep those paddles in retirement, huh?"

He huffs a laugh that sounds like it hurts. Nothing is funny about Meemaw hitting me with the paddle — I loved Meemaw, but she was kinda crazy — but her paddling Dad is pretty damn funny. I laugh it up too, just happy he's happy, and then like he throws his arm around me and I know that he really is happy and like so am I, really happy, but I know that something wrong is coming, filled with hurt and disappointment, because it seems like that right after the happy feelings something wrong comes next.

"I really miss you, son. It's not easy for me to be away from you and your siblings like this."

"Not for us . . . not for me, either. I like live in Sesame Street here, but I'm about to turn sixteen. I don't belong here, Dad."

"Son," he goes, and it's like he doesn't know what the fuck to say. But I also know he'll cop out. He always does. And he doesn't disappoint: "We should've just taken a real vacation. We should have gone on a family vacation." It's so lame that I can't fight him. I just go along. "It's still summer, Dad, it's not too late." In a way, I'm thinking how nice it would be if we did have a vacation, but I don't want everybody else with us. Just me and him, like it used to be. Maybe the others for like a day or two.

"Yes, a vacation, that would be nice," he says, freeing his arm. "Let's get out of here."

The doctor gives him his official discharge. I carry his things. There's like a few minutes of paperwork, and then we stroll right out of the hospital. It's bright outside, and he reaches into his pocket for his sunglasses and puts them on, looking kinda cool for a dad.

The Jaguar is in the parking garage, and we head in that direction, Dad saying he doesn't want to wait for me to swing the car around. But like there's a man standing near the hospital exit, a tall white man with a horseshoe-shaped bald spot.

"Mr. Saunders, I need a word with you."

"Yes," Dad says, looking at the man's chest. Dad then looks at the man, at me, at the man again, and then sends his words to me: "Jewells, you get the car. The attendant knows, so just tell them you're my son. I'll wait right here."

The Jaguar is parked very close to the garage exit and the walk bridge to the hospital. The grandpa attendant is hovering around all the parked cars, and he stares at me suspiciously when I stop at the Jaguar. I say, "Griffin Jewells Saunders."

"Mr. Saunders?"

"That's right," I say. "I'm Mr. Saunders."

He studies me for a second.

"That your car?"

"Yes, it's my car, the silver Jag. I'm Griffin Jewells Saunders."

I'm like waiting for him to ask for my driver's license, and then I'll be fucked, but he doesn't. I walk over and see that the passenger side, from headlight to taillight is smashed in, as if the car sideswiped something.

"Hey, man, what happened to the car?" I shout to the attendant.

"Sir, it was like that when it was brought in. It's noted in your file."

I get in and slow-drive over to where Dad is still talking to the bald dude, probably some lame reporter wanting info on Uncle Chief. I settle into the seat, relaxing like this really is my ride, and I'm like, this will be my ride someday — well, not this ride, but a ride that is kick-ass, sound system and all, not a girly Miata. Then, as I watch Dad still talking to this dude, I'm thinking whatever car I get, it won't be from Dad buying me one, fuckin' Stepmom's made sure of it. And then I'm thinking that LoQuan is right, you want shit, get it yourself.

"Dad, the car's messed up. It's been hit," I go, when he finally gets in.

"I know. I had a little accident."

"Like, you sideswiped somebody, hit a tree, what?"

"A guard rail. Just before the panic attack, when I started feeling bad . . . "

"Okay. Not because you were talking on your cell

or texting, right? Because, Dad, you know that's like dangerous?"

He doesn't respond, but looks in the direction of the dude he was talking to.

I go, "Dad, who was that?" The expression on his face makes me think we should like go back inside the hospital, so I say more as a joke, "An FBI agent, the CIA, ATF?"

"Same difference," he says, trying to smile. "Let's get out of here."

My dad's like fuckin' smart, still he's wrong, even I know they're not the same, but I don't correct him. I'm scared for like a millisecond, and then I see how I'm being manipulated by him and Stepmom. I know what's coming next, but I wait till we're off Goodman Street before I say anything.

"When you gotta go back to D.C.?"

"Too soon." His black sunglasses stare straight ahead.

"Tonight, tomorrow, Thursday, Friday? When?"

He doesn't answer. Like, I knew it!

"Dad, I need to know. Like, I have my driver's test on Wednesday. What should I do?"

"Reschedule it. I'm back in two weeks, we'll revisit the issue then."

"Dad . . . ?"

"Jewells, son, get off it . . . I can't control this. If I could, I would."

A bus speeds toward us, it's like two lanes over. I get this fuckin' crazy impulse to drive right into it.

But then I'm like, "Dad, don't worry about it. I got a Plan B. Lots of my dudes got cars, so . . ."

He goes, "Jewells, I said reschedule it."

He's breathing like he's going into heart-attack mode. I'm like scared and reach over to touch him. Then he goes: "Don't write me off just yet, no matter how disappointed you are in me. I'm settling something and real soon you're coming to D.C. and we're gonna make plans and check out schools for you. I'll be there for you, promise."

"Cool, Dad."

"But I need you to help me out. I need you to do your part. Stay out of trouble! I can't finish what I'm doing if I'm all the time worrying about you."

"Okay, Dad."

"Because you, Jewells, mad as you might get sometimes, you don't wanna kill me, do you?"

"Naw, Dad. You're all I got."

I thought I should explain myself, just to be on the safe side, but then Dad goes, "You're all I got, son."

At home, I hug Dad and to make him think I got his point, I chill out with him, Stepmom and the clan, which like almost never happens anymore.

Four years ago, the shrink I was going to told me that whenever I feel sad I should try to visualize my best memory of Meemaw. I have a shitload of best memories of her, but the one I think about most includes Dad. It was my eighth birthday, and for my surprise present he came down from Chicago and took me and Meemaw to Kings Island Amusement Park for the day. I was so surprised, I couldn't believe it. My last three birthdays, what I got was a box with filled with Nintendo and devices and some clothes, shit he knew I liked. Then he would show a week later, and we would celebrate, but I would be mad 'cause like, who the fuck wants to celebrate their birthday a week late? Not me.

So me, him and Meewaw were at Kings Island, and the day was like a rainbow on a Hallmark greeting card, and I was like so fuckin' happy to be with dad and Meemaw. Only, we barely got through the entrance to the park when shit went wrong. Meemaw used to take me to the Cincinnati Zoo and she could handle that, no problem, but the ginormous amusement park was like too much for her. On the big avenue just past the entrance where thousands of people and Snow White and the Seven Dwarfs were dancing, I felt her grab my hand like she was scared of the cartoon character. I remember passing a row of wheelchairs and thinking to myself we should get one for her. An hour later, she was tired from all the walking, and so we went back for one. Then we had to roll her around and go on rides that were made for the old folks. She couldn't fit on any of the cool rides — not the rollercoasters, not even the spinning teacups. I was like, why did you even come with us? The lines for the rides were really long, and Dad wasn't going to leave Meemaw alone, so he waited with her and I went on the rollercoasters by myself, which was cool but sucked at the same time. Like, I think she must've seen my frustration, 'cause we stopped someplace to get lunch and a soda and she said "I'm gonna sit right here under this umbrella and y'all ride all you want."

Much as I loved Meemaw, I was like "Fuck me, we should have left your old fat ass at home anyway," which was like crazy of me to think, 'cause I love her more than anybody except my dad but I wanted to have a great day and it was turning shitty 'cause of her.

The restaurant was in Hanna-Barbera Land, and I was so like totally not interested in riding the Scooby-Doo and the Haunted Castle or Der Spinning Keggers, simple kiddy shit like that. Then I saw the the giant slide. From where we were, you could see it over the treetops, which was kinda cool.

Dad wanted to keep both me and Meemaw happy, he was down with the slide, so we left her talking and laughing and feeling sorry for herself with another old fat lady.

Looking at the slide, Dad was like, "It's pretty high."

I was like, "Yeah, I'm psyched."

I don't remember looking at Dad, and I think I thought he was like agreeing with me that the ride was gonna be a lot of fun. The closer we got, the more the ride, called Scrappy's Slide, looked like a building, it was so tall. You had to climb all the way up, and it was like twenty flights of stairs, but because the line was long and slow, we just inched our way to the top. Took us about twenty minutes to get there, and I guess I was talking most of that time, telling Dad about basketball, which is what I was playing then. Near the top, I looked out at the view and I could see the whole park, and then I could see Meemaw. And I like pointed to where she was sitting, the umbrella leaning far enough away from her that I knew it was her for certain. Dad, who I guess hadn't looked out, turned and he was like sweatin'. He put his arm around me, and he goes, "Jesus, we gotta get down from here. It's too high."

He turned so that he was facing the last few steps, and an attendant gave us what looked like a big sock to get into.

Dad went, "We need to get down."

"Okay," said the attendant, "But you're gonna have to wait until the line thins out. The steps go one way only, and for safety reasons we can't have you go down the steps when people are coming up. We'll hold the line, and you can go down when it's finished. In another half-hour."

Dad, sweatin' hard, goes, "We can't wait."

"Then you'll have go down the slide."

Dad looked at the steep descent, and the five humps that you flew over to reach bottom.

I'm like, "Dad, you scared?"

He goes, "It's too high. It's too high."

"You afraid of heights?"

"No, but this . . ."

People got their socks and bumped into us as they moved out farther on the platform to get ready to launch. This bothered him and he locked his arms together and looked like he was about to be sick.

I was like worried but at the same time I kinda wanted to rub it in, 'cause it was weird that Dad was afraid of anything at all . . . but a giant slide!

So I was like, "Dad, we can't wait up here like this. Maybe we should go down the slide?"

"I can't."

"What if we get in the sock together, and if I like sit in front and you can hold onto me and close your eyes and I'll make sure we get down to the bottom without flipping over?"

He didn't say anything at first. He just stared at his feet, sweating and changing colors, like clouds passing over the moon.

Then I got the sock, and I sat down at the launch closest to us.

"Dad," I said. "Dad come on. Ride down with me. Please, Dad."

He nodded, sweating and shaking, and sat down, spreading his legs and scooting into the bag. I could feel his hands lock around my waist and his head dig into my back.

"I got this, Dad. Don't worry."

What the fuck! I had this feeling he was crying and I was like really weirded out by that, but I figured if we didn't go now, we wouldn't. We scooted to the edge and then I saw Meemaw. She would later claim not to know what I was talking about, but it seemed to me, just before we went over, that she like opened her arms like she was going to catch us.

My stomach was like between my ears and I felt like my rib cage was being crushed as we flew down the first descent, then leveled out and dropped down the next descent, and I was like thinking to myself I was gonna pass out before we reached the ground. We finally got to the bottom, and Dad scrambled to his feet and totally threw up, and I was like trying to catch my breath.

"Thanks," he said, putting his arm around me and we towed each other back to Meemaw. "I panicked up there. Don't know why."

I figured I shouldn't say nothing about the fact that he nearly broke my ribs.

"I'm glad you were there. Cool as a cucumber. You saved me." He kissed my head with vomity lips. "Thank you, son."

Tite!

8

All I really know about D.C. is the Redskins, Wizards and the Capitals. And duh! . . . President Clinton is there and the government and the courts and Uncle Chief. I did get to go to Uncle Chief's swearing-in ceremony. Dad took me, Percy, Stepmom and Oma with him. Basically we flew in, went to big boring parties, and flew out, and even though I didn't get to see any of the city, I did get to connect with Uncle Chief's son, and me and him kinda clicked. So even though I didn't get a chance to vibe in D.C., I've always thought it could be the right place for me regardless of Dad.

That was like three years ago, and I haven't been back. Never mind at least four of Dad's promises . . . surprise! In the past, I just got mad and frustrated. I don't now. I feel that this time could be it.

Seems like a good idea to get the ball rolling. I call Uncle Chief. I'm guessing he's still in fuckin' Europe someplace, but I'm like I'll just leave him a message.

But he answers and I stutter. I tell him I'm surprised and he goes, "Jewells, my boy, I'm glad you called because I was just thinking about you."

"That's cool. I was like just thinking about you, too,

Uncle Chief . . . that's why I'm calling you now."

"Thought equals action. How you doing?"

"I'm great. Me and Dad are going to celebrate my birthday, he got box seats for the Reds/Cardinals game."

"That should be riveting. Two last-place teams battling it out for loser of the year."

"Yeah, right. I mean, like, can't wait!"

"But you'll get lots of quality time with your dad . . . bet you're excited about that, huh?"

"Yeah, I am."

"I hear you might be coming this way?"

"He told you?"

"I can read my brother's mind. I know what he's thinking even before he does."

"Cool! I mean, that you know about me coming. I mean, like, I thought he might be just . . . I don't know . . ."

"Just what?"

"Getting my hopes up . . . it wouldn't be the first time. Uncle Chief, I really wanna come to D.C. with him."

"I've been on your dad about getting you here with us for a long time. It's going to happen this time."

"For real?"

"For real. It's not good for you to be there when you could be here. A boy your age needs his father."

"That's right, Uncle Chief. I'm glad you've been like looking out for me. Dad doesn't get it, but maybe he does now."

"My father had a couple of wives and well, you know, he had a couple of women on the side, like your dad's mom for instance. I know how it feels to have to deal with the other family."

"I didn't know that. I mean, like, so you felt they didn't want you either, like you were in the way?"

"Yeah, son. I sure did, only my father and I were inseparable. The difference is that he also took me with him when he temporarily relocated. It worked. Look how I turned out."

"Yeah, wow, Uncle Chief, you're the man."

"That's what I want for you, son . . . a victory over adversity."

"Did you have a stepmom who like totally hated you?"

"Put it this way . . . and the feeling was mutual, right?"

"Right!"

"Don't sweat it, Jewells, your time is coming. D.C. is where you belong. You need to be in a place where you can thrive, that's what I think about you, Jewells. We'll put you in a good school. Lots to do. We'll put you on a glide path to Georgetown. The football and basketball coaches are buddies of mine."

"Tite. Thanks, Uncle Chief, for . . . for . . . advocating for me."

"Jewells, I consider you my son, and I would advocate

for you like I would my boys."

I try thinking of another impressive word, and nearly say that I consider him to be the coolest uncle ever, but there is a squeak of weird laughter in the background, and I'm like suddenly grinning too, even though I'm not sure they…we…aren't laughing at me.

"How's your dad since the heart attack?"

"He said it was a panic attack."

"Excuse me . . . guess that's what it was, then. I've spoken with him, but in your own opinion, how is he?"

"He's kinda of weird. I mean, I'm pretty worried."

"Is he doing anything strange?"

"No, but there's been some strange people coming around. Some like scary FBI-looking dudes, and I'm like, these dudes are going to give him a real heart attack."

"Interesting. Well, guess then he really needs you here to look out for him."

"See, that's what I'm saying."

"I hear you. As long as you understand that the moment you start being a problem you'll have to go back to your loving, doting stepmother, I think it could work."

"I definitely won't be a problem."

"I know that. Your dad . . . well, we'll both be looking out for him."

"Is there some kinda trouble, Uncle Chief?"

"No, just the usual."

I don't know what that means, and I don't ask and it's like we've pushed the pause button. I hear him mumble something I can't make out to someone, and then he goes: "Listen, you keep an eye on your dad, and you call me and let me know what's going on. And the FBI-looking dudes … you tell me if they keep coming around . . . I wanna hear everything about them."

"I will."

"I'll be seeing you next week then."

I go, "Cool," even though I don't know what's going on — if Dad's leaving me or taking me with him. Fuck, I wouldn't be surprised if he's packing right now for an escape without having to face me.

We hang up and I'm like fortified and pumped up like Coach McGlad wants me to be. I'm like on top of my game.

My dudes are calling me, leaving messages, but I text back — thank God, Stepmom has not canceled my text messages — and say hell no to every request to meet here, there and every-fuckin-where. My dudes that got cars let me practice driving and I know the driver's manual already, so they are really calling to hang out. I'm like so tired of this lame shit, even though I like my dudes and they're like so cool. Much as I like LoQuan I know I'd better leave his Bora Bora ass behind too, and like soon. Never mind the money… I can't even believe I like kissed and jerked off with him. Wow!

Now comes the hard part. I practice my best-behavior

game face, and intercom to find out dinnertime, all armed with charm for Stepmom to answer, but it's Oma, and she's like surprised and suspicious of me.

Oma goes, "Jewells, you come willingly, huh?"

I like laugh a little, and she goes: "Whatever you're up to, please don't upset your father."

And I'm like, "I'm not up to anything, I'm trying to help."

She goes, "Okay, that's good. But I hope you mean it. I really do. Honey, now is not the time."

I'm like, What the fuck! Is everybody fuckin' crazy?

Then I go, "I do mean it. I really do."

"Come over in half an hour. Your mother and father are going out this evening."

"They're not eating with us?"

"No, they're having an early dinner with friends. Then there's a reception at the mayor's for the governor and his wife."

"But Dad just got out of the hospital."

"I know. They're just making an appearance. It's business and they'll be among friends, too — that's what your mother says. It's part of the reason your father came to town . . . plus your birthday, of course."

I'm like, wow, I see the future and it looks all bright and shiny.

"What time are they going?"

"The reception starts at 7:30. They'll probably leave at 6:30."

Tite. I know just what I'm gonna do.

I'm cool, I always clean up good. I was planning on some square khakis and an oxford shirt, looking preppy and normal in the way Dad would like to see me, but then I put on some black pants and a white shirt and my good shoes . . . not my fave sneakers but hard-soled dress Kenneth Coles . . . and I'm looking clean-cut and conservative like the dude that sometimes picks Dad up in a Lincoln Town Car and drives him to the airport when Stepmom can't or won't.

The Jaguar is on the side of the house where it usually is. The keys are kept on a wall hook near the side door Dad usually uses. I go inside to get the keys, then I go to the car. It's hot as fuck inside the leather and plastic interior, and I start the engine up while putting the windows down. Stepmom's Suburban is right next to Dad's car, but on the side of it that blocks the Jaguar so that you can't see it so well from the house. I put the car into reverse, and I'm backing up, swinging it around to bring to the front of the house. But then I think, Dude, Dad wouldn't drive a wrecked car to the mayor's house, that would just be tacky. Then I think, I should just park the car where it was. That's what I do.

Like, I walk back to the house and put the keys on the wall hook, and I'm like staring at the keys to the Suburban. I've never driven it 'cause Stepmom won't let me. I think about going up to ask Dad if I can drive them to the party, be their chauffeur for the evening, but then I'm like that's going to fuck up my surprise. Then I think, just go for it. They're always talking about how selfish I am, and now I'm like ready to give up my evening — so what if I'm on curfew. That definitely makes out a lie of that lame theory.

So I like get the keys and slip out to the Suburban, installing myself in the cockpit. I get a little rush, all the buttons and settings. I stick the key in and the engine coughs to life, as the mirrors and seats adjust to Stepmom's preferences. But damn, I can't really see the side view mirrors that well, the view skimming over the top and the side of the Jaguar. I think I know, though, and put the car in reverse all the same. I'm like making a hard right turn, when there is a sudden bump. Shit! I stop, jump out the car, and fuck me, I've hit the Jaguar. I panic, shifting the car into drive and ease it back like it was — only wrecked! I slip out on the passenger side and I can see a big dimple in the molding near the Jaguar's rear taillights, but I don't care about that, Dad's car was already beat up. Looks like I haven't been seen, and I run back into the carriage house, set the keys down and take a leak, and then head over to the house again, nervous as hell.

The boys run up to me when I come inside, and they're like "Jewells, Jewells." Oma smiles and I know she's pleased at my getup. In their highchairs, the twins giggle and finger the air as I kiss them on the head. I'm about to tussle with the boys, when Dad and Stepmom, looking very dressed up, make an appearance.

Oma says, "Aren't you the couple?"

"Mommy's pretty," says Percy, already such a homo. "I like the ribbon."

"Thank you, Percy. It's the Oscar de la Renta."

"I love the Oscar de la Renta."

"Yeah," I chime in, feeling ridiculous, "the power couple."

"Thanks," she says, giving me a very ungrateful look, as Dad grins.

I go, "A big night, huh?"

But Dad is like, "Just business as usual."

Stepmom goes, "Mr. Saunders, you never take me out, so I say thank goodness for business as usual. It's always nice to mingle with our friends."

Kissing the girls' heads, Dad goes, "We need to get moving." Looking at Oma: "Is there anything I can do for you?"

She goes, "Well, we'll be just fine, now that I have Jewells here with me the whole evening, we'll be just fine."

I go, "We will," as if I'm the most eager babysitter assistant ever.

Stepmom looks at me and offers one of her glittery attitudes, and Dad pats me on the shoulder. They are speechless, and I'm like silent, and thank God, one of the girls squawks and they stop staring at me.

So, they leave through the side, only I don't hear the

door open. Instead I hear Stepmom go, "I put the keys here, just as I always do."

"Maybe they're in the car?"

"No, they should be right here."

I'm like, Fuck me, I forgot to put the keys back, I left them sitting on my dresser. Not good! The Pamper screwup all over again!

I stew in my seat while pretending to play rock-paper-scissors with Fletcher.

I then walk over just as Stepmom and Dad approach the Suburban. Stepmom climbs inside and goes, "No, they're not here, just like I said they wouldn't be."

Dad then looks at me, and goes, "Jewells, go into my study and look in the top left drawer. You should find my keys to the Suburban."

I do. I'm practically shaking when I run through the house. Oma shouts "What's wrong?" and I yell out the problem. I get the spare keys and hand them not to Dad but to Stepmom as she climbs into the passenger seat. And she like gives me a look that says that she knows, but then she goes, "I appreciate you helping out. Thank you."

I go, "Sure. Not a problem. Mom. Have a good night."

Dad's like, "Thanks, Jewells. We should be home no later than eleven."

"Cool. I'll be here."

Dad smiles and seems like Stepmom does too, only with

clenched teeth. Soon as they're gone, I run back to my place, grab her car keys and then drop them on the garage floor, just about where Stepmom gets in and out of the Suburban, so she thinks it's her fault.

9

All my friends are like, "Dude, you got your own house." The carriage house isn't exactly my own house, and my dudes all got good setups too, but I take their point. What they don't have is privacy, and I got plenty of that 'cause the beauty queen's clan is like over there, and like I'm over here, all alone. I mean, like your house could be so big that you could get lost in it like my dude Manning, or you could like hide out in the family boathouse like my dude Chuck, but you always get found. Me, I hide in plain sight. I know they're always checking on me, watching me coming and going, and I have to come over for dinner every night. There was an old video camera mounted on the carriage house to monitor the property 'cause like a lot crime was coming from Evanston where the poor blacks live, and I think it's been busted since the neighborhood hired a private security firm now.

Like, I know I live where the help should live, like the nanny or even Oma if she wanted more privacy, but it's tite 'cause I got a space that's like a loft with a little-ass kitchen and bathroom, but I have to listen to the racket of the garage door opening and closing. Dad always parks the Jaguar inside, and in the winter sometimes he like leaves the car running while he goes back into the house 'cause he forgot something. It doesn't matter if the garage door is open, the fumes still seep through the floor into the apartment, so it's like fuckin' toxic. In the summer he leaves the door open, which wouldn't be cool if we didn't have a gravel driveway. I always hear when someone is coming my way, even if they're trying to sneak up on me. Dad used to all the time, but now that's the beauty queen's job. There is a way to surprise me, though, if you cut across our neighbors' properties or climb the hill and come up through the back.

Like Sophie does.

She like always texts me that she's on her way over, but 'cause I'm like asleep I don't see her message until I practically hear her feet on the squeaky stairs and I'm always like, What the fuck!

This time is no different except I'm like paranoid. I think it's Stepmom showing up to question me 'cause she doesn't believe she dropped the keys in the driveway. But she wouldn't like wander over here after nine, even though that's like when she should if she were ever going to catch me up to shit. Then I think Dad, since he's in town, but he wouldn't come over here this late either. And then I grab my phone and see the text at the same time I hear Sophie's voice calling up the stairs.

"Jewells, dude, you better not have some other girl in there."

"Sophie, it's three in the morning, what the fuck."

"Don't you read your texts?"

"I can't always hear that little beep when it comes."

"Dude, you have to train yourself. It's Pavlovian. Like, text comes in the middle of the night, you get up and get ready because you know it's Sophie. You know what Sophie wants."

Tiiiite!

It's like that too. What Sophie wants, I want. She is a sight, with her blue jean shorts cut off at like pussy level, and tits sticking right into her muscle teeshirt like her nipples trying to burn holes in it. Sophie's like a reminder of why I'm never gonna be a one-woman dude, not unless she is the last woman on the planet 'cause civilization has been like wiped out, so we'd be fuckin' wiped out too — I mean, like what kind of survivors would we be, not knowing how to do shit when fuckin' humanity's on the line?

With the last night on fuckin' earth in mind, I figure we could like copulate — we're good at that, real good. She pulls her shirt off and there wasn't much holding the shorts up no-how. Her pussy is shaved and it makes me think of the baby-sis drama for a second, but then I get over it. Like, I have complained before, but Sophie's like, you do whatever you want with *your* pussy, this one is mine. Once she let me shave it, and I was like, tite. By the time I was done with the razor, I was like crazy to fuck her, but she knew it. She was like, "It always works." And I'm like, "How many dudes shaved you?" And she's like, "None of your fucking business."

And all of it just makes me want her more, the hell with my other girls. Guess I'm a little crazy like that.

"Sophie, what's up? Something's wrong, I can tell."

"Nothing I want to talk about, Jewells. Just fuck me, okay?"

I had a hit of a joint before going to bed and I'm like still high, and she says she's buzzed too. Her gloomy side like totally doesn't faze me though, and I poke my finger in the spool holding her hair on her head and blonde sunshine falls and floats down all around me. Soon she like bounces on my dick and flips her hair back and then whips it around over me, her titties etch-a-sketching on my chest, and kisses me hard on the month. We like chew each other's lips, grinding away, when she climbs off me and flops back and does one of her famous cheerleader splits. I put my tongue where my dick has been, and I'm like this might be the closest I ever get to knowing what my own dick tastes like — I pulled a muscle trying to suck my own joint once — and get her to cum good, her blue eyes rolling in the back of her head like the Exorcist girl, and then I'm ready to finish the job when all of a sudden I hear:

"Dayum, so this where the party is?"

"LoQuan, what you doin just showin up like this?"

"I was in the hood."

"Dude, you liable to get picked up for trespassing in this hood."

"And I'll just say I'm visiting the Griffin Jewells Saunders family, which is true."

"Hi," goes Sophie, sitting up, snapping her legs together like scissors, all shy suddenly.

"Hey babe," says LoQuan, inching toward her.

"Oh my God, your hair is like fuckin' amazing," says Sophie. "It's real. It's so thick and shiny."

"Come and touch it."

And before I know it, she's like unzipping his pants and his dick is in her mouth.

"Dayum, nigga, dayum."

"Fuck me," I say, and I'm like, now what?

And then she takes us both in hand, and I'm looking him in the eyes, and Sophie goes like, "Y'all can kiss, I really want you to. I like watching boys kiss. It gets me wet."

There ain't shit more to say, our mouths meet and when we take Sophie to the floor, Sophie straddles me again and I plant my feet and use my thighs to fuck. This time, I feel what I think is his dick rubbing against my balls and butthole just before I cum. I'm like, dayum — and when he pulls his dick out of her he squirts on her pretty hair and on me — it's warm, kinda hot.

"Like, I know spooge is protein-filled and supposed to be good for my hair, but nigga, *don't* do it again!" Sophie snarls, then runs to the shower, ass jiggling mightily.

"Dayum, oh, myjesusmaryjoseph. So this is what it be like in Hyde Park."

"East Walnut Hills, nigga."

"Jewells, my man, you holdin out on me?"

"What you talking about?"

"All this bounty, all this booty, and you never invite me?"

"You invited yourself. And dude, if you ever come here again and the security police pick your black Asian ass up, you better hope they just take your word for it and not call my folks . . . "

We like lay there, and I'm like, fuck me, I've got to get up in two hours, and Sophie comes in and says, "What's your name, dude?"

"LoQuan."

"Now, secrets please. What kind of conditioner do you use?"

"Nothing but the best, Cream of Nature."

"What's that?"

I go, "It's for black people."

"Are you black?"

"Yeah, he's a nigga," I go.

And Sophie's like, "I just called you nigga as in my dude, but I didn't mean it like historical racism — don't take it personal."

"I didn't, no problem."

"Cool," goes Sophie. "I figured you were like a dark Filipino, Mexican or Puerto Rican. It's all sooo confusing."

"I'm all of the above and whatever else you like," goes LoQuan.

"Your mother must've been beautiful?"

"No doubt, but you are the cream of nature. Wanna be my babymoma?"

"Nigga, please."

LoQuan cracks up, and I'm like, "Dudes, y'all wanna good laugh?"

I'm fuckin' tired as hell, but I pull up a digital clip on my Mac. It's of Stepmom on the talk show *Sunday in Cincinnati*. The second Kitty Vanderhoven starts talking, we flop back on the bed and are laughing our asses off at her umbrella hairdo. She says, "Ladies, many of you will remember my good friend Margeaux Saunders from her days as co-host of *Today in Cincinnati*. Since Margeaux left that show, she and her husband Griffin have become quite the power couple around town, sitting on museum boards and helping to raise money for their favorite charities . . . and there's speculation about a future mayoral candidacy.

Margeaux is five months pregnant with their second child."

Smiling Stepmom goes "hi" and waves to all the people in TV land, and Kitty says, "Margeaux, you look so amazing. How do you do it?"

Stepmom goes, "Thank you. I feel great too, and that's very important during pregnancy. I've been lucky, no morning sickness — it's been pretty smooth, but I also have a strong fitness regimen that keeps me energized and feeling terrific. All those endorphins, you know."

Kitty says, "There are lots of beauty benefits during pregnancy — prenatal vitamins and power surges of estrogen. Have you found that to be true?"

Stepmom: "Well, yes, my hair has never been fuller or shinier. It's really amazing, even my hairstylist says there's nothing for him to do. Some would say, renegotiate his fee, but I say no, because it isn't his fault I'm low maintenance."

"What about your nails?" says host Kitty Vanderhoven.

"There's so hard I can open boxes without a box cutter."

"Have you cut back on salon visits?"

"Yes and no. I didn't do any hair perms or coloring or highlighting during my first trimester. As far as nails, I make sure the salon I go to is well ventilated — that's an absolute must!"

I go, "Is it an absolute must for you, LoQuan?"

"Man, shut up, your Mom is wacked!" he says, as Stepmom then like lists all the face and body creams and astringents she uses, plus the day spas she goes to, and the "pleasant rubs that delight her and baby."

Sophie goes, "Wow, she's like the Martha Stewart of pregnancy, huh?"

Kitty Vanderhoven says, "Margeaux, I saw a photo of you in a gorgeous stunning Christian Lacroix dress, wearing a brilliant red lip color. A very unexpected choice for you. Off camera, you're usually a nude-lip gal, or a soft red at the most, aren't you? What made you decide to go with that intensity?"

Like, Stepmom sounds like the English teacher explaining the subjunctive, "I just felt that a vermilion lip was the perfect counterpoint to the blue-black Lacroix. I knew I would feel very mischievous, even though I was bursting at the belly! Chanel Rouge Vermilion can be very dramatic and elegant. And a bold lip, like a compelling piece of jewelry, draws the eye away from the belly. Pregnancy is a beautiful time in a woman's life, but I don't advise making the belly the center of attention anymore than it already is."

"I wouldn't advise it either," I say, hopping up to press pause.

"Listening to your mom turns you on, huh, Jewells?" Sophie says, making big eyes at my big piece.

"Yeah, baby." I like make a big deal of grabbing my balls, and notice that LoQuan's got his in hand, winking at me.

"She should've spent some time talking about cumming with a fetus sitting on your joint," says LoQuan, petting

Sophie's nipple. "That would have made a really interesting topic that a lot of bitches in Cincinnati would have loved to hear about."

"Bitches? That's like totally gross, dude," says Sophie.

"Yeah, bitches. For real, I'd just like to know, I mean," says LoQuan, as straight-faced as I've ever seen him. "I mean, like, if you getting it hard, would my dick like be beating up the baby?"

I crack up, and Sophie has LoQuan by the hair. "Bitch, I would beat your ass first."

"I bet you would," he says, his voice soft. I put on Portishead 'cause Sophie likes it, but LoQuan erupts, "What the fuck is that?"

We agree to disagree, and soon meet in the middle with Sophie sandwiched between us, LoQuan in one hole and me in the other, like a mad Oreo cookie.

Tite!

10

One of my dudes shouts — "Eat too much pussy last night, Jewells, is that why you can't see straight?" — after I like overthrow the ball out of bounds, and then get slammed in a hard tackle that clips me at the knees, flips my shoulders down until they hit the wet spongy grass, followed by the rest of me, hydroplaning and slow-mo spinning. The popping sound in my ears is like being on a plane. All of a sudden, I feel dizzy and can't breathe, and yank the helmet off. Two of my teammates grab my underarms and haul me up. "Dude, you alright?"

"I'm good." I see pink bubbles in the gray sun, and like red ones in the green grass.

"You sure?"

"Yeah, I'm sure."

We were like thirty yards out, but my teammates, playing defense and offense, now go in different directions. I like wobble, not sure which direction I should go — fuck me, I don't even know where I am. I feel my legs go limp and my whole bulk hit the ground. A couple dudes lead me to the bench.

"You alright?" Coach McGlad is holding a pair of binoculars, or so my brain thinks.

"Just a little dizzy," I nod, still seeing bubbles everywhere.

"A little dizzy is okay. Sit here awhile. If it gets worse, we'll get a doctor."

"I'm okay." I'm like, shit, Rusty the quarterback, the concussion that ended his career.

He goes, "Good, and don't worry, I don't think your dad saw."

"My dad?"

"Yeah, he was here."

Coach McGlad pushes his binoculars so I see them again. "I saw him drive off just after your second down."

"Oh, well, that's good."

Adding surprise on top of being dizzy and vomity doesn't help me stand up spin-free, but it does make feel better.

Later at dinner, Stepmom says something urgent came up and "your father had to go back to D.C."

All of a sudden, I fuckin' lose it: "Sur-prise, sur-prise, sur-prise! So predictable!"

"Jewells, please."

"I'm just saying . . . I mean, Fletcher, Percy, are y'all surprised?"

"No, Daddy's always gone," says Fletcher, the feather in his pirate hat shaking.

"Alyssa, Ariel — y'all surprised?"

Ariel shows off her two teeth as she slams her cup on her high chair.

"See there, and she can't even talk. No fuckin' surprise!"

"Cut it out, Jewells. I mean it. Now."

I jump up from the table. She follows me out into the hallway.

"Listen, you really can't act out like this in front of the

children."

"Well, I just did."

"You think he wanted to go. He didn't. He'd much rather be here."

"Yeah, yeah, yeah."

"It's not about you. Why is it so hard for you to understand that not everything's about you?"

"The problem is nothing is ever about me."

I was like planning to mention the concussion, but I'm like fuck it — maybe it's better if I go to sleep and not wake up, so I don't say shit. Well, I apologize, but only to get her off my back and me out of there because I so fuckin' feel like disappearing. I look at my phone, and in two hours I will be sixteen years old — on punishment, no driver's license, no car, concussed, and nobody fuckin' cares. I tell her I'm going back to my place, and she says goodnight. The boys do too, and then the babies.

Back in my space, first thing I do is like light up a joint Sophie gave me like a while back. After I start mellowing out, I look up at this poster of Dad playing college ball and I'm like pissed again. All the posters in my room show basketball players, not football, and this one is like the biggest. Dad is doing a layup for the UC Bearcats. I used to to think it was taken at a live game, but it's like one of those fake shots, where he jumps up and tips the ball in. The picture like snaps him the split-second before the ball leaves his fingers and goes in. The team uniform looks like something some chick would like wear to aerobics class, his shorts are so tight you can see the outline of his stuff. The fro is low-carpet, and he has like these shoe-tongue-like sideburns and is wearing visors instead of his usual glasses. I always thought that Dad's so-so stats were 'cause he maybe didn't see so well, until I asked him one time and he said, "No, I just wasn't good enough. I knew I wasn't, that's why I focused on school instead."

That poster always made me want to be like him. Fuck, I'm like better at basketball than he was, and that's according to Dad himself. Despite my Meemaw jinx, I played my first year of high school, which was last year, but my stats were like no better than his. At a lame school it wouldn't have mattered, but at Roger Bacon, one of the best in the city for everything but especially for sports, hell no. Name the sport, good enough isn't good enough. It used to to piss me off that I don't got game, 'cause I should — and I think that's why Dad says I'm better than he was, 'cause I fuckin' should be. I watch Michael Jordan and I think I should be playing better than I do, but I'm just not good at it. Not for trying though — I guess I just don't have the right hustle. And like I don't know why either, tall as I am, and fast too — like Dad. The B Coach swears I got speed and agility, but for a player to have game he's got to have mad defense too, at least as good as his offense, and like that's where I'm short — that's why I'll never have game, or maybe it's 'cause I'm gonna be haunted forever by Meemaw

dying by me playing basketball. Watching Jordan shows me
what it takes. You have to rule — fly, forward and backward,
whether you've got the ball or you're trying to get it. Fuck,
I definitely don't feel like a god out there. What throws my
hustle off is like when dudes are coming at me super-fast. I
wouldn't have lasted in football if the coach hadn't said I got
a great arm. Fuck me, I like quarterbacking, 'cause like it's
really the only thing I have to do — like, I've always been
better at offense; well, not getting tackled before passing the
ball is a priority too. The best part is I get to stand out, 'cause
like the QB's the star — and I should be the star. Fuck, I mean
it's not easy at all, but I'm good too, I know it. Sometimes,
though, like when I see them all rushing at me, I think they're
going to like fuckin' trash me, break my bones. I try not
to think that, but I can't help it. Mostly, I try and keep the
football field in my head like the screen of a video game, and I
try to see where everybody is and nail a pass, or run like hell.
I've scored a few points by taking the ball in for a touchdown,
running my ass off smoking the dudes chasing me. Everybody
cheers a touchdown, but you don't get much cred for running
the ball for points like you do for throwing it. And all I want is
to do something that's fuckin' great.

I look at my golf trophies and grab one of them and like
I swing directly at Dad in the poster and CRASH. It fuckin'
falls to the floor, glass every-fuckin-where.

I lay there in bed. First I'm laughing my ass off, but then

I know he'll be really hurt and that makes me sad.

What's wrong with me? I'm like gonna cut my toes off, so I go and clean the glass up before laying down and feeling like a loser.

My phone rings, and I'm wrong in thinking that it's Dad calling because he remembers he forgot me.

"Hey Uncle Chief."

"Happy Birthday, Jewells."

"You never forget me."

"My boy, never, not in a million years." The line sizzles and crackles and sounds like it's breaking up. "Shoot, I remember all my children's birthdays . . . and I love you as if you were my own flesh and blood."

"Thanks, Uncle Chief."

He always says this, and now I wish I *were* his. I wonder if he'd be a better dad, but at least I wouldn't be stuck here, I'd be in D.C. or in New York.

"I wish I could come and visit you this summer, since Dad obviously doesn't want me with him."

"Your cousins are already at the Vineyard. Your father and I will discuss it."

"Looks like Dad doesn't have time for me this summer."

"You'll be here, I'm working on it."

"When?"

"Be patient. I can't say just yet. Leave your father to me."

I think I say thanks but don't hear myself say anything.

"There's a present on its way to ycu, it should arrive tomorrow."

"Wow, cool, Uncle Chief."

"I'm in Singapore and I'm traveling all day tomorrow — that's why I'm calling you now."

"Thank you for remembering me."

"Your father go to D.C.?"

"I guess."

Uncle Chief gets quiet. "Okay my boy, happy birthday. I'll work out the visit with your old man. Good night, son."

Now I don't see myself being anywhere but stuck here all fuckin' summer. I look at the wrecked poster of Dad, and like I'm already so sorry for what I've done — I don't have impulse control sometimes, that's what the shrink said, and I guess he was right. Dad had that poster specially framed for me. There's like no way I can hide it; he'll know. I run over to look at it, and a piece of glass I missed buries into my heel. I limp around bleeding, and by the time I get the shard out of my foot, I'm pissed off all over again. Everything fuckin' sucks.

I finish off the joint, buzzing over the fuckin' treetops, and it seems like a cricket is in bed with me. I'm like asleep and dreaming I'm hearing my name whispered.

Only the nightlight is on, and the room is dark as Guinness ale. I dream I look up and there's LoQuan, standing over the bed, with a cupcake and a burning candle.

"Happy birthday, nigga."

I don't say anything, but stare at him, and I keep staring at him until I know I'm not dreaming, and then like I'm wondering what the fuck!

"Sweet sixteen."

He sits the cupcake on the nightstand.

"I got some Ecstasy to go with it."

"What the fuck?"

"It's like coke when you sniff it."

"I know. That's tite."

"And I have two other presents for you, but I'm saving the last one for later."

He hands me a piece of paper.

"What's this?"

"Your credit report. Yo, you one rich nigga."

"What?"

"See, it's like, you own all this shit — houses, apartment buildings in Over-the-Rhine. Man, you ass been bankrupt a few times too. But not now, your company, GJS Enterprises, is sitting sweet, you a mo'fuckin' Donald Trump, only your black ass didn't even know it."

"What? They must got me mixed up with my dad?"

"Naw, nigger, more like your dad got your Social Security number and been using it all over the place."

"No."

"He's been making you rich and is fuckin' you up big

time at the same time."

"Your cousin told you my business like that?"

"No, I was in her office and she went to the bathroom, and I saw it plain as day on her desk. Then I did a little research."

"Probably a mistake."

"Social Security numbers don't lie. She gonna call herself. The application is approved, so we get the Miata."

"We do?"

"Yeah, man. All we got to do is get you your license and go sign the papers and pick it up. And we've got the first payment after Saturday."

"Tite, but . . . I don't know. What if my dad finds out?"

"You tell him that you know what's up, that he stole your Social Security number and his ass is going to jail."

I turn away. I don't want him to see me crying, and I want his ass to leave — how did he even get in here? — but I don't want him to go, I'll be by myself. Then I feel him sitting on the bed.

"He's my dad," I say. "I couldn't do that."

"Jewells, look at me," he says.

I feel his hand on my shoulder, and it's pushing me toward him. I wipe my face and stare at him.

"It ain't about your dad. Dads ain't shit, far as I can see. Naw, nigga, it's about you and me. Like I was driving around and I was thinking about you . . . " he pulls his shirt off, and his hair drops around his chest. " . . . and I was like, Jewells is my nigga."

I watch, and I'm about to suggest I text Sophie, but I know I don't really want her to see me all crying and shit. And maybe I wouldn't want to see her 'cause . . .

"Am I your nigga, Jewells?"

Then he leans over me, his hair falling over me. I reach up with like both hands to push it away from his face, and my fingers get tangled.

"You heard me, Jewells. Am I your nigga?"

"Yeah," I say, his mouth pushing onto mine, his hand in my shorts.

"I'll do anything for my nigga. Cuz I know my nigga would do anything for me. Am I your nigga, Jewells?"

"Yeah, you my nigga."

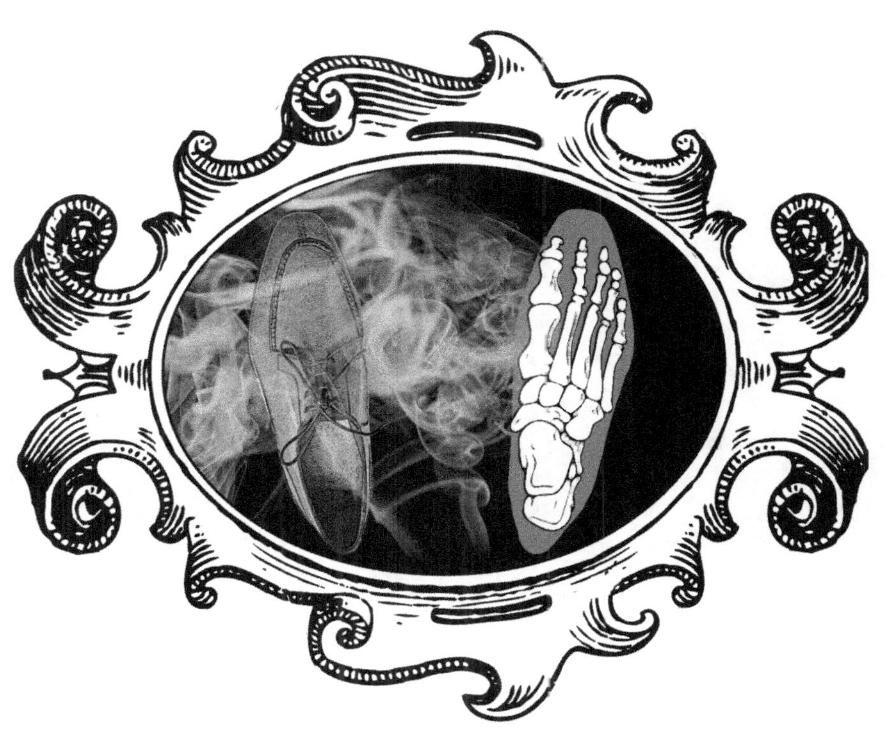

Mr. Saunders

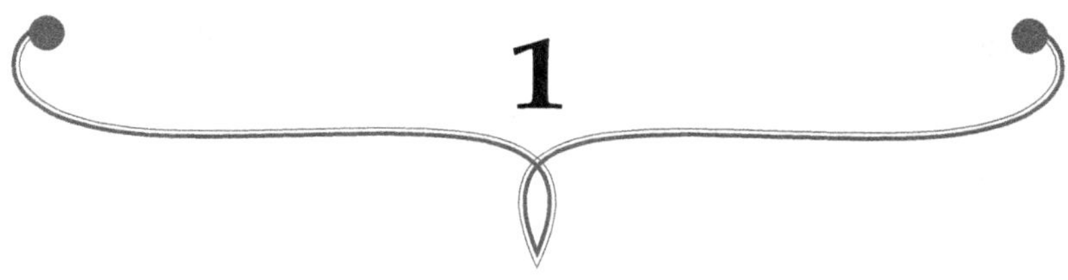

1

It could be the light in the Bentley showroom, but the darkly tinted windows of the Arnage seem excessive, and the mirrored versions extreme. Passersby curious about such a car might think its passenger a glittery entertainer or lesser sheik, and wonder why such a person would bother with the harsh glare of Washington, D.C.

Fitted blinds, on the other hand, say a gentleman is aboard; likewise, curtains drawn exactly to Downing Street effect. Unfortunately, none of the showroom models is outfitted with either type of window treatment, nor is there a dressed-up custom order collated among the parked inventory. Solomon, the sleek Bentley salesman, has just claimed that your average rich American considers window dressing "too fey. But, in fact, Mr. Saunders, you and I both know there is nothing average about the man who drives a Bentley."

"I'll say," Griffin has responded, as wary of suck-up Solomon as he is of certain people in D.C., the ones pressing his need to obscure himself in public. He has countered that the real problem with blinds or curtains is not "feyness but exposure: You wouldn't be able to see who's looking within without also being seen." Further, he points out, Griffin has implied that it is important that a man with very rich clients be seen in the right light, and equally that he get a good look at who's watching.

Solomon reminds Griffin of the 1998 Arnage's built-in video surveillance, a little technological feat of omniscience that renders all window treatments a matter of vanity rather than of security, whether the car is in motion or parked. Griffin refuses to own that the surveillance feature is the reason he is here in the first place, but he suspects that it would be the case with most men of his ilk willing to place down such a sum. Moreover, the windows frame a bigger issue that bothers Griffin even more. Regardless of the Bentley window fashions, the available color palette for the Arnage lease models is lacking: black with matching interior and red-leather trim, white with cream interior and white trim, and silver with beige interior and black trim. Solomon, with his Mediterranean hair, hummus-toned skin and the telltale lips of a black man, has previously mentioned that, because of the remarkable number of athletic teams in the nation's capital, Bentley proudly offers a sapphire lease model with peacock blue interior and trim: "You know how the brothers like to strut."

"Isn't that the reason you make the Rolls . . . for strutting?"

"Not everyone can afford a Rolls. In fact, few can . . .

only your superstar athletes, Persian Gulf dignitaries. The rest flock to the Bentley instead."

"Or strut to it," Griffin smiles.

But he is still irked by the lack of suitable Bentleys for lease for an operative like himself. Other lawyers and lobbyists typically drive the Lincoln Town Car, Cadillac Sedan de Ville, or the Jaguar; vehicles nearly always black, with a black man taking his instruction from behind the wheel.

It is obvious what is going on. If Griffin really wants to drive a Bentley that is signalized to his personality, he will have to buy a custom-designed one. He reminds Solomon how accommodating Lucien at Masarati is, to no avail; likely, Solomon knows that Griffin's second car choice lags way behind the Bentley, and ties with his third favorite, the Rover. The Bentley takes Griffin back to his first experience in the Cayman Islands, there last January to check on his offshore bank account. A liveried airport official escorted him from the plane to a male-chauffeured white Bentley, courtesy of the bank. The exquisiteness of the Bentley's glide through the landscape of citrine, whitewash and emerald was all the more perfect because he had been expecting a Mercedes-Benz, Lexus or BMW — the usual suspects. He also had been expecting to be met by your average middle-aged male bank representative, not a woman as wondrous as the Bentley, with a name that conjured the Greeks: Athena. He can yet see the shaft of afternoon sun that cast her in glittering beams, as her creamy cleavage pressed up through the opening of her loosely buttoned blouse when she veered from talk of the seasons in the Caymans to call his attention to a landmark. "I beg your pardon, Mr. Saunders, but over there is the old port where ships would come in . . .," she said, sliding her sunglasses up in a gesture that sent her lavender perfume aloft in the cool white leather cabin. No mention was made of the export and import of slaves, the real reason the port existed, Griffin knew. Though that history was irrelevant in this supreme moment of paradisical possibility, it was not hard to picture ragged human cargo roped and chained together like bait for the sharks. His eyes were willingly led by her flowing gestures pointing out landmarks and their significance, but they eagerly traveled back on their own, along the route that began at her lacquered fingertips and crossed the isthmus of outstretched arm, wandered up along the narrow of neck with a brief stop at glistening coral lips before lingering on the elegance of coppery clavicle, and then plunging down the slope of her breasts and along the ravine of hips. She lifted one leg to slide it over the other, and the long hemline of her white skirt teased upward, revealing a wedge of inner golden thigh. The heel of her foot freed itself from the white strap of the taupe high-heeled sandal, and the arch of her instep steepened, allowing the creases between her tanned toes to peek out from patent leather. "Ours is a beautiful island, without equal in the Caribbean, wouldn't you agree?" she said.

"Amen," he said.

Three months ago, with Athena in mind and under bluer, clearer sky, Griffin had Solomon draw up a custom order for a deep gray Bentley Arnage with beige interior, only to place it on hold pending the 1998 models' arrival in the showroom. Just last week, Solomon had called to press for a decision about the custom car, but by then Griffin managed to put the order completely out of his mind, to the point where he could actually climb in and out of the Lincoln Town Car without feeling cheated, less-than, let down. It was the Arnage's price that pressed his foot on the brake. How to justify what even Chief would scream was "extravagant goddamned frivolousness"? Griffin told Chief about the Cayman Islands, and the spectacular beauty of both the island and the bank emissary, and Chief said, "Lil'Bro, you don't need a Bentley to get your johnson sucked. A car like that is like a wife you always have to worry about because she's just too goddamn fine — it looks bad." Griffin had not put much stock in his response; Chief as much as said the same thing about Margeaux. He had been wrong, his words revealing his jealousy, then and now. Without question, Chief might be the better looking of the two brothers; but in Margeaux, Griffin had the finer wife, hands down . . . and with the Bentley, the finer ride.

A tempting new Bentley model, the Continental Sedanca Coupe, now lures Griffin over. It flirts in rich cream, with a hardtop and rounded rear end. There's a hint of glint in the swell of red leather interior. He imagines speeding down that pale highway under a lapis sky and beside the turquoise sea, with the goddess Athena beside him, chattering about the view.

Giving in to Sedanca temptation, he turns to see Solomon now standing near the front showroom window. He is talking to another man, presumably another sales agent, with the haircut and demeanor of someone paid a commission. Both smiling men look Griffin's way, and Griffin reciprocates, peering over the rail of his reading glasses. He thinks these men are not to be trusted. The hard stare of the other man suggests the FBI agent who had accosted him as he had been leaving the hospital after his heart fright, with Jewells:

"Mr. Saunders, you will need to talk with us," the guy had said.

"About what?"

"Your half brother, Samuel Tecumseh Black II, the U.S. Commerce Secretary, is being investigated."

"For what?"

"Misuse of his office, kickbacks, accepting bribes. We know what's going on, and you're an accessory to his crimes. The only possibility you have of avoiding prison is by talking with us."

"For God's sake, I've just come out of the hospital after a possible heart attack. Are you trying to kill me?"

"We'll be in touch."

It is the darkest and the heaviest of the balls Griffin must juggle. He glides his hand over the sloping rear of the Bentley Continental Sedanca coupe, and puts his shoulders firmly forward. He then notices a television monitor in a room for employees a few feet away. On the monitor is Chief's face. Griffin wanders over to the coupe's passenger side for a better view of the TV. Neither Solomon nor his colleague is around.

The television says, "A groundbreaking trade agreement with China was announced by the Clinton Administration today. A priority of the administration since its first term has been the broadening trade agreements, and China has been within its sights as having the potential to open up trade between the United States and Asia . . ."

Griffin stares at footage of China — the Great Wall, Tiananmen Square — then of the President of the United States shaking hands with the president of China. Then, presciently, Chief is shown in an inset like a little jailbox floating within the television monitor.

"We join the press conference now . . . "

An image of the President and Chief now dominates the TV screen: "Today, we are excited to embark on a new path that will bring the destinies of our two nations together. The

United States and China have entered a new era, as friends and trading partners with common interests and hopes for the future. I would like to thank Secretary Black for his efforts to bring this about."

The President yields to Chief: "As a representative of one of the youngest nations in the world it's been an incredible experience being here in one of the world's oldest nations. We share many values and ideas with the Chinese, but what inspires me most is our common understanding that every new idea is an impossibility until it is realized. We rise to the challenge facing our nations with ingenuity and the goal of prosperity for our people."

A speechwriter probably deserves all credit for that gem, but Chief is both eloquent statesman and crude, potty-mouth, trash-talking low-life at the same time. He may have grown up in Strivers Row, Harlem, but he certainly knows his way around the streets. Harvard Law School may have given brilliance to his golden-boy sheen, but beneath it all is a cold-blooded, bad-mouthed con man.

"He's a sharp guy, that Secretary Black," says Solomon, smiling more than usual, while his colleague stands at a distance, watching. "He's a customer. Or will be some day."

"Really," says Griffin, feeling suddenly as if he were a shoplifting suspect. The colleague leaves the showroom, just as Chief leaves the TV screen.

"Yes. He was here, in fact, just after Clinton won the

presidency. He was seriously considering a Bentley — the coupe, in fact. Then he was appointed Commerce Secretary. He said it wouldn't look good for him to be seen riding around in such a car, not good for the President's folksy image. I told him, in fact, that it wouldn't look good to the racists among us, no matter what he drove, frankly, him being a black man — and with the surname Black, well . . . 'Secretary,' I said, 'you might as well look good.' Mind you, the Secretary looks good. He's a handsome, impeccably dressed man, and way better-looking than Clinton."

Solomon excuses himself to take a phone call, and watching him walk away, Griffin knows he is right in his observation about Chief's assets. It is precisely what makes Chief such an excellent front person. In this town, Griffin is strictly back office, willing and even happy in his invisible role as the brains behind the business.

Chief is long gone from the TV monitor, though Griffin stares as if his brother has only stepped away to the men's room momentarily. Peter Jennings offers a tidbit that redirects his attention: "In Cincinnati, a child pornography ring has been uncovered. Two men in the area are in custody, and arrests have been made in Minneapolis, Los Angeles, Sweden and London."

Disgusting. As mayor, Griffin would like his beloved city to make the headlines for good things, important things, rather than the usual sordid and violent — most recently, the

1991 riot, with its burning and looting of the black downtown, an event Griffin himself had witnessed, his gun at the ready as the enraged rampaged. His trigger finger had trembled and the fresh sweat released the pressure of his own anger. All that he was — from having pulled himself up by his own bootstraps — made it impossible to understand why any vandalism to his property or threat to himself deserved less than a bullet, no questions asked.

Someday, there may yet be a Mayor Griffin Jewells Saunders II. D.C.'s perennial felon Marion Barry is living proof that even a prison stint need not preclude public office.

Just now, the long-lingering matter of what to do about the car is resolved. Griffin can see the perfect photo-op Bentley (blinds or curtains?), how it will look on television — and even better, he can imagine Chief cursing a blue streak, Chief asking to borrow the car for certain events involving certain women of his acquaintance, to which Griffin will respond no — and best of all, Chief will be envious and bitter.

"Boss man," says his driver, Horace, running into the showroom, interrupting Griffin's Bentley reverie. "There's a phone call for you. It's the Secretary, he says it's urgent."

"Thank you." Griffin looks very closely, even crossly, at Horace, and can't quite imagine him driving the Bentley. Horace is unsophisticated, with his "fuck the white man" pout, and he sounds like he never set foot in school before ten years old. True, Griffin took exception to Horace's remarks about the curtains — "Boss man, I don't know, it's like we're driving around in a coffin, or like you some old English fag . . ." — and it is also true that he has had to scold him too many times. The Bentley deserves a foreigner, someone Greek or darkly Italian with a strong accent and other languages at his command — and with an appreciation of the fine touch of curtains, and the good sense to keep stupid opinions to himself.

On the other hand, Horace is trustworthy, and it is essential yet near-impossible to trust anyone these days, Griffin thinks on his way back to the car, mumbling to himself.

Instead of taking Chief's call, Griffin disconnects the car-phone line. Then he phones Solomon and tells him to place the order. He does not want to wait three weeks for delivery, because he has important business this week, is it possible to get a rental? The loaner sedan is two grand a week, four hundred less than the coupe. Griffin goes for a cream sedan and says he will come by in the morning to pick it up. But a couple of minutes later, he phones Solomon and puts the order on hold, again, and cancels the rental too. He explains he is normally not so indecisive and that he's under a lot of pressure, and Solomon lowers his voice, "Look, Mr. Saunders, I shouldn't be saying this, but because you're you . . . I'm losing money on this . . . in fact it's already a loss financially for the company . . . but here's an offer. I've got a possible deal for you on last year's model of the Brooklands R. Mulliner. To a Bentley aficionado such as yourself, you may find that the

Brooklands R. Mulliner is a little more stylish than the Arnage, and it's limited edition."

"Yes, the dramatic tail lights."

"Plus, the wing mirrors, mesh under bumpers and side vents — not as extreme as the Turbo but definitely modern in feel."

"Yes, I like it."

"I think the Brooklands R. Mulliner is for you — in fact, more so than the Arnage: all the luxury of Bentley without the formality. It's the car to carry clients in but also for everyday living. I'm happy to say, we have number twenty-five in our inventory, in silver with cream and gunmetal interior. Of course, it has the hardware for curtains, plus an advanced video surveillance system — it projects an image field around the entire car and sends a live video feed directly to your laptop or your phone or even the police, if you choose. The only drawback is the steering is British . . . you know, righty. It's perfectly legal on the road here, but most people feel too odd. It was intended for the British embassy, but in fact the order was canceled before the car shipped. Believe it or not, the car was considered a bit flashy for the embassy — a new ambassador in the post-Thatcher era, you know. We were going to ship it back to England. If you are interested, I'll look into it."

"Tell me about the surveillance system."

"It may interest you to know that the surveillance

system was developed with M16 technology, and M16 is of course the British Secret Intelligence Service."

"That's impressive," Griffin says.

"It will be nearly $75,000, in fact. It'll most likely be a cash deal, of course with the full backing of Bentley. Shall I look into it?"

"What's the mileage?"

"In fact, it has two miles on it."

"Two?"

"Accumulated here on the premises."

Griffin hangs up and says to his driver, "By the way, Horace, did the Secretary ask you where I was?"

"He did."

"What did you tell him?"

"That you was looking at the new Bentleys."

"Never, ever answer my phone again," Griffin says, his spit quivering in the corners of his mouth.

"Sorry, Boss, but he ast me."

"And never, ever tell anyone where I'm going or where I've been . . . what I'm doing or what I'm driving or whom I'm driving, talking to, eating with, et cetera."

Horace's hangdog nod is not good enough.

"Black man, you got that?"

"Yessir."

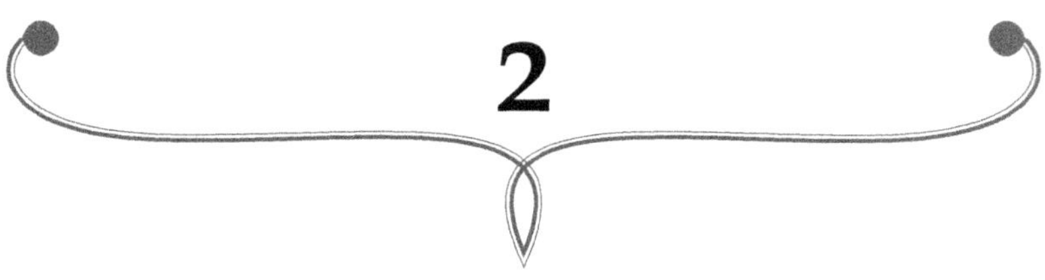

2

The Washington house is a Craftsman bungalow that disappears into the landscape. Ashwood trim on a low-slung brick single-story that seems slipped into the acreage of shrubs, fir and pine. In certain light, depending on the time of year, even the driveway hides in the margins of a two-lane highway that daily claims wildlife near the northeast D.C. border with Maryland.

Two years ago, Griffin acquired the property in a blur of quick, insider-trading-type moves, thanks to a rezoning tip from an old business-school acquaintance now heading a D.C. city planning commission. More than the required $10,000 thank-you, Griffin's trump card had been the false suggestion that the property would jointly belong to none other than Chief. To Griffin's way of thinking, any venture involving the most esteemed black man in America deserved to jump the queue of other minority business owners vying for the same opportunity. At least that's how it would have worked in Cincinnati, where no one in his right mind would dare do anything to attract scrutiny into the process of awarding minority business contracts. A drought in government funding would benefit no one.

Not so in the nation's capital: The swift outcry of
the "jumped over" elicited a *Washington Post* reporter
wanting to know how Premier International, a Cincinnati-
based company, could be competing with local minority
businesses for D.C.-area projects — and, more importantly,
how Secretary of Commerce Samuel Tecumseh Black II's
owning a stake in that company was not a conflict of interest.
Griffin denied advance knowledge of the land deal, insisting
he purchased the house because he loved it. Moreover, it
was acquired not through Premier International, his cable
company, but through GJS Holdings, his real-estate concern.
The GJS Holdings portfolio included twenty-three properties
in the Greater Cincinnati area, four in Indianapolis and now
one just outside D.C. When the reporter pressed whether
Premier International was listed as one of the prospective
land developers, Griffin conceded it was not at the time,
but insisted Premier International was in the process of
incorporating in the D.C. metro area, and that, regardless,
the Commerce Secretary, "or Chief, as we call him," had
nothing to do with any parcel of land and had, to avoid
the appearance of impropriety, sold his interest in Premier
International before joining the Clinton Administration, in
1993. Whether believed or not, it was true — that is, Chief was
not involved.

For his part, Chief had been in Brazil at purchase time,
a distance that seemed to give just enough wiggle room for

Griffin to feel independent. In hindsight, with a phone call he could have consulted him on both the real estate transaction and the bribe and thus avoided Chief's rage over being thrust in the spotlight of "Your Amateur Hour Shit Show." "Lil'Bro, looks like you got took for ten thousand goddamn dollars! I know everybody in this town, and these chump muthafuckas can kiss my black ass. If it wasn't for me, there wouldn't be minority set-asides — zilch!"

The blacklisting was sure and complete, and the minority set-asides pie would never serve P.I. — their nickname for Premier International — even a crumb. P.I. was doing just fine in Cincinnati, and it was at such times that Griffin regretted letting Chief talk him into setting up among D.C.'s hostile factions. What was the point in staying in the nation's capital under the circumstances? Enduring such slights as "the parvenu from the Queen City in the Buckeye State" — a snide remark Griffin overheard a new acquaintance make to another gentleman during a cocktail party.

"Lil'Bro, we're going to make even more money. I didn't ask you to move this way for the same small-time shit, I mean, these motherfuckers here are after FM radio stations, car washes and Kentucky Fried Chicken franchises. We're way ahead of the curve, Lil'Bro — how many cable stations we own or have we bought and sold . . . ten or twelve, whatever? We're going international — that's the reason we called the company Premier International, right? Just don't make a move until I tell you, and for Christ-fuckin-sake, don't get into any business with the Negroes around here. Lay low."

To that end, moving into the Craftsman house was not entirely about saving face. The overpriced apartments in the Georgetown and Capitol Hill areas were reason enough to check out the Craftsman, then sitting empty for months while a land deal suddenly became mired in public hearings decrying the proposed development of an unneeded and unwanted shopping mall. That was two years ago, and now the project is stalled indefinitely, and the ten grand seems to have been his initiation fee into the D.C. minority business club. Griffin is glad he bought the house — now the official headquarters of P.I., once he discreetly transferred the property when the furor died down. There is no shingle out front, only a listing in the index of active companies in the nation's capital.

"Smart," Chief agreed. "It's looks like P.I. is in hiding — not exactly the impression you want to give business prospects. On the other hand, it's better that I'm not seen so this is good. When Bubba is impeached from office, I'll be kicked out too, and then we'll move to K Street and make a shitload of money."

Regardless, Griffin refuses to use the house to entertain clients, and that's where the Bentley will come in, a kind of stylish, steerable equivalent of a suite on K Street. A Mercedes Class A or BMW 700 Series would cost even more than the Bentley Brooklands R. Mulliner. Still, given the murky future, it may make more sense to hold off buying the car, or anything else for that matter. On the other hand, he has always wanted a Bentley. Maybe he should enjoy the ride while still a free man? That is, free in the nation's capital, without wife and children.

The driveway, where the Bentley Brooklands R. Mulliner will be on view to exactly no one, is L-shaped and ends on the lush side of a high hedge of lilac flanked by a rock wall. There is a garage too, one big enough for a full-sized car and the storage of junk, from patio furniture and a riding lawnmower to ping-pong and pool tables. The very junk that came with the purchase, and that Griffin is now discarding for the Bentley's sake, in the heavy, perfumed heat of early July evening.

Sweat drizzling off him cannot be mopped from his brow quickly enough. The labor is not depleting, but exhilarating, even liberating. There are no nosy neighbors on either side to observe that he is shirtless as he drags a chaise longue to the main road for garbage collection. In Cincinnati he would not risk being seen moving furniture or clipping hedges, lest he be mistaken for a laborer or servant — a danger awaiting any black man living among the rich. The Berendts, Aranoffs, Tulsans and Zemlowskis know the Griffin Jewells Saunders II family well enough not to mistake them for the help or the help's offspring. Moreover, it is as much a matter of keeping up appearances as avoiding an indignity — a questionably legal immigrant in the yard doing the edging is foolproof, a sign of power and position. Here in the farthest reaches of the nation's capital, though, he basks in new anonymity, feels free to do as he pleases. Help with moving the heavy objects can be had at a moment's notice. Local Guatemalan day laborers loiter a couple miles up the road. The business cards of handymen, housekeepers and contractors in the area occupy a "local" file on his desk. As yet, Griffin has no intention of giving up the chores, as he calls them — all so easy, and even soothing, without the joys of children around.

Griffin imagines that the Craftsman's previous owners, a childless elderly couple who perished en route to their winter home in Fort Lauderdale, passed their days planning every detail of the land. The grounds were completely wild when he first saw the property, but the evidence that it had been fussed over was still present in the unnatural brightness of the grass and roundness of shrubs. Inside the garage, walls contain the stuff of yard work, tools precisely grouped by use. Those for gardening dangle on a far wall, neatly organized as if by a surgeon, while those for landscaping dominate two walls from ceiling to floor, on the side where their riding lawnmower and mulch wagon stay parked. He imagines his predecessors would probably disapprove of his changes. The biggest was the removal of the cinematic grass — more appropriate for a football field. It took nearly three days to scalp the yard and graft variegated ivy that blooms with tiny lavender flowers in spring.

Griffin passes the back porch and can see his cell phone flashing. The house phone is set to mute, and filled with messages too. They are all from Chief. Griffin has listened to each of them carefully. The new one says:

"Lil'Bro, Griffin, I need you to call me immediately . . ." — hissing breathing — "Griffin, I know you saw the news . . . I think I looked pretty good, Lil'Bro. Pretty goddamn amazing looking" — and sharp breathing, like he is swearing — "Look, Lil'Bro, my main man, my nigga — Griffin, so I'm leaving L.A. tonight. I want you to cancel whatever you've got going tomorrow morning, and we'll have us a little breakfast meeting, cool?"

The message before that said, "Lil'Bro, it *is* all fucked up, but we'll make it right . . . so don't go having another goddamn heart attack. I need you, and love you, man — but I could wring your fucking neck right now."

Before that: "Sorry, call me."

Before that: "Nigga, if you don't pick up this muthafuckin' phone, I swear to God . . ."

Griffin has told nothing to the FBI so far, but the fact that he will have to makes him afraid to speak to Chief, as if Chief will instantly know.

Hopefully FBI technicians are listening in on Chief's various rants, and even recording Griffin's reactions —

both possibilities could be good, ultimately, playing to his advantage, because Chief just might do himself in, sparing Griffin the task of betrayal. He is no Judas, although Chief, with his insults and profanity-laced tirades, has yet to deserve his loyalty these many years. Money — and they have made lots of it — was, is and always will be the tie that binds, he feels strongly, but the well dries and the parched bottom is within sight.

After saving the message and hanging up, Griffin nervously looks around the house and feels the presence of digital others — listening bugs, specifically, likely planted while he was in Cincinnati having a panic attack. The security video cameras do a pretty thorough surveillance and the tapes promise the house is as he left it. Yet such are the times that cell conversations can be snatched from the ether, e-mails can be received on the other side of the planet in a split second, and who knows what all else technology can do. He had the Town Car swept just this morning, and it is doubtful Horace, who has been chauffeuring him the last two years, is a turncoat. Equally, the place where the car was swept; it's the very same one Chief uses, coming highly recommended by a billionaire Brazilian wise in these spy matters.

Griffin's heart now flutters. He and Chief were on the phone when the Jaguar hit the guardrail and what he thought was a heart attack began, Chief saying: "This crew of white boys came through my house and my car with their little wands and waved them all up and down the walls, over the furniture and even through my mutherfuckin' underwear, and guess what they found? Bugs. One in my goddamn office phone, and the other in the goddamn living room. These sons-a-bitches — Who? Who? Who? — have been eavesdropping on my goddamn conversations, and they've probably been watching me fucking. No bugs on my dick, though."

"Cameras too?" Griffin said, nervously laughing.

"No, aren't you listening to me? They found microphones, not cameras. And it was a joke, you know, bugs as in crabs on your dick . . ."

"You said watching . . . Never mind."

"And just so you know, Lil'Bro, you owe me ten grand. I know those Vietnamese muthafuckas paid you twenty, they told me, and you said they paid ten."

"I said fifteen, and I deducted five grand for expenses. Remember, I went all the way to New Orleans, wine and dined them, and . . ."

"What exactly did you sell them anyway?"

"Just what you told me to sell them . . . access."

"Lil'Bro!"

It seemed to Griffin that Chief himself was forcing the Jaguar into the guardrail. Just before impact, Griffin no longer saw the road but a plane of white as he shrieked at the top of his lungs. After careening back into the lane, the Jaguar lurched to a complete stop, and Griffin's cell phone, then lying on the floor, shouted up to him, "Lil'Bro, what the fuck?" along with the furious horns of a chorus of cars behind him. Griffin jumped from the Jaguar, shouting and flailing his arms, "Go around!" The damage left him shaking . . . and then the chest pains and short breaths. He went back to the car, screamed into the phone, "Damn you, damn you!"

After hosing down the garage floor, Griffin heads back to the house, removing his work boots at the door. In the kitchen, with its handmade cabinets that remind him of chemistry class a lifetime ago, he thinks there is no point in having the house swept. It is quite expensive, even more so on short notice.

The answering machine clicks and Griffin impulsively takes the call. "Hold on," he says, as the machine whistles and trumpets till he hits the off switch.

"Chief."

"Well, I'll be damned, if it isn't Griffin Jewells Saunders the second. It's about time you picked up."

"Sorry, I can't talk. I'll see you in the morning, though."

"You goddamn well better, Lil'Bro."

Griffin hates nothing more than being called Lil'Bro, but protesting never amounts to much — a reason to betray Chief, though? He coughs loudly into the receiver, feels a strange desire to apologize for screaming at him in the car after the crash.

"You still sick? Still having a heart attack?"

"No, I'm fine, no thanks to you."

"Sorry, so much shit's going on I just freaked out when I didn't hear from you. And we're cool about the money."

"I can't believe you accused me."

"Like I said, a lot of shit's going on. I'll tell you later. You up for a game of bowling tomorrow, or will it kill your ass?"

"I'm up."

"You never said if the Jag was totaled?"

"It wasn't."

"Family good?"

"Yes."

"That boy of ours in jail yet?"

"I'm bettin' you'll get locked up before he does."

"Ha-ha-ha-ha-ha, that's good, Lil'Bro."

"Forty to one odds, Bigbro," Griffin, grinning, says.

"I can beat those odds. You call him for his birthday?"

"Of course I did." Griffin is careful not to overdo the indignation bit. Jewells loves Chief and maybe one day will learn the truth out of necessity — for instance, a medical-related emergency such as organ donation — and will have an affectionate relationship to build upon. "Hard to believe he's sixteen, a big strapping young man-child."

"Nothing like growing children to make you feel old."

"And worry you to old age. He wears me out."

"Yeah, I say don't fight unless you've got to knock some sense into them. He's upset over the driver's license, so now if I were you I'd buy him a nice a little car and threaten to take it from him everytime he fucks up . . . carrot and stick, carrot and stick, Lil'Bro."

"Good advice, Chief. Now, if you could pencil him in for the driver's test, that would be great."

"Yeah, well, there are companies that do that, and then there's you, Lil'Bro." There is yawning. "Fuck, I'm beat! I've back to backs all goddamn afternoon, then dinner tonight and then the red-eye. Yet you're the one having heart attacks and shit."

There is laughter. Griffin is unamused.

"What time tomorrow? I have a three-thirty."

"Noon then?"

"Noon it is."

"See you then."

Griffin's reply is to hang up before Chief does.

He immediately calls Solomon at Bentley to reschedule the signing and pickup for the Bentley Brooklands R. Mulliner later in the afternoon.

Next he phones his office in Cincinnati for a necessary check-in. D.C. has shuffled his priorities to a degree unimaginable, and right now he feels his Cincinnati assets lost in a thick deck that includes repairs to various buildings, government subsidies for the repairs, taxes, and so on . . . and on and on. Though excellent with the books, even after twenty years Therosine is incapable of running things at GJS

Enterprises. Therosine is his mother's second cousin — the only reason she still has the job — and as much as he hates repeating himself he must frequently do so, because she is both dense and dull and yet of a sweet disposition that reminds him of his mother, who would never forgive him were he to fire her or be mean. Early on, either possibility was very real. Therosine made the mistake of addressing him as Griffin, when she should have known better, given that even his mother called him Young Mister as a boy, and just plain Mister when he was grown up. There have been many other necessary correctives, and twice she has fled in tears. In all, the years have provided patience when there is little understanding, and blood-empathy where there is little sympathy.

After they finish going over building repair details, Griffin says, "Is there anything else?"

"I don't want to trouble you, Mr. Saunders."

"What is it, Therosine?" Griffin and the phone head outside, and he imagines the Bentley Brooks R. Mulliner turning into the driveway and rolling up to the house. It will look perfect here, he thinks.

"You forgot to leave the receipt again?"

"What receipt?"

"Remember, the receipt for the autographed Barbra Streisand picture you gave me for my birthday?"

"Oh, shoot! Therosine, I'm sorry. I don't remember what

I did with it."

"You know, Mr. Saunders, tell you the truth, I don't care for Barbra Streisand that much, and I appreciate you giving me the picture though."

"But Shauntay told me you did . . ."

"Shauntay ain't right, Mr. Saunders. We was just sitting there watching TV one night, and this commercial come on about the Barbra Streisand Collection, and all I said was I like her voice. Next I know, everybody's giving me Barbra Streisand for my birthday. Nine CDs — three of them are *The Way We Were*. I also received two biographies, and this funny-looking Barbra Streisand doll, which kinda scairt me!"

"I'll never consult with her again."

"No, never listen to Shauntay, Mr. Saunders" — sniffles and a crack in the voice — "she's always trying to undermine me. Well, at least she's outta high school now, with a diploma. And now she has a certificate from Delpha Drug Rehabilitation. The graduation ceremony was last night."

"That's something, Therosine, and you can build on it."

"I know, but" — sniffles and now wobbling voice — "it's just hard with a chile like that."

"There, there, Therosine, you're not alone. These kids today are not like you and me when we were kids. No respect, no sense of pride or achievement. Everything comes easy to them, where we had to work and work hard for it against all kinds of obstacles. And they want, want, want, more and more and more."

It feels good to say it.

There is a shudder of indignation that sends him headfirst into a state of dread over his next call, to Margeaux, for an update on his own Shauntay. What to do with Jewells?

"It breaks my heart. I just try so hard with the chile, and still she just won't do right."

"You'll get results, just hang in there. Therosine, I have to go now. But I'm going to e-mail the number of the place where I got the Barbra Streisand picture and you can just explain to them what you need. I assume you're planning to sell it?"

"That's right. I hope I don't hurt your feelings. I have to have the receipt so the picture can be authenticated, then I'm going to put it on Ebay."

"They may even buy it back so you don't have to put it on Ebay."

"That's wonderful, Mr. Saunders. Thank you."

"Oh, and Therosine, before I forget, I'm going to have a large expense here, it's about $75,000."

"What is it?"

"A vehicle," he says. "Since we can't open an office in the city until after Chief finishes with the Clintons. I need a vehicle to get around here, one more appropriate for our image and suitable for taking clients in."

"What kind you get?"

"A Bentley."

"Ohhhhh my, a Bentley, have mercy!" she says. "Michael Jordan has one, I think. Oh, your mother would be so proud of you, she just might have to come down from heaven for a ride in it!"

"Wouldn't that be something?" Griffin says. There is the zinging of a insect, and now a chigger bite swells on his forearm. Bugs everywhere, nature-made and man-made.

"Amen."

"By the way, when will the repairs be complete on the Jaguar?"

"They said by next Wednesday."

"Let me know. When it's ready, I want you to make arrangements to have it delivered to my house."

"But Jewells said he'd pick it up, now that he has his driver's license."

Griffin grumbles. No wonder Jewells has not called him back.

"On second thought, Therosine, have the car delivered to the office and under no circumstances are you to give Jewells the keys."

"Yes, Mr. Saunders."

3

A truck bounding up the driveway would normally mean little. FedEx is clear in orange and blue letters, and yet just the sort of FBI disguise to take a man off guard. Griffin opens the front door, his knuckles kneading flabby waistline.

Rain has not come in weeks, and driveway dust billows and levitates around the truck. Griffin puts a smile on his suspicions, and goes down to the meet the driver.

"I'm not expecting anything."

"It's from Margeaux Saunders, of GJS Holdings," the driver says.

"Okay." Griffin stares at the large, flat package, troubled that he has so quickly forgotten about it. Dodo-bird Therosine, who organized the shipping, should have reminded him. He will speak to her about this.

"I would like a call before you deliver in the future, is that possible?"

"No worries, Mr. Saunders, I would have just left it here."

"That's not what I mean. I mean I would prefer a call first."

"Sir, you can always track your packages. Just go to our website and enter the tracking number."

"What if you don't know a package is coming?"

"I can't help you there. If you prefer, you can also have packages kept at our dispatch office. That way, you'll be notified if something comes."

"That's what I want. And you can just leave that there. Thanks."

"If you say so, but it's pretty heavy. I can handtruck it to the porch. How's that?"

"Fine," Griffin huffs, annoyed at both message and messenger.

A box cutter opens fresh irritations. Staring at him is the Griffin Jewells Saunders II family portrait, taken early spring, in an elaborate, gilded frame that must have cost a fortune — and $557 to ship! Griffin specifically requested Margeaux not have the photo framed, that he would do it himself, since it was unimportant to him that the artful presentation matched the one over the Cincinnati mantelpiece in the dining room. He could be accused of not ever coming down hard, but never of being unclear.

What did she not understand?

Griffin looks at his watch and thinks she is probably just finishing tennis — at least she gets her club membership's worth.

"Mrs. Saunders, I know you're still on the courts — I've just finished working out myself — but I wanted you to know the FedEx people delivered the photograph. Sweetheart, thank you for sending it." He wants to add something stinging, but can't, so he hangs up.

Five minutes later, though, his phone rings, and Margeaux says, "Good morning, Mr. Saunders, I'm just getting into the car. I'm so glad you're feeling normal. How much time did you do?"

"About a half hour on the elliptical machine. Then I rowed for another half hour."

"I hope you alerted the staff to your medical . . ."

"Why would I do that?"

"Just in case."

"Margeaux, it was a panic attack . . . that's all. That's not angina or an early sign of congestive heart failure. It's not even a medical condition; it's a phenomenon. How was your game?"

"Still, dearest darling, informing them would be as much for their benefit as your own. And my game was fine. Beverly isn't that good — not that I'm that much better, but we're not evenly matched. It's so hard to find the right partner, isn't it?"

"Yes, it is. But at least she's there."

"You're right; I can always count on Beverly. And I appreciate it, but I really need to upgrade. I want to be challenged."

Margeaux is smarter than he is, a quality that makes Chief suspicious of her: "Man, your wife should never be the sharpest knife in your drawer. She will cut you at the neck, take everything you've got and leave your ass high and dry, bleeding in the wind." Margeaux is also unsentimental, a quality that unsettles Griffin — shouldn't a woman, a mother of five children no less, be sentimental . . . always? The problem is Griffin appraises himself as about ninety percent unsentimental, but that only makes her lack starker. Even with a large family, he suspects she is far more likely to walk out on their marriage than he is. As an example, a more emotional woman might have argued against his principal reason for setting up in D.C.: "I can't afford not to be where the opportunity is. Chief and I have a plan." Jokingly, he added, "We'll be broke if I don't bring in more money, and you won't be very happy then." She did not counter-offer to downshift their lives from pure platinum to sterling or plated, although some adjustments were made.

The family photograph is a case in point. For the sitting, clever Margeaux repurposed her wedding dress, having it chopped, dyed and shortened into something pewter and perfect for a gala at the museum or formal party at the mayor's. Griffin donned a tuxedo, and Jewells, too, while the boys did bowties and jackets, and the girls little white dresses stiff as paper cutouts. In the photo, husband and wife sit on a gilded chaise together; the children are configured around them, on three benches, like a deck of cards fanned out to feature only those of high rank, jacks to aces. To their left and right, a baby is beside a boy. Jewells stands just right and slightly behind Griffin — a handsome Jack of Spades, or perhaps even an ace, a trump card. Or a joker.

The photo was composed in the living room of the Cincinnati house. It was taken by a team of art students from the local university, and whenever dinner guests comment upon it, in particular the fact that it is in black and white, with an austere royal quality about it, Margeaux maintains that it has all the formal elements of great portraiture — capturing some fundamental quality about the subject.

"What would that quality be about the Saunderses?" Griffin once asked her.

"That we are a dynasty."

"A dynasty?" Though he loves the idea of legacy and heritage, he immediately thinks of dictators he has met through Chief.

"That we are anchored in history and tradition, and we know where we come from."

"Yes, I see," Griffin said, looking at the overly dark, moody photograph and not seeing a dynasty at all. He did see something, however, but it was about Margeaux specifically, and then only like a chimera of odd, bold color below the crease of her otherwise dark eyebrow, as if some part of her own radiance would not surrender to the starkness of black and white. Griffin thinks it an ugly photograph, and all the arty pretense very oppressive, but it is enough that Margeaux is a beauty and has given him caramel children that seem, so far at least, to lean more to her side in striking looks. The children will be an amalgam of good genes, they will attend private schools and graduate from the Ivies, accruing all the silver-spoon benefits his own life was denied — essentially what most men want for their offspring.

Even Chief now congratulates Griffin on Margeaux, in itself a reason to see his wife as his best victory. In all fairness, though, there was never a real contest, as Chief was trapped in marriage from the very beginning, to the dull daughter of a New York labor boss, thanks to the political calculations and manipulations of their father. Chief was the first to say his nervous Ernestine gave him children and kept a beautiful home to surround them, while his mistresses filled the pleasure void. "Pops had ladies all over the place, and I guess our daddy's appetites are mine too. In the blood, Lil'Bro."

A by-product of the men's dalliances with mistresses was unwanted, unacknowledged children, like Jewells . . . and even Griffin, too, but the brothers don't go there. Griffin is now fortunate to have moral thoughts that he stands by in action and deeds, and he cannot discuss without sounding censorious of the base behavior of his brother. Recently, Chief has taken to crowing about one of his girls — who is by day an interior decorator, but come night a hooker in bed, from fellatio to anal sex, a beauty without limits. Two weeks ago, Griffin stood in the presence of her dangerous

Belizian magnificence, when Chief showed up at Griffin's
house at three a.m. Instantly recognizing the car and thinking
something wrong, Griffin, armed with a pistol, charged out
in his underwear, only to find the two of them naked, tangled
and sweaty in the backseat of the limousine. In the low-radiant
car light, she sprawled across the bench, Chief's head between
her splayed legs at the end of which were the dagger points of
glittering stilettos. The startled Griffin lingered long enough
to grab a glimpse of her makeup-smeared face — ecstatic or
demonic? — and flattened breasts and a swirl of thick black
hair flowing from the seat to the floor. In the house, he waited
for Chief to emerge with a crude laugh, but the limousine
sped off, not a word.

Must Chief be so slimy? So without limits?

As a man with limits, Griffin appreciates a complementary
wife like Margeaux. Such antics were beneath her. Not even in
private would she appear unbuttoned and mussed — and
never whorish, and it would displease him immensely if she
ever did. Still, Margeaux is unshy. Their bedroom can feel
mysterious to him at times, but she seems to understand the
alchemy of pretty lace panties and satin slips and red toenails,
how they conjure a fantasy of seduction, on the one hand,
while lifting him to her level, in an aspiring if conventional
way, on the other. Athena fantasies aside, Griffin desires
nothing more than his wife's perfect menu of pleasure, he is
certain.

Still, it is remarkable to him the cost of quality. He cannot help the small rumble of unease at the price tag, really — the half million dollars sunk into decorating the house with custom furniture, draperies, the state-of-the-art kitchen with fancy appliances . . . her designer clothes, her tennis trainer, her day spa trips. An accountant by training, Griffin's large black eyes are always arranging the abacus, sometimes with grunts of displeasure. Lately Margeaux has gotten into the habit of pointing out that she is cutting corners. The family portrait, for instance, would have cost five times as much had she hired a celebrated art photographer, purchased a new gown, had the children's clothes custom-made. Griffin thanked Margeaux for her thrift, and left it at that — it is beneath her to account, he feels, but he wants to know she can. Pushy is not his style; neither is issuing decrees. Delicate nerves could be within her core of steel. They have never discussed it, but several properties Griffin owned years back previously belonged to her father, Britton Chenault. Griffin knew him, if only briefly, and last communicated with him just before his dry cleaning processing company went up in flames. The fire department alleged deliberate arson, the insurance denied payment, an arrest was imminent, and Mr. Chenault swallowed a bullet himself in the garage on a balmy July afternoon. That was a period Margeaux would understandably wish to forget, if also one a mere scratch below the surface. Mrs. Chenault, or Oma, as the children call her, has confided that Margeaux's father was a profligate man, with giant dreams and little skill to pull anything off. She has also owned up to enabling him, having been helplessly in love. Griffin suspects the same insanity in the habits of Margeaux, as well as in his enabling indulgence of her, and feels it is in the best interest of his children that his fortune is safely in a trust, completely out of her reach . . . forever.

Margeaux also has sent a copy of the family photo via e-mail, which Griffin proudly forwarded to Chief. Chief has observed that Margeaux — her choker of pearls, diamond and pearl earrings and glittering rings — and Griffin, with "your fudge brownie complexion, look pretty goddamn Idi Amin . . . and what's with the black and white . . . from the 1930s?"

The brothers have laughed. Griffin has held back the admission of having mused over similar dictator thoughts, too.

Chief had worked at a Washington, D.C., law firm for ten years. His specialty had been lobbying on behalf of problematic wealthy African dictators, despots and war criminals who might feel more comfortable being shaken down by a suave beige African American with a Harvard pedigree. The firm's clients included Zimbabwe's Robert Mugabe and Angolas's José Eduardo dos Santos, but it was Uganda's Idi Amin that captivated Chief. His Excellency had amused and charmed him in London, and Chief would have visited Uganda in 1977, had the world not got wind of the

dictator's serial murdering of his people. The mad Amin —
also known as Lord of All the Beasts of the Earth and Fishes
of the Sea and Conqueror of the British Empire in Africa in
General and Uganda in Particular — had been deposed and
in exile a decade before Chief honored his acceptance of the
invitation. He had brought Griffin along to size up the money-
making opportunity in Uganda, but equally for the strange
comedy of it all: "It'll be the first time in your life you've ever
felt like you were light-skinned." Between Griffin's breathing
difficulty in the suffocating heat and shock over the in-your-
face poverty it had registered as pretty awful in his mind.
Neither brother had harbored romantic ideas of a reunion
with the Motherland from which their ancestors had been
merchandised into slavery, so it had not shocked them to see
dead bodies on the street, when it should have had. Rather,
they had been troubled more by the idea that there would
be no way to safeguard an investment here, contrary to what
they had been told. Griffin himself could not have been more
relieved when they had hopped the private Boeing jet out of
the country for the real reason they had gone to Uganda, Chief
later had confessed: a new client, Muammar Muhammed Abu
Minyar al-Gaddafi. Turned out, the President of Libya had
been an acquaintance of Chief's from his Harlem days. It had
been an act of treason for the brothers to set foot on the plane,
to say nothing of alighting Libyan soil, and they probably
would have been arrested upon their return to the States, had

Chief's firm not been one of D.C.'s most powerful. The visit to Tripoli had been just a long weekend, in a palace sheathed in gold and guarded by black-clad gargoyles with machine guns. Gaddafi himself had never bothered to show up to meet them in the palace; they were never sure he was even present. Plenty of amusement made the weekend fly. "Wall-to-wall pussy, it's heaven," Chief had said, in the fullness of bliss, sleeping all the way back to Uganda, then on the journey to London and even the final leg to Washington, D.C. Griffin himself had attended business. Beyond oil, what opportunity could be extracted in a country a snap from violence. He had marveled at the ease of making money in the absence of red tape and where life itself had little value. Not long after the visit, P.I. had sold cable technology to the dictator, for one hundred million dollars, their profits now safely banked in the Cayman Islands.

It had also surprised Griffin just how universal were the preoccupations of rich men. Beyond the fripperies and toys money bought, and the back turned to the suffering masses their wealth depended upon, the bottom line was beautiful women, whether wife, wives or mistresses, and in the extreme, a harem of both wives and mistresses. The tally would always be high — the lifestyles to woo them, the homes to showcase them, the cars to transport them, the baubles and trinkets to dazzle them. From dictator to entrepreneur to real estate magnate to superstar athlete, you paid. It had not been until marriage to Margeaux that Griffin really understood the red ink of a rich man. The lesson had been worse for Chief. The low salary of a Commerce Secretary could buy very few of such luxuries. Chief's Belizean beauty's decorating skill quickly soured him to her other charms: "She's already fucked my house up. I'm gonna have to hire another decorator just to put it back the way it was." Griffin could see that Chief was, in his way, proud to have such a beautiful problem in his life.

Margeaux offers where she thinks the family photo should go in the D.C. house. Griffin quickly agrees the dining room is ideal, given the hunting-lodge style of the living room fireplace, with its taxidermied wolverine crouching as if about to seize prey . . . or fight for its territory. Margeaux was quite far along in her pregnancy with the girls when Griffin purchased the D.C. house. Now, unwilling to leave the babies behind, she has not actually ever seen the place, only pictures of it, a fact which makes the expensive frame job even more galling, and her hanging suggestions too. The plan is, she will come up for a long weekend in September and return home first thing Monday morning. Only then will he let her undo the simple, quiet, monastic quality of the place by crowding it with pillows and rugs and couches. 'Til then, Cincinnati is hers, this place his.

The conversation traces the usual protocol. After some talk of her recent lunch and dinner with their friends, Margeaux goes on about the children, about the girls' teeny-tiny accomplishments and the boys' chasing around the yard like squirrels. News about the boys delights Griffin, for he fears the eventual result of Percy's girlish proclivities, both encouraged and indulged by Margeaux. Not to say he would ever force his child to be other than his true self: As long as he is successful Griffin will keep both his disappointment and disapproval at bay. At the very least, if there are no Jewells-like problems, Griffin will be agreeably accepting of his child.

"And Jewells?"

"Jewells is Jewells. He's respecting the curfew we imposed, which is saying a lot, but I don't know, he just . . . One morning I saw this kid leaving the carriage house. Some Asian or Indian-looking kid. He disappeared by the time I got to the driveway. I asked Jewells about him. Jewells said he was a teammate, that he was dropping off a playbook, but I don't believe him."

"Why?"

"He's up to something."

"I suspect so. He hasn't returned my calls."

"No surprise there."

He hears her breathing impatience.

"Dear, you need to make a decision. I have the other children to think about."

"Yes," he says. Griffin glances at Jewells in the photograph. His aloof, princely problem child. It will do no more than aggravate tension if he brings up the driver's license.

Inviting a critique of his parenting is the last thing he needs to hear.

"A decision soon, Mr. Saunders."

"I'm trying to figure things out here. I have to meet Chief tomorrow."

"I thought he was in Europe."

"No, just coming back from L.A."

Griffin would rather speak about the FBI, but he is frightened to, for all kinds of reasons, not least that they might be listening to his every word and conclude Margeaux is somehow involved.

"Chief's son comes to D.C. in summers too. It's too bad they're all at the Vineyard now. Tek and Jewells get along, despite the age difference. I'll plan something, and soon."

"Yes, before it's too late."

"Yes, we will, before it's too late." He does not appreciate her dramatics.

She says, "I love you," and he repeats the sentiment.

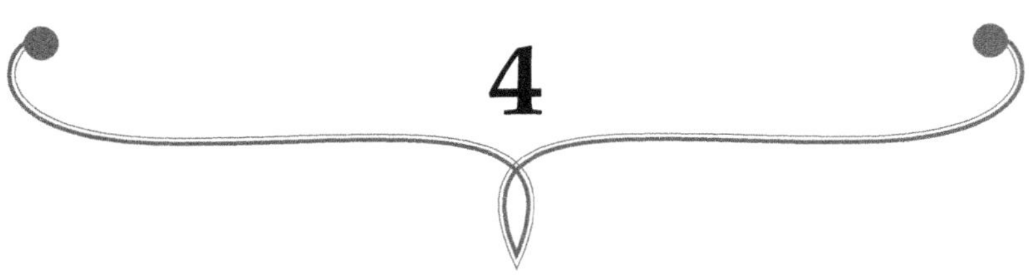

4

Griffin's bowling ball is a Quantum Raven, a glossy sphere of black resin with an odd, mushroom-shaped core that gives its roll a hard Sugar Ray Leonard hook. Old, oiled wood lanes ideally conspire with the uppercut of the power bowler for shattering strikes and wins.

Pinky's Lanes is old style, the establishment around since the segregated 1940s. Back then, blacks wishing to bowl took to makeshift lanes in floodlit basements, beyond the reach and retaliations of Jim Crow. Harold 'Pinky' Porterhouse was a D.C. pioneer. He set up Pinky's with a staff of three boys running from lane to lane setting up pins, until automation put them out of work. Black nightclubs were abundant then, but the combination with modern bowling proved irresistible. After-hours jitterbugging, singing and comedy acts were a typical weekend at Pinky's: Martha and Vandellas and comedian Nipsey Russell are said to have all rolled through on the same night. Telltale high-heel scuff marks spoke of randy dances that overflowed up to the Naugahyde couches in the bowling area. True, the bowling was never all that. Though buffed and polished, the lanes are dry and it is difficult for a bowling ball to gain traction —

disadvantaging Griffin's roll and Chief's too, although for different reasons. No question, White Oak Duckpin Lanes is better all around, but it is in Silver Springs and the folks there do not have Chief's back. These days, as of old, count on Pinky's for handshakes and well-wishes of the brothers and sisters of working-class D.C., plus a daily menu of fried chicken, pork chops, collard greens, black-eyed peas, macaroni and cheese; and holiday offerings of hog maws, chitlins and oxtails.

Griffin is on time, and assumes Chief has preceded him. A likely hired Lincoln Town Car is parked in Pinky's lot, but also Chief usually arrives early to commune with the locals. Before he was Commerce Secretary, he was a lieutenant in the Democratic Party, and Griffin has seen him glad-handing from lane to lane, as if he were on the campaign trail. The people never fail to eat it up; he is their very own chitlin. These days, though, Chief rightly takes no chances and now pays others to watch his back. He is usually flanked by a driver armed with a SIG Sauer P228 pistol. According to Chief, this make of weapon can fire thirteen rounds in a blink, and is the choice of the Secret Service; Chief's cabinet rank does not qualify for Secret Service protection.

At the bar, Chief is holding court with two men, while his driver/security pointman hovers never more than ten feet away and sometimes at point-blank range. Chief's gestures are nearly always in motion, a sure sign he is tipsy. One hand alternates between a Bloody Mary and a sausage biscuit; the other grazes a napkin over his mustache and goatee after each bite, then waves around as Chief makes a point, laughing, talking and chewing at the same time, spreading biscuit crumbs like fairy dust. The stool he is perched atop makes him appear short, when just his torso is short and compact; his legs are long, his butt high and hips narrow, creating a silhouette not unlike an inverted bowling pin. Griffin has seen their father in person only once, and then he was lying in state on the day of his funeral. There are photos and television footage to draw upon, and now of course Chief. Chief is the spitting image of the dapper New York congressman, in 1952: endowed with their father's golden skin, lady's-man hazel eyes, the inky curls, the handshake-friendly smile, the impeccably tailored appearance sharpened by flourishes of profanity, as dapper as dangerous. Griffin has convinced himself that Chief lacks the old man's renowned cunning — the quality that made him rich, respected and feared.

"Hey, Lil'Bro, let me introduce you to my new friends. Fellas, this here is my little brother, Griffin Jewells Saunders II. He's come here for an ass-whuppin' on the lanes."

"Stick around, and you'll see whose butt gets whooped," says Griffin, shaking hands and clapping shoulders. He looks at the peppercorn-like moles along Chief's jovial cheek as he swings back to his point.

"Lil'Bro, we were just jawing about Bubba's blowjob.

Like I was saying, fellas, I don't know any man that would turn down a pretty pair of lips on his johnson, and I'll grant you, goddammit, this is *not* the time to be caught with his pants down, Bubba being the number-one man in the country and the world for that matter, but shit . . . a man is a man is a *man*."

"You right about that," one of the twosome says. "But see, I could understand this situation more if the pretty lips were attached to something even prettier . . ."

"Come now, brother, any lips will do when your johnson is dry, and you know it . . ."

They erupt in mirth, with Griffin pretending to be amused. He finds the indignity of Chief's public conversation unworthy of his position, and the vulgarity too much. Their old man cannot have been as crass, or as big an ass. There are no recordings of their father in his element to prove it, but Chief has said about Big Chief, as he called him: "Our father would cuss out God if he got in his way. Me too."

Chief comes down off the stool and shoos the men along: "Getting impeached over a goddamn blowjob just can't happen. That would be un-American. This is America!"

Chief signals the bar for another Bloody Mary, and sends his armed man Floyd to fetch it. The brothers head to their usual spot, in the very center of the bowling alley. The lanes themselves appear backlit in sunset tones, amid the soundtrack of crashing, clattering bowling pins, overlaid with

Martha and the Vandellas singing "Heat Wave." Also bowling is a small number of afternoon diehards, mostly second-and-third shift workers preparing for weekend leagues, Griffin guesses. It feels safe here, and if he should find himself under house arrest and Chief behind bars, joining the local league could be his biggest sport, now that he has made many enemies on the fairways of the capital's exclusive country clubs.

"Baby, I'm burnin', burnin' inside . . . Heat wave!" Chief croons, removing his wedding ring and one with a shimmering diamond at the center. Griffin has an identical one too, though he never wears it around Chief, not since Chief's wife once joked they were wedding rings. "Trapped in another bad marriage" was Chief's slapping sally.

"I don't blame Bubba, shit. But I suppose that's the point. The first black president is too black. Fuck, too bad the bitch wasn't black, then at least we could turn it around and make money."

"How?"

"Guilt, Lil'Bro . . . guilt equals opportunity. Shit, can't you hear Sharpton crying about the master raping the slave, and laughing all the way to the beauty parlor for a wash and set? Damn, Lil'Bro, we could at least got some legislation passed through the stonewall Congress. But Bubba, hell no . . . that muthafucka just had to fuck up everything for everybody, not least of all his damned self . . . Shit, he's the reason these sonsabitches are always sniffing up my ass now."

"No kidding. I'm getting paranoid. I feel like eyes are all over the place."

"Eyes and ears too. It's Bubba they want. I mean, you ain't worth jack shit to them, and I ain't either beyond getting to him. Well, there might be some satisfaction to lynching a black man like me, but Bubba's the prize And they can have his pseudo black ass, far as I'm concerned. I'm done."

Griffin thinks he would handle the Clintons a lot better than Chief has, Chief with his zipper problems. On the other hand, perhaps to work for America's First Black President means to acquire similar afflictions and perfidies.

"By the way, Lil'Bro, anybody reaching out to you about me?"

"A reporter now and then, but that's it. I'm not returning calls."

"Yeah, you're not even answering the phone."

"I think the phones are all bugged," Griffin says, calmly. He inspects his bowling ball, rubs a cheesecloth over it to restore some of its black gleam . . . holds, shines, then gently places it on the carousel.

"You've had the house swept?"

"Not since I came back, but yes I have."

"That's all you can do, Lil'Bro."

"Yeah," Griffin says. "By the way, you did look pretty good on TV, with the president. You and Bubba are quite the team. Like Magic Johnson and Michael Jordan."

"Except I can't stand his ass, and that Frankenstein wife. She can't wait to get rid of me. But they need this house nigger because all of Black America is watching. And you know, Lil'Bro, I'm not worried about the Clintons at all. I mean, I've been all over the goddamned place, around the world twice since I took this big muthafucking albatross of a job. I should be tired but I love it. What makes me tired? Republicans, dick-headed, pussy-deprived muthafuckas can't think about shit else but how much they can't stand the niggers in charge, especially Bubba and yours truly."

"It does seem so."

"It is so!"

"You should be careful. I mean, especially with your phone messages, Chief. All you need is for some recording of you cursing up a blue streak to get in the hands of the media."

"I know, I'm just like my daddy . . . our daddy," Chief says, removing his own bowling ball. "But like I always say, always wear a rubber when you're fucking, because you never know."

"That's right, you don't."

"Like I don't have enough to worry about, and now microphones and cameras trained on every move my ass makes. Maybe we should like make up some words to throw people off. Shit, I knew a little pig latin as a boy, but I guess we'd have to create a new fucking language."

"Your profanity is another language at times."

"And there ain't a black muthafucka in the United States of America that doesn't understand every word I say, including your puritanical ass. It's encoded in us."

The brothers laugh at this, both the absurdity and the plausibility at once funny and appalling.

Griffin is first up. He rolls the ball in a way that pitches his tall body forward as if he too will catapult down the lane. The ball swings to the lane's edge, but arcs hard into the strike zone, for an eight count but also a split like gapped teeth. This is the downside of his Quantum ball, but one worth it, even when his second roll fails to make the spare.

"Looks like this game is over already." Chief retrieves his ball, holding it in the air like Atlas. It's a dark green Brunswick, and called the Anaconda. It tends to break mid-lane, and mostly holds steady on Pinky's hostile lanes. Chief's delivery though — swinging the ball behind him as if he were going to send it down a fairway — propels the ball in an erratic way that leaves its result up in the air. Which doesn't mean Chief loses; on the contrary, he usually wins. Indeed, he rolls a loud, clattering strike.

Griffin's next-up is a strike too. Chief's an eight count, but his second ball easily takes down the spare.

Chief sings a medley concerning business, from China's premier to recent Asian pussy, and they are five games in, and he is ahead, when he changes the tune: "So, Lil'Bro, I need to be advanced twenty-five grand."

"Okay. Anything I should I know?"

"No, I just need some extra dough. The decorator —
she's having some problem with her mortgage."

"Don't you worry she has loose lips?"

"The better for sucking the johnson . . . ha, ha. But no,
she's getting clients from me. And let's just say her loyalty
was bought when it started."

"You and Bubba . . . " Griffin shakes his head. "Your
kingdom for a cunt."

"That's good," Chief laughs but then asks when he'll
receive the twenty-five grand.

"How soon you need it?"

"Like now."

Griffin only pretends to ignore him. He bites his lip,
watches Chief finger and grab his ball, then step up to take
his stance. His arm is arced into a high backswing when he
suddenly seems off balance and balks the ball as if aiming for
the lane to his left. Doubtless, a strong, Bloody Mary-inspired
delivery. He gets a three count as the ball slides into the
gutter. "Sonabitch," Chief hisses. His second roll leaves three
pins standing and victory in doubt. Though Griffin suspects
he is being greased by Chief, a surge in confidence helps
his next roll take out nine pins, followed by an easy spare.
Steadiness versus inconstancy usually prevails, Griffin thinks.

"Is the lady in question in foreclosure?"

"No, not that that's any of your goddamned business,"

Chief snaps. "We still meeting those Singapore gentlemen on Thursday?"

"Yes."

"Those Burmese chumps pay us yet?"

"No."

"Uncivilized, greasy assholes. Everybody knows to bring a nice gift but not those two ignorant muthafuckers. How much they owe us anyway?"

"Technically nothing."

"Fuck technically. They owe us ten grand, and I want it now."

Griffin has pretty much seen it all with Chief, but the brashness and brazen mercenariness are new. His sort of power drunkenness would fail a breath test, and will probably take them deep into trouble. Still, Griffin feels calm . . . even carefree. Let the dice roll as they will.

Not long after the brothers first met, Chief was in New York interviewing with a law firm. He invited Griffin for the weekend, all expenses paid, to celebrate Griffin's just finishing undergrad, at 30 years old. It was their second outing since meeting at their father's funeral; the first was a Bulls game in Chicago, each man taking the other's full measure after a back-slapping good time. Back in Cincinnati, Griffin, already with a successful real estate portfolio, had arranged for them to jointly acquire a property, which he then flipped for a handsome sum. The brothers celebrated, partying, clubbing, gaming; essentially they indulged in all the antics Griffin atypically denied himself. Three days into their debauchery, the brothers found themselves in a hotel room with a boney little black girl sandwiched between them. Nostril rims burning from cocaine, and stratospherically intoxicated, Griffin could not and still cannot remember exactly how this scene came to be, only the images of the girl; on her knees taking turns sucking them off; of her fish-lipping Chief's dark brown doorknob-like head, then Chief watching as the girl straddled him, reaching over and sucking her pacifier-shaped breasts, his hard johnson grazing against Griffin's side. He remembers Chief's fingers inside her traveling the shaft of his own dick, grazing his balls, and then prying and lingering in the space of his asshole. He remembers Chief shouting: "Tear that pussy up, Lil'Bro. Make our daddy proud" — and then his body's uncontrollable, the nearly violent outpouring as Chief's erupted all over his chest.

Next morning, he had been confused and worried not just about what they had done but about the girl still lying between them and looking very underage. When they got rid of her — she wanted a McDonald's Egg McMuffin as much as she did the $35 — Griffin threw up and snapped at Chief: "I'm not into your threeways and freak sex," to which Chief responded, "Don't be a fuckin' prude. We just having fun."

"I'm not into that kind of fun. I'm not like you Blacks, I wasn't brought up as one, I was brought up a Saunders, and we Saunders are not Blacks. If you want to be brothers, fine, if you want to do business together, fine, but not this kind of shit. I was raised better than that."

"You trying to say I wasn't?"

"Fuck you, I said what I'm trying to say perfectly clearly."

"Well, I wasn't. Ha, ha. And I don't remember seeing no baby Jesus sitting on your shoulder, nigga."

Grabbing his shirt, Griffin said, "I'm getting outta here."

"Okay, Lil'Bro, I heard you, loud and clear."

"What was she — 13, 14?"

"17 she said . . . and she's a fuckin' whore, what difference does it make?"

"Probably about 10 years in prison."

"Okay, I can see you're an eternal-damnation kind of guy, just don't start preaching your gospel to me."

"Fine. I said all I have to say about it."

"I just gotta say, you definitely don't have our daddy's genes."

"Guess not." Griffin went for his sneakers.

"Man, our daddy was always screwing somebody, one way or another. With the women, sometimes I'd be in the next room, looking through the fucking keyhole. When I was fourteen, he watched me get my first blowjob. Lil'Bro, he had morals, I have morals, just not your goddamn morals."

"It's not your fault."

"Damn right it's not, just how it is. My middle name

is Tecumseh, not Running Water, and not just because his momma was a Cherokee Indian, but because I am the Chief, that's what our daddy used to say to me."

"A good thing I wasn't raised in your house."

"You middle name would've been 'Stick Up Butt.'"

"We're statutory rapists . . ." If there had been a moment to go off the deep end, it was then . . . when it had been all he could do to hold back the punches he felt like aiming at Chief's face. Griffin made for the door, although not before hearing: "Yeah, rapist, you sure were having a good time. Was it the finger in your ass, Lil'Bro? I apologize, I thought it was her hole."

Yet also, if there ever had been a moment of clarity about what he had been denied as the bastard child of a famous man, it occurred just then, while staring incredulously, murderously at the chosen son, as he slammed the door behind him. In that instant, Griffin had seen clearly that he had missed nothing. Unfortunately, he had not been able to hold on to this thought any longer than it took him to have it, before the longing and the jealousy had returned, full on.

To be forever longing is the birthright of bastard children. Especially when there is dynasty involved. The allure of having come from a long line of "somebodies" proved irresistible to a "nobody" like Griffin, almost from the moment he first glimpsed the man who had sired him emerging from a limousine on television. The father-filled dreams of a young boy grew into the obsessions of a teen. Long before he had had driven overnight to New York from Chicago to see his father in the flesh, however necrotic, he had delved into the history of the Blacks and discovered the very sort of past he longed to be associated with, not just the tradition of education but also of stature: A great-great-grandfather who was a Cherokee chief, a celebrated uncle who traveled the country as emissary of the government of Abraham Lincoln to speak on behalf of the rights of Negroes post-Emancipation Proclamation, in 1863. These were his people, not the long line of washerwomen, maids and slaves linked to his mother. He may bear the name of his maternal grandfather, a garbage man, but Griffin Jewells Saunders II belongs to the powerful exceptions, not the powerless meek.

Griffin has often thought he and Chief are two sides of the same coin, one good, the other bad. Ironically, their Janus relationship has bound them together, inspiring trust they have taken to the bank many times over.

Apparently, their relationship is the perfect state of bound-by-blood conviction for the FBI to exploit. Griffin knows this to be true, at least on some level. Their arm-twisting, back-stabbing, backroom-dealing father, pitting both adversaries and friends alike against each other, had set Griffin in the world to envy and covet what he had not been given. Still, betraying his undeserving half brother, and by extension besmirching their tyrannical father, does not exactly mean Griffin is a Judas. Perhaps a half Judas. Griffin reminds himself he is an empire builder, not a wrecker. He has a family to worry about, and no stomach for revenge, even as his hand is being forced.

"Maybe I should just handle the Singapore meeting myself," he says, when Chief makes his easy tree-pin spare. "It's a little too dangerous for you to be meeting them, under the circumstances."

"Maybe you should, I'll let you know. But it's like this, Lil'Bro, if I show up, those muthafuckas will pay more, not that you can't deliver the bacon, I just get more. And I want more. We don't know how long this gravy train is going to last before the Republicans derail it. Otherwise, it will be Idi Amin and Gaddafi for our asses again, or back to small time fried-chicken-franchises bullshit."

"I understand, but I think it's too dangerous."

"Shit, I gotta get Bubba to let the Riaals stay at the White House. We'd be set for life. Those muthafuckas are worth almost a trillion. Do you know how much that is? I'm lost in all the zeroes."

Griffin nervously looks around, notices a couple of black men glancing their way.

"Two things. First, stop being so fuckin' paranoid! Before your ass has another panic attack." Chief snaps him with his bowling ball cheesecloth. "Nobody can hear anything in this place, unless you're recording everything I say. Are you, Lil'Bro?"

"What kind of question is that?"

"Of course you aren't," Chief says. "So don't worry, be happy. Ain't it the goddamn truth!"

Somehow, smiling prevents breathing. Griffin plays new anxiety off with a shake of his head and roll of his eyes. They are in the tenth frame, and Chief rolls a strike and an eight count but then nicks only one pin off. Still, he has prevailed, but winning is and never will be the point of these games.

Griffin is unbothered by the braying. "You said two things. What's the second?"

"Oh, I was so busy whipping your ass I forgot . . . Lil'Bro, we need to bring everything down a couple levels. Hit only the opportunities with a big payday; fuck the rest. I don't want you using my name for anything that has anything to do with cable or fucking cable encryption."

"I won't . . ." Griffin feels sweat sprouting on his upper lip.

"In fact, don't use my name at all. I'll use my name. Got it?"

"Got it."

"And Lil'Bro, about the Singapore dudes: You make sure it's twenty-five thousand. My time is precious." He sneers at Griffin. "And by the way, what was your ass doing at Rolls Royce/Bentley yesterday?"

"I'm buying one. It's for our new clients. Plus the Bentley has a video surveillance system that records the car, inside and out. Anyone tries to put a listening or video device in or on it will be caught."

"Good," he grins. "You even have to be careful where you put your goddamn dick nowadays? All kind of bugs out there." Then: "You need to make sure that nigga driving your car isn't telling folks where you are."

"I handled it."

Griffin nearly brings up Solomon, but instead re-emphasizes the need for security as his sole motivation, given the caliber of their new client roster.

"Is it bulletproof? Because these muthafuckas we dealing with are used to everybody trying to kill them in their countries, so unless you got something that can take a hard hit like the White House limo, nobody's impressed."

"They won't be the only clients."

"Whatever, Lil'Bro, but you know you just want a Bentley, admit it?"

Griffin grins — but in the spirit of gallows humor.

"Look, long as it's not outta my pocket, what do I care if you want to drive around looking like a fruit or some towelhead. Pointing to his bodyguard Floyd, he adds, "That's better security for my money."

5

Solomon at Bentley has offered a courtesy pickup, and Brodey the Scottish driver turns out to be as "proper" British as the sleek, black Bentley Arnage limousine he stands beside. Ruddy-faced and scrubbed, and dressed in gray livery jacket and matching hat, Brodey opens the rear door with "Good afternoon, sir," his gray eyes dipping slightly in a bow of deference.

"Afternoon," says Griffin. Griffin eases into the backseat, and Brodey brings the door shut. Once installed behind the wheel, Brodey then appears on a small video screen on the seat in front of Griffin. Griffin smiles; video Brodey eye-bows.

"If the gentleman would please sit back and relax. He'll find the *Wall Street Journal*, the *New York Times* and the *Times of London* in the pocket directly behind my seat. If he prefers to use the carphone, he'll find it just above the pocket. Push the privacy button, and the glass between us will close. The phone is calibrated for a soft speaking voice, guaranteeing the gentleman's privacy, sir, but he should feel free to use his own phone device and speak as loudly as he likes. If he would desire tea or coffee, he'll find a demitasse service in the drawer of the lower part of the seat in front of him, as well as

wee bottles of Perrier, Glenlivet Scotch and Chardonnay, if it
pleases the gentleman. Any questions, sir?"

"No."

"Is there anything I can do to increase the gentleman's
comfort?"

"No, thank you."

"Then I'll have the gentleman at the showroom shortly."

Here, at last, the dream chauffeur. Griffin wants to
ask where are the Brodeys of the world. Reserved for the
gentlemen who can afford them . . . of course!

His mother's brother had been chauffeur to a wealthy
downtown Cincinnati German family that also summered in
Indian Hill. When Griffin was a boy aged ten, Uncle Wilbur
urged her to take a seasonal position at the summer estate.
Domestics wanting to escape Cincinnati's rising crime in
the black quarters jumped at the chance to work in Indian
Hill. The hitch was the Beerman estate was so far away that
staff were required to stay on-grounds — hardly ideal for a
devoted church lady of the United First Baptist. Should the
Beerman family decide to stay at the house all year round,
however, the job offered permanent employment. Regardless
of the duration of her stay, she could flirt with a summer
worship or settle down indefinitely at an Indian Hill church.

Still, she dawdled over her decision . . . until her young
son insisted she say yes.

Already a realist, he had understood the bottom

line: Meemaw had had no job for several months, after her
previous employer, a bakery, went bust and had fallen behind
in rent. Yet she had no fear: the Lord would surely provide,
finding a way for her and her boy. Griffin, however, wanted
more than just "a way": he wanted the best way. If she could
not grasp the possibilities Uncle Wilbur was alluding to, he
could. The sliver of Indian Hill occupied by the black servant
class rightly boasted that their two lone schoolrooms had
churned out a few generations of young black teachers and
tradesmen, plus a few lawyers and doctors, who in turn
became professionals throughout the quaint towns between
eastern Ohio's two biggest cities, Cincinnati and Dayton.
Other than restaurants, liquor stores, pony kegs, beauty
parlors, bars, pulpits and funeral homes, mostly what the
downtown blacks laid claim to were a mess of problems.

The precocious Griffin planned to be among the
professional-class success stories, and here before him was the
perfect way forward and a chance to be inspired. Indeed, his
first impression of that summer was sight unseen. From what
he understood from Uncle Wilbur, wealth meant a man could
have houses for different times of the year, and that he could
move between them as whim or season dictated.

A train shuttled commuters between Indian Hill and
downtown Cincinnati with minimal difficulty, but Mr.
Christian Elder Beerman preferred the privacy of his car and
vagaries of traffic to the crowded, clattering efficiency of the

train. The entire Beerman family usually decamped to the Indian Hill countryside in early May, and for the next four or five months, Uncle Wilbur ran between the summer estate and the Beerman office and house in town.

A bachelor, Uncle Wilbur lived off the estate, in an area called Silver Springs. Somehow Mr. Beerman hardly knew it, so careful was Uncle Wilbur to appear at the ready, there at six a.m., gone around nine p.m. nearly every day. His father had been houseman to the downtown-Cincinnati Beermans, and the job of chauffeur came to Uncle Wilbur almost as a family legacy. Gentlemen like Mr. Beerman were a vanishing breed, and so were the chauffeurs at their service. "I'd be lying if I said there was nothing in the world I'd rather be doing than rolling that ole farting man around town in this kung-fu suit, but it is what it is," was how he had put it to Griffin and his mother.

The job interview had been a success, thanks to well-spokenness of both mother and son. The next day their migratory lives began when Uncle Wilbur rolled up just hours before daybreak to pick them up, and an hour and a half later Griffin first laid eyes on the fancy house in a bright, lemony sunrise. Next the migrants were assigned a tiny room in the dark, north-facing wing of the attic. A delightfully dazed Griffin gave little thought to the three large, sun-soaked rooms they left behind in North Avondale. He put his head to the thick lead glass window, marveling at the swimming pool and what he soon learned was a tennis court. In the distance, shiny horses grazed in the fields, and lush hills rolled both east and north as far as he could see. This dreamy view perhaps had been shared by the wealthy who arrived in the early 1900s, to dwell in this village that incorporated in the 1770s as little more than a tract of farmland undulating between the Ohio and Miami Rivers. The vistas and breezes of this precious land had been stolen from native Seneca Indian tribes, to become a weekending and summering antidote to filthy Cincinnati.

Not long after arriving, Griffin saw what Uncle Wilbur described as the one thing he loved about his job. "I got summin' to make you feel you done died and gone to heaven. Watch from the window."

Five minutes later, abracadabra: The 1957 Crown Imperial Ghia Limousine sVr.

Uncle Wilbur rolled it out of the garage, but it was as if he were escorting a lady for her entrance . . . a Lana Turner premiering on the red carpet at the Academy Awards in a sky-blue evening gown with a white mink capelet. Mr. Beerman owned a department store, and the staid Cadillacs of bankers and brokers were neither tasteful nor sexy enough.

"Heaven's chariot, my boy, that's what you got here," Uncle Wilbur said to Griffin. He then rhapsodized over all the details: the landau roof, skirts, fenders, headlights and more. About his outfit, what he called his Chinaman's kung-fu jacket buttoned up to the neck, a flat cap snug on his head, "It was made for the car. Now that's class."

For the impressionable Griffin, Lana Turner had nothing on the glamour of the Beermans, with all their grand homes and fancy cars and tennis courts and pretty horses.

"You get in the front seat and you can ride along while I take Mr. Beerman to his office."

Though big for his size, Griffin could barely see over the dashboard. His head bobbed above the door handles, just high enough that he could perceive the small, bespectacled man emerge from the house, in a wheat-colored linen suit and bowler hat the blue of the landau roof. Uncle Wilbur pivoted from his post beside the car, offering "Good morning, sir," as Mr. Beerman passed into the cool leather and spongy world of the cabin, with a cold "Good Morning, Wilbur" swatted as an afterthought. No sooner had he sat down, than a scowl parked on his face as he pored through the newspaper and the coffee service Uncle Wilbur had set up. The air-conditioning was going, and the car's window curtains were partly pulled to block the morning light. The glass partition between the cab and the cabin effectively sealed him in, like a rare exotic bird in a luxurious cage.

Uncle Wilbur winked at Griffin, putting a finger to his lips to suggest silence, as if speaking somehow would disturb Mr. Beerman. But how could Mr. Beerman even hear them? Griffin desperately wanted to turn around in his seat and watch the funny old man, a Jiminy Cricket come to life. What did a man so little need with such a big car? Such a big house?

Then Griffin heard a strange sound, and a few seconds later a voice crackled to life from within the car. Uncle Wilbur pushed a button on the console.

"Yes, Mr. Beerman?"

"Pull over, please. Something doesn't agree with me."

Uncle Wilbur sent his finger out like a switchblade that only Griffin could read. He then glided to the side of the road. The car had hardly rolled to a stop when the passenger door opened and Mr. Beerman stuck his head out and threw up.

"Goddamn ulcer," they heard through the speaker.

Twenty minutes of crackling and mumbling passed before they pulled up to the west side entrance of his building on Fountain Square.

"I think it'll be an early day for me," the dashboard spoke, just as Uncle Wilbur bolted to get the door. Griffin turned and watched Mr. Beerman exit, speak to Uncle Wilbur and then vanish in the revolving doors of the store. Uncle Wilbur was just about to take off, when suddenly Mr. Beerman was tapping on the window.

"On second thought, be here at five," he said.

Griffin suddenly felt the old man's trout eyes dimple upon him.

"This your nephew?"

"Yes," said Uncle Wilbur.

"Train them early, I say," he smiled at Griffin. "A good

chauffeur is hard to come by."

"Yes, sir."

Once they pulled into traffic, Uncle Wilbur said, "Poor Mr. Beerman, he's scared to death to thow up and now every morning he thows up. We lucky he didn't mess all over the car. But I tell you what I hate. His boy's craziness, him with his girls and him getting their pussies in the back seat, whether they bleeding or not. Excuse my language, but it's just nasty, just nasty! Well, leastwise Mr. Beerman know it ain't me, though I sure could have a good time with a car like this."

On Elm Street, Uncle Wilbur pulled over, removing supplies from the trunk: "You get on back there, and clean up after him."

As the car sped along, Griffin cleaned, and afterward he leaned back into the spongy comfort, in exactly the same spot Mr. Beerman had occupied, observing the world outside the window passing in blurring and colorful shading. One evening while watching TV with his mother and Grandma Saunders, the two women argued over a black man on the news; he was getting out of the backseat of a fancy car, a chauffeur holding the door for him. Grandma Saunders had said, "That man is a prince of the devil, but I'll grant he sure still is nice to look at. Musta been hard to keep your panties on. Ast me, you was lucky to escape and that the nigga gave you Griffin, when he could have gave you a demon." She then gum-smiled at her grandson.

That man was Congressman Samuel Tecumseh Black I, a man so important he was on Ed Murrow.

When she had run out of the room in a rush of tears, Grandma Saunders had said, "Griffin, that man is your daddy, and he's important, and you better grow up and be sumtin' too, 'cause you got it in your blood to be somebody. Otherwise, what would be point?"

This sense of himself — of his roots stemming from an important man — had given Griffin a unique vantage point from which to see everything, including Uncle Wilbur's dilemma with the vomity Mr. Beerman.

"You can maybe drive for my daddy . . . Congressman Samuel Tecumseh Black is his name," Griffin offered, thrilled for having thought of it.

"Drive for your daddy, huh?" Uncle Wilbur mused. "Boy, look at you . . . ackin' like you always be riding around in a big fancy car with a chauffeur. Like you a little nigger Fauntleroy on a radio. Ain't you something, little man . . . or should I call you Mr. Griffin?"

"Mr. Griffin," Griffin said. "No, Mr. Saunders is better."

"Oh is it now, Mr. Grif—Mr. Saunders? Yeah, you must be the son of the congressman. Though he wouldn't know your little black smartass from Buckwheat. In case being a big man don't work out for you, better you learn your place. Now come up here with me, and I'll teach you a thing or two."

Griffin did as told. He shimmied through the small sliding pane in the glass partition separating driving and passenger. He then climbed onto Uncle Wilbur's narrow lap and gripped the blue, ridged steering wheel, vibrating with all the power and mystery at his fingertips. The road became more than strips of white lines and the city gave way to spans of space and rolling hills. He felt the oneness of man and machine, but also the wonder of the world around him — thrilling in ways never imagined.

Then a strange, not unwelcome sensation traveled along his body. Uncle Wilbur's breathing came with a moaning sound and gripping that forced Griffin to hold still, followed by a pulse of energy and shaking and breathing and a grunt. Uncle Wilbur's two-toned lips kissed the crown of his head for being such a great driver. Griffin wished to ride on the congressman's lap, to show him what a good driver and son he could be.

A few weeks later, summer seemed to drift by in slow-motion miles on the same well-traveled routes, until it took a nasty turn when Uncle Wilbur forced Griffin's head into his lap. Unable to breathe, Griffin jerked the steering wheel so hard they sideswiped three parked cars. The only person more displeased than Mr. Beerman was Uncle Wilbur. Thereafter, the summer was filled with pain.

"Good day to you, sir," says Brodey, holding the door as Griffin emerges from the Bentley.

"And to you . . . thank you," says Griffin, almost forlornly, as he watches the true gentleman's dream drive away. Solomon, who is holding the showroom door for him, seems to read his mind.

"Isn't Brodey a treasure? He's what Bentley is about — a gentleman's comfort, ultimately."

"Yes," says Griffin.

"By the look in your eyes, you're a member of the Brodey fan club. Believe me, everyone wants him."

"I'm sure," says Griffin, as Solomon leads him to Griffin's own little purchased world of Bentley.

"And curtains, just as you wanted — a small gift from me to you."

"Curtains, yes. Thank you."

Solomon gives him a tour of the car, and though Griffin mourns the absence of the video intercom, he is awed by the high-tech security — the whole point of this purchase, he reminds himself. Once behind the wheel, though, he is tentative with the disorienting steering. His experience of London was not from behind the wheel. The driving on the wrong side of the street was confusing enough, but this feels worse somehow; a reversed image of the way things are, like reading text in a mirror while in motion at forty miles per hour. No surprise that the immense car handles like a dream, as if all the bumps and holes in the road smooth out at the car's supremacy. There is, however, a sense of veering and tipping when mounting corners, and especially turning from the center lane, but it is more an issue of the righty steering. Also, with the curtains drawn, there are unnerving, unforeseen blind spots. They prevent a rear view, a frightening prospect given the speed at which things rush around a car in motion and, he thinks, a life in turmoil: cars, trucks, buses . . . surveillance, scandal!

Griffin could pull the curtains back, but then what would be the point of having them? Not even Brodey would be able to talk himself around the absent rear view. How does a chauffeur account for what he cannot see? Is it even legal to drive so handicapped? Uncle Wilbur's driving with Griffin on his lap was almost certainly against the law, and Griffin remembers passing many a policeman, and yet nothing was ever done. Chauffeurs of rich men can skirt the law too.

Solomon assures it is the very reason chauffeurs have a special license, but Griffin remains puzzled, and once on the highway, all his worries about the car grip onto the steering again. Solomon reassures the sensation Griffin is experiencing will pass quickly enough. Should it not, however, in the worse-case scenario, the steering can be re-oriented, in about eight weeks, but at considerable expense: $12,000, excluding freight to and from Manchester, England, where the Bentley was crafted. "It isn't just the steering, it's the wiring, the

upholstery . . . everything. We don't do that here. In fact, Mr.
Saunders, that's the reason you got the car at such a steal."

"Yes," says Griffin.

"Second thoughts are understandable," adds Solomon.
"Not to worry, you'll only be charged a $5,000 courtesy if
the contract is null and void. It's standard procedure for all
Bentley purchases."

Griffin does not immediately reply, wondering if he
has been taken for a ride. By the time they return to the
dealership, he has got the hang of the steering and a handle
on reality, firm enough to know that he will look like an
idiot — out not $10,000 as before with the house bribe, but
ninety thousand and counting. A thick blob of nausea works
its way up his throat, and Griffin, fearful of vomiting, now
worries why this peculiar condition comes upon him at the
oddest moments, without warning, lately when the issue at
hand concerns money, sex, children or even bowling. At such
times, he pictures Mr. Beerman in the open car door, bent over
in reverse peristalsis, but unlike the old gentleman, Griffin
chokes the vomitous feeling back down.

"I have no second thoughts, Solomon. This is exactly
what I want. And thank you for all your help."

"Excellent, Mr. Saunders, it was a pleasure. I'll just need
your signature, and you'll receive the registration and title,
and then you can be on your way."

After minutes and meaningless small talk about

the many reasons to join the Washington Bentley Owners Club, Griffin signs on the proverbial dotted line. A second glance makes him think his own signature lacks clarity and conviction . . . just as his new Bentley will lack Brodey. Alone, on the Beltway, his driving is lacking too, and he narrows his options to the slow lane and minimum speed. He can sense the curiosity and admiration of cars passing him, but there is also the feeling of being not so much in the pack as beyond it, even above it, and therein is the pleasure of Bentley ownership, with or without a Brodey.

That particular reassurance glides along with him up the driveway of his beloved home, but it vanishes when he sees a car that clearly does not belong on his property. It's the man from the hospital in Cincinnati. Griffin looks around. Who else is here, watching, and for what reason?

"That's a nice car, Mr. Saunders. I'm pretty fond of the Bentley myself. It's simple, not flashy, very distinguished, but at the same it says who you are without shouting. It says you value quality."

"You should work for Bentley," Griffin says, amused that the homely fellow would fail the good-looks test and likely end up in a stockroom. "What are you doing here?"

"Following up on our last conversation. I realize you were just coming out of the hospital, but you said you were going to contact me when you returned to D.C., but you didn't, so here I am . . ."

"My attorney, Irving Finkelstein, did. My attorney speaks for me. If you've got some warrant for my arrest, show it or get off my property now."

"I don't think you understand me, Mr. Saunders."

"I understand, but I'm not interested. Whatever you're attempting to do to Chief, you'll have to do without me."

"No, I don't think you understand, Mr. Saunders. You're in it deep and there are no options left."

"Are you threatening me?"

"No, just telling you like it is."

"What do you want from me?"

"As I said before. The Secretary of Commerce for the United States, Samuel Tecumseh Black II, also known as your half-brother Chief, is our target. And like I also said, Mr. Saunders, you can choose to cooperate or not, but you will be prosecuted either way. The question is not if but how seriously we go after you, that is, if you don't find yourself suddenly on a holiday."

"I've done nothing wrong."

"The word I'd use is illegal. At the hospital, I mentioned financial improprieties. I believe the example I gave was income tax evasion. Now that you're stronger, here's a little more of what we've got. There's the matter of identity fraud, illegal real estate transactions concerning properties throughout Cincinnati. I could mention minority business funds obtained under false circumstances, and I could also mention bribery, extortion — but that's the secretary's part of what you've done wrong."

"I don't know what you're talking about."

"Mr. Saunders, you and I both know what the deal is … and frankly, people in your situation have been tied up and carted off in the trunk of a car and red-eyed to Bogotá — that's in Colombia, in South America, home to Pablo Escobar, who would gladly be your host. Trust me, those unfortunate fools are never seen again."

"So you are you threatening me?"

"Just helping you make an informed decision."

Griffin's stomach trembles as his eyes linger on the Bentley.

"Just for the sake of argument, let's say we do this your way. The lawyers can go back and forth, back and forth, and you'll still end up in jail, after considerable expense, but the big difference is you'll have to deal with all your friends, family and enemies reading about your sins or watching them on TV, over and over — you know how the news cycles are."

Griffin swallows hard.

"Or, if we do it my way, you give us what we want, and your name, and that of your family, and your assets, will be kept out of this as much as possible."

"What exactly do you want from me?"

Griffin feels the sweat breaking the surface of his skin, as a picture is put in his face.

"You know this man?"

With the dynamics of a burp, Griffin says, "Mankit Huang, he represents this Hong Kong family called the Riaals. That's all I know about him, but he could be anybody. Is anybody who they say they are?"

"How do you know him?"

"As I'm sure you already know, my company Premier International develops and sells cable technology. The Riaals, the family Huang works for, are from Singapore, but they are strongly tied to China and Vietnam. They own shipping yards and ocean freighters, papermills and textile mills, media, and who knows what else."

"And . . ."

"They want to get into cable, that's how I know them."

"And the Riaals want an introduction to the White House, and would pay you and the secretary for the introduction. That's how the quid pro quo works, isn't it?"

"I don't know what you're talking about," Griffin says. "Now . . ."

"And we know you're meeting with Mankit Huang . . . very soon, Thursday." He consults a little black book. "Yes, Thursday. Where?"

Griffin looks at the house, then at the car, concluding he is cornered.

"Why even bother asking me anything? You're obviously listening to every conversation I have."

"I need you to confirm when and where, Mr. Saunders."

"Why, so you people can bug the place?"

"Something like that."

"That's all I have to do — confirm the details?"

"Yes."

"You do whatever you have to do, but I'm not wearing any gadgets or doing anything like baiting him . . . I won't."

"I'll be in touch."

"Will it be enough? Will you leave me alone then?"

"We'll see."

"I want it in writing, and I want you to communicate with my lawyer."

An hour later, sitting in the backseat of the Bentley, with his attorney, Irving Finkelstein, on the phone, Griffin pictures the trap in all its hardware, as precise and inescapable as a Swiss-made watch.

"Griffin," Irv says, "sounds like you don't have a choice but to deal with them directly and hope for the best. I don't know what all else you're involved in, and never mind your brother's business dealings, you're looking at three years and a possible half-million fine for just the identity fraud alone."

"Jewells is my son. What's his is mine, and mine is his, until he is of age."

"The court won't see it that way."

Griffin tried to think of something to add, but nothing came to mind that did not make him come off a complete shit. Then: "I couldn't get loans because of some bad debt, so I made a fresh start. End of story."

"I'm sure you meant well."

"As a businessman yourself, you can appreciate that I didn't do it to 'mean well,' I did it to make money. Far as the government is concerned, my kid is rich . . . even richer than I am, on paper anyway."

Griffin could almost hear Chief say "slumlord," for all the run-down properties in Over-the-Rhine and Avondale, plus in Indianapolis, in Jewells' portfolio. The imagined slight, on top of the FBI, the accident, the Holt monitor, and everything else now angers Griffin.

"And you know what the punchline is to this sick joke? Jewells isn't even my biological son."

"And you've raised him as your own. That's very noble."

"That's debatable. To him, I'm the worst father in the world. There are worse, I know, but I don't exactly feel like a model father either."

"I've seen these adopted kids on TV. It's difficult knowing you're adopted."

"Jewells doesn't know, nobody knows, really, except . . . "

"You have no contact with the parents?"

"Never heard from the mother again. But the real father . . . he pretends he isn't the father. His public image, you know." Griffin mopped at his forehead, knowing he should just shut up.

"Poor kid — Jewells, that is." Irv clears his throat. "Griffin, it speaks to your character. You're big-hearted, clearly loyal. Now listen, Griffin, I can appreciate how difficult this is for you. For what it's worth, I've always admired you, and I'm still a big fan . . . and not because you pay me to be either."

"Good to know. Perhaps I'll avail myself of your pro bono services once I'm behind bars."

Both men chuckle, and then agree to speak again soon.

After hanging up, he phones Jewells, leaving what is the seventh unreturned message in almost as many days. "Jewells . . . I know you're disappointed, but son, things happen."

He then phones Therosine, engages in a half hour of small talk, including the Barbra Streisand debacle and Shauntay's drug-free run, before they move on to property issues: broken generators, boilers out, rodent infestation, roof replacements, backed-up sewage, unpaid rents, evictions, court dates.

"Did the Jaguar get repaired?"

"Yes, it's supposed to be delivered to your house tomorrow."

"Did Jewells ever phone back about picking it up?"

"No."

"Good. Please phone Jewells now. If he answers, just say that the Jaguar is being delivered to the house tomorrow."

She does his bidding, and a few minutes later, to Griffin's

surprise, she phones back.

"I just spoke to him. He was pretty sassy, as boys his age can be. Your mother used to say Jewells had to be reminded of his manners all the time."

"What did he say?"

"That he was coming to pick it up. I told him that the dealer wouldn't release the car without the owner's permission, which is true. He didn't say anything after that."

"Good. Please make sure that Margeaux gets the keys to the car. And you call me if Jewells gets in touch with you about anything, no matter what it is."

"Yes, Mr. Saunders."

6

The summer barbecue is a familiar tradition, although not Griffin's thing. The typical paper plates and picnic tables with benches without backs are synonymous with slovenly dress and lax moral rectitude.

This particular cookout invitation is one Griffin should not refuse under any circumstances. He has been advised by the FBI to behave normally, keep to business as usual, as if nothing is wrong.

Even Chief agrees, although for different reasons.

If only there were a way to know in advance if there would be real tableware.

Unlike in Cincinnati, Griffin may know D.C.'s elected officials on a first-name basis, but few know his. He has met the higher-ups, even drug-addled Marion Barry, thanks to Chief's introductions. Inconstancy is not what kindles warmth and familiarity in such relationships, however. Birthday flowers, an invitation to lunch, a "God bless" at church, and the dropping in at parties count if not endear. A well-timed sympathy card, even in the most extreme cases, is an ace in hand. Chief has even argued that the FBI videotape of Mayor Marion Barry snorting crack cocaine warranted a show of support, just as Clinton's fellatio peccadillo did.

"It could happen to anyone, even you, Lil'Bro."

"Really? Me?"

"Really, you. I know you, and you haven't always been the goody-two-shoes you are now. Nobody is. Not even those fuckin' right-wing Christian hypocrites, so goddamn certain about the sins of other folks."

"Whatever your point is, Barry isn't making your case. I mean, you're saying because he got busted in the commission of a crime he deserves pity?"

"No, the point being, no man thinks the FBI is analyzing the goddamn pussy cum on his boxers and offering his girlfriend, poker buddies or weed dealer a plea bargain."

"But crack, Chief! He was caught smoking crack! It's on video."

"Look, Barry's one low-class, old-school nigga, but he's running this muthafuckin' plantation, not them, and that's what you need to never forget if you're going to make money in this town. And, goddammit, how hard it is to show some love with a phone call, a card?"

"Not at all, call 1-800-FLOWERS and you're done."

"Flowers? How punk of you. Of course I didn't send no muthafuckin' pansies, so there." Chief clutches Griffin by the scruff, like they are boys on the ball court. "And unfortunately Hallmark doesn't make cards for a sorry-ass Negro getting busted smoking crack . . . Yeah, so I wrote him a personal note and said something like, 'Man, this too shall pass. We bros are not many so we've got to stick together. Let me know what I can do for you.'"

"I'm touched."

"The point being, so was he. And you know, Lil'Bro, who would have thought that, here we are, four years later, on the eve of his ass about to be mayor again? Do you realize that the only reason he hasn't been mayor nonstop is because the law says he can't run for reelection while serving a goddamn federal prison sentence? That's something — that's power. The crackhead motherfucker got chutzpah. The election is a formality. He's already won."

It certainly appeared so.

In saying yes to the barbecue, Griffin had sensed something in the air . . . perhaps barbecue smells of a pre-celebration for something momentous to come.

Carter-John Workman, or C.J. for short, is the business-school connection whose tip got Griffin his beloved house. Chief recently let on that C.J. is expected to be appointed deputy mayor to the office of Planning and Economic Development. Griffin thought nothing of it until C.J. personally called with an invitation. C.J. essentially confirmed Chief's assertion. "D.C.'s scope needs to be more international, more global, more Africa-friendly. I'm really interested in your ideas, and so is our Mayor to be. Think about what you want to do, and let's talk. He'll be at the party, I'll introduce you," C.J. added.

Introduce him as what? The chump you took for ten grand? Griffin would not be fooled again.

That conversation was two weeks ago, and Griffin still is uncertain what C.J. meant or intended by the remark. He heads out to the cookout, not feeling quite as crisp as he looks in pale blue seersucker trousers and pink polo shirt. The addition of a sky-blue blazer and black shield-sunglasses lends a debonair quality, he thinks. But when he observes himself in the Bentley rearview mirror, he is displeased, certain that he looks as if he were headed out for a game of golf. Without the jacket, he appears on his way to the groomers to have his poodle shampooed. The very idea disgusts him, as he runs back inside to change into a white blazer. Unless he is sporting a gray or dark or white suit, the Bentley is a hard car to dress for, he concludes.

Margeaux would solve this dilemma in a split second. Her voice is the absolute last voice he wishes to hear.

Just as he is leaving, Jewells' voice erupts on the answering machine, and Griffin lunges as if the boy himself were within easy grabbing.

"Jewells, Jewells, son . . ."

"Hey, Dad, I was about to try your cell."

"Glad you got around to calling me back."

"Sorry, Dad, you know how it is . . ."

"I don't know how it is . . . why don't you tell me how it is?"

"I've been busy."

"Jewells, when I tell you to call me, it's not an option. And it's not something that you should do when you feel like it."

"Yeah, I know . . ."

"It's been a week, and I really can't have this immature payback."

"I've called you back, Dad. I can't help it we're playing telephone tag."

"Jewells, son, I didn't leave town because I wanted to skip out on you, I left because I had to."

"So you said before. Sorry, I didn't call persistently, but like I said, I was busy, just like you, Dad."

"Doing what, exactly? Let's see, football practice. No driver's ed since you have a license now. And what else?"

"I picked up the summer reading list from the library and have been trying to get ahead so it won't be so hard to keep up."

"And what are you reading that so engrosses you that you lose all track of days and time?"

"*A Farewell to Arms, The Crucible*, and *Invisible Man*."

"Which have you read?"

"*Invisible Man*."

"Don't know it. What it's about?"

"It's like weird and trippy . . . about a black dude that white people can't see. I could relate to the feeling of not being seen. And I could . . . "

Griffin does not dodge this dart of criticism, but neither does he acknowledge it. In fact, he muses, the cloak of invisibility would be just the thing right now . . . and the perfect fashion for the Bentley.

"Dad . . . you there?"

"Yes, I'm listening to you . . . "

"And I'm like just glad it wasn't a book about slavery. In eighth grade, we read *Sounder*, but I didn't get why that was on the syllabus, I mean, like it's only a handful of black kids at the school anyway, and just me and Davon in the class."

"Maybe that's the point. It's not so much about the black kids but about the nonblack kids."

"Maybe," said Jewells, "we were like over it already. Like, what do we care? I mean, it's like embarrassing reading how the slaves were treated. I know they couldn't help it, and that's what slavery did, but I mean, like, why can't we read *The Virgin Suicides* and cool current stuff?"

"What's that about?"

"These sisters that commit suicide. I mean, though, it's like really cool . . . not sad, pathetic or anything like that. It's romantic. Better than slaves."

"I don't want you reading anything like that."

"Too late, I already did. And at least I'm reading, right? Isn't that what's important, huh?"

"Jewells . . ."

"Oh, and Dad, as you just pointed out, I got my driver's license. A friend helped me out. I didn't cancel my road test and this friend picked me up from practice and we just went out there and took it."

"What friend is this?"

"He plays on another team."

"Does your mother know?"

"No, and she would have said no for me to go take the road test, and she'd be upset about me having the license."

"Because you're on punishment!"

"I know that, Dad. I know that."

"Jewells, why do you insist on testing us? You'll lose, son, you'll lose."

"It's not a big deal, Dad. It just isn't. And when I get off punishment, I plan on getting a job and I'll get my own car."

"We'll talk about this later, but I am sorry you couldn't wait, I was looking forward to it."

"Yeah, well . . ."

"I'll be home in about two weeks."

"Cool."

"How's football?"

"Football. I mean, I'm like looking forward to the scrimmage, even if I don't get to play."

"Why wouldn't you get to play?"

"Coach McGlad's always got something to say about me. Before it was that I was late, now it's that I'm not concentrating. I get headaches every day I'm thinking of the plays so hard."

"That's what it takes to win. That and sacrifice."

"Yeah, I know."

"I don't think you do," Griffin says. "See, Jewells, you shouldn't think that I love having all this responsibility, because I don't. But I've chosen a certain life, and I have to play the game as best as I can. I'd rather spend all my time with you, but I have to support our family and I have to be here."

"Yeah, dad" — a trio of fast sneezes — "When do you leave for the trip . . . Transylvania, right?"

"Croatia, and I'm not leaving. I'm not going. Something

is happening here, so it's better that I stick around."

"See, I could've come back with you then," he says, giggling.

"Yes, son, turns out this would have been a good time, but you have football anyway."

"Yeah, so . . ."

A shaking that rises up from his gut forces Griffin to pretend his cell phone is ringing. In cutting Jewells short, he promises to call again before the weekend, and he feels as if he is suddenly burning up. He snatches off his blazer to spare it staining, and makes his way to the Bentley, blasting the air conditioning. Just then it seems to him, there really is no escape — no fixed price that he will pay forever and ever. And it should not be thus.

On the drive over to C.J.'s, he finds himself thinking of the Cayman Islands, how sweet it would be to be motoring along the coastline, Brodey behind the wheel, the pinkish beaches against the turquoise sea, the perfect specimen of woman sitting beside him — Athena — on his way to a motherlode of money.

The Cayman Island-inspired calm does not leave him at C.J.'s. C.J. lives on D.C.'s Gold Coast, but not on or near choking 16th Street; rather, on the far edge of Rock Creek Park. The plateau of backyard tumbles down into a ravine neatly laced with a ribbon of shimmering stream.

Griffin's smile and hand are at the ready for greetings,

and there are so many people to meet — all organized in clusters like pastel bowling pins, and there is porcelain table- and glassware.

As he eyes the crowd and plots where to strike first, a hand touches his shoulder blade, and he feels the game has officially begun.

C.J., a copper, medium-sized man of Griffin's years but retouched with the sort of constant grooming that makes him appear much younger, assures that he is delighted Griffin has come. "I can imagine shuttling back and forth between D.C. and Cincinnati must be pretty taxing?"

"Not at all," says Griffin. "Not at all."

"Guess it works for some people more than others. For two years I did it, between here and Atlanta, where my family lived at the time. I didn't know which was worse: the strain on our marriage or on our finances from having two mortgages."

"It's not a problem for us. And I'm so close to BWI airport, it's nothing."

"When am I gonna meet your wife?"

"She'll be here in September. We're going to make like we're on a little holiday somewhere, without the kids."

"Sounds nice. She was in television, right?"

"She was indeed."

"Well, right over there is Robert Johnson, president of Black Entertainment Television."

Griffin feels a tugging at his pant leg. It is a toddler, a

little chocolate bar with arms and legs in a sailor suit. Griffin instinctively reaches down and lifts the boy, and finds himself nuzzling in a memory of Jewells.

"Sorry," a white man says, reaching for the child. "Little Max seems to really go for you."

"And I for him . . . " says Griffin, grinning as another man, a black man, comes, touching C.J.'s shoulder.

"That's what happens when you're missing your own children," says C.J. "You've met Max, and this is his dad, Josh Winterbottom, and his other dad, Duggins Robertson."

In the instant that Griffin is confused, and just before he shrugs it off, C.J. says, "Duggins and Josh just got married in Hawaii . . . isn't that marvelous?"

Griffin grins, nodding.

"We're actually suing the District of Columbia," Josh says.

"He's a lawyer," C.J. says, adding, "Duggins and I work together on the Urban Planning Commission."

Griffin hears but is not listening and at times not breathing but inhaling as if on life support. He senses thousands of confetti-like chits falling through sunlight and vanishing in the emerald green of trees and lawn. The talk is about law and logic and discrimination, and he feels himself going along though understanding little, and his thoughts wandering back to the Caribbean. Finally, he excuses himself to the restroom, and there presses down a panic, daubing the sweat from his brow. A few deep breaths, and he is fine; swell, even.

On his way out, he passes a man he knows, and almost immediately he turns, as does the other man, pulled into orbit.

"Griffin, isn't it?"

"Yes, Griffin. Spencer?"

"That's right. The War Crimes fellow." He smiles. Griffin thinks, if Harry Belafonte were a diplomat, he would be Spencer — elegant, eloquent, fatherly, with a serene look that holds you in his aura.

"Arusha — I remember you said you were about to move there. Did you?"

"That's a good memory you've got. I did move there. I'm just passing through, checking on a few things. I have to be in New York tomorrow, and a quick pop back into D.C., and then it's back to Arusha."

"Is it as beautiful as its name?"

"It is. A little oasis of calm and beauty, you should come visit while I'm there. I love having guests. I don't get many . . . the distance."

"I need a holiday."

"It's the perfect place. It's high in the mountains, but the climate is decent. The U.N. presence means it's pretty easy to get around, and very safe. It's quite international, and yet your money goes far. A big house, staffed, a car and driver for pennies on the dollar. It's next door to the best of Africa — Mt. Kilimanjaro, the Serengeti. Kenya and Uganda are neighbors."

"I've been to Uganda, post-Idi Amin."

"Unfortunately there are many like him in that part of the world. After Rwanda, he seems a gentleman. One power-hungry madman, versus an entire population gone mad."

"Sounds like Washington, D.C. The corrupt mayor and all the drugs and crime here."

"Maybe you're right on some level. Although it's really impossible to get one's mind around the murder of over 800,000 people in the space of five or six weeks — which is what I'm talking about. A smattering of murders that add up to a horror versus a genocide that happened — and still is happening — practically overnight and right under our noses."

"At least you're on the right side of justice."

He reaches into his pocket and hands Griffin his business card.

"I remember feeling you and I were kindred spirits when we met the first time."

"I felt the same," says Griffin, allowing his hand to be taken and held.

"It's too bad I'm leaving this weekend. But perhaps we can continue our conversation another time?"

"In Arusha," says Griffin.

"Maybe I can manage a week off and we can travel together?"

"Yes," says Griffin.

Spencer excuses himself to the restroom. Griffin

wanders out among the guests, and is soon pulled into a
conversation about zoning and planning. The topic bores him.
He wants, and is waiting, to hear more about Arusha — in
Spencer's bedtime-story voice. No sooner does Spencer rejoin
the party than he is pulled away by the host, among others.
The two men make helpless eye contact, and the distance and
the guests between them grow. The barbecue quickly has
become a who's who of local power and celebrity. The craggy-
faced Marion Barry arrives, surrounded by arch men suited
in black who are surely sharpshooters. Out of the corner of
Griffin's eye, he watches Spencer, and when Spencer seems
to nod at him, he first believes they are acknowledging the
scallywag mayor, but when their eyes linger he suddenly
understands that they really are kindred spirits. Griffin thinks
of Chief, and then switches fully to autopilot. He finds himself
grinning, clapping shoulders, pumping handshakes like a pro,
and with brio speaking so many untruths about how much
he loves D.C., how great it is to do business in the nation's
capital, a place of sophistication, opportunity, black culture,
achievement and connectedness, at a level he has never
experienced, among the kind of accomplished black people
he has always imagined but never found, not even in Atlanta,
a place he very much dislikes for all kinds of reasons he no
longer even remembers. He pretends to feel so at home with
his "peeps" that when someone has the presence of mind to
ask about an investigation soon to loom over Chief, he feels

himself straying into the margins of Chief style, and as if referring to the felonious Marion Barry, he says, much to his regret, "Hallmark doesn't make sympathy cards for lowdown niggas like him."

7

Just beyond Mr. Huang's head is a snapshot of the nation's capital from the Virginia side of the Potomac River. The lineup of landmarks begins at the Kennedy Center, with a straight shot down to the Washington Monument and the Mall. Depending on the angle of Huang's head, the view crops the Watergate Hotel. The hotel gleams, and Griffin more than once loses his train of thought, feeling the sway of tacky bamboo stenciling on the room's wallpaper. It is not at all that he even likes the Key Bridge Marriott, in Arlington, Virginia. Chief once told him that it is an affront to be seen in a hotel in his town and not be greeted with "Good afternoon, Mr. Secretary" or "Good evening, Mr. Black." Griffin has always wished to have that problem, but not now. As he looks around the room, he wonders where the cameras are installed.

"Thanks for coming all the way over here," says Griffin,

when Mr. Huang enters the hotel suite a half hour later. "But you know, seems the secretary is in the news so much, it's better to keep a low profile."

"Yes," says Mr. Huang. "Fly under radar. I know what you mean."

"I was going to suggest we go for a drive in my car, but I've given the driver the day off."

"Hotel nicer."

"It's a Bentley."

"Too much traffic today."

"A Bentley is nicer than the Ritz, but you're right, there is lots of traffic today."

"And bathroom in hotel."

The knock on the door stops Griffin's heart a split second; he knows he must act natural, or else blow everything.

Chief is dapper in cream-colored light linen, the creases in his trousers holding firm as he glides in, clapping Griffin on the shoulder, shouting to Mr. Huang, "Good to meet you at last."

"Likewise, Secretary Black, it good to meet you too."

"I was just saying to Mr. Huang," Griffin says, glimpsing the view from the window, "that it would have been nice to meet in the Bentley, such a beautiful day."

"And I was saying to Mr. Griffin, bathroom not in Bentley."

"There goddamn ought to be a way for a man to relieve his bladder in the car other than in a piss jug." Chief clapped Mr. Huang on the shoulder again and both men laugh.

"What is piss jug?"

Chief heads to the table and grabs a whiskey glass and points it toward his crotch. "Piss jug for car."

"Oh," Mr. Huang squeals.

"All kidding aside," says Griffin, "we have a nice view here. See the Watergate over there? That's the kind of place you would expect to find Chief. Cross the river, though, and it's complete anonymity."

"That open?" Chief says, nodding in the direction of a bottle of Scotch on the table, there thanks to Griffin. Three glasses stand on the table, along with the Bentley keys, the "B" insignia in full view.

Griffin tends bar while Chief wanders to the window and back again toward Mr. Huang. "Nobody knows me here, and that's good. I'm a people person, but it's nice not to be recognized."

"You're anonymous," said Mr. Huang, smiling.

Mr. Huang accepts a glass of Scotch, and Griffin wonders if he's going to have to control a crazy Chinese who can't hold his liquor . . . or is it the Japanese that can't hold their liquor?

"And you look very different on TV, much bigger," Mr. Huang smiles. "Big handsome Negro, but Air Force One make even you look small."

"I am a big handsome Negro." Chief contorts with mirth.

Griffin fills his own glass for show, and Chief and Mr. Huang sit at opposite ends of the sofa.

"Big handsome Negroes to protect them is just what the Riaals need when they visit Washington," says Chief.

"We have security."

"Big handsome Negroes work best in Washington, it's best for business. Are the Riaals in town now?"

"No," Mr. Huang smiles. "They see Broadway. They see *Cats* the musical."

"When they come to Washington, Griffin here will arrange all the security details," Chief says, straightening his tie clip, its diamonds sending out smiley faces.

"Yes," says Mr. Huang.

"Mr. Huang . . . may I call you Mankit?"

"My close friends call me Manny."

"One of my closest friends is named Manny." Chief smiles, finishing off his Scotch so Griffin can refill it.

"I'm disappointed that Mr. Riaal didn't show up here today."

"It couldn't be helped."

"Yes, *Cats* couldn't wait."

"Tickets hard to get."

This meeting could trend in the wrong direction. Griffin

himself likes doing business with foreigners. The best times of his life occurred while traveling in foreign lands, with and without Chief. The highlight: beautiful Athena in the Cayman Islands.

Chief used to like business with foreigners too, before his new role in the Bubba administration. Now he has drawn a line at dealing with foreign nobodies, no matter how deep their pockets. Griffin sees him looking at Mr. Huang's Tag Heuer watch, and making sure that the flicker of his own platinum Rolex dazzles in the hotel light. Mr. Huang seems to take the point and angles his head in such a way that the view of the Watergate Hotel dominates Griffin's vision, again. As he pulls the drapes closed, Griffin wonders if Mr. Huang knows about the scandals that brought the Nixon administration down. Foreigners know so little about whom they are dealing with . . . and that's a good thing, he thinks.

"Manny, you are aware that the Negroes suffered, and still do suffer, horrible crimes against them because of their skin?"

"Yes, I'm aware of it . . . a little. I born in Shanghai, I here just two years now."

"Got it. Let me bring you up to speed. Of all the millions of black men in the United States, there's only one Negro like me. And it's not because I'm so exceptional … well, I am … but because the calculus of the laws and the culture of the United States never added up for black folk. No matter what you do, you hit a wall, and it's a zero-sum game — you're familiar with that expression, I'm sure."

"I am."

"Zero sum, if that's your luck — gets zero. Goddamn zero. Now, Presidents Kennedy, Eisenhower and Nixon all knew the worth of minority votes, and our luck changed a little. Now, with President William Jefferson Clinton . . . it's a game-changer. Bill understands how we continue to be disadvantaged and uses the government's full power to make amends. Negro Americans — Black Americans — can deposit his check in the bank because they know it won't bounce. Bubba's one of us."

"Bubba?"

"President Clinton, beg pardon. President Clinton is a personal friend — I call him Bubba — and we go way back. The president and I together created the Office of Minority Business Affairs, and now the factor of zero is removed. Let me speak frankly: It's the gold rush for entrepreneurs. Well, for women, blacks and other minorities too, including you Chinese."

"We Chinese is businesspeople. We understand success."

"I admire the Chinese as much as I do the Jews."

"Thank you."

"You know, your Chinaman Square incident is very much like our Birmingham stand-down, only they didn't have tanks."

"You mean, Tiananmen Square?"

"Oh goddammit, I always do that. I mean Tiananmen Square. You know, I'm a person who has to see a thing to know it."

"I agree. We will be good partners."

"I think so. I like you Chinese. I like the Koreans, too. Not the Japanese, though. They are racist."

"Yes, they are, in my experience. In my country's experience too."

"Erase racism from all the societies in the world." Chief waves his hand like he wiping something clean. "Erasism."

"That's very unforgettable. I like that. Erasism."

"Erasism. That's my motto. When I meet a man, I don't see skin color but an opportunity."

"I may please call you Samuel?"

"All my friends call me Chief."

"Chief, I know you busy man, so I arrive at the point. The Riaals do not wish to stay at the White House. They wish to meet with the president. That is their wish. They would like to meet him in the fall."

"Not on Air Force One, unless they want to travel as freight."

"The Rose Garden is fine."

"Good. Griffin here will establish all the security for the their visit."

"Of course," Griffin says, as Chief goes to the restroom.

"As you know, a thirty-thousand-dollar advance is required."

"I will speak to the Riaals, but I'm sure there will be no problem."

"We will arrange all the details later."

Chief returns just in time to see Mr. Huang leave an envelope on the table.

"Erasism," Mr. Huang smiles at Chief, and then makes a gesture with his hand as if he were erasing Griffin. "Very catchy."

Chief smiles, but Griffin knows he is not amused. Griffin thinks Mr. Huang is being ironic, and Chief enjoys his own sense of irony, not that of others.

"God bless America," says Chief. On that salutary note, he explains that in the morning he will begin a trade commission junket to the former Soviet Bloc and he must prepare for it now. They shake hands.

"You didn't tell anyone you were meeting me?"

"Just Mr. Riaal."

"Good, can't be too careful," Chief says, clapping him on the shoulder and making his way toward the door before adding, "I'll leave first. Griffin will be in touch. Till next time."

Possibly out of paranoia, Griffin takes Mr. Huang's hand and gently pulls the stout Chinese toward his chest, making sure to let his hand glide down his arm and side for evidence of a plot, but Mr. Huang mistakes the gesture and brings his hands to Griffin's butt. There is awkwardness as

Griffin repels a confused, heavy-breathing Mr. Huang away.
He says he is feeling a little light-headed and he will call about
the Riaals' security needs, then shows Mr. Huang out. He
is sweating and soon discovers that the hotel room window
appears stuck. He has an impulse to break it, but instead
his attention narrows on the Watergate, as if the infamous
structure has something to do with the stuck window and
intensifying odor. He covers his nose with a handkerchief. He
checks to make sure Mr. Huang is not waiting at the elevator,
and is about to make his way to the lobby when Chief phones.

"Did that smelly muthafucka do right?"

"Five grand."

"Griffin, Lil'Bro, you kidding me?"

"That's all."

"The goddamn nerve!"

There is a tall young black kid standing near the hotel
entrance. Griffin sees him from the back, and is drawn to the
flashy sneakers. For a terrible instant he thinks it is Jewells.
He is about to turn in the other direction when common sense
argues that whoever this is, it is not his son. Their eyes meet
as Griffin passes through the doors. He hands the keys to the
car attendant just as the boy shouts, "Dad, Mom."

Chief appears near the hotel entrance at the same time
as a parent-like couple approaches. They clearly recognize
him.

"Good afternoon, Secretary Black," says the man,

shaking Chief's extended hand. "I'm Rollins Gaines and that's my wife Patricia, and our boy Kofi."

"Nice to meet such a beautiful family," says Chief. "How are you people on this fine day?"

"Very well. And yourself?" says the woman.

"Beautiful. The sun is shining."

Griffin smiles, admiring Chief's glistening aura.

Says the woman: "I think it's a shame what those Republicans are doing to you."

"Thank you for that, ma'am."

Says the man, "It's just another witch hunt. Let us get a little power, and they can't stand it."

"The truth shall set you free…." says Chief. "My innocence is real, and justice will prevail in this glorious land of opportunity."

"Amen."

On this note, Griffin heads to the Bentley, figuring he will pull up and stop all conversation. Steering toward the party, he eyes the couple's kid — still standing at the entrance, squirming with impatience, arms akimbo. Griffin idles at the entrance, letting the window down.

"Wow," says the son, apparently appreciating the luxurious distortions. "The steering is like weird, don't you get confused?"

"No," said Griffin.

"Nice ride," says the father.

"Umm-hmmm," says the mother. "Kofi, come get a picture of the Secretary of Commerce for the United States."

The first flash captures Chief in front of the Bentley, the second standing beside the boy, and the third shoulder-to-shoulder with the parents. Griffin, unwanted and unsure where to go, hunkers down in the seat.

"God bless you good people," says Chief. "I've got an important meeting and you know Washington traffic. It was a pleasure. And keep a close eye on your boy. Don't let him out of your sight. Ever."

"It's open season on our children," says the father.

"But it's the parents, that what's wrong with these kids," says the mother.

"It's all our faults," Chief says.

Griffin smiles at this statement but is not looking at the statement makers.

Chief continues: "We as parents have to do a better job, and pray."

"Amen. Amen."

When they walk away, Chief climbs into the backseat, and says, "Take me to the office, goddammit."

"As if I'm a chauffeur," Griffin mumbles.

"Griffin, Lil'Bro, you know I'll drive this English muthafuckin' fag-mobile into a ditch."

"I'm not a fag-mobile. It's not the chauffeur."

"What? You're not even making any goddamn sense.

What the fuck's wrong with you? And what the fuck were you thinking, buying a goddamn Bentley with the wrong steering? It's goddamn wrong, wrong, wrong!"

Griffin does as told.

Later, panic. A pricking sensation on his skin draws sweat, but it might as well be blood. Deep breaths. A headache waylays him, a nap energizes him.

Spencer's card is on his desk. Griffin phones, hoping, praying the kindly man is back in D.C. Yes.

"I was wondering if you had time to get together . . . tonight?"

"Well, I leave tomorrow afternoon. I'm in the middle of packing."

"Oh, sorry . . ."

"But yes, it would nice to chat . . . if you want to drop by?"

So eager to get out, Griffin grooms without the usual care, hurrying into jeans, a crumpled polo shirt and sweat-stained blazer. So hungry to not be alone, he pushes the Bentley harder than usual, appreciating however that the car purrs seductively the faster it goes. Solomon has mentioned the Bentley is built for speed.

On Connecticut Avenue, N.W., reside some of Washington's most illustrious citizens in some of the city's most expensive real estate. Spencer's address heralds a stately, unassuming building, exactly the kind of situation Griffin imagined the gentleman would live in.

Upon entering the apartment, Griffin is clumsy with self-consciousness — after all, at this hour, why is he visiting a stranger, granted a charming one? What exactly is it he is here for?

The elephant in the room trumpets softly. Griffin says, "I suppose this seems a little bizarre to you, my asking to see you like this. . . and you about to leave tomorrow?"

"It had occurred to me, but then again I looked forward to the opportunity to have a real conversation with you, almost from the moment we met."

"I feel the same. I have no friends here, and I don't especially like this city."

"I hate to disappoint you, but I grew up here."

"I'm sorry."

"Don't be. It's my home but mainly because of my work."

"You're nothing like the people I meet here."

"A good thing."

"You talk about other things, important things. I'm tired of the usual self-centered, power-obsessed D.C. bull."

The explanation sounds good, if thin. If surprised, Spencer is gracious to a fault. A potent vodka martini quickly goes to Griffin's head, as they talk about litigating a genocide.

"Forgiveness is a powerful tool. It, along with unconditional love, is the one thing in a situation such as this that can overcome the enormity of the crime, a crime that is quite beyond anything you could ever imagine, even in your worst nightmares."

"I find it is difficult to forgive. I can't imagine myself in such a situation."

"It's really the only thing you can do. What happened in this massacre is far more complicated than portrayed."

"How do you do it?"

"Well, it's my work. And I never married, and have no children, so I'm flexible."

"It's noble work."

"No, and the bottom line is I needed a job. Five years into this, I'm not sure if what I'm doing matters at all. Mass murder, perhaps not on this scale but equally egregious, happens all the time. It's all rather dispiriting."

Not *Schadenfreude* exactly, but the feeling that comes over Griffin makes light of his own predicament.

"I hope you don't mind my saying, Griffin, but I sense that you are troubled."

"A little, but less so, now, thanks to you." Mentioning he will likely be in prison soon feels a bad idea, but connecting the dots to their talk seems the right thing to do, even if pat. "I think I see the wisdom of forgiveness. I struggle with it, but I realize it's maybe the only way to move forward when you are at such an impasse."

Spencer leaves the thread unpursued, with a quick glance at his watch.

"It's getting late," Griffin preempts.

"Unfortunately, I have a long day tomorrow. Of course I'll sleep most of the flight, but I confess I'm a little tired."

"Yes, of course."

As they make their way to the apartment entrance, Spencer offers, "Griffin, you can always contact me. It's not exactly cheap to call Arusha. But if you have a landline, I could call you."

"Thank you, but you've far more important matters to deal with than my issues."

"Don't be ridiculous. I want to stay in touch."

"I do too. I wasn't joking when I said I'd come to Arusha. I'd like that."

"Let's make it so."

"Yes." Then: "You would've have been a great dad."

Griffin gladhands, grins warmly at the surprised Spencer. A feeling of bereftness, that this is the last time, takes him. His eyes well up, and Spencer reaches to caress, only to be enveloped by Griffin's hulk and need. Griffin breaks. What passes in the embrace and the warm touching of cheeks is the result of tenderness, and it is only later, lying in bed in the dark of sleep, that its implications sweep over him. Before Griffin had left, Spencer had asked if he would like to stay over.

But for all that Griffin was, he might have.

8

It is not the Pepsi commercial itself that fixes his attention, but the suspicion that something deeper lurks within the TV. It makes sense: People watch TV; TV watches people back.

His own research has shown Griffin that video recording devices come as small as a cheese nip. He imagines that for the TV, it must be so tiny it tucks within the picture tube. He is wondering about picture tubes when Solomon at Bentley finally takes him off hold.

"Very sorry to keep you waiting, Mr. Saunders. I fully understand your concern, but as I stated before, all told it will take up to three months for the steering conversion to be done properly. At Bentley, we take these matters very seriously, indeed."

"I can't believe the car has to be shipped all the way to England, just to have the steering switched."

"In fact, as previously mentioned, it's not only about the steering, it's about the technology, the wiring, interiors, too many things to list."

"If a Bentley is crashed, you repair it?"

"Yes, of course, Mr. Saunders."

"Then why can't you just order the parts? Why can't your crew install the ordered parts?" Griffin seethes best when no one is watching. The ringing cellphone — Margeaux calling — calms him a little. He politely presses: "There are always exceptions."

"Not in this case, not at this location or any in the U.S. that I know of, Mr. Saunders, because in fact, we do not assemble our vehicles in the U.S. We just don't, because doing so would be inconsistent with the Bentley brand image."

"We're not talking about assembling a vehicle, we're talking about adapting the steering."

"Mr. Saunders, I'll see what I can do for you. New York may be able to help, maybe even Los Angeles. I'll get in touch with you as soon as possible."

"Thank you."

Griffin is still holding the receiver pressed to his ear, listening for a telling echo or hiss. He remembers this from a thriller movie or a TV show. He walks toward the Panasonic television, a brand he has been loyal to, peering at the wide screen, holding the phone like a wand, and for an instant he hallucinates himself over the image of ABC news host Peter Jennings. Peter Jennings is chattering about economic developments at home and abroad, when suddenly Chief himself is in the middle of the TV. Chief and a crew of Eastern Europeans, walking across the tarmac of a sooty airport, with mountains wreathed in fog in the background.

The TV voice says: "U.S. Secretary of Commerce Samuel Tecumseh Black II arrived in Zagreb today, the third stop on his tour of the Balkan region on a mission for economic development, the first ever such visit by a non-State Department official from the United States. This trip comes on the heels of major success in Asia, where deals were signed with China and Indonesia. Globe-trotting Secretary Black has logged thousands of miles traveling to countries where the U.S. sees its future interests and potential trading partners."

Chief leaves the TV, and Griffin too steps away, finding it curious and even wondrous that Chief appeared just like that. The cell phone rings, and Griffin hesitates — Chief spying from Zagreb, lying from Zagreb, cussing from Zagreb, through both phone and TV?

But it is Solomon's voice ricocheting through the ether.

"Good news, Mr. Saunders. In fact, the steering can be altered in Palm Beach, there's apparently a market there for the conversions, usually from left to right, though . . . those retirees, you know. Imagine my surprise: I've been at Bentley ten years and this is the first I've heard of it. You'll need to get the car to the showroom there, unless you want me to ship it."

"No, I'll take care of it."

"The conversion can be done in just a few days, apparently. I'll email all the contact information to you."

He mentions fixed costs, and Griffin agrees to it with a firm grumble of thanks.

The TV is again saying things, but Griffin cannot hear. The networks will replay Chief in another forty-five minutes or so. The news cycle, over which Chief has no control, will be his undoing in his absence. He will return in another week, and be taken into custody, and Griffin imagines the scene on TV: Chief in handcuffs, being led out of his office by a block of grim government officials. The FBI guy has not said this — two weeks, and he has not said anything, in fact, but he has left Griffin alone to ponder all the possibilities. His conclusion: Surely after the Riaals' bonanza of illegality, nothing stands between Chief and prison.

And Griffin will be in Palm Beach, a place he has never been.

He remembers that the father of the Chicago Bulls' Michael Jordan was shot in the head during a robbery on I-95, the very highway Griffin must travel to reach Palm Beach. Jordan senior's napping in a Lexus at a rest stop was not a smart thing to do, and quite inexplicable for a successful businessman with a superstar son too.

Caller I.D. reveals five calls from Margeaux, none of her messages listened to. There are no calls from Chief. Travel never stops Chief from calling, and Griffin senses a sea change has occurred. Again he looks at the TV — is it possible that Chief is recording Griffin's every move?

Margeaux's first message, received the previous evening, at 9:15 p.m.: "Griffin, oh my God, something's going on over at the carriage house. A fight or something . . . I was sitting in the study with a book, and I heard this shouting, and then a crash. I called over there, but Jewells didn't answer. I'm scared, I don't know what's happening. I'm calling the police."

The second message, received at 9:45 p.m.: "The police went over to the carriage house. The door was open and they found Jewells crying. He was on the bed, beaten up. They said I could come up, so I did. The room was completely torn up. He said it wasn't a robbery or anything, just him and a friend roughhousing, but whatever happened, Jewells was pretty banged up. One of the policemen asked me if he was on drugs. I didn't even know what to say. After the police left, I told Jewells I was taking him to the ER, but he insisted he was fine. He refused to come back to the house with me. I had earlier seen someone running down the driveway, and I asked him about that. He screamed I should leave him the 'eff' alone."

The third message, received at 11:45 p.m.: "It's almost midnight, and Jewells is gone. I'm standing in his room, and he's gone. He doesn't answer his phone, either. Should I call the police again? Oh, Griffin, what should I do?"

The fourth message, today, at 7 a.m.: "Your son definitely didn't come home last night. I'm standing in his room. I called his coach about what happened here last night, and he said Jewells hadn't been to practice in over two weeks.

I have no idea what's going on. What should I do? Where are you? I'm worried."

The fifth and final message, five minutes ago: "Griffin, of all the times for you to bow out on your responsibility. It's just ridiculous, and I'm so angry and fed up. I have no idea where Jewells is, and I need you to help me. You need to come home and deal with your son."

"Bow out?" Griffin hisses. She should not leave messages that reflect poorly on him. He erases her from the machine — erasism — all of her defaming remarks have probably been intercepted anyway, if not through the phone then the TV. There are probably satellites speeding around the earth pointing directly at him, recording the sweat and stink on him, the swell of gas in his upset stomach.

He knows what he must do, yet does nothing.

He thinks of the Cayman Islands. Yes, that's where he could go. No one would know. Well, except Chief. But Chief is going to jail. And if not to jail, then he will hit the wall of his career, resigning in disgrace. Griffin can always threaten to tell the world Chief's secrets. Griffin knows that he himself will come off looking the complete fool, and a morally corrupt one at that. Worse, the lucrative business he and Chief have built together will implode, and fast — which will happen anyway if Chief goes to jail, and everyone will know everything . . . as they will.

He wonders, How can I get away? I can start by running

out the door, deep into the woods, live off the land — not this land, but land in the middle of nothing, nowhere.

It would be so much better if he had a purchased an SUV instead of the Bentley; then he could head south and cross the Mexican border into the life of a fugitive. He could travel to the Cayman Islands from Mexico and no one would know.

Eyes and ears are everywhere and watching.

A rifle leans in his closet bedroom. He climbs the stairs to get it. He thinks he could shoot himself out of these troubles. It would like busting out of a bank of trouble. He remembers Margeaux's father, pictures him first trying to extinguish the blaze in his dry cleaning shop, then pulling the trigger. How bad had it been? This bad?

Then he thinks, there is probably a better way; he should wait till it reveals itself.

The ringing phone chimes his thoughts into the moment. It is Jewells — the ace of spades.

"Hey Dad, guess where I am?"

"Jewells, what in God's name is going on? Are you alright?"

"I'm fine. Guess where I am?"

"Son, I'm not —"

"— I'm here, in D.C. Well, not where you are. I'm at Uncle Chief's. There's nobody home, so I'm sitting on the front steps — all these bees. The police keep coming around, and I like tell them I'm his son and I came home to surprise him. I would have come to you, Dad, but I didn't know how to get there."

"What are you doing here?"

"You said this turns out to be a great time for me to stay with you. You said you weren't going to Croatia with Uncle Chief. "

"I did." Griffin stares at the TV. "I know, son."

"I spent my money on the bus ticket, so I figured Uncle Chief or somebody would be here and you could come and get me or I could take a cab to you. Dad, will you come and get me? Please."

"I'll be there in forty-five minutes."

"Okay, Dad."

"Son, are you hurt?"

"No, I'm fine. Glad to be in D.C."

Griffin immediately dials Margeaux, bracing for a grilling. Though relieved, she is not her usual understanding self — "Griffin, there's no more negotiating about Jewells. I've had it with this situation — with your passive, missing-in-action fathering. I'm glad he's with you now, because he's not welcome here anymore, unless you are here to deal with him — and I mean all the time, not when you get around to dropping in. That's how it is, and that's how it's going to be."

"Margeaux, I'm sorry. This is my fault. I've been —"

"— it isn't all your fault, but a lot of it is, he's a screwed-up kid and you need to deal with him . . . obviously."

Griffin dares not say anything about the tone of her messages, or the harshness of her critique, or the fact that maybe it was unwise for her to call the police, because if marijuana or another illegal substance was involved, there could have been an arrest, police record and bad press that might loop back to Chief.

"Sweetheart, we'll discuss it later. If anything more comes up, just text me to call you and I will ASAP . . . and unless it's an emergency, don't call the police."

"He's on your turf now. You deal with him."

Griffin has a set of keys to Chief's Georgetown house. He has never had occasion to use them. It is not a large house, but there is room for Jewells, Griffin thinks. Or better still, the house in Atlanta. Atlanta is ideally where Jewells belongs, where past wrongs could be righted in the embrace of family. Chief's children — two daughters and a son, Jewell's biological half-siblings — live there with their mother, and he himself even agrees that it is a good idea for Jewells to be nearer, and that all the children should be closer. Only in this way could Jewells overcome what Griffin believes is an instinctive insecurity about his birthright. Had Griffin himself been given such an opportunity with his own father, and a chance to live among his father's powerful people, imagine the man he could be today.

Chief's family would never welcome Jewells, however.

Jewells does not exist to the father as his son but rather as his nephew. Why would he be anything other than a cousin to the family?

Jewells' mother was not like the nurturing Meemaw, she was a child — likely Jewells' age, possibly fourteen. She needed protection, not a child to mother. Certainly the law was on her side. Stupid little gold-digging black girl or not, her seducers were the sons of a famous man.

Griffin frequently thinks of her; Bianca was her name. Her bright plum of a face, her pretty giggles and squeals, like a girl flying high on a swing in a flouncy summer skirt that reveals the full shape of first ripeness. He had never met her before she sucked him and Chief off in that hotel room in Manhattan, yet, through the haze of booze and cocaine they had consumed, he felt somehow he had known her. Perhaps she had come to him in a dream . . . The sort of dream where he is suddenly falling, spiraling, going down.

Griffin thinks there was a cruelly ironic justice in Bianca's dropping the kid off on the porch like that, in a fax machine box, just as Griffin and Chief were laying the foundations for their cable technology business in D.C. On that day, the brothers been had sitting in the kitchen of Chief's parlor-floor apartment, having coffee and danish and poring over relevant international laws, when Griffin heard a thump that might have been the closing of a distant car door. Nothing unusual in that. Then an hour later, Griffin heard a baby's cry very close by. The brothers stared at each other, puzzled. Chief went to the window, and Griffin to the front door — which, he now thinks, was also fortuitous, as if he was meant to bear witness to the child first, for there was no telling what Chief would have done had he alone discovered the infant.

Bianca's blunt note: "I told you I would, you sorry punk ass muthafucker!"

It was not unlike the daze and confusion of a car crash.

Trying to grasp the meaning of the child in a box on the porch, Chief was now the injured party: "That stupid little cunt," he roared with his hands smashed against his ears as if to block his own sound out. Then: "No, she didn't leave a goddamn baby on the porch . . . is she gone?"

"What the hell is going on?" demanded Griffin, staring at the baby, which, with its blue filmy eyes, stared back.

"Bianca, that little bitch we dicked in New York, this is hers . . . She tried to say it was yours or mine, and she wanted me to pay her some money, and she said, she said . . ."

"She came here from New York to abandon her baby on the porch?"

"Do I look like I know the mind of a crazy fucking black bitch?"

This much was certain: Chief's wife was on her way from Atlanta with the kids. He panicked — "Just drop the kid off at the Salvation Army, or wherever . . . or better still, drop it in the Potomac, for all I care."

"She's right, you are a sorry muthafucka!"

"For not letting some goddamn, cocained-out kid I don't know shit about wreck my life, hell no!"

Griffin lifted the warm, wriggling infant into his arms and, not long after, laid it across his lap as he drove to a hotel, stopping only for Pampers, baby food, juice, a bottle, pacifier and wipes. They holed up until he could figure out what to do.

In a little under thirty-six hours — the time it took for Chief to finally show up at the hotel — Griffin had made up his mind, with the child cooing and nuzzling against his chest. Chief argued, "Think about it. What you gonna tell that kid when he's a grown man. That you and me gangbanged his cocaine-head mom, and that the bitch dropped him off on the porch in a fax machine box? I don't think that's gonna make him feel too good about himself."

"I'll worry about that later," Griffin said. "Right now, we're not throwing this kid in the Potomac, as you would prefer."

"I was kidding."

"Yeah, I know."

To keep the boy until Bianca came back — hopefully settled down with some good sense — required Griffin to think bigger and bolder.

After driving all night with the screaming child alternately squirming in his lap and the crook of the front seat, the next morning, when he showed up at his mother's door with the baby in need of mothering, she said she had had a dream and that the inky-eyed chocolate baby bundled in blankets really was a Saunders. Strange that she did not ask a lot of questions, as if she knew her son of a sinful man was righting a modern version of the original wrong, or that her destiny was to care for misbegotten children linked to her by seduction: "This baby's staying right here and we gonna raise little Griffin. Ain't a woman alive that could bring such a beautiful chile in the world and not love him. And he looks just like you, son."

That's what Griffin thought too. The boy could be his — the eyes, not in color but shape, dark complexion and the thin length of body, as if the infant would unfurl into a full version of Griffin. No son of Meemaw would publicly admit his skepticism about God, but Griffin could not help but see this development as providential. All those years of tuning out pulpit bombast and foot-tapping on the rhythms of hymns came down to the shining black eyes of the infant in his arms.

Then at age nine, Jewells's face molded into a dark-complected version of Chief — or possibly even their omnipotent father. Maybe by some miracle the sperm of both Chief and Griffin had teamed up to produce the boy; despite foolproof science the whims of a mysterious, mercurial God had won out. A paternity test confirmed what ten minutes of due diligence would have revealed the moment he had first stared down at the baby in the box. Griffin not only shared a blood type but also genes with the baby — "I'd say, you're probably an uncle," said the doctor.

Griffin decided to hold tight to this information. What good would it do, after so many years, and so much love, and with Jewells firmly grounded?

One day many years later, Chief himself brought it up. He had been considering a position as the Democratic Party Chair of D.C., and understandably worried about scrutiny.

"You know they'll be turning over every goddamn rock to find some dirt on me. There's nothing extra-legal in the way you've been running our business that I should know, right?"

"No, it's all above board. You probably should be more worried about your women."

"Shit, everybody respects a man with a few bitches on the side."

"What about Bianca?"

"Who?"

"Jewells' mother, the girl in New York, the one we . . ."

"Shut up about her. She's not a problem, she's been taken care of."

"You pay her off?"

"Something like that."

"I can't believe she never got in touch with either of us about Jewells."

"It was money, that's all — and that's what the bitch

would have been calling about if she had bothered."

"It's a terrible thing, you know . . . what we did. I regret it."

"Yeah, but just as there's a God above, she sure was a pretty little black thang," Chief said, looking away. "You know, I can't help myself, I just have sweet spot for 'black' black girls. I like the fancy women too, in their fancy panties and froufrou, they're the trophies, but there's nothing like breaking in a pretty, dark, dirty little filly."

"You knew her before I met her in New York, didn't you?"

"Yeah, well . . . I seen the little ho before, other times I was in the city, but I didn't know she was plotting. There's no telling who Jewells' father is. You shoulda dropped him off at the Salvation Army like I said."

"You also said I should throw him in the Potomac."

"I was just talking shit, and you know it."

"Chief, is it ever hard for you to sleep at night?"

"Nothing but pussy and money keep me up at night!" he laughed, clapping Griffin on the shoulder. "And, Lil'Bro, just for the goddamn record, I never thought he was mine."

"Even though he looks like you? Even your wife said so, when we were at Martha's Vineyard last year, remember? She said he looks more like you than me."

For once, Chief had no comeback — throwing his hands up to block further talk.

No paternity test was required. Griffin knows that none would ever be gotten without court order. Chief has a thousand legal reasons he would never prove paternity, but to Griffin any one of his refusals is as good as DNA confirmation from a hair follicle, swab of spit or semen.

"I am and always will be his father," Griffin said. "That's all that matters. I couldn't love him more if he was my own flesh and blood."

That thought touches Griffin now, as he readies to gather up the teen version of the abandoned infant he brought to Cincinnati over sixteen years ago. He instinctively reaches for the Honda's car keys, but Jewells would get such a kick out of the Bentley. Griffin does not bother to dress himself up, shave or change out of T-shirt and flipflops. He does not notice the eyes admiring his car's regal glide along the Beltway, nor does he care about those searching his careless appearance, so unworthy of such a car.

What Griffin sees as clearly as the shaft of the Washington Monument thrusting into the skyline of this arch city he does not like but cannot leave, is a new chance shaping into the perfect and pure. It is unclear what the chance is, exactly, or what it means, but it guides him right over the obstacle between him and his boy. The slab of black-and-blue bloody bruise on the right side of Jewell's face might as well have been a blow struck against his own person, for Griffin feels so deeply he nearly throws up. All he can do for balance is hold, wobble and kiss his one and only namesake: "Oh, my boy, I'm so sorry, I'm so sorry."

9

The sound of spraying water awakens Griffin to an early morning surprise. He goes to the window with reason to worry, but instead his heart is glad. There, he sees no leaks or anything untoward, just Jewells hosing down the Bentley. A plume of water sends mist in the air, into yellow and blue ultraviolet light. The rainbow that comes hovers and bends toward Jewells — shirtless Jewells, too deep in his dance to notice. Wires of a Discman feed from his ears into the back pocket of droopy shorts, and his long brown torso twists and bends, as if conjuring the god of suds. The bow of Jewell's skinny arm then stretches over the Bentley's hood, while spatulate fingers soap its silver steel. Head bobbing, body bouncing, he seems content in the way of little boys, with his Tonka trucks and trains.

Jewells has encamped on an air mattress in the room opposite Griffin's. The door is ajar enough to show a wedge of new mess — the jumble of his few clothes, the sprawl of shiny pocket junk, the sneakers kicked out the way. A kid with something to hide would not be so careless, especially under the circumstances, Griffin thinks. Though this is a good time as any to go through his things, the sight of his son's dance with the Bentley bodes well. Griffin is certain he did not ask that the car be cleaned. It has not even crossed his mind, given the near thousand miles between D.C. and Palm Beach, a distance that makes Jewells' gesture all the more touching.

"At last, inspiration," Griffin shouts. A smile comes over his face as Jewells points the hose in his direction. The force of water does not reach the second floor window, instead drumming against the inset roof. Griffin swells with laughter, and equally with pride.

"Come on down, Dad," Jewells shouts. "I'll inspire you with a wash and wax job."

"Will you now? Polish your old pop off." Griffin is happy, feels young. He wants to join in, he really wants to — thinks it would be good, joining in is fun, a great thing to do actually . . . and he will, he thinks, but first . . .

Margeaux. He phones not to boast of Jewells' deed but reassure that the dark splotch on the boy's stomach is nothing more than a serious bruise, and that there are no fractures in his facial bones — according to the doctor who checked him over in emergency care last night. "Your son was obviously kicked and punched repeatedly and maybe struck by an object like a broom stick. He's lucky no bones or organs were seriously injured," the doctor had said.

If Mrs. Griffin Jewells Saunders II is relieved, she does not show it. And it seems certain to Griffin, his son is not the only one altered. No sooner has she answered the phone than Griffin realizes that no words, good or bad, can cap the outrage. He wants to tell her to shut up, that what happened is not about her. He imagines Jewells' demanding she leave him the "eff" alone, and while he is troubled by such aggression from his child, a part of him understands, a part of him is gleeful.

Instead, when the flow slows to a trickle, enough to allow him a word, to justify beginning again, Griffin says, "You're right, of course, sweetheart."

"Right now, I feel like we're in the middle of a ghetto drama; something lurid, drug-related, as if we were some common black criminals from Cabrini Projects in Chicago. Contrary to what you might think, I've been to those kinds of places, as a news reporter, so I know. Any minute I expect some reporter to start calling us. It's just outrageous, it's embarrassing."

"Yes, you're right, dear."

He wonders that she does not see her father's blowing his own brains out as evidence to the contrary. She has never had a pass on the horrible, and she has not only stood in "their shoes" but walked in them, and more. And Jewells, whatever his faults, is not "the horrible" by any measure of comparison. He is a child. His Griffin Jewells Saunders III.

"Imagine my dilemma. I mean, if I hadn't called the police, there's no telling, whoever he was fighting might really have hurt him."

"You did what was best."

"I've hardly been able to sleep because I'm so angry at him over this. And now, I'm paranoid. I think we should install cameras around the property. I keep seeing things in the yard now."

"We'll discuss that when I'm home, but if it'll make you feel better, why don't we ask the neighborhood security watch to drive by in the evening. I'm sure they will. I'll call."

"Thanks."

He wants to hang up, but feels the need to let her go on, and she does, about the neighbors, what they must think — Susan Erkenbridge specifically, because she dropped by in the morning to ask what all the commotion was about. Griffin has always cared about what others think, and he realizes he does not want to hear about East Walnut Hills in any way, just now. He looks toward Jewells' room, focuses on the emptied-out bag, then walks to the window again. Father and son lock eyes, and Margeaux's voice is like the far-off whine of a tree trimmer. Jewells waves, and Griffin waves back, but he feels they are waving as if they are both departing, leaving something behind, maybe going separate ways, into the future — or perhaps it is to Margeaux and Cincinnati that they are waving, waving not hello but bye-bye.

"Margeaux, Jewells feels bad about swearing at you. You should talk to him, let him apologize."

"I can't just yet, I just can't. I know, I need to be a

parent, but I just can't right now. Maybe later, maybe this evening, just not now."

"Whatever you think is best, dear."

Griffin hears a cry bubbling up, only he does not want crying now.

"Sweetheart, I'm as worried as you are. I'm not going to let him out of my sight. I have to be in Miami Tuesday, and I'm taking him with me. We'll drive there. We're leaving after breakfast today."

"Miami? Another one of your mysterious business trips?"

"If there's time, we'll swing through Cincinnati on the way back, and grab some of his things."

"Good. Because, Griffin, I meant what I said."

"I know you did."

"Do you? Really? Because if you do, then you'll also understand that it's not just Jewells, it's everything, really. We need to decide what we're doing. Are we staying here, are we going to live in D.C.? Your three years are up. Which is it?"

"Of course, dear, you're right."

She asks about Chief, but Griffin puts her off. "I can't say now. I'll tell you when I'm home."

Neither says, "I love you," before hanging up.

Showering, Griffin tries to imagine the family filling the small space of this house — the children ruling the rooms with their toys and loud, demanding ways. The family will not live here, though. Margeaux's mind has already been made up, and she only pretends that the matter needs to be resolved.

He then pictures himself and Jewells re-inserted in the Cincinnati house, the most likely outcome. At the same time, he cannot imagine life in Cincinnati again. Not even as mayor of the city, the zenith of his ambition.

Dressing, he looks outside for Jewells, and Jewells, looking up from the tire he is polishing, waves again. A hint of smoke provokes Griffin, but he smiles and waves back.

If his Meemaw were alive, would Jewells be this way? This sea change in his son's behavior began when she died, but it is as possible that the badass gene was there all along, just needing a match. Griffin could have made her life a hell for deceiving him about his own father. He chose instead to be an even better mamma's boy, one all the more deserving of what he was denied in fatherly love. If only she had lived long enough to see his success, how proud she would be, he thinks. He often thinks the same of his father. If Samuel Tecumseh Black senior had only known what a good, upstanding, righteous man Griffin turned out to be, he would regret what he had done in not claiming him as his son. Griffin as often wonders about the seduction of his mother — maybe it was just an inebriated error in judgment, an undressing and laying down without intention or conscience, or maybe it was a kind of power grab that failed miserably and sent her back to

Cincinnati in ruins. Not every woman would have stood up to her responsibility, as she had. It makes Griffin know that, while the circumstances of Jewells' birth are not to his credit, he has done his best to do right — and he will do right from now on — and that is all that a man can ask of himself.

Looking at Jewells, though, he wonders if a man should not ask more of himself.

There is no answer, only the want of wisdom.

Griffin has never felt so alone in the world, so uncomforted. He thinks of diplomat Spencer. He hears the silky voice: "I felt we were kindred spirits . . ." Griffin thinks, I have done terrible things, and hopes Spencer will say to him, Come to Arusha and all will be well. He pulls the diplomat's card out of his wallet, and feels the gentle touch of his hand, wishing for the touch of his father, but then he thinks of things he should not be thinking and feels certain elemental forces in his body that he should not feel.

He calls Therosine. She understands because she just does — her way is cushiony soft, just like his mother's. She intuits the details of his woe — the sadness of children, and the shame. After this exchange of breathing and beating hearts — a seance really — he is not ready to speak of it. Instead, they chat about business, she tells him she has FedEx'ed stuff to him that should arrive by noon. In the pouch, there is something from Secretary Chief, as she calls Chief. Griffin puzzles over why Chief would send anything to Cincinnati, but then decides it does not matter.

Then he puts words to the woe, "There was some trouble over the weekend. I have Jewells with me now. I took him to the hospital just to make sure he was okay, and had the doctors do drug tests, but I won't get the results till this afternoon."

"You did the right thing."

"I have to go to Palm Beach. I'm taking him with me. If there's any sign of drugs, he's going to a treatment place or one of these bootcamp places, to get himself clean."

"That's a good idea."

"I'll keep him up here with me . . . It's funny, he seems like a little boy to me, all six-feet-three-inches of him." Griffin grins. "I don't know if it's an act, or what — but he isn't like he is at the Cincinnati house. He's always so smart-mouth, so . . . belligerent."

"You mother used to say Jewells was a daddy's boy. Maybe he just wanted to be with you."

"Yes," Griffin says, feeling his son's need is so much, too much. "He'll be okay . . ." adding, enigmatically, "one way or the other."

In the kitchen, Griffin fusses over breakfast. He has never fixed a meal for anyone other than himself in this home. Before the era of Margeaux, father and son would have a huge meal of pancakes, sausage and eggs before meeting his mother at church most Sunday mornings. Today's adhered-to low-cal life offers little of the butter and sugar and fat comforts of old, yet Griffin manages to whip up whole-grain French toast, hash browns and omelets with Muenster cheese and broccoli. He goes to call Jewells inside to eat, and there is a moment of unease when he does not at first see him. Then the shower upstairs turns on. Griffin wants to tell him to wait till after breakfast, and finds Jewells naked, about to step into the stall. A surprised Jewells turns, revealing a shaved pubic area and a bright gold ring on his penis.

"Hey, Dad," he says, smiling, as if it is too late to make an effort to cover up. He pulls the shower door partly closed, and pokes his head through the opening. "You surprised? It's now spanking new again, like it just left the showroom."

"That's great, son," Griffin looks at him, from disembodied head to his nakedness made shadowy by tempered glass shower doors.

"I'm almost done, and I know you wanna leave soon."

"Okay, but be quick, breakfast is ready," Griffin says, looking away from him again.

"Two minutes is all I need."

"That's fine."

Griffin returns to the kitchen, but his mind stares at the cock ring and shaved privates, wondering and worrying.

As promised, Jewells is quick. He barely sits down before Griffin says, "What's with the ring down there?"

"Oh, nothing. It's like a tongue ring, or an eyebrow

ring . . . just jewelry. It's cool."

"Someone give it to you?"

"No, I got it myself." He airlifts three pieces of French toast to his plate, and crowds them with the omelet and hash browns. "Any ketchup?"

"Is that expensive?"

"It was."

"Where did you get the money for it?"

"I worked for it."

"What kind of work?" Griffin snatches ketchup from the refrigerator door, but closes the door calmly.

"Yard work."

"When did you have time for yard work when you were on punishment?"

"It was before punishment." Jewells upends the ketchup bottle, slapping it. "I've had it since summer started. I always wear it. It's cool."

"Cool? Maybe, but I don't want you wearing anything like that."

"No biggie, Dad. I'll take it off."

"Now."

"Right here at the table?"

"There's the bathroom. And bring it back with you."

As Jewells drags to the bathroom hissing under his breath, Griffin grabs a Ziploc sandwich bag and waits. When his son emerges, he opens it to receive the ring. Mesmerized by the glinting metal as he seals the bag shut, his mind turns to Chief.

"Jeez, it's just a cock ring, Dad. No need to freak out."

"I know what it is." Then: "We'll dispose of it later." As if evidence could so easily be gotten rid of.

Jabbing at the pile of French toast, his son breathes hard but says nothing, and Griffin reads the silence. He thinks it will not take long before they can be as they were, return to the time just before Margeaux's arrival, when Jewells seemed happiest. He thinks this because he just does — Jewells is not hard or beaten, he is just a boy. But how long will it take, how long before the surly, sassy boy is checked by reality? It cannot be just father and son, there are four other children to consider, and a fed-up Margeaux, ready to wash her hands of them both.

Griffin visits the bathroom where he checks his phone for a call about Jewells' blood tests, then goes for the maps on the living room mantle. He drops them on the kitchen table and kisses Jewells on the forehead.

"You've got a lot of driving to do, son, so we should start figuring out our trip."

"Tite, Dad!" Jewells smiles, the space between his busted lips filliing with bright teeth. "That's real tite."

10

It is hard to imagine that any work could get done in a piloted Bentley. The comfort is excessive, and so is the desire for a martini and the tendency to nap, releasing the stress of accounting, calculation and cunning to the leather cushions designed to embrace and massage the back, and "chill," as the kids say. Griffin cannot pinpoint exactly when he switched from the front seat to the rear. He remembers seeing a neon cowboy and hotdog and then the hump of a raggedy rollercoaster and the churn of a ferris wheel in a fairground just off I-95. He also remembers a perfect cloudless canvas of sky above the road ahead, a kind of blank slate reflecting his state of mind at that moment. It seems he was dozing off, and then Jewells was pulling into a rest stop, insisting, "Dad, you chill in the back, let me do the driving."

He awakens to a sign indicating the bypass to Charleston, South Carolina.

"Dad, this is so cool."

"Jewells. Sorry, it must have been that big breakfast. At the next turn off, you can pull over."

"Sure, Dad, but you probably have some calls to make and work to do. I know, like, it's Monday and that it's a business day for you."

"I do have a few phone calls," he says.

"It's cool with me. Just yell when you're done, I'll pull over."

"Sure you don't mind?"

"Are you kidding? Being a chauffeur is like in my blood. It's like tite."

"You know where you're going?"

"Don't worry. It's a straight shot. Dad, I got it."

The pouch Therosine sent is full of the stuff that normally gives Griffin pleasure: details about money and property, the line items and balance sheets of success by his definition. There are maintenance contracts to review, there are legal notices served. There is a photocopy of the Barbra Streisand receipt.

And there is the package from Chief. Griffin stares again, but does not open it. He could have legitimately traveled with Chief as an American business emissary representing cable technology. Of course, it would have looked bad, or be made to look bad, still it was a chance worth taking. He wonders just how much of their business he could actually do on his own, without Chief the star. Has he allowed himself to be made into a lackey, Chief's henchman? And of the questionable business deals and dalliance they have done together, how much of it would earn little more than a wrist slap of punishment versus prison time? Only Chief knows the extent of the holdings in Jewells' name, and forged signatures to acquire them, but he knows indirectly; same is true of Therosine. Therosine is far too frightened to speak off script with anyone, and if she had ever committed such a foolish act, she would have told him immediately. Not Chief. Fearless Chief. Throw-the-infant-in-the-Potomac Chief.

"Jewells, you know, son, I'd rather we got ourselves some lunch. I'm starved."

"Okay, Dad. I pull off at the next food stop."

"Cool."

Griffin is surprised by the traffic. It feels bumper to bumper, and intrusive with the eyes of every passing car staring at the Bentley. He wonders if it would actually be better to drive at night, but of course that is when Michael Jordan's father was robbed and murdered.

Griffin is not a Big Mac kind of man, but neither is he a Denny's. It seems to him that it might have been better had they plotted the trip with eating in mind. Nothing can be done about it now, on the highway in the middle of nowhere . . . sixty-five miles east to Charleston, about seventy-five to Savannah. What lies immediately ahead looks a lot more tasty. Just off the exit, nearing a Burger King Griffin spots a sign for Smokehouse BBQ three miles away.

It must be the very late hours of lunch, just before dinner, because the restaurant is empty but for them and a couple of families scattered around the dining room.

Griffin should not have bread or potatoes, but he orders

a grilled ribeye steak that comes with all the no-nos. The salad will hopefully offset the damage, he thinks. Jewells goes for a cheeseburger and French fries.

"I sure wish I could eat like that," says Griffin. "Things happen as you get older. Your body just changes and does what it wants."

"You're not active enough."

"You're right, son." Griffin wonders, waits. "You know, Jewells, I was raised by your Meemaw and Grandma Saunders, so I was one of those boys who behaved all the time, and if I even thought about stepping out of line, there was Grandma Saunders' paddle, which Meemaw inherited for you."

"I don't remember Grandma Saunders."

"She was a nice woman, she was a teacher. Your Meemaw was to have been a teacher too, but you know she got pregnant with me and had to leave college. Those were different times, it wasn't so easy as it is now. You make a mistake and swallow a few pills the next morning, and presto, you're done."

"Well, there's AIDS now. Not so easy, is it, Dad?"

"That's true, son. It's easier in some ways, harder in others."

Father and son appraise each other, and Griffin is the first to look away.

"Yeah, Dad, if you're wondering if I'm sexual, I am. But

I'm into protection."

"That's good, son." They will stray into gray area, which maybe is a good area to be in, a sort of Switzerland for the cold, hard truth of fathers and sons. "With your Uncle Chief, I sowed my oats — I had a good time, like I never had a good time. I never had a brother before, and he was kind of wild, and we did things . . ."

"What kind of things?"

"Things I would never do again. Drugs, sex and rock and roll. Youthful indiscretion, and it was a lesson for me. I think that's how to look at our mistakes, you know, as something we can learn from."

"Yeah, I think so too, Dad. It's how you learn to throw the ball perfectly, you note your errors until you get it right."

"Jewells, I want you to tell me what happened to you."

"I . . ."

"What have you been doing?"

"I just got into some trouble. Youthful indiscretion, as you say."

"What kind of trouble?"

"I was hanging out with the wrong crowd."

"Drugs?"

"Yeah, Dad. It was drugs."

"You were selling drugs or using them?"

"Using . . . but not seriously. I mean, I'm not like an addict."

"What kind of drugs?"

"Cocaine and pot, some pills. Like, nothing serious. What kind did you do?"

"Same as you, plus booze." Griffin does not especially want to revisit his past, yet must for this teaching moment. "I came up in the late sixties, early seventies, and it was wild, but I have always been pretty sober and suspicious about these things. A drink now and then was about it for me. But I guess in the back of my mind I was curious to try just to see what it was like to be high, and about that time I met your Uncle Chief, and well, I went all out because we were celebrating the success of our first joint venture. Cocaine, marijuana, hash, and serious drinking, partying an entire weekend. I blacked out and don't remember most of it . . . and the parts I do remember still make me sick. Honestly, I'm surprised it didn't kill me — not him, though, he's used to it. The experience taught me a couple of things. It's not exactly a productive way to live your life. And you end up having to deal with the mess you didn't know you made when you were cranked up and out of your mind. So, no, partying wasn't for me. What about you? You like being high?"

"Yeah, I do. I mean, like I said, I'm not an addict or anything, it was just fun. I feel good. I feel really happy. I feel like nothing matters, like I can turn my mind off for a while. I like that."

"Are you on something now?"

"No. I haven't been since . . ."

"Since what?"

"Since the fight, since I got beaten up. Like I said, I'm
not like a druggie or even a pothead. Like, I had some pot, but
I figured it wasn't too smart to carry that on the bus in case
there was some police crap or something."

"That was smart thinking." Griffin warms and feels
relieved somehow. But it is short-lived, for the configuration
of words arranged in Jewell's comment imply worse, that
in fact his son would be the object of the police. Keep calm,
Griffin says to himself. Then: "Jewells, my son, is there
anything else you want to tell me?"

"No, Dad. No . . . "

He is a child, Griffin thinks, as he watches Jewells
suddenly fold into himself. "I'm sorry, Dad. I'm so sorry."
Then his face, battered and bruised, scrunches into pain. "I
really fucked up. I don't know why — I don't know why I did
it. I'm not even like that."

"Like what? Jewells, what did you do? What happened?
Who beat you up?"

They are sitting in a booth. Jewells slumps down in his
seat, and Griffin, frightened, slides over and pulls his child
into his arms again.

"Listen, son, it's gonna be alright, whatever it is. I know
I haven't been there for you like a good father should for his
boy, especially his best boy. I'm sorry for that. But I love you,

son — and you and me were always good buddies. I miss that. We'll be good buddies again. You're gonna stay with me, and we're gonna figure everything out, me and you. We will. I promise."

"Ok, Dad."

"You'll tell me when you're ready. And it'll be okay. You and me are best buddies, and we'll always be, no matter what, son. Always."

Jewells wants to drive. He wants Griffin to do his work, and Griffin thinks it is a good thing, as he climbs into the backseat, only there is something wrong here, something very wrong. He thinks of the Bentley limousine Brodey drove to pick him up, and he wishes now for such a car, so that he really would have privacy. Surely Jewells' blood test results are in now.

Griffin pulls his work into his lap. He is thinking about his boy. There are three messages on his cell from Chief.

The first message: "Oh Lil'Bro, I'm gonna die. This muthafucking plane is flying through a goddamn cyclone or something … up and down, up and down, I'm sick as a dog … and I just know, I just … in case I don't make it, I just want you to know, Lil'Bro, that I know, but it doesn't matter now… These honky muthafuckas been washing each other's hands forever, but soon as a black man does it, well, sic a grand jury on his ass. Somebody had to be the heavy, the fall guy, and that had to be you. Think about it, I make the money for us,

I've got the connections. But shit, if I'd known I was gonna die like this, I coulda been the fall guy. I'm sorry... Awww, shitttt! "

Chief's second message: "Well, I'm alive. I practically shit my pants during the crash landing when this bitch slid off the runway and the tires busted and we had go down the emergency chute. But my black ass didn't die, I'm alive, Lil'Bro. Ignore my last message, because I'm not sorry about shit . . . I'm going to London in the morning, and I'll be home Wednesday. Don't call me, I'll call you . . . and whatever you do, keep your goddamn mouth shut, you don't know shit. Cuz you really don't. Yeah, I know what you've been up to, who you been talking to — I know, because it's my people, and I had to be sure you had my back. Now I know you don't have my mutherfuckin' back, and I'm disappointed, Lil'Bro . . . but you thought you didn't have a choice, right? To hell with you."

Chief's last message: "Griffin — you're not my Lil'Bro — Griffin, there is one thing I am sorry about, just one thing . . . the kid. I just want to say . . . what can I say? Goddamn sick it is — and I didn't have shit to do with it. The authorities contacted me, and all I got to say is, thank God he's a minor and his name won't be in the news."

Griffin has always been slow on the uptake, and he does not understand Chief's ramblings — then again, Chief's ramblings and rants are not meant to be understood as much as suffered. He replays the second message and is clear. It has been Chief spying on him, Chief threatening him into betrayal. Griffin has offered little more than the date and time of a meeting; that's it. But the fact is, he should not have. He should have just kept his mouth shut, at least until he was forced to play a card. And now, it would seem, the game is lost. He leans over, unable to catch and push back the vomit this time, much less to get Jewells to pull over to avoid a splattery mess in the car. Mostly it lands in the plastic bag he covers his mouth with in the nick of time.

The FedEx mailer sits on the empty seat beside him. Griffin drags the little silver metal wand that pulls the curtains shut. The light in the car dims as if to offer the sweet spot of the day, the moments just before something beautiful happens, only it will not be so, he thinks. He pulls the pouch tab of the mailer, tearing along the seam. Inside is a manila envelope, very official looking. He imagines a legal matter, he imagines it is proof of Chief's betrayal: photographs of him talking to the fake federal agent, perhaps procured by a spy in the shrubs, or a high-altitude aircraft armed with a satellite. Maybe even evidence of Griffin's own perfidies, from taxes to Jewells' Social Security number.

Nothing so simple comes close to what he sees.

It is not quite a seizure that breaks him out in sweat and uncontrollable shaking. There is, however, a sense he is in the clutches of something he cannot control, and of the coming to a full stop. Griffin sees no mountaintop and no glory, as

Meemaw's unflappable faith in God always promised; nor does he see his own life flashing before his eyes, as he always heard he would. He sees instead only the white column legs of an overpass, dug deep into the green of low grass, and he sees them as twin destinations for a man with such problems as his. He reaches over the back of Jewells' seat, grabs earplugs that send a beep of hip-hop sound rushing out. As if parting a silent wave, he pushes his arms through and wedges his body between the seats, not daring to look at his boy, refusing the pleas of "Dad, Dad" — this Jewells, the terrible boy in the pictures, naked, his ringed dick in some Chinese boy's mouth, in some white man's ass, in the clench of his own hand, his mouth slobbering on that of another man's, a tongue in his buttcrack, getting fucked.

Griffin's left arm methodically pinions his son's neck, while the hand of the other commandeers the steering. There is a moment of confusion over what the force of his embrace means, and what follows is a terror of struggling and thrashing that Griffin also only ignores. Ever so clearly he stares at the bisecting plane of the overpass, like perfect opposing diagonals converging to hold up the folly of life. He zeroes in on what seems like a score zone, as if it were a hoop he must sink a three-pointer in to win. He pushes past all obstacles in his way, and all odds. It is probably the struggle for breath that suddenly mashes Jewells' foot on the accelerator, and even after the crack and snap of his neck his foot holds fast, as his head lolls in Griffin's tough-love embrace. The Bentley speeding faster, faster, the engine sings loudly along, its inner and outer luxury making one last, enduring impression, living up to its heritage in the most supreme way, its body and bonnet the shimmering silver of a shooting star. The roundness of the one concrete column comes so close that it squares into a lone wall, but one widening and lengthening and pulsing like a beacon to bring the Bentley in.

Mrs. Saunders

1

Afternoon comes, and the chorus of cicadas. Bug skins shine in low light that maple trees in the backyard dapple and blot. The first insects awoke ahead of the swarm by a day. To Margeaux, the cicada looked like a hair barrette, so prettily colored and perfectly shaped, glimmering in new grass, undisturbed. The attraction was mutual until desire took wing, with Margeaux flailing and screaming for it to get away, before finally backhanding its ardor down. The insect's doting is now succeeded by armies that bide their time deep in the trees, then tangle in the hair of little girls and courage of tender boys. Their epic hunger has made a mess of the garden, spoiling the flower beds while gorging the appetites of wasps, grackles, robins, bluejays. A squadron of molted cicadas now cling to tree bark, at times pretending like something comely in the dusk. The fallen among them are a dead giveaway, carpeting the grass with a layer of dread. The only thing worse than their flying and crawling is the unavoidable stepping on the living and the gone. The gardener Jorge rakes them into a writhing mulch pile, only not fast enough.

The timing troubles Margeaux even more than the menace. Today marks the midpoint and their numbers will go down. But today is also her big moment. Ed Bradley and the crew of *60 Minutes* are on the way over, due any minute.

"My husband and I were of one mind where our family was concerned"; "He was an exceptional man caught up in exceptional circumstances"; "We are bereft without him." Such lines are rehearsed before a large ornate compact mirror, with a purposeful tremor of feeling along her perfectly penciled lipline. The trick will be to let tears well up without spilling over into a mascara run — and definitely not into a full-on cry, always a risk when the camera is rolling, the eyes a smear, the skin a foundation fright as the face pulls into ugly puffy sentiment. Her rescue is at hand: Shiseido has the perfect emotion-proof mascara and eyeliner. Still, Margeaux is not one to leave a dream moment to chance, having mastered tearing on cue and sharpened her vocal precision by reading aloud. The effort has carried her beyond the usual *Winnie-the-Pooh* and *Knuffle Bunny*, with the added beauty that *Wuthering Heights* and other masterpiece English literary classics have purpled a sense of love and loss.

Just last evening, the performance and precision-enhanced Margeaux had a run-through over dinner with her cousin Mitchell Chenault. Mitchell is a corporate-malfeasance lawyer in the District Attorney's office and an encyclopedic man with batlike ears and chronic dermatic dryness, a condition immune to all but the best moisturizers and presumably inherited from her father's branch of the family tree. He has been prepping her on the noncommittal ways in which she might discuss Griffin for the *60 Minutes* interview.

The restaurant was a Griffin favorite. All proceeded smoothly enough, until the main course arrived. Fabio the chef personally delivered a surprise plate of Bolognese for table: "In memory of your husband, a great man."

It's always the unexpected, the unprepared-for that does a girl in!

But not Margeaux . . . after a small shudder in her breathing and a quiver along her lip, the length of her finger touched just under the lower lashline, as if to hold back a burst. "'Fabio's Bolognese is the best,' that what's Griffin always used to say. Thank you," she offered in a fraught yet clear, in-control voice, with an endearing caress of his hand, winningly heartbroken. A quick, discreet glance at her finger revealed not a trace of tears, mascara or eyeliner. And, no sooner had the chef left the table than an equally quick, though more thorough look at her reflection in the blade of a butter knife showed unsmeared eyes glittering with grief. Proof of a triumph of poise over problematic, unpredictable emotion, the clear-eyed determination to prevail in the most wrenching of circumstances.

Of course, Ed Bradley and *60 Minutes* must naturally prefer she fail when the camera is rolling. Nothing wins viewers more than a woman reduced to teary blubbering. Research on viewing audiences has shown that female audiences require a breakdown, however small, at minimum.

"Jorge," Margeaux calls from the screened-in veranda, her practiced voice now much louder and shriller than she means. "Can't we burn something — citronella, garlic, anything to make these beastly bugs go away, just for a few hours?"

"No, Señora Saunders . . . three more days and they dead."

Her gardener, Jorge, has frequently explained why he is eschewing poisonous insecticides and now, once again, echoes statements overheard on the local NBC *Nine's Got You Covered* news. In his best English, he loudly quotes: "Cicada plagues last a week at most, to be followed by a slumber of seventeen years, before hunger sends the bugs swarming again." He removes his cap, revealing a cicada kabobbed on an inky spike of hair, which he then flicks away. Most summer days, he is shirtless and since the invasion, ten, twenty, thirty cicadas orbit him, evidently drawn to his sweat. Margeaux keeps a safe physical distance, even as emotionally she has lately felt herself drawn to him. Parts Native American, Spaniard and Italian, with a soupçon of Senegalese African — "all Mexican," he likes to say — he is aware he is iconically handsome, as much man as totem figure, with a complexion the chic brown of a Louis Vuitton. Overconfidence in his looks may explain his apparent inattention to the many moods of Margeaux. He waves a gardener's glove as if to shoo her away, and heads to the carriage-house garage, out of sight and incommunicado now that the garage intercom link is broken.

The weather also refuses to cooperate — it is breezeless and cloying like liquid foundation in 100% humidity and 100°F summer.

Nothing is going right.

Granted, three months of planning have fostered an obsession with the perfect *60 Minutes* interview. Her ideal storyboard includes a charming chat with Ed Bradley, free of legal or vocal missteps during a stroll in the garden, a sit-down in the living room and a light-hearted moment in the playroom — the camera and sound crew flowing with them, scene to scene, and the skies above a Tiffany's periwinkle blue.

It is hard not to feel a male conspiracy at large. That she has been turned against, from dead husband, to plague-hurling God, to ridiculously late hair stylist!

But playing victim ill-suits Margeaux, a role at odds with her indomitable spirit. She resumes her facial exercises in the study, occasionally sipping from a glass of room-temperature honey and lemon mineral water. A bottle of nail polish — a purple-black called Vamp — is on the table at her side. Her darling Percy loves the dramatic vamp touch. During their last beauty spree, he selected this purple-black shade at the NARS counter at Nordstrom's. She now thinks the defiant hue may be too much for even a stylish widow to

wear. Her nails are presently a slick creme, the tips Frenched-
up in shiny quarter-moons of white, an effect she loves
but worries may also be too trendy for the kind of gravitas
required. It is good that Percy is not yet home from summer
preschool: A fashion prodigy just shy of six, he does not like
being contradicted, overridden or having his taste questioned.

The cicadas hurry in and out of view, and Margeaux's
attention wanders toward the busy street just beyond the
copse of woods. She notes that Jorge has yet to relocate
the cicada pile to the other side of the yard, to redirect the
feeding frenzy away from the house — offering only "no
good" as his reason. The house, carriage-house garage and
driveway belong to the golden age of private chauffeurs, with
the distance from door to car just close enough for a cicada
squadron, and all the creatures that love them, to amass, in
mess-hall fashion, ruining one's arrivals and departures. The
moles — blind, shy and silly-looking with diabolical claws —
warm to the tires of parked cars and clatter around the cement
driveway in the dark sunset. The wasps hunt in trees and
bushes, flitting through the air like glinting hatpins. The blue
jays hound anything moving, two or four-legged. They need
only glimpse Margeaux to give chase: Sometimes an especially
surly pair taunts her with bullying cries, occasionally striking
her umbrella when it is open. Jorge says they are protecting
their young, but Margeaux feels they are maniacal and cruel.
Ugliness has always unsettled her, whether an unfortunate

face or unbecoming behavior or tasteless style, and the bug-eyed cicadas, in their rude millions, are an inescapable affront. The Dustbuster is her weapon of choice, even in moving traffic.

Where she goes, the bugs follow. TV cicada experts, and Jorge too, have suggested avoiding perfume, but her only concession has been to switch from full strength to Eau de Toilette. Just now, at least fifty of the six-legged monsters lay siege on the veranda screen. She is reminded of the media swarming the property after Griffin's death, only the bugs clearly are there to bask in her aura. Their fiendish red eyes glow as the alchemy of Opium by Yves Saint Laurent swirls on her pulse points. The heady effect is immediate and intense, hitting all the high notes for both her and the enraptured creatures. In twenty minutes, the scent will arc into an alluring, mysterious hint of what was, on its way to what it will be, before vanishing altogether late in the night. The gross, parfum-intoxicated bugs will keep their vigil . . . glowing, glowering, and perhaps warning that there will be a price for parading her late-husband's perfidies before millions of judgmental Americans.

60 Minutes producers first contacted her over five months ago. The proposed segment would be devoted to the one-year anniversary of her husband's death. Explored would be its implications in his brother Chief's troubles in the Clinton White House, from his imminent resignation as

Secretary of Commerce to a possible indictment by a grand jury.

Margeaux said she would consider it.

The pros: A chance to own her story, as the media would certainly come down on her anyway, once Chief's troubles reached a head.

The cons: A slip-up could inspire a subpoena forcing her to testify against her famous brother-in-law, risking her prospects for a solvent future.

As she saw it, any move dangerous to her own self-interest was a wrong one to make. An ill-considered word could jettison her to the bad side of an already ruinous financial situation. Griffin's will had given Chief complete control of their three-hundred-million-dollar cable business, despite the fact that he would likely lose the company in the almost-certain grand jury takedown. And, while Griffin did name her as the beneficiary of most of his possessions, the possessions themselves were not his to give. Through some unfortunate mix-up, his irresponsible, reckless, sneakers-obsessed namesake was the heir to the estate, including not just investment properties but the main house too. All Griffin's local and Indianapolis assets were held by GJS Enterprises, which was registered in Jewells' name thirteen years ago; as Griffin Jewells Saunders III, when it should have been II. Had it been a clerical error, made by her overly fastidious husband? Cousin Mitchell suggests the use of

Jewells' Social Security number was pure identity theft, and that, either way, the ostensible motive was most likely money, accomplished by the commission of fraud. Moreover, the incriminating paperwork was an oversight, evidence of sloppy thinking, even if the ploy was intended only to mislead. That Jewells has died in the accident that killed her husband meant the estate would almost certainly go to her, assuming there was anything left after the paying of mounting debts. All Griffin's business affairs were put in probate, a normal process that, however, given the extraordinary complications and wealth involved, could go on for the next decade, all but guaranteeing a balance of zero.

There is not even car or life insurance to count on. The suspicious deaths of father and son emboldened their blue-chip providers to justify denying payouts in the millions by claiming foul play; their most outrageous allegation was a suicide pact. The evidence gathered at the crash site supported such a theory. Any fantasy of making Bentley/Rolls Royce pay for a design or manufacturing defect was just that.

And, compounding the horror of it all, two weeks before the accident, Griffin named his office manager executor of his estate. The logic of such a move would normally have been unassailable but for his untimely demise. This person, this homely, Bible-thumping person, relished the wielding of her long-simmering disapproval of Griffin's wife through the rankling power of the word no. Margeaux — a woman unused to be being denied — suddenly found herself in the severe confines of a stingy stipend for the family to live on and having to account for every expense, even nail polish and lipstick.

Clearly, the climate was too anti-Margeaux to risk a *60 Minutes* interview. On the advice of powerful friends and lawyer kin alike — all seemingly motivated solely to protect Griffin's image or Chief's — Margeaux told the producers no.

The lone voice insisting that she say yes came from Parris. Parris is a former colleague who has proven so much more than a silly makeup artist, stylist and gossip. Margeaux had not wanted her life to become more fodder than it already was, and for nearly eight months into her widowhood, she kept her few friends at bay, not returning phone calls, even declining all invitations, regardless how fabulous.

One evening not long after her initial *60 Minutes* decline, she bumped into him at the James Galanos trunk show at Saks. The surprise had been all hers — Galanos, designer to former First Lady Nancy Reagan, could hardly be described as a Parris favorite. The thrill was all hers too — such fond memories of the good old days, when his artful makeup brushes and endless catty-chatter entertained, encouraged and consoled her during her brilliant rise and fall on *Today in Cincinnati*. Naturally, years of working together had given him clever keys to her usual guardedness. After one too many glasses of champagne as they eyed the so-so collection, carelessly emboldened emotion let slip private details best kept secret. When she might have said sorting her husband's business and legal affairs was complex, she instead described feeling as if tangled in a vast spider web, about to be devoured by a hairy tarantula. Parris had a keen terror of spiders, and clutched her hand as both grew teary. Margeaux's truths poured out, as their glasses kept being refilled, and five hours later, they were still in the thick of her skein, untangling and unknotting the mess, including the *60 Minutes* offer, when he raced right to the heart of what had been tormenting Margeaux for months now:

"Hon, let's face facts here, your husband had plenty of time to set you up, so accident or not, out of his mind or not, he fucked you over! Period, end of story. I mean, like, screw him and think about your future. Like, thanks to him, you have to go back to work. You should seize the opportunity and give Ed Bradley and *60 Minutes* a hard-on, so you can claw your way back to an anchor position or better still, your own show. Make it your best audition ever, and get yourself a slot on national news or in Chicago or New York or D.C. or Houston. You're way too all-that for this shithole."

Never mind she despises being called hon, and that the graphic, dirty language offends, she followed the argument to its flattering conclusion because she knew, deep down, he was right.

"My brother-in-law is the problem," Margeaux

whispered, as if speaking at a normal voice would conjure Chief himself.

"To hell with her."

"You know who *he* is?

"No, but screw *her*."

"*He's* the Secretary of Commerce of the United States, a Clinton man. *He's* about to be indicted. *He* owns my husband's company and all its assets. My future is in *his* hands."

"Wrong, your future is in *your* hands."

"There's no way around talking about him in an interview that's really about him."

"Repeat after me: No comment! Hon, make this interview about you."

He had a point. And to prove just how viable she herself still was as a media topic of interest, within just three days, Parris, pretending to be a publicist, had aroused interest in interviews and articles about the newly brave Margeaux Chenault a.k.a. Mrs. Griffin Jewells Saunders II, reentering the world. His pitch: "Life of a local Cinderella one year after the tragic loss of her Prince Charming. They ate it up," Parris had claimed.

So, yes to *60 Minutes*!

At the time, Margeaux had also been told the focus of the interview would be wide-angled, starting with a montage of Griffin truths: Small minority businessman makes the big time and becomes a wheeler and dealer in Washington, D.C., with his famous half-brother, Samuel Tecumseh Black II, the Secretary of Commerce for the United States of America — whose power connections to the Clintons and lucrative foreign trade made the brothers a fortune. Margeaux was advised she need only appear at her local affiliate to do the actual interview. A pity! She had hoped to be flown to New York, with the chance to fit in friends and shopping at her favorite stores, the B's: Bendel, Bergdorf and Barneys.

The scope of the interview changed, however, when the investigation into her brother-in-law had taken a prison-likely turn. Glaring across national headlines were details about Chief and Griffin accepting bribes from two Singapore businessmen, and suddenly there were cameramen in the shrubbery and journalists at the door. Neighborhood security services were insufficient, and additional protection had to be hired to keep the media away. The *60 Minutes* producer emailed that they now wanted to bring the interview into her home, to make the family hearth of Griffin Jewells Saunders II its centerpiece.

Margeaux got the producer on the line: "Are you insane! There will absolutely be no *60 Minutes* interview here with me and my family caught in a circus."

Cousin Mitchell: "A good move, best to stay out of this mess, let it all just die down."

Parris: "You're a fool to let this opportunity go!"

Mutti: "I don't want to be on TV."

Percy: "I want to be on TV."

Even gardener Jorge weighed in: "I'm illegal. What I supposed to do?"

It was show-host Ed Bradley himself who decided the matter. He personally put her mind at ease with assurances and an outline of the ten-minute segment. He promised the story would still be about her, but the interview would be on the house grounds, in the study and the family room with the children. They would discuss the pressures Griffin may have been under that could have driven him into a bridge, from his brother's business affairs and his struggles in Washington, to the Clintons themselves. Collaged into the segment would be scenes of the nation's capital, the epicenter of her husband's and his brother's undoing.

What really sold her, though, was his acknowledgement of her background in television journalism and hosting, and his delicately hinting at the the glory of this opportunity to cast herself professionally in a new light and on a national stage — almost Parris's exact words. As he spoke to her through a raspy voice afflicted with a cold, she could almost feel her dormant ambition zapped fully into life, a broken butterfly with newly mended spectacular wings unfurled for primetime.

Indeed, Margeaux was "ready for her close up."

Now, two vehicles turn in the drive. The first, a black

van, tucks the second, Parris' lipstick-red sports car. The vehicles separate at the loop, Parris toward the front of the house, the van toward the carriage house in the rear. Griffin, she thinks, would have wanted Parris to park his sissy car in back, whether a film crew was coming or not. Her husband was good in that way, holding highest how a thing might look — never mind his aback-taking dislike for gays.

"Parris, late as ever," Margeaux curdles into her cellphone.

"Oh my God, that's Ed Bradley in the front seat. Hon, did you see him? I'm so gonna ask to do his makeup."

"Don't. He travels with a woman."

"How do you know?"

"Parris, please."

"It's so exciting? You'll be a star, I can feel it."

"Can you really?"

"Can I, can I? . . . of course, Hon. I'm going to have to charge you more if you don't promise me this instant to take me with you to fame."

"Please . . . we'll jinx everything by talking about it."

"Maybe you've noticed the cicada armageddon?"

"Isn't it horrible?"

"Biblical."

"Of all times for the wrath . . . or is it the rapture?"

"Rapture is the new Givenchy collection . . . think about it!"

Margeaux giggles. "Parris, what would I do without you?"

Before disconnecting, she explains he must move his car because the film crew will need to get an unobstructed shot of the main house. Jorge has swung the Jaguar out of the way for just that reason.

"Okay," says Parris, blowing a kiss as bugs crisscross her view, his car backing up and lurching toward the carriage house. It occurs to Margeaux she should have warned the camera crew about the acute cicada invasion in her yard. She has seen *60 Minutes* episodes filmed in terrorists' dens in the Middle East, the crosshairs of gunfire in Sarajevo, the winds of killer tornados in Oklahoma.

"CBS *60 Minutes*," one of the cameramen calls out, waving at her or swatting cicadas, it's hard to tell which.

"Yes, come in, please." Margeaux hears the cicadas thrashing the door and watches as black-clad Parris and his purple zebra-striped makeup weekender bag spring from the sissy car, cross the yard, his arm pressing against his chest as if holding down jiggling breasts. He wears a headscarf in Muslim hijab style, and removes it once inside, revealing gold-tinted hair scraped into a ponytail. Parris insists he has the same bone structure as his first cousin, the classic American beauty model Cheryl Tiegs, and sometimes Margeaux sees it, most times not.

"These horrible bugs love my mousse. I can't go without mousse, it's just not going to happen."

"Tell me about it." Margeaux watches the yard, as the

crewmember makes his way toward her. "Calm down. We'll get through."

"It's really like old times, isn't it, Margeaux?"

"It is."

It is not worth adding the good times ended badly.

A man tanned nearly a complete shade of rawhide, from hairline to fingertips, and with piercing blue eyes, arrives on the veranda, swatting a helix of cicadas.

"I'm so sorry about these awful bugs. They're everywhere."

"Not a problem, Mrs. Saunders. I'm Chet of *60 Minutes*. Ed's in the van, on the phone, he'll be in shortly, but if you don't mind we'll just start setting up our camera equipment."

"Of course not."

"If you could take me to the study, we'll set up there. Our cameramen will take pictures of the living room, the library and the house too, if that's okay?"

"Certainly. And just so I know, how long before we start?"

"About an hour. Ed will fill you in."

Parris offers lighting suggestions that are more favorable to Margeaux's complexion, but Chet seems to ignore him and goes for more gear.

"Excuse me, Hon, but *60 Minutes* really is the ugliest show. I mean, like, I see dead people, okay — everyone on *60 Minutes* looks like a cadaver, and it's like they have something against beauty."

"Their audience skews older."

"No surprise there, okay! We'll just have to animate you a little more, I guess, to compensate."

Margeaux wants to lock Parris in her powder room, but he insists on a corner where the action is — "So I can work with the lighting we've got."

"Okay, but, Parris, you must stay calm, not get hysterical if there's criticism. Please."

"Yes, madam."

"I'll bring the dress down."

Margeaux leaves him, finding Ed Bradley standing in the entryway. He seems startled.

"Mr. Bradley, Margeaux Saunders," Margeaux greets him with her hand rising to a handshake.

"Please call me Ed."

"It's a pleasure."

"What a beautiful home. Really. I've visited Cincinnati before, when I came to cover the 1968 riots after Martin Luther King, Jr.'s assassination. I remember being impressed by the stately homes. Yours is a knockout — and the grounds, my goodness. The river can't be too far off, am I right?"

"How nice of you to say. Thank you, Ed." She debates whether to acknowledge the most recent riots, an unpleasant subject she wishes not to banter about. Then: "You're right, the river is not so far off. Our property is just three acres, but the backyard and the long slope down to the woods make it seem bigger; there are other properties between ours and the river, and in the winter you can see them clearly, their rooftops and a sliver of river."

"'Sliver of river' . . . I like that."

"My husband used to say that."

Margeaux nudges him along with a touch to his elbow. The gesture is forward, but she knows that when he speaks of the beautiful house he in fact is talking about her. Powerful men are prone to double entendres. She has always preferred clever flirtation over the crass.

"It may surprise you to know that, unlike the stately homes you noticed, the style is not German-influenced but French Chateau," she says. "It was built in 1931, as part of the Wurlitzer estate — if you remember the Wurlitzer organ, it's that family. The Wurlitzers were German, with French tastes. While the English have nothing to do with this house, my first experience here was very British. I can still remember the day Griffin brought me to see it, it was our fourth or fifth date. He had purchased the house at auction and had been living here with his little boy, our Jewells, when I met him. I felt like Elizabeth Bennet, in Jane Austen's *Pride and Prejudice*, when she first sees Pemberley, Mr. Darcy's estate. 'Of all of this I might have been mistress,' she says. Of course it's not so grand as even the Pemberley stables, but it's my favorite place in the world."

"I love that story, Mrs. Saunders."

Margeaux knows it's lovable . . . it's why she said it . . . even though she has only recently read the Austen masterwork. "My marriage was like a fairy tale in many ways."

"Everyone loves a fairy tale."

"Especially one with tragedy. It's cynical of me to say . . ."

"Maybe true. Although I think people love a story of redemption just as much, if not more. Something about rising above petty, arbitrary circumstance appeals to our sense of justice and hope for happiness and a promising future."

"This isn't a story of redemption."

"It could be . . . your redemption."

"Yes, I suppose you're right." Margeaux is at once stilled and electrified.

Chet and technician crew plant themselves before Ed Bradley, pulling him away. Margeaux dashes upstairs for her wardrobe — a white Bill Blass with a black rose petal inset, to which she will add a black diamond brooch — and drapes it in Parris' work station. Water is running in the powder room; she assumes it is he. On the way to the study, she is summoned by Chet's crew with questions, and faintly hears the boys yelling outside, being chased and hopefully not outpaced by cicadas.

"Excuse me, day camp's out and my boys are home. I'll be right back."

The rear veranda is the entry point the boys prefer most.

Margeaux finds Mutti there to gather them up.

"My handsome darlings." Margeaux opens arms as they file up to kiss her. "The camera crew is here already. I want you to help out by washing and dressing yourselves. Your clothes are already laid out." Mutti seconds the request, adding that they come right back down to the veranda when they are ready.

Percy stares at all the long black wires and big cameras and insists he will not play television interview. "I want the Dior runway."

"We'll play Dior runway soon as this one is done."

"I want to play Muppets interview." Fletcher chimes in.

"We'll play that too. Percy can be Mr. Poodlepants and Oma can be Camilla the Chicken."

"She's Oma Mrs. Piggy," smirks Percy.

"That's right," seconds Fletcher.

"That's not nice," chides Margeaux, even if true. In her youth, Mutti possessed not quite Jacqueline Kennedy's beauty but something not far off . . . poorer, less polished, but no less foreign; German to be exact. Now, a hyperactive thyroid has piled on the weight and she is porcine-colored, lumpy and swollen — just another statistic of poor health.

"Or we can play Hansel and Gretel and put bad little boys in the oven," says Mutti.

"Given the history of your country, ovens are nothing to joke about."

"Really, Margeaux!"

"This obesity isn't good for you, Mutti. Soon as the weather cools, you can push the girls in the stroller around the track. Get yourself in better shape."

"Yeah, get skinny, Oma," says Percy. Then, throwing hands to hips: "I don't want to walk around the track. I'm not Miss Piggy."

"Boys, let's get through *60 Minutes* now," says Margeaux. "Now go upstairs and dress yourselves like proper gentlemen. Percy, no accessories, please."

The boys head for the kitchen stairs.

"Margeaux, I realize you are nervous, but your jabs at me are cruel and not appreciated. It inspires the boys to be impudent."

"I'm sorry. You're right, of course."

"Dearest, it'll go just fine. You're a pro. Just pretend you're on your old television show."

"Maybe that's not a good idea. The viewers didn't like me: 'She's too pretty, her hair's too long, her hair's too short, she's too white-sounding, she's not black enough' — they tore me to pieces."

"That was then, and this is now. You know who you are, and people all over the country will be watching, because they're interested in your story."

Ed Bradley joins them on the veranda.

"This is my mother, Mrs. Chenault."

Extending his hand and eyeing her appreciatively, he says, "Beauty runs in the family."

"Oh, please," Mutti says.

"I'm more like my father," Margeaux murmurs, hoping she will not have to say there will never be an on-camera mom-and-daughter moment . . . ever.

"My daughter is afraid that my figure is in her future."

"Lucky is the woman who retains perfection in her late years," says Ed Bradley.

"Oh, you're smooth."

"I hear the faintest accent. I'm very good with accents. Let's see . . . German?"

"Yes, you are good."

Glancing at Margeaux: "It's my mother tongue."

"Where?"

Hesitating: "Near Bavaria. I came here with my parents when I was quite young."

"This is great. I would like to include you in the story, if you don't mind."

"Oh, no," she says, looking at Margeaux. Then, "Absolutely not."

"If not an interview, then just a shot of you with the kids should do it. So everyone in America can see Margeaux's beauty heritage. And frankly, we don't do enough stories that reflect the true racial character of our subjects."

"You are saying a picture is worth a thousand words?"

"Yes."

"No, but thank you."

Margeaux's jaw quivers with annoyance. She will take a hardline with Mutti afterward for daring to step into the foreground and possibly provoking an unnecessary probe into her past, however innocently.

"On to the business at hand, I have questions." Margeaux smiles over her annoyance and nudges Ed toward the study. On TV, the gaps in Bradley's teeth make him seem more sincere, but not necessarily more handsome. She pictures him in braces; lots of adults are wearing them these days, although probably few television newsmen among them. They move to the living room, stopping at the fireplace, above which the Griffin Jewells Saunders II family photograph looms. Margeaux refuses to look up, leading Bradley beyond this emotional quake zone with a touch of her hand.

"Margeaux, just as we discussed on the phone awhile back, the interview will be pretty straightforward."

"Nevertheless, I'd like for you to show me the final storyboard, so I can understand the flow of the segment."

"You realize it could be very different after it's edited?"

"I do, but indulge me anyway."

"Okay. There'll most likely be, as I said before, a montage of images about Secretary Black's rise to prominence, imminent indictment and then a quick cut to your husband. The voiceover will go something like: "We begin today's program with Margeaux Chenault Saunders, the widow whose husband is at the center of a grand jury investigation that is looking into the business practices of the Commerce Secretary of the United States." It'll say that your husband and the Secretary were half-brothers and co-owners of a company called Premier International; it'll say that the company was a cable-industry frontrunner that bought and sold cable rights throughout the United States and was becoming a major international player. It'll say that the Secretary sold his ownership of the company to your husband, but among the prosecutor's many allegations — bribery, extortion, perjury — it is alleged that the Secretary received hundreds of thousands of dollars in kickbacks from lucrative domestic and illegal international sales that he helped the company obtain as a Clinton cabinet member. It'll say that your husband and brother-in-law were snared in a sting operation with the FBI when, one year ago today, your husband was tragically killed in an accident, along with his teenage son, on a highway just north of Savannah, Georgia. It'll say that many in Washington wonder if what your husband knew about the secretary's dealings with the Clinton administration cost him his life."

"Tabloid sensationalism," Margeaux says, as they walk toward Parris and his arsenal of palettes, tubes and brushes.

"It's real, it's in the headlines in papers and television news throughout the country. It's part of the context of this interview — your husband's death is part of the story of the secretary's fall. Looked at another way, it's a story about the rise of African Americans as true power-players in the worlds of business and politics. It's true that there have been more powerful African American businessmen than the secretary — Reginald Lewis of Fannie Mae/Freddie Mac comes to mind — but no African American has ever risen to such political heights and wielded so much power."

"Yes, I understand. But Ed, let me be frank. I realize that *60 Minutes* is an investigative news program, but I don't want to come off as some paranoid widow waiting for justice. Believe me, it's a love/hate relationship with my brother-in-law, but I know the harm speculation can do."

"I understand."

"And of course there's no evidence to suggest my husband's death was anything more than a tragic accident, whatever forces were at play."

"The coroner's report states your son was asphyxiated before the accident. His neck was broken. There's also evidence that the crime scene was tampered with, that things were removed."

"Certainly not by either my husband or son."

"That point isn't in dispute."

"Not yet." Margeaux thumbs her wedding ring nervously. "Ed, I also don't want to be presented as if I was my husband's business partner. I wasn't — I wish that I had been more engaged, so I'd at least be on top of what's going on now."

A squad of four shiny cicadas quietly dangle on the drapes near where Ed stands. Margeaux's eyes linger there long enough to see the spider, trapezing toward the bugs. The moment requires action, not panic, and a fearless Margeaux politely nudges Ed away from the imminent war zone, saying: "There's the grand jury inquest. The findings will be released soon enough. I certainly don't want to end up subpoenaed in the future. Also, to make matters worse, my husband's local company GJS Enterprises is tied up in probate."

"Margeaux, I promise I'll only raise issues the audience expects to hear addressed. You're a pro, just as I am. Shall we get down to it?"

Behind every prominent TV host or anchor is an agent and a well-connected executive producer. Margeaux once could claim to have had both when she was riding highest, cinching the journey from city TV reporter to Sunday morning talk show host in less than two years. Now she is lucky to get a timely return call; even then, there is only polite interest.

After much brooding over why her own colleagues were ignoring her, Margeaux tells Parris, "Maybe they think it's unseemly — you know, Margeaux Chenault reduced to begging for representation."

"Begging? Who's begging?"

"I am, just by calling. They should be calling me."

"Okay, first, wrong attitude. Who cares what they think? You need to knock on as many doors as possible, and as loud as you can, until one opens for you."

"You think?"

"Yeah, I think."

"I know I'm being a bore."

"I can see that a big part of my job as head of Team Margeaux is keeping you on point."

"Team Margeaux . . . you're so fabulous."

"I know, but let's adore each other later. Right now, I feel a strong need to deprogram you so you are thinking straight. First, Oprah Winfrey you ain't, so spare me the victim diva act. Second, you are not an old ass, and yet you act like my mother . . . in her sixties, hello! Okay, you want a career in today's world, so you need to know how to operate. It's the synergies that matter. That's what'll get you noticed. You need a publicist, you need a press release, you need a website, you need email updates, and most of all, Hon, you need an attitude that says Margeaux is back, more fabulous than ever."

Who knew Parris had pluck beyond makeup?

Her media career ended just as the new technology had begun to change everything, and now Margeaux is far down on the learning curve of self-promotion. Agents are paid to handle such things, and it is inconceivable that she herself could engineer a similar result, although it is pretty of Parris to think she could. In the past, beauty reliably generated its own synergies, from pageants to international fashion runways, editorial shoots in *Vogue* and the like, to the host chair on a morning talk show. Time was, she needed only to show up, all poise and sparkle, and naturally and engagingly deliver her lines, sometimes in little more than a bikini. Opportunities, if not twinkling crowns, followed — all, leading to this crisis in confidence!

A quick study, she is more than eager to learn this new, technical stuff, so long as someone else is doing the heavy lifting. She feels exactly the same about children. It is enough that she has borne them. A team of a nanny, housekeeper, tutors and private schools must do the rest.

In much the way Mutti assumed control of the Griffin Jewells Saunders II household during Margeaux's first pregnancy, Parris takes the reins of Team Margeaux, his commission a mere $15,000, due once she lands her first anchor or host chair, and the position as her executive producer or chief hair stylist or exclusive agent, whichever opportunity yields the greatest benefit. Soon her phone begins ringing not with offers for a new pilot or TV role opportunities, but talk of her *60 Minutes* spotlight, due to air in six weeks.

Everything seems to be fast-tracked. On a Monday morning, Parris finagles a profile in *Cincinnati Magazine*, and two Wednesdays later, both the interview and photo session are done. Standing near enough to the magazine's photographer to watch the high-tech digital images appear on screen, Parris directs Margeaux for the most light-flattering effect by angling his head this way and that. It is also his idea that she sail right over the dark shadows of her dream marriage, and give only a sidebar to her husband's flawed greatness and the imperiling troubles of Secretary of Commerce Samuel Tecumseh Black II. She is not the only one won over by this new all-knowing Parris. Even difficult Percy submits to his authority during the photosession, in exchange for an exclusive lipgloss Parris invented — and cooperates while a magazine photographer takes a loving, bright-yet-bereft family photo. On a fashion note: At Parris' suggestion, Percy even wears a pink polo shirt and black clam diggers, punctuating Margeaux's noir tank top and silver-iridescent shorts, and the girls' sunsuits and Fletcher's white denim. The photo is snapped on the stairs of the side veranda, where the dead cicadas now molder in a vast blackened mulch pile, Margeaux is horrified to note.

The magazine story is slated for August. Sly Parris

wrangles the editors into seeing that they would be missing out on the perfect promotion opportunity, unless they bump the story to the July issue, to be on the newsstand and in homes a week before her *60 Minutes* "breakthrough" goes live. Unknown to Margeaux at the time, the bait is — surprise! — her brother-in-law Chief. Parris has falsely given the impression that the grand jury verdict is imminent, and the magazine story would be a prescient first.

Next, an editorial for the Cincinnati Inquirer is commissioned, to be penned on the subject of women's triumphing over seemingly insuperable adversity. A month later, the deadline looming, Margeaux loves the idea of writing such a piece much less. Speaking to a live video camera feels natural, whereas the written word intimidates. Video inspires artifice and a brand of creamy insincerity that smoothes over every flaw like the perfect makeup primer. Written words do not — words shimmer on the surface like a trick of light, at once revealing and obscuring meaning. The essences she has jotted down in her notebook to describe Griffin — liar, thief, cheat, con man, bankrupt, absent, coward — are rogue enough that she is unable to speak them publicly, despite years of TV programming for women having shown that audiences would relate to her evolution, from careerist, to wife of a prince, to happy mother, to a young widow wearily assessing the legacy of her tarnished man. Looked at another way, going public about her marriage's tragedy means admitting to failure, all the more so given the circus to come when Chief's grand jury indictment is handed down. Never mind the scandal, just thinking about her lapse in judgment in marrying Griffin Jewells Saunders II provokes feelings she is uncomfortable with. Scientific research has proven that anger and bitterness are unkind to all women, but especially those with bread-and-butter looks. Anger prematurely wrinkles and furrows one's skin, while bitterness dulls one's sensitivities to color and even to taste — not at all good for the new high-definition video cameras.

"I've had to dive deep within myself to find the strength to go on, for the sake of my children, first and foremost, but also for myself. Who am I?" Her editorial includes such sentences. In sentiment and meaning, they are opposite the harsh words she had written about her husband, fully six months ago, as if anticipating this spate of publicity and self-reflection. They allow that she is deciding instead to focus on picking up the pieces of a life shattered not by her husband's perfidies, but rather by his smashup with fate.

Jewells is given but a few words of false praise — far more than he deserves.

The newspaper refuses to run it: "Though heartfelt, this piece is little more than self-reflection on a shallow pond . . . we had hoped for the details, the controversies, all laid bare, to show real adversity."

Neither Parris nor Margeaux takes the rejection, or its

meaning, to heart, for the editor also recommends placement in the metro section as an essay. Further, the local NPR affiliate wants an interview, to air on the actual day of the second anniversary of her husband's death.

It is thrilling how it all could come together in a news-cycle splash. A comeback, always a longshot, suddenly feels within reach. If only she were employed before Griffin's good name putrifies in the headlines. Dare she hope he was cheating on her? As disgusted and aggrieved as she would be were it true, a viewing audience might rally to her side. Maybe a discreet hint of his adultery could pave the way?

Margeaux is thinking about a preemptive strike when her phone's caller I.D. reveals her former co-host on *Today in Cincinnati*. She decides to screen.

"Margeaux, Magda here. Girlfriend, how are you? … It's been ages… Where has the time gone since we got together?… We have lots to catch up on, but for now I want to personally invite you to be a guest on my new cable show… Yes, a cable show. If you haven't already heard, it's a talk show, with a shopping network component. It's not about HSN or Walmart junk, it's more expensive merchandise, and we're going for the sexy attitude of this new series, *Sex and the City*… I'll tell you all about it when we speak, but you'll have a chance to reconnect with your fan base, and by the time *60 Minutes* airs — Parris mentioned it — producers will be on your doorstep trying to lure you into prime time. I gotta run. I'll wait for your call. Meanwhile Lilith — remember, she interned us at TIC? — she's now my own very excellent executive producer. She'll be in touch."

Margeaux immediately rings Parris.

"I can't believe that cow has a new show. Why didn't you tell me? And don't pretend you didn't know . . . she gave you up! You've been working for her all along?"

"Hello, because you hate her. TIC is in the past."

"Don't call it TIC. I did not work on a show called TIC."

"*Today in Cincinnati*, then . . . okay."

"And cable too! — she has all the luck."

"Hon, I know you wanted to do your own cable show, so I didn't want to upset you."

"I am upset. And I hope you haven't told her about my down-and-out existence?"

"Of course not, Hon."

"Right." Margeaux seethes. "And how does she get an opportunity like that?"

"High ratings, of course. Jerry Springer people approached her."

"I hope it fails. A big fat flop!"

"Since you're taking it so well, Hon, you might as well hear it all. It's starting off as a weekend show, but there's a national potential. Magda's larger than life, a real fun big girl in every way. She'll do for Cincinnati what Oprah did for Chicago. And . . ."

"And?"

"She's offered me the job of head makeup artist, and if the show succeeds, I'm taking it."

"I thought you wanted to go with me?"

"Where are we going? When you have something concrete lined up, I'll consider it. Makeup has been good to me, but I aspire higher. We'll see."

"Greed!"

"Hello, I don't have a multimillionaire husband, dead or alive."

"Lest you forget, I've been trashed!"

"Hon, do you want to hear about the show or not?"

The pause seems to Margeaux pregnant with distrust and suspicion. At such times, she thinks he, without eyeliner and contacts, is beady-eyed and bears neither bone-structure relation nor resemblance to Cheryl Tiegs. Homely is the word come to mind.

Several days of recovery later, Margeaux plans to speak with Magda directly. First, she endures five episodes of the *Jerry Springer Show* as part of her research. The world is a ghetto!

Despite nausea and concern over the possibility of being ambushed on the show, she immediately agrees to a taping. Her real worry is the show's set design. Cincinnati may be its home, but its décor suggests Miami tropical warmth and brightness. Not good. Later, Parris confirms her

worst fears, insisting such lighting better flatters a tanned
or darker complexion, or a ruddy roly-poly like Magda.
Margeaux's creamy golden tone holds unsteady in such
lighting, tending to wash out and flatten. He points out that
The Magda Show was designed by the same team behind
Today in Cincinnati. To avoid looking Latina, regardless of the
ever-growing demographic, his remedy calls for a foundation
secret weapon called Summer Walnut, along with dark eyes,
strong lips and big hair, as opposed to the clean elegant
look for staid *60 Minutes*. *The Magda Show* will run Saturday
evenings at eleven — an hour perfect for lingerie looks, Parris
reminds — as a smart alternative to the men-centric, late-night
and porn fare in full swing.

"I'd go feral, with animal prints, leopard, zebra, tiger."

"Parris, you know I don't do feral."

"Maybe you should. TIC — sorry, *Today in Cincinnati* —
is so over."

Later, she pens in the margins of her notebook: "Past is
not present or future."

Stylists and makeup artists exist for a reason, but
Parris's fashion taste troubles. Overwhelming evidence that
he has none abounds, plus a certain demographic — deciders
in the television industry — will be paying close attention to
her every move. On the other hand, high glamour invariably
backfires in this Middle America backwater of a city, and
the audience will turn on her again. Past polls of viewing

audiences revealed that everyone in TV Land had hated her, except young and educated white women. Her only ardently loyal fans had been a tiny percentage of men, ages twenty-five to forty. Men exactly like Parris — Cincinnati queers — Margeaux had been convinced at the time.

She is confused. Which demographic to please? And with just three days before the Magda interview, a full-out crisis feels imminent.

Only her buddy Drexel, a women's sportswear buyer at Saks in New York, and a former model and stylist, can help.

"Margeaux, please say you're here?"

"If wishing could make it so, I would be, but no, Drexel, no . . ."

"You sound so sad."

"I am, not as much as before, but still."

"Zero trips to New York, and it's at least six years already — how can you stand the deprivation?"

"It's not so easy to just get away for the weekend."

"Four children — I'd've killed myself by now."

"Drexel, there's so much to say and share, but I'm calling because I need your help. I've got this interview . . . and I need you to dress me, sight unseen."

"What's the job?"

Margeaux explained, not omitting the Jerry Springer link.

"That's easy. Just get a hazmat suit because you know

somebody's going to throw vomit or poop on you."

"It's a sexy talk show with a shopping component. My segment is an inspirational interview about my life after loss."

"That's sweet . . . hopefully they won't send out models in mourning outfits."

"You make a good point, I should ask what else is being featured that night . . . not that that would stop me from doing the show."

"Missing the spotlight?"

"Something like that. Well, let me be honest with you, I wouldn't do the show for a million reasons but I will anyway mostly for my sanity — and the money. I need to get back to work. For the interview, I need to look confident, shaken but confident, like I have it together or will soon. Frankly, I'm out of my depth, which is why I need you."

"I see. Making lemonade, are we?"

"I'm trying. I need . . . I desperately need to get back to work."

"Not as rich as you thought? How bad is it?"

"Pretty bad."

"Are you broke?"

Margeaux's redacted truth-telling leads Drexel to sum up her plight up: "Scaling Mount Bitterness, are we?"

If only he knew how steep the Himalayan slope before her!

"Well, 'Ain't no mountain high enough . . .'" He coos but she is uncharmed.

Rather than go there, Margeaux tells him about
the *60 Minutes* interview, about the wacky rumors about
assassination and conspiracy that she will inevitably have to
combat. She does this while emailing shots of her face, hair
unspooling like ribbon, and of her body in a leotard, as in the
runway days of old. She hears her email dinging its arrival
to his computer, and when he exclaims, "Oh, fabulous," she
is in the middle of saying that Chief is a monster but not so
much of one to murder his own brother. Drexel adds, "You
look soooo good" and "That body could still start a bidding
war. God help anybody who gets in your way." "That's right,
a bidding war to save poor stupid Margeaux," she deprecates.
"Oh, a pity party, is it?" "Yes." "Margeaux, like my Auntie
used to say, 'Don't let your pity put you in a pickle.' I think
you should be very careful what you say about the big scary
Chief. He's probably not the man to fuck with, and you don't
want to be on his bad side." Margeaux rejoins, "He's at the
bottom of my worry list. He's on his way to jail for reasons
that have nothing to do with me. My only priority right now
is the future of four children that I am solely responsible for."

Thank goodness, the email with the navy Lanvin photo
arrives before she leaks truth from the awkward thought
bubble above her. She exclaims "fabulous" just as he says,
"Isn't it fabulous?" — and she is spared the indignity of
blurting out a confession of her latest take on the truth: That
her husband, the stiff, humorless and downright spineless

man whom she had learned to love, had left her unable to afford the dress . . . or any dress, really.

"Drexel, I knew I could count on you," she says. He says, "You might tell that ninny Parris to have a look at the fall campaign for Bobbi Brown. That's the right direction, not circus clown." Margeaux loves the campaign and agrees, though she knows she would never dare relay Drexel's thoughts, Parris would bristle, Parris knows best. Indeed. It is always interesting to her that her two best gay friends, one black Caribbean and the other white American trash, still compete over her and loathe each other after all these years.

Much-needed calm comes in the imagined drape of the Lanvin. She pictures herself walking onto *The Magda Show* set, the flounced hemline dancing above the knee. Elegant but not too elegant. Figure-flattering but not too sexy. In three-inch heels, Margeaux stands at six-feet-one, the perfect height at which to remain above the fray.

All evening long she feels carefree with the children as if nothing is wrong, even when Alyssa says "dada" with her little hazel eyes darting about. Fortunately, Alyssa is not babbling to Margeaux, but to Mutti who understands how to handle such significant sad moments, not to mention managing the messes, tantrums and demandingness — the very things about children Margeaux would just as soon avoid. It is amazing that they are so lacking in understanding, and so overwhelming, such psychopaths. Yet how hard to imagine not having them! Especially Percy. Where Fletcher is a miniature Griffin, only fairer in complexion, Percy is so in her own image — well, in fact, he shares many of Mutti's genes, from dark blue eyes to chestnut hair, but in all other ways he is so her. Unsurprisingly he lights up over the Lanvin when Margeaux presents the photo to him at bedtime.

"Mommy loves this most," says Margeaux.

"It's chic," he says. "Chic, chic, chic."

Not just for his but for all of their sakes, Margeaux must pull off something big, hold steady while drawing upon her inner powers as she braves the stares and judgments of critical people, loving you one moment, loathing you the next.

As promised, Drexel overnights the Lanvin, along with two other "surprise" possibilities, to Saks downtown. Margeaux heads out in the late afternoon pre-rush-hour, two grackles tailing her to the car. The birds seem to have had their fill of cicadas weeks ago, and are now just spiteful, ignoring the insect burial mulch mound as yet unmoved to the outskirts of the property. She has not seen Jorge the last two hours and then, with suspicious timing there he is — shirt open and chest out — coming from the carriage house just as she slams the car door. Jorge nods; Margeaux points to the pile. He nods again, smiling. He seems to shoo away a wasp, swings with a mean forehand, followed by a serve. Nosy Susan Erkenbridge next door thinks "he's a little hot tamale, isn't he?" possibly referring to the fact that he at the time was shirtless in the broil of summer. Vulgar Parris has gone even further: "What I wouldn't do to get him in the sack. Probably uncut Bratwurst . . . yum!"

It is not long before Margeaux crosses the threshold into Designer Sportswear and is swooning into the phone to thank Drexel. The Lanvin is less fabulous on than the photo led her to hope, but the surprises — a bold aubergine Narciso Rodriguez sculpted to her lean curves, a silver Jil Sander chemise that funnels slightly at the thigh — win the day.

"You've thrown my budget out the window. I have no right to ask, but could this be a celebrity loan or product placement? And if not, with your discount, how much for . . . oh, I can't even decide."

As she is peeling out of the Narciso, Drexel's text says the discount equals $3,250 for all, but "No celeb or pp, and no returns! If you do, I could lose my job. Should that happen, I'll jab the voodoo doll I keep of you right between the eyes."

What an awful thing to say; Margeaux is superstitious and he knows it.

After a brief stop in Designer Footwear and two pairs of Manolo Blahnik pumps on sale, the tally is a little shy of $4,700. Margeaux is resigned — she must, this is a career investment. Besides, she has been good — how auspicious that she did not cross the five-thousand threshold! Long gone are the days when she could think only of herself, without a financial care in the world.

As she is handing her credit card over for the second time in less than an hour, Drexel texts: "I know you. After the taping, return the Weitzmans or Blahniks or whatever you just bought. Wear only on the set. Swear?"

"Swear!" Margeaux rejoins, resigned. It is embarrassing. Unlike when they first met, Margeaux does not feel young or free — qualities that framed their friendship in gilt and shimmer, in what were truly the halcyon days. From Guadeloupe and with a Jorge-like glow, Drexel goes back to Margeaux's undergraduate days at Wellesley College, where she majored in media studies. An architecture student, Drexel attended Boston College, where he dandied around in ascots and spats and a Caribbean-British-tinged accent. They met on a cheap flight to Manhattan, to put their exotic looks into runway service during Fashion Week. Although they bonded and kept in touch, they did not become best "girlfriends" until he took a job at Saks Fifth Avenue in Cincinnati. After a harrowing experience as a crime TV reporter in Chicago, Margeaux returned to the city for a plum features-editor-role on *Today in Cincinnati*, arriving just in time to help then-ailing Mutti manage after brain cancer surgery. Neither had the patience for boredom, and their balms — a quick dash to shop in New York or Los Angeles or a long weekend in Paris or London or Italy — held it at bay. But after two years, Drexel moved on, first to Dallas and then New York, leaving broken hearts behind like old clothing. Margeaux still wonders "what if," and often wishes she had been as smart, to put career first, leading men on short leashes and leaving certain obligations — read Mutti — behind. If the co-host position at *Today in Cincinnati* had not offered her a spotlight, she might have packed herself and Mutti up for good.

Love him, but Drexel is an "I told you so." His prescience about her life as Mrs. Griffin Jewells Saunders II was uncannily accurate. Having flown into town on work-related business, he was with her the night she was introduced to Griffin, at a party at the mayor's. Griffin's cool, reserved, even formal six-foot-four presence inspired Drexel to comment at the time: "Could he be more Episcopalian?" Intrigued, Margeaux did not understand, but perfectly got what followed: "Margeaux, I doubt he's enough man to handle you. Something is up with him, and not necessarily in that department." She sipped her wine, batted her eyes over the scene and spectrum of men, from black to white, Greek to Latin, old to young, flabby to fit. Whether too Episcopalian or not, from the media she knew Griffin Jewells Saunders II stood above them all — handsome, self-made, rich, a cable-industry pioneer. Just what Margeaux loved. The city deputy mayor was a friend and brought Griffin over to her, describing him as a future mayor of Cincinnati. After cocktail laughter and small talk, Griffin was no more interesting than any of the other guests. But later in the evening he placed himself squarely in her mind. She saw him coming toward her and allowed him to separate her from Drexel with a touch of his hand and "May I have a word with you?" With an angelic look in his eyes that bordered on reverence, he said, "I have to tell you something. You probably don't remember but we met before. You were probably all of nine. It was at Lakeside Methodist Church, Easter 1975. You were sitting between your father and mother, and I was with my mother and grandmother, and we shook hands. You were wearing this yellow lace dress and white Maryjanes, and there were white ribbons in your hair. You said, 'Enchanté, monsieur.'" "It's incredible that you remember that," Margeaux replied. "How could I forget the prettiest girl I ever saw? You'll laugh, but I thought, I'm gonna marry her someday. The fancy of an infatuated boy." Margeaux was rarely if ever speechless; she had the feeling he would never lie about such things. "But what I really wanted to tell you is that I admired your father. My mother used to take our good clothes to his dry cleaners once a year, at Eastertime, and she thought the world of him and he was always nice to me. I wanted to be successful like him, he was my role model." Touched tears encircled Margeaux's eyes, filling, then spilling over, so caught off guard was she.

Fairy tales have such beginnings.

Several months later, Margeaux confided to Drexel, "I think he's exactly the kind of man who can handle me."

His reply: "Uhn-uhn, don't say you weren't warned."

In hindsight: Knowing that her first fateful encounter with Griffin had occurred in church, when he was eighteen and she less than half his age, should have alarmed her, not made her feel moved and honored.

Now, entering the world of cosmetics at Saks, Margeaux senses the damp of a cloud of gloom. Life would be so much better if only she had no money worry, if only she could just keep the purchases she loves. That she must return them only fuels the obsession, and so the cycle goes.

If only Griffin were here . . .

Not even the new sheer high-shine YSL crème lipstick glistens enough to bring her attention back to beauty. Batting back tears, she is nearing the Shu Uemura counter, blind to the posters of mascara and foundation models pouting for her notice, when she hears "Excuse me, Mrs. Saunders."

Margeaux is soon looking into the paperclip eyes of a unnervingly handsome black-and- Asian-mixed kid, reminiscent of the iconic male-model Tyson Beckford, with hair coiled like a long tentacle along his chest. He seems familiar in another way, but she cannot put her finger on how or why. Nearly half of Roger Bacon High School turned up for a memorial service for Jewells, but she cannot place this seemingly unforgettably handsome boy among them. And even afterward, when she could manage the despair and had made contact with all of Jewells' friends to discover what her stepson might have been up to, he was not among them, and none of them mentioned anyone like him as Jewells' friend.

"I just want to say I'm sorry for what happened to Jewells and Mr. Saunders."

"Thank you." She puzzles over his curious looks, what crash of cultures, genes and chromosomes could produce a face like that. "You are?"

"I'm LoQuan. We've never actually met each other."

"Yes." She lifts her sunglasses, just as a burbling of tears erupts. "Excuse me, I'm in a hurry."

"Look, I ain't trying to upset you. I seent you in the store before, and I just wanna say, we didn't know about the pictures. I figured y'all was like, what Jewells and me was up to, but we didn't know. We was tricked."

"Tricked?"

"Yeah, they hid the cameras. Me and Jewells, we wouldna done it if we knew."

Then, it comes to her. The male figure running down the driveway the night Jewells had been been beaten up. What she thought had been a jacket hanging off his shoulders could have been hair.

Pulling her sunglasses down and gathering her wits, the dormant journalist in Margeaux shakily reemerges, as if she were suddenly stranded by a teleprompter. "I did wonder. What did you expect they would do?"

"Pay us, and that's it."

"You obviously didn't know who you were dealing with." A tightening sensation travels up through her throat, ending in her mouth.

"Yeah, but the po-po busted them and we got ours, so it's all good, right?"

"Po-po?"

"Police." He grins, making him even more beautiful. "Yeah, but hey . . . like I was saying, I seent you a couple times now, and I wanna do Jewells a solid by letting you know that. He wadn't no thug."

"I thank you. I'm surprised I never met you before, given you were good friends."

"Well, yeah, it woulda happened, I guess."

One thing is clear: If he was the person she saw that night, then he also assaulted Jewells. Margeaux decides to let the solution reveal itself at another time.

Lifting her glasses, "I've been a little sad today and my eyes are puffy."

He smiles, flirtatiously. "I never seent you on television, but you are even finer in person."

"You work here?"

"Yeah, in the stockroom."

"I'll look for you next time I'm here."

Lowering her sunglasses, she thanks him, turns away certain of his lingering stare.

In the car, after checking her eye makeup, she phones cousin Mitchell at the D.A.'s office: "I won't bore you with how I am today. But something just happened at Saks I thought you should know about." She relates the incident in detail and what she remembered from the night Jewells was beaten up.

"What kind of photos?"

"Apparently of an incriminating kind . . . if the po-po — the police — were involved, it sounds like they were caught doing something they shouldn't have been doing. Typical Jewells stuff."

"What do you want me to do?"

"I don't know, Mitchell, how about checking him out? His name is LoQuan. He didn't give his last name, and I didn't think to ask."

"You don't know it was him."

"I do. I just have a feeling about him, that somehow he had something to do with what happened to Griffin and Jewells. Just see what comes up, please?"

He promises and will be in touch, one way or another.

3

Nearly all the women Margeaux knows at her then-level in television are childless. The notable exceptions have all-powerful nannies. Or mothers.

As a rule, Mutti handles crying children in the middle of night. Her room is next to the twins, with the boys just across the hall. Margeaux has never liked her beauty sleep interrupted, nor her calm or meditation. The master suite is at the far end of the hall, with a sitting room that buffers against infantile tantrums and tears. Griffin preferred children quiet however the effect could be achieved, and Margeaux agreed.

The first cries penetrate Margeaux at about three a.m. She rouses, eyes guarded in an Natura Bissé age-erasing mask, and waits. It seems a false alarm. Five minutes later, more cries reach her, and then the ringing cellphone. Margeaux pulls herself awake and pads down the hall. The girls.

"Mutti, wake up!" Margeaux pushes her finger into the flabby arm. "Don't you hear the baby's crying?"

"I'm so tired. I can hardly move. You'll have to manage without me."

"But . . ."

Margeaux fetches a febrile Alyssa and carries her across

the hall to Mutti, worried she will catch a cold or some sort of infection.

"I think she's sick." She wishes she had grabbed a mask and rubber gloves first.

"The playground today. The Goldsteins' boy has something . . . he may have given it to us all."

"That's not good. Not good at all." Margeaux observes Mutti's unusual pale doughy face and is frightened the brain cancer has returned. Who will manage the children?

"What about the boys?" Mutti says.

"They're asleep."

"That's good."

"Can I get you some tea or something else to drink?"

"If you would just heat up a glass of water with some lemon and honey."

"Of course."

"And some Tylenol."

"Okay."

". . . and, I've got some Tums somewhere. Hand me my purse."

An irked Margeaux goes to retrieve agitated Ariel. The younger of the twins immediately begins pulling at the age-erasing mask, taking its corners into her mouth. Margeaux is about to hand the child off to Mutti, but thinks better of it. "Let me get her back to sleep."

"You might not want to put her down in her room all

fussy as she is."

"But you're not well enough to take her."

"Why don't you?"

There is a small, evident visible panic, for Mutti says, "Just take your time dear, I'm not going anywhere."

Against Mutti's advice, a defensive Margeaux carries Ariel back to her room, plops a bottle in the child's mouth. Passing the boys' room, she sees Percy is wide awake.

"Mommy, I don't feel well."

"Oh, darling, just a minute."

His impatience is expressed with near house-penetrating crying. The nursery station is equipped with everything from formula to first aid, but none of these things are what Percy needs. With Ariel on her hip, she runs to her own room, bringing back the new issue of French *Vogue*. Percy naturally calms to whimpers as he rifles through the pages, but shrieks the moment Margeaux leaves. In his red Polo robe, he follows Margeaux and Ariel to the kitchen. As his baby sister is installed in the high chair, he points out that it is the wrong high chair and babies are stupid.

"That's not nice, Percy."

"Why? It's not her chair. That's the other stupid baby's."

Margeaux is microwaving a cup of water when Percy goes over to the back door and picks up an envelope on the floor.

"Look, Mommy."

"Give me that."

"No."

"Percy, it's three o'clock in the morning. Mommy will be a wreck and so will Percy. Little boys get bags under their eyes too. And little boys don't go to galas like Mommy does."

Percy acknowledges this by handing her the envelope. On it is scribbled "Mrs. Sanders" — even Jorge knows how to spell Saunders. Inside is a Polaroid of a black sleeveless tuxedo dress on a hanger. On the back it says, "Ralph Lauren Black Label. Your size. I know you want it. LoQuan, 513-235-7632."

Surely stolen merchandise — from Saks? Ralph Lauren is not Margeaux's taste at all, even if that particular dress sings a love song. What kind of person steals ready-to-wear? What kind of person buys it stolen? Perhaps this is the kind of trickery he and Jewells were involved in?

With Ariel at the hip and Percy on her heels, Margeaux runs to the study and checks the security cameras, wondering if she will need to rehire the service to guard the property. The motion detector is off, but the video is rolling. The feed appears on the computer screen. She scans backward three hours approximately, before she comes across a hazy image that surely is LoQuan. . . coming up the driveway, attempting to enter the carriage house, and then crossing the yard to leave the envelope at the back door.

The nerve!

What she needs is the absolute proof of a face shot. On the property there are several cameras, but Margeaux realizes that she does not know their positions or the focus at which they are shooting. She will contact the security company about camera placement.

Percy says, "Who is that?"

"A personal shopper."

"What's that?"

"Somebody who buys for you because they know exactly what you like."

Back at the kitchen, Margeaux adds lemon and honey and rushes upstairs with Mutti's drink in one hand, Ariel still at the hip and Percy puttering close behind.

"Here you are, as ordered," says Margeaux, noting that Alyssa lies beside her, smiling and flushed.

"It'll make you feel better, Oma," adds Percy.

"Yes, it will, and thank you both." Mutti sips as Percy climbs in bed beside her.

Margeaux and Ariel do as well, the adults as large bookends to the little ones. She does not recall sleeping or the moment she too became febrile, only that she awoke in a state.

The pediatrician cannot make an immediate house call, and Margeaux is outraged.

Mutti is the voice of reason. "Calm down, dear. We'll all survive. It's just a bug."

"Yes, I know." Margeaux thinks of the creepy cicadas. "I

need antibiotics before it gets worse."

"I think we'll survive a few more hours."

"You know best."

"Mothers do."

The occasional jabs are just. Margeaux takes it in stride. Not because she is a poor mother, but because Mutti is a great mother — Margeaux herself is the proof.

"But darling, I do think we need someone, a younger girl who can keep up with the children. I can't do it anymore, it's too much for me. Four young children are more than a notion."

"I know, Mutti." Margeaux wistfully glimpses herself in the mirror. "You're not young."

"Unless you want to handle them in the evenings."

Margeaux does not dignify the question. "Maybe Jorge can recommend a girl."

She does not suspect laziness when Mutti claims she is too weak to make breakfast. Mutti is only fifty-four, having had Margeaux at age 18, but does appear uncharacteristically senior-citizen-like and fragile. Other than the thyroid that has plumped her, and the brain tumor that was successfully removed, she has been in good health. What gives?

Margeaux phones the security company about the cameras and is promised that someone will come out today. And after a quick phone-message update about the new LoQuan development to cousin Mitchell, she rallies enough energy for cereal for the boys and the girls, and corrals everyone into the playroom. Fortunately the daybed is comfortable enough for Mutti to lie on. Margeaux and the sick children soldier on with games and lots of TV and lots of crying. At some point, Percy suggests they play TV interview, and Margeaux modifies the game to focus on her different outfits.

Late afternoon arrives before the pediatrician bothers to show up with his apologies, antibiotic prescriptions and optimistic prognoses. Jorge is more helpful, and cheaper. The boys like tacos and the girls guacamole despite grossed-out faces. Margeaux and Mutti make do with tostadas. By five in the afternoon, a pretty brown girl Jorge claims is his cousin is taking orders from Mutti. The children all instantly adore the sparkly eyed America. After initial confusion as to whether she is also "the United States," Percy seems bewitched by her chic, impossibly straight hair and hypotenuse bangs. Margeaux is pleased too, in sync with her brood, and admiring of the ever-accommodating Jorge. Turns out, he even knows where the other video cameras are. A fast study, he figures out how to access them on the computer in Griffin's study. Together they watch LoQuan in action. Jorge does not remember seeing him before, but confesses he had witnessed Jewells smoking marijuana with friends from school and a blond girl — "her name Sophie" — who would come by for sex. Margeaux had interviewed Sophie and did not imagine the extent of their relationship, and now blushes at the thought. Jorge smiles.

It had been a mistake letting Jewells stay in the carriage house alone.

America costs less than a so-so daily manicure. It angers Margeaux that she will have to haggle with tight-fisted Therosine for thirty dollars a day. It would be pointless to argue that Griffin promised their children would not want for anything. She is glad she did not fill all the bedrooms with his sire, as per his wishes.

Mutti would be much better at handling Therosine. The women like each other, and naturally each adored Griffin and, she suspects, are in agreement he could have done better in his choice of a wife. A strange thing to say about Mutti, but nevertheless true. Like Drexel before her, Mutti had warned Margeaux about marrying Griffin, although not because she would be disappointed: "Sweetheart, he is a wonderful man, but do you really want the life he offers?"

"Of course I do, don't be ridiculous. He owns a cable empire."

"He wants a wife and mother to his children."

"I can be that."

"You've never wanted to be that. You're reacting to a career setback."

"I'm not. Not completely anyway . . . this is the time." She hesitated to add that Griffin was agreeable to the idea that

Mutti could live with them, in fact saying he intended that his own mother would have had she not passed way. "Griffin and I are in agreement on nearly everything. It's a good partnership, we want the same things."

"Are you really sure, Margeaux? Because it's not just the children you will have, it's Jewells, too."

"Yes, I'm sure. And I get along with him just fine. It'll take time."

"Think seriously about it."

"I have. I am. Griffin can handle him. He'll have to."

"And you're going to be a stay-at-home mom?"

"No, of course not, I have every intention of having a career. He's fine with it."

"I don't think Griffin cares a hoot about your career or TV personality."

Nonsense.

And yet Margeaux had sensed the same. After several dates, Griffin had brought her to see the house. The Jane Austen *Pride and Prejudice* moment she described to *60 Minutes* Ed Bradley was complicated.

With unusual bluntness, as they admired the elegant architecture, Griffin said, "There are six bedrooms here, and only two are now in use. How many children do you want?"

"Certainly not a litter." A burst of silly laughter belied the pressure she felt. She had not mentioned her recent firing from *Today in Cincinnati*. Despite the media chatter about her abrupt departure and the shakeup on the show, she rewrote her professional sputter, spinning her sudden state of flux as more a tussle between her career and desire to settle down and have a family. Of course, Griffin was no fool; if anything, her version reflected her inability to say to herself she had been fired. The end came swiftly and suddenly. No interviews were requested of her, no job offers came.

"I think you know how I feel. That I have chosen this house pretty much says it all."

"It says other things, like you got the price you were looking for."

"True."

"And I don't know how you feel. Why don't you enlighten me, Griffin?"

"You do know how I feel."

"I want you to tell me."

"Well . . . honestly, as I told you six months ago at the mayor's party, I've known since we were kids that I would marry you. You've been in my heart since that day in church. I'd do anything for you, you can count on me."

"Is this a proposal?"

"More a statement of fact and declaration of intention."

"It's sort of strange to me that you swing in two different directions at the same time. So sure of yourself and yet you hesitate."

"I only mean that when we're ready, we can settle

down." He reached for her hand. "I've dated more than a few women, all of them wanted to get me to the finish line, but I always remembered you. I think I pledged my heart to you. You alone. Margeaux Chenault."

"Pledged?"

"Devotion."

"Are you sure that's what you mean? You haven't asked me to marry you. You've sort of backed into the issue."

"Well, I was never good at parallel parking." He chuckled and Margeaux pretended to.

As if he were afraid of what she might say, he looked away, but soon returned, resolved. "Seriously, Margeaux, you haven't spoken of me with the kind of conviction I show you. And you haven't told me if what I offer is what you want in marriage, or even if you want me at all."

"I'm here. There's no one else. I do."

"Do what?"

"Want what you want."

"So you don't love me?"

There was no way around this sticking point. The men who came before him should not factor into this moment, and yet the lessons they taught her pointed fingers, warning "he's a jerk," "men are all jerks." But of course, he was not like any of her past relationships, measuring up in every sense, if not excessively then exceedingly. Even in passion, he was thoughtful, considerate, gentle, accommodating . . . the very opposite of passion, really. To her surprise, he seemed to enjoy most being dominated, pinned down, with her on top. This suited Margeaux's alpha side just fine. Only once had she been a submissive; her then-lover was a dominant sports star figure, and it had ended badly. In hindsight, excessive relinquishing of control and indulgence in wantonness invariably ruins a girl, for the obsessive ascent to frenzied ecstasy is almost certainly followed by a precipitous drop. Nothing worse than a man with an unequal, nonexclusive passion for you, posturing over you, toying with your heartstrings, spellbinding your clitoris, a hand ready to clutch your throat.

What she admired most: Griffin Jewells Saunders II struck her as a paragon of the modern black man, his education and accomplishments standing for something that did credit to both his character and his race. Before ever understanding the politics of her parentage, Margeaux had been a daddy's girl — and in every way proud of it, boasting of the beautifying black genes in her blood, when she could have passed for white or Latina. She could do her father's memory no harm by marrying a man in his image. Surely he would approve.

But none of the things she admired about him tallied up to I Love You. Margeaux was unconcerned, noting that she had picked an ideal man *not* to be in love with. A certain power firmly in one's hands is a good thing.

"Griffin, you have my heart. I trust you, and I adore you. And I also believe you and I would make a great team."

Where there may have been disappointment, agreement prevailed. Griffin offered. "I feel the same. We would make a great team."

"You are the only man I've dated in the last decade that I would even consider marrying."

"Really. That's inspiring."

"Yes, I'm twenty-nine, you are thirty-seven, we are not getting any younger and this is the perfect time to start a family, I suppose."

"That's right."

The deal-breaker: Margeaux mapped out a scenario in which she would be resuming her career after having a couple of children. He did not object, and in fact added that her career could be a boost to his prospects as an eventual candidate for mayor of Cincinnati.

"You're serious about it. Why?"

"Because I have something to contribute. I know I don't have one-of-the-boys personality, but I'm honest and could run this city well. And I really want to contribute."

"That's exciting. That's noble." Even as she said it, she wondered if he was pliable enough, deceitful and double-dealing enough, for a life in politics. "My gallant Griffin."

"My beautiful Margeaux. You would be an asset in every way, and not just in the love and happiness you bring to my life."

Then it came: "I do love you, Griffin. . . how could I not? I do."

Silver wedding bells heralded a spectacular event that captivated the social set of the city — some highlighting her daring pairing of a backless silver Zandra Rhodes cocktail dress and a tulle Vera Wang veil that trailed some five dazzling feet behind her, carrying the romance and the promise of love. Perfection truly would have been achieved if only had her father been there to hand her off. Her cousin the famed actor Raymond St. Jacques flew in and performed the task with aplomb. That Chief was the best man ensured a clean sweep of all the society-page headlines and talk at parties.

All seemed right from the start.

The one wild card was Jewells. Whatever concerns she had about him dissipated after his adorable performance as ring carrier, and in the fullness of marital felicity and mothering warmth of Mutti's bosom, the boy seemed to settle down. The newlyweds were ripe with fertility and pregnant days after exchanging vows. Percy's birth seemed to awaken a meanness in Jewells that, a year and a half later, came to dominate his personality with the arrival of Fletcher. Griffin necessarily kept him on leash, carving out time for just the two of them.

After five years of marriage, Margeaux had no reason

to regret her decision. Her plans to relaunch her career were on schedule. With Percy already in kindergarten, Fletcher on his way to day school, and Mutti fully in charge, she was ramping up for her return to television. She began making more frequent guest appearances on local shows, chatting about her life in motherhood and marriage, fashion and beauty, all her favorite topics. Then, during a taping of *Sunday in Cincinnati*, she felt that tiny-feet patter in the soul that precedes the pregnancy test, and was all but ready to schedule an abortion. That same evening, while lying in bed together, Griffin said, "I know that look, we're having another child." At first she pretended not to have noticed — and she would know such a thing, but she was on birth control. All the same, Griffin sped to the drugstore for a pregnancy test kit. The result was confirmed by a panicked visit to the doctor, news the equivalent of binding Margeaux's feet. Mutti reassured her they would be fine, she would handle everything. That was before a stethoscope and sonogram revealed two heartbeats in squirming dollop-sized amphibious bodies. The joy was all Griffin's, and Margeaux suspected his goal all along was to chain her to the house for another five years. Not long after the twins' birth, he began part-time living and working in Washington, just when she needed him most, if for no reason than to manage Jewells, whose slide into a troubled teen was well under way.

How convenient!

Negotiating with Therosine about America can wait.

The technician from the security company both affords her a stronger sense of safety and compounds financial problems. He installs a high-powered zoom-in digital camera on the veranda, its powerful eye able to take in the full length of the driveway and garage level of the carriage house, offering images at such high resolution that even close-ups with enough detail for a skin diagnosis are possible. While hardly the cheapest, the $6,200 choice was the price of security for The Griffin Jewells Saunders II family.

Newly bitten by the buying bug would normally make shopping seem inevitable. Instead a wiser Margeaux phones Parris, with the photograph of the Ralph Lauren tuxedo dress pinched between fingers.

"What would you say about a sleeveless tuxedo dress?"

"For Magda? Are you kidding? Too *Harper's Bazaar*; we want *Cosmo*. Animal prints."

"No, no animal prints. I won't do it."

"They may make you, you know. It's their image they care about, not yours."

"Drexel sent over this amazing wine-colored Narciso, maybe I'll just wear it. Percy will never forgive me if I don't."

"Drexel, huh? Well, I would listen to Percy over Miss Saks Fifth Avenue any day!"

"Yes, well, *Mr.* Saks Fifth Avenue knows my taste and what looks good on me, and can arrange product placements and celebrity loans."

"You've been warned."

More to change the subject, Margeaux says, "I can get that dress I mentioned before, if I want. But I think it's hot."

"Maybe, maybe not. Hard for me to say without seeing it."

"I mean stolen, it's probably stolen."

"You, you would wear shoplifted ready-to-wear?"

"No, of course not. I was at Saks yesterday, and I ran into this exotic young man; he was a friend of Jewells from school. It was strange, too strange to even get into. Anyway, this morning, there was this Polaroid of the dress slipped under the kitchen door. Percy found it. Of course it's been in bed with him."

"How do you know it's stolen?"

"The note on it pretty much says it's for sale. It includes the young man's name and a number. He works for the store, but this smells like hot merchandise, not that I know anything about hot merchandise."

"A shoplifting ring, how fun. That's just the kind of thing people want to know about. Maybe you should buy the dress, just to find out about the theft ring, and then you could help bring the whole organization down?"

"And have to enter a witness protection program and move to Alaska!"

Later, Margeaux emails Drexel about the tuxedo dress, and soon after comes his response: Yves Saint Laurent did the tuxedo first, three decades ago. The value of the Ralph Lauren reimagining is "$7,200 and five years in jail for receiving stolen merchandise, so, if it's hot, don't."

For publicity's sake, as well all manner of personal reasons — most TV personalities align themselves with du-jour causes that keep their calendars full. A high-profile marriage similarly seeks benefits for its beneficence.

As befitting their status in Cincinnati, Mr. and Mrs. Griffin Jewells Saunders II always maintained a hectic social schedule, even with five children and the demands of his various enterprises, including, early on, the burgeoning Washington career. He sat on the boards of two local companies and a national one, and helped spearhead the funding of the new sickle-cell anemia research center, on the campus of the Cincinnati General Hospital, in tribute to a close cousin who died of the disease at twenty-six. Her obligations included the boards of the city's musical hall and art museum, and a charity that helped to keep teen mothers informed about prenatal care and raising children — roles in which, granted, she had no expertise, but ones nevertheless she felt at ease talking about with the teens and even better, to the public to raise awareness. More often, the in-demand couple compared and coordinated schedules than meaningfully discussed their respective causes, for, as he made clear from the beginning, the mayor's office was their ultimate destination, not the little "pesky stops" along the way.

The past year, Margeaux has avoided public life altogether. So devastated, so unsure of herself, she could not bear public glare. Keeping up appearances was pointless, as was clinging to obligations out of fear of disappearing from the A-list. Almost from the moment she had heard about Griffin's death — from Chief, who had been contacted by the FBI, Georgia and Cincinnati authorities, he claimed — she had kept expecting that at any moment her husband would chuck Washington and come home, even after the bits and pieces of him were collected and encoffined. The irreality, the senselessness of it all — took apart the put-together Margeaux. On the bright side, mourning provided the perfect respite from the genteel hurly-burly, a kind of lugubrious molting in which she could take stock and contemplate what went wrong, until ready for takeoff in a new life.

Mostly, she missed making entrances and exits . . . the unbreakable habits of a high-fashion runway model.

In the spirit of her butterfly-like reemergence, Margeaux

has said yes to an invitation to the gala of the Taft Museum. The institution was an eponymous gift by Cincinnati's equivalent of political royalty, a line descended from William Howard Taft, the 27th president of the United States, in 1873. Griffin sat on the institution's board, despite Margeaux's deep ambivalence about the Taft family Nevertheless, she has cinematic memories of herself flowing in Armani Privé, in vintage Norell, and in an original Hubert de Givenchy (thanks to Drexel!).

How stunning would the tuxedo dress look descending the cascade of stairs into the museum lobby!

Margeaux now curses Ralph Lauren and LoQuan — as much as she does probate, Jewells, Therosine and her late husband — rummaging through her suite-sized closet and coming up short. Given the impossible situation, what should she do?

Picking up an outfit at Saks would have been tempting fate, although at Saks Margeaux's actual purchases far exceed her returns.

The purchase-to-returns ratio is reversed at Neiman Marcus, where she heads instead. There, she quickly fixates on a sleeveless black silk-satin three-quarter-length sheath from Valentino Haute Couture, $9,300. Brigitta the saleswoman knows Margeaux from her television days and has never questioned her returns. Naturally, it is the sort of dress photographers love, but then so is Margeaux's beauty.

Ducking the cameras will not be enough; she knows she will have to return it at once, before images of her appear in the society pages. Saleswomen like Brigitta read the society pages, scouting for clients. Worse still, the Magda interview will tape late the next morning. In a sure sign of her clear thinking, she writes in her notebook's margins: "Mention gala on the show only if asked. No elitism!"

Her date, Thornton Childs, is a scion of the lordly family. The Taft Museum, a charming mansion modeled in the style of their White House, was the family home once upon a time. Set on what was a plantation, the structure resembles no less than a mini version of Tara, of *Gone with the Wind* fame, or the ubiquitous one on the Colonel Sanders fried chicken box.

Margeaux and Thornton go back to their youth at Summit Country Day School. There had been an infatuation, a boy-meets-girl moment that must inevitably stand as a symbol of the shared history that binds white and black together. Her father's simple inquiry about the boy whose face was inside her locket became a pointed story of the institution of slavery. According to him, many of his relatives were once property of Taft descendents. An allegation of this sort should not have been shocking, given the region's history: The slave state Kentucky and free state Ohio were shackled to each other with only the Ohio River between them. Their tense coupling was borne out in a riotous history, involving kidnapping, bounty hunts, raids, rapes and murders before and after the Civil War, and right up to the Civil Rights Act of 1963. Practically every day, the local news still teemed with stories of violence and protests.

This polarized world seemed an alternate universe. Margeaux had been a sheltered girl, with her Latinate beauty and privileged life of private schools and upper middle-class neighborhood. Daddy's girl or not, she accused her father of fabricating the bondage-ties bit to break up her relationship with Thornton. History could not be unwritten, and the proof of the accusation needed only to be pulled from shelves of Taft family history encased at the downtown public library.

Crushed by her first crush.

Though very young, it had occurred to Margeaux that their relationship might have stood as an ideal symbol of racial equality. Her father made hash of the thought: "Your mother and I will introduce ourselves to his family and you'll see just how ideal your relationship is."

Today, Thornton is recently divorced, although not because of another woman, or a man for that matter, according to Parris' sources. There are three children and a solvent financial services company. Always good to do due diligence before sticking the toe in or withdrawing altogether.

Griffin and Thornton were acquainted; the Tafts and the Saunderses rank on similar A-lists in town. Margeaux never disclosed to her spouse her ninth grade fling with Thornton, and doubts seriously Thornton confided in his wife, Bunny, a Princeton graduate with gray eyes encircled with stress. At the time of Griffin's death, the condolences of the Tafts arrived with a bouquet of leaning tan lilies and bursting white peonies. The arrangement was nearly identical to those sent by everyone else on the A-list. Margeaux noted the card was signed "All my love, Thorn." He still maintains he was in love when they were kids.

What does a twelve-year-old know about love?

Margeaux doubted it was of the undying kind . . . and at any rate, it was unshared.

Earlier, stubborn Percy was fixated on the red Donna Karan, refusing to see how the Valentino would complement Margeaux's sunkissed skin. A teachable moment: Margeaux explained she would rather wear the sleeveless tuxedo dress in the Polaroid, however impossible. Percy did not buy her explanation . . . any more than Margeaux would stolen merchandise.

Now, Mutti and the children hole up in the playroom on the second floor until she leaves, lest she be distracted and exhausted. Percy's anger and shrieks will certainly travel downstairs, interrupting Thornton's deserved experience of Margeaux's entrance. She exits the house just as he is turning into the driveway, and puts herself in a model state of mind, imagining how she will be seen. The arrival of a beautiful woman is always exhilarating. Margeaux still finds the runway thrilling: The girls come and the girls go, arms following swinging hips, insteps at the brink of snapping.

The gravel driveway adds elegance to the house, but is hostile to high heels. Just in case, Margeaux has switched on the porte-cochère lights, offering Thornton a directional beacon. He pulls up just as Margeaux begins her catwalk saunter: flowing and gliding and glimmering down the three steps in the burgundy sunset. Unknown to her until she is in front of the sports car, a two-seater Mercedes Roadster, the children and Mutti are perched in the window and waving at Thornton. She is annoyed that he appears to pay more attention to them. In an instant he is door-side, gallantly waiting.

"Goddess Margeaux!"

"Thornton."

Margeaux artfully aims to kiss cheeks, lingering long enough to envelop him in Guerlain perfume and withdrawing only when his hand inches along her satin waist, the naughty boy. His glance toward her décolletage provokes issues of memory versus desire.

"The gods smile on me tonight. Sweet sixteen."

"Oh, Thornton, we're practically old people now."

"Hardly," he says, exuding a whiff of gin. "Not you anyway. Not beautiful Margeaux . . . goddamn! My father said you were glorious."

"'Glorious negress' is what he said."

"He didn't mean anything by it, you know — that was

just his generation talking."

"The greatest generation."

"You could captivate even the most ardent racist."

"I'm relieved . . . Enough about our past, and please, you don't need to cheer me up with all the flattery. Really, it's not necessary, really."

"Margeaux, I mean it," he says, swinging the two-seater out of the driveway in a way that flings pebbles about and stirs up a small dust cloud. Jorge will ask about it.

"It's you cheering me up by coming out. It's been a rough year for both of us — much worse for you, of course. I've been nostalgic a lot these days. You know? I want to be Thorn, not Thornton — Thornton has toxic waste to deal with all the goddamn time. Thornton means feeling suffocated, choked by the hands of life. Thorn wants to breathe again. Thorn was all party and fun. Remember, Margeaux? Remember Thorn?"

The facts: Margeaux always hated "Thorn," refusing to call him by his nickname. He was not so much fun as the rugby-handsome son of a name-brand family. Rather than a telltale locket, Thornton's sister Zoë had blabbed to the Taft family about Margeaux, then had relayed to Margeaux their response, emphasizing that while "you might be very 'comely' my father says your 'daddy is a coon, period, exclamation point.'" Neither she nor Margeaux knew what a coon was, nor that Thornton's father would become a congressman a few years later. Nor that stopping the young lovers would prove as easy as as shipping Thornton off to a private academy somewhere in the Pacific Northwest. Unsurprisingly, as happens in such cases, absence bound them in ways being in each other's presence never would have. Three years of longing later, a chance encounter in the summer of their junior year in high school ended in a failed condom that gave Margeaux existential worries up to the day of the abortion.

The senseless cruelty of the congressman's comments scarred Margeaux's psyche with the knife blade of reality. About her looks, Margeaux had only ever heard how beautiful she was, so it was impossible to understand how anyone could see in her the black girl they so reviled, or the hated coon in her wonderful, adoring father. The whole point of attending a private school was to be spared the trauma of being of mixed-race parentage in the cold, cruel world of public education in a city that was never far from its slavery roots.

Yet for Margeaux, the eternal question did and does still run deep: What is the right shade of beautiful? Margeaux the pageant runner-up, Miss Ohio 1977; Margeaux, winner, Miss Cincinnati 1975. Margeaux the runway, showroom and print model. Margeaux the weathergirl and co-host of *Today in Cincinnati*. Margeaux, Mrs. Griffin Jewells Saunders II.

Past is past, and revenge is sweet. All the various Margeauxs have prevailed, beauty intact — perhaps fortified by her triumphs over petty adversity.

Not so with Thornton. No longer handsome — grief?
bitterness? alcoholism? — he is now the opposite of it.
Glamourous Margeaux is riding shotgun to a balding, bulbous
version of the prince charming she once knew. Still, she
entertains the idea of an encore romp just to see how it would
be, satisfying needs long neglected, assuming it is possible to
find inner, deeper beauty in the absence of the outer . . . and
whether this wreck of a man was worth the bother.

"Our lives are too complicated," he says, turning lips
tilted to send his burp out the driver's side. Stirred into the
smell of strong gin is Vachetta leather and Marlboro smoke,
creating an aftershave of blunt scent. "You know what I
mean?"

"I was surprised to hear you divorced," she says,
wanting the dirt, only sanitized. "I hope it wasn't too
painful?"

"Blood-sucking leech! But let's not talk about her."

"How are the children?"

"I don't want to talk about them either. Tell me about
you? How've you been coping?

"It's been very difficult," she says. "I was considering
going back into television."

"Never saw you on that show."

"That's encouraging."

"I don't give a hoot about what's going on today or any

lousy day in Cincinnati."

"Tell you the truth, I don't either."

"What's there to know? A bunch of backward right-wing retards are running the goddamn place on the high level, and the backward black people shooting each other up for blue jeans and Nikes on the low level. It's damn awful, Margeaux. I know what's wrong with the white people, but what's going on the heads of black people, Margeaux?"

"Thornton," says Margeaux, "I wouldn't know anything about that."

"That boy of yours, Jewells, wasn't he a handful? Wasn't he in jail?"

"No, he wasn't. There was a day in juvenile detention, but that's not jail. And for the record, he was Griffin's son, not mine."

Saying it made her feel heartless and the need to amend: "I loved him, but he wasn't my child. We had problems bonding. He was very difficult child, anyway, and a worse teen. Maybe I was a little immature in the beginning, I don't know . . . " Her eyes water before she realizes what is about to happen. "But . . . "

"Kids are all screwed up . . . all of them, and guess what, it's always your fault."

"Thornton, Thorn, I didn't come out tonight to go deeper into gloom. I came out to have a good time."

"I'm just a dumb stick in the mud."

"So far you're not, but you might be getting there fast." She squeezes his hand on the console. "Seriously Thorn, there's something I need your advice on."

Explaining the tie-ups binding her in place, she leaves out the more incriminating intricacies — her husband's fraud, tax evasion — and finds herself tangled in the skein of truths and untruths. Thornton though, seems to have a firm grasp of the financial and legal gossamer as he takes the curves along Gilbert Road, down which they are driving a little too fast, passing the Old Wurlitzer piano and organ plant.

"Here's what I'd do: I'd liquidate some of the assets and pay myself a nice fat salary."

"How can I do that?"

"Well, you just said one of Griffin's companies owns a lot of property in the city and a house in Washington and beachfront in the Dominican Republic. Why not sell?"

"How?"

"I'd march into that office, figure out what the hell is going on. I'd put the staff on notice, find the best real estate agent and then put the properties on the goddamn market."

"But I don't work for the company."

"No, you own it. And even if you don't at the moment, the staff won't know the difference. You're more than a pretty face, I've always said that about you."

"Is that legal?"

"Legal, shmegal. Unless there's something you're not

telling me, like a prenup, the probate will be decided in your favor anyway. That's the way it goes."

"What if the staff resists?"

"Fire them all."

"What if the staff is only one person, and she's your husband's cousin, and she's executor of your husband's estate, even though you're to inherit it? And, if all that isn't galling enough, what if you have to rely on her for a check just to get by?"

"Situation all fucked up!"

How things go is a mystery, Margeaux thinks. I-71 crisscrosses overhead, its concrete legs pulling her to thoughts of her husband and the speeding Bentley. What had he been thinking? Suicide? Why? A $200,000 car?

At the gala, Margeaux lightens her burdens and brightens with possibility. Old and familiar alike feel new and fresh, and the puffed and fluffed-up tiresomeness of it all seems not quite so tired. Her usual cynicism for these inflated gatherings is as unlikely to ruin a newfound sense of fun as the periodically quarrelsome Thornton is. A Latin jazz band rumbas, and beneath a towering chandelier of teardrop crystals Margeaux cha-chas to a percussive samba, to the fullest extent such high-heeled glamour allows. Her partner is a handsome ruddy Irishman she has never previously met, with eyes the green of spring shoots and a sensual hand on her hip that quickens both pulse and pace. The night takes

a dark, mysterious turn when Thornton vanishes without
a trace, last spotted in the men's room splashing his face.
A ride home comes by way of the Grinigers, owners of an
air-conditioning manufacturing company, the husband a
golfing pal of Griffin's. Both husband and wife have the long
snouts of legendary gossips, and inevitable questions about
Margeaux's circumstances and coping skills are asked, about
which she offers only that time heals all wounds, including
financial and emotional, one way or another. The awkward
allusion to money lends focus to an unexpected whiff of her
own perspiration, surely a warning that a full refund for the
Valentino is unlikely. She frets as silver organza clouds sweep
by, fringing the treetops along the ledge of River Road. New
gloom fully descends as they climb up the winding road to
Hyde Park, when she notices the little intaglio identifying the
Grinigers' car as a Rover sedan, a sharp make of the stylish
model that sent Princess Grace of Monaco down a fatal cliff.

"It's always important to keep things in perspective,"
a sleepless, dreary Margeaux jots down in her notebook after
hanging the Valentino up to air out.

5

With only three weeks left before the *60 Minutes*
interview airs, the buzz is loud and the local pressure is on for
a piece of Mrs. Griffin Jewells Saunders II.

On the set of *The Magda Show*, Margeaux feels fabulous,
from low-slung ponytail to painted toes peeking through taupe
Maud Frizon column-heeled pumps. Despite the Miami-like
lighting onset, she has every reason to feel confident her
interview will appear elegant and easy, as polished as Parris
makeup — a more mascaraed eye, lined red-peach lip and
NARS neutrals set with matte gold finishing dusting powder
that give her skin an ebullient sheen.

The host Magda herself is dowdy and overdone with
cheek blush applied like road paint. Margeaux instantly
senses that the gravitational pull of beauty turns the cameras
toward her, but when has it it not been thus? The studio klieg
lights stare with harshness, but she is unfazed by the intensity
and worries of high-definition digital video. Her smile is
creamy but firm, shiny but not slick, and her clasped hands,
the wedding ring in full view, suggest eternal love. Her
ponytail (Percy's idea) is held not by a band, but by a black
silk scarf suggesting lingering grief, albeit chicly appointed,
and her tears are on standby for a heartwarming cameo.

"I'm especially happy to be sitting here with Margeaux Chenault Saunders. Many of you will remember Margeaux as my co-host on *Today in Cincinnati,* from 1985 to '89. If you don't know already, Margeaux nabbed one of Cincinnati's finest, most eligible men in what can only be described as a fairy-tale love affair gone wrong. Griffin Jewells Saunders II was a successful local business leader and pillar of the African-American community, and all of Cincinnati, but he also was the half-brother and business partner of Samuel Tecumseh Black II, the Clinton-appointed Secretary of Commerce of the United States and possibly the most powerful African American to hold political office in U.S. history. One year ago today, Margeaux's husband and their eldest son Jewells died tragically in a car crash outside Savannah, Georgia. Margeaux has shunned interviews and the media until now, and I'm pleased that she's with us today to talk about healing and moving on.

"Welcome, Margeaux. I think I speak for all in Cincinnati who love and admire you, it's wonderful to have you on *The Magda Show.*"

"Thank you, Magda. It's so wonderful to be here. Like old times."

"Awww. . . It's nearly seven years that you've been off television, and we've not seen you for two and a half years now, because, gosh, a lot's happened to you, and not all of it good. Your storybook romance ended on a tragic chapter. Was the crash that killed your husband and son an accident?"

"Most certainly, it appears that our son was driving and lost control of the car. He'd just gotten his driver's license, and the car was new and the steering was on the right-hand side, in British style, instead of the left because the car was made to be driven in England and the Commonwealth. They were on their way to have the steering reoriented to the left side, during a little bonding vacation for just the two of them."

"Ooohhh, that makes it doubly sad."

"Yes, but if this had to happen, I take consolation in the fact that they were together."

"You're saying then, that this was no accident?"

"No, I meant as in God's plan."

"Well, there are reasons to believe that it could have been no accident. For one, the car, which was traveling at a high speed, in excess of 120 miles an hour, may have been being pursued when it crashed into the bridge?"

"There are all kinds of rumors, but that's what they are, just rumors."

"There has been more than one allegation of foul play leading to the deaths of people linked to the Clinton administration and his Democratic machinery before. Vince Foster and Chandra Levy come to mind. And while your husband was not in the Clinton cabinet, his brother-in-law was and still is. The basis of the rumors is that your husband knew things and was about to go public. The secretary is the subject of a grand jury investigation."

"As I said, it's all rumor, but . . ."

"Come, Margeaux, we're all anxious to know what's happening. Do you believe in your gut that your husband and son were killed as part of a Clinton conspiracy?"

"I don't," Margeaux says. "It was a tragic accident. Not today, but tomorrow will be the anniversary of the deaths of my husband and son. Griffin was the center—"

"—but Margeaux, that the accident report has so many inconclusive findings puts the possibility of foul play in the spotlight. Many of our viewers know I once was a prosecutor, but it doesn't take a lawyer to understand that with your husband's death, a material witness has conveniently been removed. Now, I know this is upsetting . . ."

"It is . . . very," Margeaux said, dabbing at her eyes. "I don't dwell on what has happened, I can't change it no matter how much I want to. Instead, I try to live for the present for my children's sake. And as you, Magda, have no children, nor a husband, you probably don't understand how tragedy of this kind shifts your priorities around. Because if you had children, you would know what it means to have no choice but to focus on what matters most!"

Turning away and speaking more for the cameras, "One of the things that surprised me about what was going on during the process of coping with my family's sadness and even my own sadness, was the toll it took on me physically. Ladies in the audience who've gone through a hellish experience, whether a loss of a family member or even a job you loved, will know what I mean. Of course, it's understandable that you feel uninspired and depressed, the professionals would tell you that. Still, I'd look at myself in the mirror and just feel so much worse. I've always been in top form and this brought me low, but now I know better . . ."

It is a bravura performance.

At the segment's conclusion, Magda applauds and Margeaux stands up, turns her microphone off, growls in whispery tones, "What an ugly thing to do — but then, considering the source" — and marches off the set.

Speaking with Parris in the break room, she says, "I knew she'd try a takedown. I can't wait to get even with her. Somehow. Someway. Someday."

"I think you just did."

"I should have walked off in the middle of the segment."

"Hon, unlike the *60 Minutes* interview taping, where you were a weepy bore with that grave, gap-toothed Ed Bradley, this time you won the battle and put your flag down for victory in the war. You were captivating."

"Defiant is more like it," she said, swapping the heels for flats, and graciously smiling at a similar, insincere compliment from the producer.

"In the most polished way," Parris said, following her

out to her car. "You could have slapped the fat bitch in front of all the people in TV land."

Time and again Margeaux has made clear that she does not go for vulgarity — a big factor in her preference for Drexel over him, though Parris will never know it.

Triumph is fleeting. Nearing Neiman Marcus, grim reality greets her. She has several shopping bags in the trunk, filled with merchandise to be returned, each representing a humiliation weighing on her. Fortunately the perspiration stains on the Valentino and the speck of gum on the bottom of Jimmy Choo slingbacks go unchallenged, a full refund immediately given. A lucky Margeaux goes straight to cosmetics to discover a new anti-aging breakthrough that she has seen in the French, Italian and American editions of *Vogue*, *W* and *Harper's Bazaar* — the trinity of her favorite reading. Soon the power of planifolia bananas from Madagascar promises miracles to her skin . . . revitalized, regenerated, radiant!

The esthetician, a chipper woman who says she is from Romania but sounds as if from Erlanger, Kentucky, chirps away. Margeaux is in the beauty zone — what Griffin called her senseless shopping state of mind — and soon finds herself leaving Neiman Marcus with costly skincare purchases, tearfully on her way to Saks. There, she returns several items — all the new purchases for the interview, plus a Nanette Lepore forgotten in the trunk the last month. The kid LoQuan passes through her thoughts as if through mists of annoying parfum being spritzed at the fragrance counters. In designer apparel, a full credit on everything is offered, no questions asked, even on the Nanette Lepore, which, it turns out, is ripped. And once again, she finds herself in cosmetics, this time for new holiday resort nail color, and in the hands of another chattering esthetician/makeup artist claiming to be from an exotic place despite her fluency in speaking Kentucky.

Margeaux thinks about her icons — Sally Quinn, Joan Lunden, Deborah Norville, Faith Daniels, Campbell Brown, Norma Quarles — and their struggles to stay on top. Kathie Lee Gifford's comeback is the latest among the sad many. It is painful to see her so aged — and the terrible rocker hair! There's the possibility Margeaux too could come across as an laughable parrot-like impersonation of her old self, with bad hair and an air of desperation.

Some things about her old career were too painful to forget. She still hears the network director's voice criticizing her: "The moment you go off script, you sound like a snob. You need to be more like Miss Average America, don't use words like 'bohemian' when you can say 'cool,' 'apt' when you can say 'likely.' Get private school and all that Wellesley out of you. Be more like Kathie Lee. Kathie Lee, by the way, is French-born, but you'd never know it, that's how convincingly middle-America she is."

Aware of the small universe of TV hostesses, Margeaux pointed out that Kathie Lee had gone to a born-again university, and that the then-new weather girl Arlene Ballantine had attended Stanford, and Magda Yale, and both had freely peppered their deliveries with upscale words.

"But they don't act like they're smarter than everybody else," came the response. "And Arlene's a blonde. Blondes can do anything they want as long as they're hot — please note that I didn't say zaftig, bodacious or curvaceous or Marilyn Monroe-esque! As for Magda, she's a Gypsy laundress at heart, and that comes across winningly. Lighten up your presentation with a little levity, you know, joke around, laugh … I know you're not a real black person, but maybe put some 'color' in your talk."

A lawsuit against the network would have spelled the end of her career forever. At the time, it seemed a better idea to suck up these tear-down sessions, which she did up to the day she was fired. By then, legal action would have come across as sour grapes. A bitter end, indeed.

All the more so because she had given up the plum career she left behind in Chicago. The beat consisted of the City Hall of Mayor Richard M. Daley, local charity events, art and gala openings and comparable glittering events serving up amuse-bouche, from one end of Chicago to the other. After she made a stunning runway-turn at the premier designer boutique Ikram's, to benefit earthquake victims in Haiti, her name quickly climbed the social register, and on invitations to events as a coveted guest. Whom she was dating became fodder for the gossip pages, effectively sealing her fate as a newsworthy curiosity. The Windy City might have been home for good but for her easily finding an on-set position at the ABC affiliate in Cincinnati, a necessary career move to bring her closer to home to help Mutti battle cancer in the brain.

The painful truth: Cincinnati has never been a good fit.

An absence of eight years seems a lifetime in the daytime talk show industry. A toolbox of new tricks would be needed for the climb up and over fresh bodies. The thought is at once exhilarating and exhausting.

Interrupting the work of the Madagascar bananas, Margeaux decides to sit for a makeover at the Stéphane Marais counter, exclusively at Saks. She calms at the attention of the makeup artist, the soothing, tickling brushes whisking over her face, the pencils drawing liplines and eyelines, with a new, fuller and more rounded brow. Nothing equals the touch of luxury, from beauty to fashion, not even, and not ever even, sex. The deeply pleasing result, showcasing the Orgasm Collection by this cult makeup genius of the same name, proves the point!

Afterward, Margeaux walks to her car, all better now. Held to the Suburban windshield wiper is an envelope, and soon several Polaroids of commonplace expensive handbags, Burberry, Coach, etc., look her in the face. LoQuan.

That he not only knows her car but has violated it is
shocking enough. Rifling through the images, she considers
giving the photos to store security, and then calling the police,
until the last snapshot reveals, upon closer inspection, white
plumage and onyx beading on a Chanel Haute Couture
clutch, changing her mind. It is not a vintage piece thrown
in; Margeaux remembers it, and the gown it was designed to
accompany, from the editorial pages of French *Vogue*.

"Mr. LoQuan," Margeaux breathes into her phone,
hardly able to speak, and then too aggressively, when his
voice is on the line. "I don't know what kind of person you
think I am that I would be interested in stolen merchandise,
which this is, isn't it?"

"Think of it as an opportunity." She can hear him draw
on a cigarette, the sound of burning paper. "It's real, and it's
real cheap, just for you."

"Oh, please." Too much anger will not help the illusion,
and taking a deep breath, she says, "You have the wrong
person."

"It's only five hundred!"

Her motivations aside, Margeaux hesitates long enough
to feel the perspiration from a true fashion dilemma, then
says, as if struggling to recover, "The Chanel clutch? Five
hundred dollars?"

"Five hundred dollars, and just for you. You want me
to see if I get the gown that goes with it? You're a size two,

right?"

"That's right."

"I'm sure you can make it work if I can get it."

Margeaux collects herself enough to think about her next move carefully . . . artfully. "Mr. LoQuan, how do I know I can trust you? I don't even know anything about you. Jewells never mentioned you. And here it seems you know everything about me, my dress size and even my tastes. I'm at a disadvantage."

"And like Jewells wouldn't have mentioned me. That much I know. I'm originally from Oakland, in Cali, but I grew up here."

"Where?"

"Evanston and downtown, then Lockland."

"What do your parents do?"

"I ain't got no parents. They both dead."

"How did you know Jewells?"

"Juvie . . . juvenile detention. I was there for a couple weeks, and he came in for the day of sightseeing and we kinda clicked."

"Why were you there?"

"Assault, but it was self-defense."

"What were you and Jewells up to when you got caught … I mean, the pictures?"

"Like I said before, we was trying to get paid. I needed money more than he did."

"Why?"

"Because I'm a broke young black man, with no parents, no momma or daddy, with nuthin' but a foster home with an old senile lady. Jewells was trying to help me. Hope you satisfied, 'cause there ain't shit else to say."

"That's so sad," she says, for reasons less about his predicament than choice of words. "I feel a little more comfortable. I like to know who I'm dealing with."

"What you need to know is I can hook you up with the clothes you love."

"Apparently. Look, I have to run. I'll be in touch about the Chanel. I promise."

Afterward, she puzzles over the enigmatic pieces of this puzzling man. Hard to imagine Jewells trying to help anyone, but in the case of this compellingly handsome delinquent, she can picture it.

On I-75, Margeaux again phones cousin Mitchell. Of course, he has no information from the police about photos involving Jewells and this kid.

"Mitchell, I am disappointed. You can't have looked closely."

"As closely as I'm willing to. Margeaux, this is an invasion of his privacy. You need to give me something concrete."

"He just tried to sell me what is stolen merchandise. High fashion. Worth tens of thousands of dollars — and you know I know."

"Probably . . . that's not good encugh. I know you know what you're talking about when it comes to clothes, Margeaux, but I can't just go snooping into this kid's life without cause."

"Okay, let's create a timeline. He met Jewells in juvenile detention; that was February, on the 15th, in 1997. That incident they were involved in where Jewells ended up black and blue, which happened a year ago. . . he said they were trying to get paid . . . which means they were trying to collect it or trying to make it . . . for him. Jewells was trying to help him. His words."

"Margeaux, he could be telling you anything. And just to remind you, I'm not a detective, I'm in the D.A.'s office, my area of expertise is corporate malfeasance — different paygrade, different priorities. I will admit there's a sealed record involving him, and were I to have probable cause, I could set things into motion."

"I'm giving you cause. Trust me, there's something here, I just know it. I might not have been an crackerjack reporter, but I know a good story when I see one."

"Then maybe you need to play crackerjack reporter, find the story, then show me something.

"Mitchell, I think Griffin kept a lot from me about Jewells . . . well, about everything, really. I need to know about my stepson, I want to understand how they ended up smashed into a bridge. I know it was deliberate, but why?"

"Okay, but for now LoQuan is off limits. I can look into Jewells; that he's family would be less an issue now, since he's also deceased. There could be something there. And if there is something, I'll get a detective in on this."

"There has to be."

"We'll see. And Margeaux, everything you've said about this kid suggests he could be dangerous. He obviously likes you, but you should be very careful."

Indeed.

Hanging up, Margeaux finds herself at cross purposes. Head versus heart. Holding on versus letting go.

6

Katie Couric is not a friend . . . yet.

Earlier this year, when the husband of the queen of morning news anchors died of colon cancer, Margeaux was moved to reach out. With just one degree of separation, getting Katie's private New York address proved easy. Margeaux even included all her personal contact info in case Katie wanted to talk. She never held it against her for ignoring the offer of friendship; clearly, her gesture was presumptuous if well intended. Margeaux can appreciate how lucky they both were not to be among TV personalities with tragic endings: Jessica Savitch's drowning when the car she was riding in flipped over in the Delaware Canal; Max Robinson's succumbing to AIDS. The list is long.

It goes without saying, colon cancer is very disfiguring. But so is being decapitated, and to say nothing of the haunting horrific pictures such gruesome violence conjures.

Margeaux tries not to compare tragedies. According to the coroner's autopsy, Griffin's body became a projectile and went through the Bentley windshield. The mass of his broken bones and charred flesh lay on what was left of the burning car's hood. His head was found in tall pampas grass more than forty feet from the crash site.

Yet Katie Couric's loss must be greater because, from all accounts and appearances, she was in love. Margeaux wonders if this is true — having never been in love with Griffin, despite appearances to the contrary, a triumph of pretense typifies the perfected image of the TV host.

Regardless of her happy or unhappy home, Katie's very public loss quickly catapulted her into the pantheon of star-crossed celebrity lovers. Apparently, grief is both marketable and bankable, and could be a career boon if managed properly.

On the other hand, Margeaux's was a double loss, if one

counted Jewells. Jewells, crushed and cooked between the front of the car and its rear, which met through the force of impact at 124 miles an hour. She often congratulates herself on never trusting him to drive her and the children around.

Only Mutti knows just how haunted Margeaux was for months after Griffin's brutal end. A sensitivity to color coordination and symmetry made her especially susceptible to the headless image of her handsome husband. Ever since, she has struggled to remember him intact, as if memory itself had been smashed and severed into bits and parts — its own kind of headlessness. Fortunately, she no longer imagines him in the doorway of their bedroom, waiting as if unsure he is in the right place. Before his death, it never occurred to Margeaux he would not want to be in their bedroom — what man would hesitate to share her bed? Undoubtedly, theirs had been a good pairing in that sense. Why would he just stand there like that?

Griffin apparently haunts everyone differently. Mutti has said she sees him in the kitchen, reading the newspaper, with his English muffin and latte. Fletcher and Percy have not reported seeing him at all — the spectre of absence.

His Jaguar still sits in the garage as if waiting for him. Never mind selling it, she has frequently wanted to give it away just to have it out of sight. But because of the will, it is not hers to give, or drive. To avoid being near it, she has taken to parking her Audi coupe under the porte-cochère, there for easy arrivals and fast getaways.

The battery is almost certainly dead. Jorge only infrequently and then grudgingly takes the car for a drive, making it clear he never particularly liked his employer, neither in life nor death. Jorge claims Señor Saunders' spirit sits in the front seat — headless? — and gets mad if he comes too close. He has no proof of this, and yet is put off by this petty ghosting, which to him is tantamount to his deceased employer looking over his shoulder. Nevertheless, they have made a deal. Jorge's new job responsibilities include looking after the family, and he will because he respects Señora Saunders and the children, too.

Of late, Margeaux has noticed Jorge has become difficult to manage, if less so to understand. Sometimes he speaks with a "this is me, Jorge" brio. Other times, an artistic temperament, and ego to match, takes over, and there is the sense a tantrum is near. For instance, Margeaux loves the slabs of stone and hedges clipped like wedges of Brie along the driveway; features and shapes Griffin would never have gone for, but that Jorge, with help from his amigos also working in landscaping, took upon himself to do anyway, without her permission. This site installation was free of charge — "from my heart, for Señora Saunders" — and if Margeaux was deeply touched by the gesture, she was less enamored of his presumption in taking such liberty, now that there is no one lording over him.

Margeaux keeps her disapproval to herself. Winter will come soon, and likely little work, making the budget axe fall, and then where will they be? She, Mutti and the children could not survive without him and America.

On this morning, her usually reliable Audi chokes. Margeaux has more or less given the Suburban over to Mutti to ferry the children about, and with America just now, they are taking a turn in the park. Margeaux is to meet with Therosine at the office. She considers hiring a car for the day, but then decides it is too expensive — proof that she can be practical, especially when the savings could be applied to a new cosmetics or fragrance purchase.

Griffin's Jaguar is the obvious option, but for her fears … and what better time to face them than now. She hesitates before going for the keys. The garage accommodates four cars, and the long, wide door is open. Much of the lawn equipment is also stored within, with Jorge always in and out — although out at the moment Margeaux approaches and warily stares at the Jaguar's rear end. If the spirit of her husband is there in the front seat as Jorge claims, he does not show himself, headless or otherwise. Margeaux is more than resolved and a little frightened. In a soft yet defiant voice, she says, "Mr. Saunders, if you are here, I want you to know that I forgive you. You were a good man, the rock of our family, and I believe you were not in your right mind, that you were pushed into a desperate decision. I'll find out, I will . . . But

Griffin, I'm in this bind now because of what happened. I'm
not blaming you, but I have to move on and I don't need to
feel tormented by this anymore, so if you are trying to punish
me, stop. Don't stand in my way. You owe me that."

His ghost clearly is reasonable, in the spirit of the man
she married.

The Jaguar roars to life and a sense of lightness
illuminates her journey downtown, perhaps appropriate for
the dark business at hand.

First stop, Green Street in Over-the-Rhine. Griffin's
right-hand woman has recently provided Margeaux with a
complete list of properties owned by GJS Enterprises. The
portfolio is concentrated in two neighborhoods, side by
side: Over-the-Rhine, storied for its Victorian houses turned
warrens of crack cocaine and black-on-black murder; and
Northside, second only to Over-the-Rhine in drug-related
shootings. Northside was also the site of Margeaux's father's
dry cleaning plant, a place she does not remember ever being
allowed to visit.

It is nearly 11 a.m., a good hour for her purposes.
According to the news most of the violence in Over-the-Rhine
and Northside takes place evenings.

Where to start?

Eeny-meeny-miny-moe picks an address of one of
four apartment buildings on Green Street. The street's name
conjures a tree-lined block, aligning with her husband's

manicured tastes, but what Margeaux mostly sees there is the soiled and rundown. 632 signifies a four-story woodframe building a shade of urine yellow and tilted leftward to a precarious degree. There must be some mistake.

A panicky turn sends her in the wrong direction, the street numbers increasing and possibly adding up to a bad situation. A hard left forces her to back up into the intersection — and the path of an elderly man, missing him only by a grizzled hair. Her almost-victim carries on like he has been hit, swinging his cane, then crashing it against her taillights. Before Margeaux can apologize, another man has posted himself at the driver's car door.

"Hey, hey, you blind? You nearly run me down too. What the fuck's wrong with you, backing into an innersection like that?"

"It was an accident. I didn't see you or him. I was making a U-turn."

"Yeah, that U-turn was with your fuckin' eyes closed. Ain't never a cop around when you need one. Folks having to worry about being shot up at night and mowed down by day."

Margeaux apologizes yet again, seeing only his heavily mustached lip and then the old man doddering toward the next street over. Car horns begin to insist she immediately cease blocking traffic. However, it is not necessarily a fight-or-flight moment, and she pulls up to the curb just past the crosswalk, with the grumbling man close behind.

Margeaux does not cower or panic. She plays the "TV celebrity" card — a disarming weapon against speeding tickets, intolerable seating in the best restaurants and unseemly behavior.

With a deep breath and pageant-worthy smile, Margeaux eases herself from the car and declares "Hi, Margeaux Chenault with WLWT. I'm here doing a story on the area." She holds up her phone as if to record their words. "I'd like to interview you."

"What? You almost run us down, and now you wanna innerview?"

"I've apologized for that. But, yes, I'm doing a story about the . . . the . . . history of blacks living in Over-the-Rhine. How long have you been here?"

"All my goddamn life. Born here and probably die here too."

"What are the living conditions now compared to when you were a boy?"

"Living conditions? Look at this place! It's a slum, a ghetto, always has been, always will be."

"Do you believe that your concerns for the neighborhood are being listened to?"

"You're joking, right? It's like some fuckin' third-world country here. Nobody gives a shit. It ain't just the streets, it's our apartments too. Ain't never missed my rent payments, but I ain't had no hot water since June, and the sorry-ass landlord is black. Black — doing this to his own people! I live right here, so I know."

"Who is the landlord?"

"It's some nigga Griffin Saunders owned this shit. He dead though — got what he deserved, smashed up in his Bentley — his money made off my back and the backs of poor niggas just like me . . . all the niggas living around here."

"Oh." Margeaux is struck by this more than glancing blow, staggering her thoughts. "My camera crew is right behind me. I think you'd be great to do an interview."

"Me, on TV — oh hell no. I gotta better idea. You wanna know O-T-R, you come back here around midnight tonight, and you'll see what it's like up in this joint. Just make sure you packin'." As he is walking away, he shouts toward at group across the street, "Hey you'all wanna be on television? It's that bitch from *Today in Cincinnati* — I think it's her innerviewing niggas."

All eyes on her, Margeaux now shies from the unwanted spotlight, reenters the car and mashes a little harder on the gas than she intends, nearly running down another old person, this time a woman. A chorus of cursing is on her tail, but safety is also near. In sight: the familiarity of Central Parkway, then the headquarters for Griffin's small empire, the ground floor of a row house near the library.

Knowing Therosine is waiting to pounce pushes Margeaux in another, more soothing direction. Saks Fifth

Avenue is also but a few blocks away. Retail therapy, though the symptom of her current woes, seems a better option with a more desirable outcome than a tangle with Therosine, given the traumas of the day.

Nearing the Saks' parking garage, the voice of guilt argues against going further. Better to go to the mall for a few books on real estate.

Ultimately, Margeaux heads home, under skies appropriately grey.

The Suburban is not yet back, and she is about to check in with Mutti when the phone rings.

"Therosine, I'm so sorry."

"I have been waiting for you for an hour, Mrs. Saunders. I was worried."

"You needn't have been. I was downtown a little while ago, but came home because I'm not feeling well. I have to reschedule with you for tomorrow. "

"Are you flu-ish? I've been reading about flus, they're around all the time. Folks think they're here only when it's cold out."

"I'm not flu-ish. I'm feeling sick to my stomach . . . I just came from seeing the Over-the-Rhine properties."

"That make you feel sick?"

Is that snickering Margeaux hears? "Yes, it did make me feel sick. Why would Griffin buy property down there?"

"Mrs. Saunders, obviously for the investment. At the

time, it was cheap, courtesy of Cincinnati and Jesus, praise Him! It'll be worth millions if it isn't burned down in a riot, which could happen if there's another police shooting. But even if it does, it'll be still be worth millions. My cousin was a shrewd businessman."

Indeed, but an endorsement of Griffin's business vision is the last thing Margeaux wants. "I'll call you if I can come by tomorrow. Please have ready a list of the properties we could sell immediately, starting with the slums."

"I can't do that."

"What do you mean you can't do that?"

"I'm not qualified to make a decision like that."

"Well, then I'll have to speak to somebody who is."

"Who, Mrs. Saunders? Ain't nobody here but me."

"Don't we have a real-estate agent?"

"No. Mr. Saunders handled everything. What we need an agent for?"

"To get rid of these horrible properties."

"Oh no, not them. Mr. Saunders wouldn't sell them until he could get his asking price, and that's probably another five years down the road. Downtown is changing bit by bit, and before you know it . . ."

"Five years! No way. I want to get rid of as many of them as possible. Those people hate him. They know who he is and probably know where he lived. How difficult would it be for them to find us?"

"Mr. Saunders was careful not to list your private residence anywhere. Now, a couple troublemakers we was trying to have evicted showed up here at the office and made a ruction, but it weren't nothing the police couldn't handle."

"That's not reassuring at all . . ."

"Well, you've been living in that house for seven years now, and ain't nothing ever happen."

"I'm still not reassured."

"Mrs. Saunders, if we was to sell those properties now, they would be renovated and them people would be evicted and wouldn't have no place to go."

"And that's what would happen five years from now, too. Obviously that's their problem, not mine."

"Well, it's not going to happen anyway, because of probate."

The tense back-and-forth lasts three more rounds, Therosine's last words consisting of "Had you cared to know about the business, all you had to do was ask your husband." The answer to that statement is so obvious Margeaux refuses to answer. She must always remember Griffin is to blame.

She notices a flicker of light coming from the carriage house. Jorge's motorcycle is parked in front, and she wanders toward the garage. Mariachi horns play loud. Closer, there's the grinding noise of hot water being pumped to the second floor. All signs point to Jorge. But he has never been so presumptuous or audacious.

LoQuan? If nothing else, the young fence for hot and/ or counterfeit merchandise may have started a trend of strays wandering across the property. She wonders if she should call the police anyway, to be on the safe side. In the garage, she grabs grass shears, then tiptoes up the stairs. The door to Jewells' room is open, and the shower going. The computer is on. Over a desk chair is pulled-off clothing, and on the floor mud-caked work boots — Jorge's? Margeaux wades farther into the room, finally stopping at the bathroom entrance. The door is open, and there is Jorge, fully engaged with drying himself.

The length of Margeaux's gaze takes the full measure of him, and in the next instant the charged look of Jorge calls upon deeper animal spirits. The drumbeat in Margeaux's ears is not a reason to run away, because something about Jorge — shining, glistening, the horn of plenty — and something about herself there — so sad, so lonely, so cornered — changes the laws of physics, in that what repels suddenly attracts, and what rises converges . . . first on the vanity, then on the very bed Jewells slept on.

Margeaux is reminded of her favorite St. John's ad: chic, overdressed older woman trailed by an oil-smudged, absurdly handsome and young fieldworker. Truth in advertising.

On her doorstep, there's yet another communiqué from LoQuan, only this time with a note atop a large shiny box, instead of the usual snapshot and envelope. She loves surprises and cannot resist even one with the gloss of criminality. A pair of knee-high Gucci boots lie side by side like priceless statues. "Waiting to hear from you. Know you love this Gucci, you make up your mind."

With the box in tow, she runs to her closet to look at the Gucci in wardrobe lighting. Authentic.

And yet, collectors and museums are fooled by fakes and forgeries all the time. If counterfeit, the pair is flawless. But how could LoQuan possibly have access to such accessories and ready-to-wear? The university has a fashion design program; an invited speaker, Margeaux once gave a talk to a class of freshman fashion aspirants about her days on the runway. Perhaps LoQuan had marshalled a team of wannabes together to make flawless fakes?

More likely, it's an inside job at Saks or other stores. But how? Mafia? Chinese Mafia — a sweatshop of erstwhile couturiers?

Jorge's gifted touch has turned Margeaux ultra-sensitive. Pressing the boots to her body, tears come. Not because she loves them so much — she does — but because she cannot have them.

Although, acquiring the boots could prove she was as determined to bring the theft ring to justice as to uncover the evil doings of LoQuan. That she has told both Drexel and Parris about LoQuan's scheme, and alerted Mitchell about a crime ring, substantiates her claim.

Parris calls just as Margeaux hears the Suburban in the driveway and the shouts of children.

"Margeaux, you're in!"

"In what?"

"The network was impressed with your appearance on Magda's show."

"But I practically spat in her face."

"I think that's what impressed them."

"Oh, Parris, what a friend you are — and just when I'm in pity mode. Thank you."

"Any chance you can get a copy of the *60 Minutes* tape before it airs?"

"I'll try."

"Hon, I wouldn't be surprised if they asked you to be a once-a-week co-host, you know, like on Regis and Kelly."

"Not with Magda, we've done the team thing before. Remember, *Today in Cincinnati* fired me and kept her."

"Well, that's why they know it might work. Staid, stupid TIC wasn't made for the two of you. But y'all dueling it out over every topic, that's another story."

"Are you serious?"

"Of course I am. It's a Jerry Springer production, he's into you. I can see you and Magda in a mud fight on the set … on a segment about spa treatments, hahaha."

"Well, if it gets my foot in the door, I could sling a little mud."

"That a girl. I think it's always important to look on the bright side."

"Me too. Even when there isn't one."

"There is always one, Hon, you just sometimes have to look where you wouldn't expect it . . . like under a rock. When you come up short, just make one up, even. Whatever it takes."

Margeaux is thinking "show me the money" but instead offers her father's favorite expression: "Make your own luck." She thinks about this as she mulls over the Chanel snapshot, which has been in her sweater pocket all along. "Mrs. Sanders," indeed.

"What's the next step?"

"Get that *60 Minutes* video before it goes live. It's your meal ticket, Hon, just like I said it would be."

"Prophet! I worship you."

In light of this good news, the Gucci fever is now past. Margeaux rushes to hide the boots in her closet, before Percy sees them, but not before snapping a picture, which she emails to Drexel with a brief explanation: "From the same thief."

Three hours later, Drexel texts: "If it isn't a fake, those boots retail for $8,500."

Later that evening, Margeaux gets him on the phone: "They've got to be fakes."

"Is there anything fake about them?"

"No, a perfect pair. Just like it would be on the sales floor. The Ralph Lauren, the Chanel clutch — they're probably real."

"Except you wouldn't see that outside the Chanel boutique. It's strictly showroom inventory — well, you might see it displayed at Bergdorf Goodman or Colette. It's the kind of clutch that is usually flying off to a Hollywood clientele, Russian and Chinese tycoons, African dictators."

"Maybe this stuff is hijacked in transit?"

"Kinda makes sense, considering their isn't any official word that I've heard about unusual thefts at Saks, Bloomies, Bergdorf."

"But Cincinnati? LoQuan? What's the connection?"

"What's he like?"

"Oh, Drexel, it's just stunning — his story reads like a typical black male you hear on the nightly news — crime, arrests, violence — except he's part Asian, Filipino, Tibetan or something . . . I mean, a devastatingly handsome face, although he's not tall enough for the runways; otherwise, he'd be a star."

"Sounds exactly not like the person you'd want fronting your hot merchandise."

"I know. It's too bizarre."

"Margeaux, you should be careful. And at the risk of repeating myself . . . just don't!"

The only response to such a caution is to suggest greater

powers are at work. "Drexel, you'll think I'm mad, but it does feel as if I'm being tested — succumbing to crime. I can't imagine why I would feel tested in this particular way, but it feels like I am."

"No, you're not. You're much smarter than to fall into some kind of dangerous scheme . . . aren't you?"

"I don't know . . . I'm having the cold sweats."

"It isn't heroin, Margeaux — pull yourself together! I don't have time for an intervention."

Laughter bubbles up.

"Seriously, Margeaux, you're not at your best. That's when we screw up, girl."

"You're right, of course. Still, I'm amazed, flattered . . . this young man knows my taste so well, like he's studied me. I wonder if he's been in the house, gone through my closets?"

"Seems like he would have."

"That horrid Jewells, I wouldn't put anything past him."

"Maybe you shouldn't speak ill of the dead?"

"You and my mother . . . If Jewells did bring him through the house, it wasn't to give him a tour."

"You can't scapegoat him for everything. Let's remember, once upon a time you were a TV personality."

"Let's remember, LoQuan is Jewells' age, which means he would have been eleven or so when I was on the air. And from what I know, he was probably in some sort of detention center."

"Fan worship is timeless and doesn't discriminate. What queen doesn't love Judy Garland, Maria Callas, James Dean?"

"That's true."

"He could be a clever kind of stalker, too."

"This is getting more bizarre by the minute."

They laugh, Margeaux mostly to sound as if she were not on edge, and bearing in mind that her dear Drexel is a master of high-fashion merchandising, not character — and certainly not her character, regardless of what he thinks. She promises to resist being "Gucci-tized," and tells him she is crumbling the Chanel photo in her hand, catching herself just as he points out that she will be destroying evidence.

She hangs up before finishing her thoughts. To one and all, she wishes to make it known that, yes, this period of life is a trial, and while her love of fashion is inviolable, foolishness is not her style, never mind recent evidence of costly compulsiveness to the contrary. Of course, deep down her good friends all must know this, but perhaps just need to be reminded that she will always return merchandise she cannot afford, a practice established long ago.

She had had to explain her practical views to the grief counselor: that her "lifestyle" spending pattern is as it always was, commensurate with her income and available resources, and that her judgment over such matters has never been clouded. She had kept to herself the extreme charging-and-returning routine at several major stores in town — so too, the credit-card-rejected attempt to simultaneously purchase a $6,500 Hermès and two Fendi baguette handbags at $3,700 each; she kept only the Hermès, picking up the Fendis six months later during a well-timed markdown. As for the ethics of returning worn merchandise, her rationale insists that, because of the life she leads and the places she goes, she does both designer and retailer a favor — and indeed, deserves a brand-ambassador privilege.

Despite her redactions, evasions and sugar-coating, therapy was most instructive. Understanding her state of mourning and shock helped immeasurably, not least by warding off excessive tendencies. If not for shopping, she might have become gluttonous, and instead be suffering from an outsized figure instead of outsized credit card debt. She had confided to the counselor that the mourning really began when Griffin moved to Washington. "Everything changed after that. Slowly at first, and then fast . . . speeding. His being there should have prepared me for widowhood, because he wasn't around anymore, even when he was here. It started with him returning every weekend, then every other weekend. When that got to be too much, every three weeks. And when that got to be too much, every month. I just got so angry, I didn't even want him here. And now he's dead, and there's no way of ever making it right."

There are moments when Margeaux sees the error of her ways in Percy. Before she can even put the boots fully out of sight, Percy is Gucci-tized. His tantrum leads Margeaux to leave a far less game-on message with its procurer than intended: "LoQuan, this is Mrs. Saunders — S-A-U-N-D-E-R-S. I want to know how to return the package you left here . . . or else I'll be forced to take other measures." Margeaux thought to imply the police, but instead says, "I'll give it to a consignment store."

She switches the phone to record mode.

Mere seconds later, he phones. "Why, don't you like them?"

"That's not the issue."

"You know you want it. I saw those boots and I was like, day-yum, that's Mrs. *Saunders*."

It is good to be coy, not to appear too easily led into his game, she knows, and yet it all feels deeply under the skin, cutting to the bone.

"Mr. LoQuan, I won't discuss Gucci, Chanel or holiday resort or any other collection or season with you. I only want to know where to send the boots."

"I'm just trying to do you a favor. Jewells told me how much you love high fashion. I always see you returning shit at Saks, and you know I work in the stockroom, and I figure it might be because money's tight — and sure I know how that be — and you know they're going to ban you from the store."

"What?"

"Because you always returning stuff worn, sometimes

with stains and rips. I heard the designer buyer and one of the salesgirls talking about it. So I'm like, day-yum, I can help you out and you can help me out."

Is there no end to this humiliation? "Please tell me where to send you the boots."

"Okay, so why don't you give me six hundred for the boots, and five for the Chanel? That's a bargain."

"No, I don't deal in stolen merchandise."

"Look, I pick shit out just for you. So, you owe me."

"You're serious?"

"Hell yeah."

"Why me?"

"Cuz I know you. And because, ladies like you wearing designer shit all the time, y'all just get compliments, not accused of shoplifting. But you don't need to worry no how, those boots and the clutch are untraceable. Fuck, buy'em and put 'em in a vault and bring them out in a few years."

"Where do you want me to send the Guccis?"

"Mrs. Saunders, just fifteen hundred for Ralph Lauren, the Chanel and the Gucci — that's like \$35,000 retail right there. Bam!"

Margeaux's thoughts push pause. Then, "I'll think about it. I'll let you know."

A half-hour goes by, in which the moral ambiguities of the situation skew in favor of purchase. A replay of the interview in its entirety changes her mind. Then she amps up the volume into the receiver of cousin Mitchell's phone. She adds: "There's your evidence. And I have what I believe are authentic Gucci boots that he left here in a box, sitting right in front of me . . . retailing for over eight thousand dollars, according to my friend Drexel, Division Merchandising Manager for Designer Fashions at Saks Fifth Avenue."

After a next-steps back-and-forth, in which ever-cautious Mitchell tries Margeaux's patience, she dares to add: "When this case is over, I hope the police would give the boots to me as a thank you. After all, one good deed surely deserves another."

A new low moment in talk show history occurred over a decade ago. Daytime Queen Oprah Winfrey announced herself a victim and survivor of sexual abuse, topping her reflections on a childhood of desperate poverty and her deadbeat mother, Vernita Lee.

Margeaux had only recently begun tuning in for the occasional nugget of pick-me-up, self-empowerment advice. She could not believe her ears and eyes, dropping her sonic undereye massager into the folds of azure Egyptian linens on the bed, as Ms. Winfrey tearily narrated highlights of a sordid tale. . .

. . . and the audience sobbing and slobbering during what Margeaux knew was a cunningly and cynically orchestrated boohoo. The bar for the modern black talk show host was thus raised. Now, success would require a harrowing history to bait the hungry millions of TV viewers around the country, with a follow-through of gospel-inspired, "we shall overcome" messages to inspire every variety of viewer.

Had she a mind to, and the courage, Margeaux knows she could corner a niche for a unique brand of suffering. Hers was not just a tale of an ancestral victimization linked to slavery, and hardly the cliché rags-to-riches or ugly duckling-to-swan story, though transformative and transcendent all the same.

Contrary to what she had been told as a child, Mutti's parents were quite alive as recently as 1971. Mutti's father was in Germany, serving out a twenty-year prison sentence. Margeaux learned about him not from her, but through research and a New York journalist she made contact with. Newspaper archives of the *Cincinnati Enquirer* at the Public Library included a mention of his arrest and extradition to Germany from Cincinnati, for prosecution of war crimes, dated November 22, 1959. Following his trial and conviction, an article in *Parade Magazine*, dated August 12, 1960, chronicled his homicide hijink that would lead to two decades behind bars. At 15 years old, Maximilian Kleidermann had joined a Nazi Youth group, helping to round up the Jews in his native Würzburg. His allegiance was less a callow, ruthless heart, than a restless, ruffian spirit in need of a fight, a rebel with a dubious cause. The zeal with which he carried out his pledge led to the row with, and fatal bludgeoning of, a Jewish shopkeeper and his wife known to all in their village. His parents smuggled him to Hamburg and onto a freighter traveling to Norway, and from there to the United States. Even as the vessel carried him far from punishment for his misdeeds, his family, including both parents and a sibling, were killed in a bombing raid in the ever-widening battle theatre in the old city. The news of their deaths reached him only after several months, during which period he was busy blending in, in America's *das Rheinland*, the Ohio River Valley, outside Cincinnati, in 1938, where he quickly mastered both English and the craft of carpentry. Intrigued and inspired by his new life though he was, nevertheless Würzburg would always be home. Hearing the news of his homeland's war-ravaged state never failed to wrench and tug his heart and inspire pining for his parents and home. Not long after the war, in 1947, without fanfare or even a goodbye in most cases, he eagerly returned to his hometown to start anew. He reunited with his teen sweetheart Helga Krank, the newlyweds becoming parents to two daughters in short

order. His saved American money set him up nicely, although
life was threadbare in a place where few had little more than
the ragged clothes on their backs, and where eggs and a loaf
of bread cost a day's wages. Even so, he would have stuck
it out, but for the activities in Bavaria of an upstart Jewish
group hunting former Nazis, calling out former SS officers
and alliances. Believing himself to be in their crosshairs, once
again he fled to America, in 1952 — for the second time setting
up his family in the Over-the-Rhine and quickly building out
the American dream until his past caught up with him.

The magazine story featured photographs of boyish,
chiselled-face Maximilian Kleidermann and his family. The
two pretty blue-eyed, flaxen-haired daughters were named
Ursula and Gudrun. Ursula died of diphtheria at age eleven,
in 1953, while Gudrun, a 16-year-old high-school junior at
the time of his extradition, was believed to have returned to
Germany with her mother.

Passionate detachment is the art of the kind of cool,
charismatic journalist Margeaux wished to be. She tamped
down her amazement as she read about her infamous
grandfather — a discovery all the more remarkable because
she'd stumbled upon it on a hunch, after Mutti refused to
provide her any details about her parents before they came
to the U.S. Margeaux's interest in her ancestry had to do with
beauty pageants, and she had gone to the library to search for
a death certificate, only to find this small trove of history.

Keeping her wits about her was especially difficult during a near breathless, out-of-body experience as she recognized Mutti as the young Gudrun in the photographs. The magazine article listed the writer, Joshua Himmelfarb, as on the staff of *The New Yorker* magazine. Gathering as many quarters as she could, Margeaux pay-phoned, explaining to the writer's secretary that she was granddaughter of a Nazi he had written about. To her surprise, a few minutes later she was on the phone with the journalist. First off, she volunteered she was no Nazi, but a teenager writing a story about her biracial — "half black" — family history when she stumbled upon the article he had written.

"You're his half-black grandchild?"

"Yes. My mother is his surviving daughter, Gudrun Elisabeth Kleidermann, and my father is black."

"Well, there's a certain justice in it."

If ever the truth came out in a career-threatening way, Margeaux could quote that very line — and of course, it made a great theme for an essay.

But a half-hour later, all she could think was how could Mutti silence away such a story? Had Father known? He must have. At the time the *Parade Magazine* story was written, not only had Mutti already been cast out by her family, and thus could not have been in Germany, but she was also expecting his child, safely nestled with his family.

Pageant pros have often said beauty contests teach

the girls equally as much about poise and polish as living
a successful life, from career to marriage. Mastering the
presentation and performance of a crowned beauty queen
required one step at a time, literally one foot in front of the
other, faultlessly hitting all the marks, the perfect balance
of confidence, humility and patience-patience-patience. The
same could be applied to the predicament she now found
herself in. Margeaux's sense of bursting was irrepressible,
yet somehow emotion, excitement and gratification had to be
delayed and the facts investigated further before confronting
Mutti and possibly parlaying this development into a
personal essay for a full offer to attend a Wellesley, Radcliffe
or Bryn Mawr. She imagined such serious news pros as
Lesley Stahl and Christiane Amanpour would approve of her
precociousness, calculations and self-control in the face of an
extraordinary, very personal revelation, as well as the scoop —
regardless that the full Nazi chapter in the family story could
hardly be the kind of revelation to broadcast, except at the
lowest frequencies.

The most alarming part of all this was how close the
story was. What inspired Margeaux toward truth had not been
personal curiosity but a series of disconnected events. The first
was the realization that, other than the $5,000 scholarship for
winning the Miss Ohio Teen USA pageant, the reign of the
beauty queen was but a meaningless, exhausting crisscross
of charity fundraisers, county parades, appearances at events

and talks no one but pageant wannabes and their mothers attended, and that a smart girl like herself should plot out a life after the crown that included a prestigious college to be trained for a career. Competing since she was 13, by junior year of high school she was exhausted from keeping the stellar kind of resume of extracurricular activities that pageant judges award points to, such as work for the National Honor Society, French Club, Young Scholars, Blood Bank, Clean Ohio River Society. And, of course, from keeping a GPA that had only once dipped to 3.9 but that kept her out of the running for even a fifth place in the top tier of her graduating class. To say nothing of the effort required to not look worn down. Her victory seemed more decathlon than beauty contest, and halfway through her reign the thrill was gone and she was eager to hand off her crown. Her interest in broadcast journalism was stoked when she learned that journalist Diane Sawyer had been an America's Junior Miss, the training for which she profusely thanked for her poise and confidence. Similar inspiration came from local TV host Kitty Katzenberg, who had also had a pageant life, although never making it past third runner-up.

The second event was an article she wrote for her high school newspaper, *The Rag*, entitled "Pretty Smart," in which she heaped praise upon the pageant experience as the perfect training for women to enter a career where they might someday be required to manage people, make decisions, and move in power circles of influence. "For me, as the child of a black father and a white mother, the beauty pageant experience has empowered me to help others look past the politics of my complexion and my ancestry."

The reaction the story received stunned. The backlash was immediate and intense, condemning the pageant life as a factory for producing vain, shallow girls who would become vain, shallow women. *The Rag's* editor suggested a followup article, in which Margeaux would look at her interracial background as a theme; perhaps two articles, one about the black side of her family, the other about the white. Margeaux agreed. Up to that point, she had given print and TV interviews in which she only mentioned her biracial background, focusing on her wholesome, all-American rearing by her dedicated widowed mother after her father's tragic death, avoiding all such disagreeables as race, discrimination and bullying by other children jealous of her looks. Lip service was given to Mutti — who sometimes appeared in photos beside Margeaux, most times not — and the struggle to afford her daughter's expensive education and beauty vocation on a secretary's salary. In these interviews Margeaux graciously extolled Mutti's sacrifice but more often doted on her father, who inspired her love of the entertainment world. Being a daddy's girl, it made sense, plus it allowed Margeaux to control the story, which invariably skewed toward the black side of her genes.

The proposed follow-up articles ignited the third event: an explosive fallout with Mutti after she refused to participate. Expecting the usual resistance, Margeaux never anticipated the slap that followed their shouting match. The tingling in the cheek resonated on another level, convincing her there was more to the story.

Before she ended her fact-finding search at the public library that afternoon, inspiration and instinct struck. Directory Assistance could find no listing for a Maximilian Kleidermann anywhere in the Cincinnati metropolitan area; however, there was an Helga Krank, in the Price Hill area.

On the way home, Margeaux detoured to a gas station for directions to an area of the city unknown to her, and after some difficulty, with at least three more stops for directions, she discovered what she believed was the residence of her newfound grandmother. She pulled to the curb on the opposite side of the street. Given its tenants' past, her home was unremarkable, a four-story white woodframe house on a crowded block of a street called Seminary Road. On the small front porch, she could see two entrances, side by side. She noticed a young-ish white couple carrying grocery bags and approaching the house; they turned onto the walkway, climbed the small flight of steps and continued toward the entrance on the right. The second door opened, and there was a brief exchange before they went on their way. Near that same entrance were two parlor windows. In the one farthest away, an old woman took her perch. Margeaux could hardly make her features out — a small head, tufted with white hair and bisected by dark-framed glasses — but could feel her focus hawking down on the street. Their eyes met in an instant that sent a shiver through Margeaux.

Perhaps a true journalist would have braved the uncertainty, with perfect calm and professionalism. After all, this woman could have been anybody, and yet Margeaux knew.

Just now, she failed this test of mettle, obtaining the proof less important than it seemed when she arrived. Far smarter to avoid another mother-daughter dustup, fortify herself, and pursue the evidence later.

On the way, however, imagination inspired by history got the better of her. Projecting herself 15 years forward, she pictured a spotlight role on a program like *Good Morning America*, plus a rich, high-powered, head-turning husband, the fantasy of women everywhere — unless the sordid Nazi past cast a long, devastating shadow. Perhaps this family history was best kept buried.

In the rush of manic thoughts and erupting tears, disorientation was no reason to slow her progress to I-75. After negotiating the tangle of exits and sloping ramps to Columbia Parkway, she was blinded in the full stare of sun, unable to see her way along the high arc of bridge that swooped down toward the Ohio River. Loss of control came

somewhere between the swerve, hard-breaking and the gasp
of inevitability. The car struck the guardrail, then repelled
sideways into the other lane, where it was sideswiped, flung
and then flipped over by a van before skidding on its roof,
screeching, to come to rest against the guardrail. Her eyes
opened to discover, in the painful scrunch against the roof
and the window, all kinds of sharp, hard things may have
just ruined her life forever. She wanted to cry out but felt a
constriction just below her throat, which seemed to her maybe
bent in such a way to prevent it. Or perhaps it was her lungs,
squeezed by the crushing of the car. Panic stopped itself
just long enough that she could see her own reflection in the
rearview mirror, now close enough to her face to serve as
compact mirror. Smiling revealed no broken teeth, and while
there was blood, it seemed to come from her head, not her
face.

The self-prognosis of her quick, calm assessment was
not far off. Despite the violence of the crash, her injuries were
not life-threatening: a serious concussion, fractured pelvis,
dislocated shoulder, long zipper-like laceration just below the
armpit. What she remembered most was not the blood and
pain but that the world was upside down.

Fortune must indeed favor the beautiful. Classmates
rallied to the pageant queen's side, detractors joining fans in
hoping for Margeaux's full recovery in time to compete for
the Miss U.S.A. crown. The black-white, double-whammy

article idea was killed: Writing about Father's past while giving Mutti's short shrift did not win her editor over. But Margeaux was invited to write about a new role on offer, that of spokesperson for Teens Behind the Wheel. Manufacturing excuses for behavior she described as reckless and distracted did not diminish the messenger's message.

Not everyone believed her explanation.

Mutti had moved into the hospital. Margeaux's fears settled down with her there, and after three days of being adored and watched over, the long-held, teenage resentfulness fell away. In its place, history stepped assuredly forward. If before the crash, Margeaux recognized its potential to be used hurtfully against Mutti, she now saw that even mentioning what she knew was just sadistic, and yet it had to be said. Mutti's reaction was unemotional, unaffected, circumspect: "I'm sorry you had to know. I hoped you never would. I accepted long ago that there wasn't a whole lot I could do to erase the past. It's always there. And my mother has been here all along, I know. It is her right."

Mutti's stated reasons for silence about her family's story were obvious enough. "My parents were stern and unloving toward me. Very cold and cruel, my mother especially. I could never have gone back to them, even if I would have had to live in the gutter, because it was I who reported my father. He threatened to harm us, to kill your father — that's why I did it. I assumed she went to Germany with him, and I was glad to be rid of them. Then one day I ran into her at Pogue's department store in downtown. We recognized each other, but we did not speak. Such hatred in her eyes. Every once in a while I call just to find out if she is dead. I look forward to the day when there is no answer."

A sugar-coating this was not. The depth of Mutti's hatred surprised, if nothing else did. What could Margeaux possibly say? Who was she to have an opinion?

"But Liebchen, if you want to meet her — that is what you planned to do, isn't it? — I won't stop you."

"Maybe I do, maybe I don't — it's so awful, so confusing . . . and maybe she's changed after everything that's happened."

"Maybe. Anything is possible."

Margeaux considered not what was possible, but whether she should or not.

"If this is what you want, I will come with you. In case she has not changed. I would never let her hurt you. Ever."

"You would? Really?"

"Yes. I have to say also, that I have always believed she and him had something to do with the fire at the dry cleaning. Of course, my father was in a German prison, but it isn't difficult to imagine he might have orchestrated it. I know it was said that your father did it for insurance, but I don't think so — I could not prove it, but I know they had something to do with it. Revenge because they knew I did it. I once threatened to report them, so they did it to get back at me."

The tearful moment that passed between them effectively ended the discussion. Not in a million years could she nor would she ever subject Mutti to such pain. Her disappointment, however, was tempered by newfound love for this woman: Father had been song and laughter, but Mutti was the true protector, defender, slayer of monsters. All powerful, all sacrificing. The glacier-like coldness between them instantly melted away. The torrent of emotion was all the more remarkable because it occurred invisibly in the natural course of things. Fall's dramas downplayed, and winter arrived bearing news of her early acceptance to Wellesley College. The announcement filled her with joy, even as her pelvis' slow recovery thwarted her bid for the Miss America title. Soon enough, Miss Ohio duty called and she was once again on the run, and the pace of life as a high-school senior returned to breakneck normal, just the way she preferred it.

Curiosity did rear its head once more. It happened just as she was packing for college. Seemed to her that now was her chance, the old lady could die in the time Margeaux would be away, and Mutti need never know. She dialed the infamous number, just as Mutti had done perhaps a thousand times. Before even the first ring, the operator's voice announced the line had been disconnected, with no forwarding information available. Later that day, she raced to the downtown Public Library to scour the obituary pages. The January 1st, 1978, issue of the *Cincinnati Enquirer* noted that the late Krank Weisendorf, aged 64, had emigrated from Germany during the Second World War, was wife to the late Heinrich Krank and mother to a daughter who died in childhood. No mention of her first marriage to a convicted Nazi. In little more than a three-line notice, history had been rewritten.

In the Clinton era, controversy and scandal as publicity tools certainly seem the modern ethic; so too, the well-timed leak for a bonanza of benefits. Margeaux now believes a time will come when it could be opportune to reveal her Nazi family secret; perhaps in her fifties, when she is coasting along in a brilliant career.

Now, on the brink of a television comeback, several other controversies might serve her well, if not on her own show to sensational effect, then on those of others as a special guest, or in magazine features about her:

Given the unending choice battle, her abortion of Thornton Childs' child after a one-night stand in the summer of high-school junior year. If presented on the topic of first-love revisited, just mentioning the abortion of a scion descended from a United States president could certainly be provocative and headline worthy.

Shocked and appalled, Mutti would have to get over it.

Of celebrity relationships: Deandre Wilbersmith, star runningback for the Cincinnati Bengals, whom she had dated throughout 1989, had fractured her cheekbone with a graze of his fist in a jealous rage. Charges were filed, but later dropped after her *Today in Cincinnati* director suggested that a loss at the upcoming playoffs would never be forgiven. Topic idea: domestic violence in professional sports or celebrated women once victims of relationship abuse.

Re. above: In addition to the implied threat, that *Today in Cincinnati* had fired her nine months later, never mind that it occurred just as she was considering her next career move — back to Chicago? National media? CNN? — suggests a deliberate attempt to sabotage her, and at a time when she was most vulnerable, too entrenched in the dull Ohio River city to have appeal outside of it. Perhaps the topic could be discrimination in the workplace.

Ménages à trois with her gay best friend + another man. A round of parties and an invitation from the stunningly beautiful Salvatore led to a weekend in Italy. Margeaux and Drexel arrived at his villa outside Rome, fully expecting a Fellini-like weekend of more parties and fun, but instead finding themselves in a scene from *Cabaret*, with their gorgeous host leaving her bed to join

Drexel in his. Margeaux's quick trip to the restroom was greeted with the sounds of heavy breathing, whereupon she peeked at its source and found her Italian slobbering away between Drexel's legs. Her reason for joining in had less to do with that she found it erotic, and more with the "when in Rome" moment and a one-time lust for the outré, never to be repeated. Topic: The allure of hedonism in the fashion life.

Re. theft: After a catalogue shoot with an in-demand stylist, Margeaux pocketed a pair of $5,000 earrings. Word of the missing jewels came from her agent, about which Margeaux pretended ignorance. Apparently, the stylist had a reputation for sticky fingers, and the matter was dropped. Possible topic: youthful indiscretions/petty crimes/shoplifting.

Scandalous dalliances with her impossibly sexy gardner. Topic: Dangerous liaisons: Crossing the border to adult indiscretion.

Last but not least, bringing down a shoplifting ring. Just thinking about it fills her with gratitude for the witless LoQuan.

Being wife of a likely philandering husband and stepmother to a teen from hell surely could be fodder. At the risk of smearing her husband, Margeaux will not go there, under any circumstances. The benefits of courting personal controversy are obvious, and the pratfalls too. Both intended and unintended consequences could be far-reaching, in ways unimaginable. Somehow, Margeaux must shield the children from the dross and detritus of her self-promotion. That she will have to say, do, and even dress in ways against her sense of decorum, style and taste would have to be seen as a sort of special Mommy twin — there's everyday Mommy and then there's the one on TV who looks exactly like Mommy but acts in horrible, tacky ways.

Margeaux's professional advice to young media women: Think twice before motherhood while climbing the ladder to success to a high-profile public career.

And then there's the issue of marriage. Find an average Joe, rather than a man in the spotlight whose history may be its own source of worry. As an example: Diane Sawyer's relationship with playboy actor Warren Beatty, and the undying rumors of her and the disgraced President of the United States: Richard M. Nixon. Jessica Savitch's marriage to a gay gynecologist who committed suicide; her affairs with Ed Bradley and yes, playboy Warren Beatty. Paula Zahn's marriage-wrecking affair with a billionaire pal of her husband's.

It is curious that Margeaux, for the second time, stands in the shadow cast by a criminal familial past she had nothing to do with. Though there are likely few closets without skeletons, it is also tempting to believe hers dangle with a certain curse that will rule her life. Unless the evil is broken.

The scandals coming to light about Griffin will have to be delicately handled: splitting him into two people: good daddy, corrupt businessman. His undoing: being half brother to the most powerful African American in the history of the United States, a dangerous rascal in a Brioni suit.

The twins are too young to have memories of their father, but perhaps they will remember sensing the discord that so painfully bookmarked the first chapters of their early lives. Perhaps the boys will tell them he was never around, living in a city hundreds of miles away. Do the boys even know how much he loved them? What he sacrificed for their sakes?

Once her career is back on track, she must make an effort to secure his legacy with his children, placing him on a pedestal above the mudslinging and gossip, as well as the crimes and misdemeanors and her own doubts about the Griffin Jewells Saunders II she married.

Before the staining and ruining of his name is complete, it is, she realizes, a good thing her husband is dead.

8

God and prayer are no strangers to celebrities of all
stripes.

Rumors abound of several leading talk show hosts and
news anchors consulting with psychics, among them the poor
canal-drowned Jessica Savitch.

Not for the first time Margeaux has wondered if there
are people empowered to know the future. Experience has
taught her that confidence shapes the future more than
anything else. How a stranger, even one endowed with special
vision, can know you requires a leap of the imagination
Margeaux is incapable of. Until a dream shakes her to the
core: Draped in black, Margeaux stands alone, in a room
decorated in red silks, satins, damasks, suedes and leathers.
She is waiting for her date and a celebration of her success to
begin. Champagne is set out in a crystal bucket on a bar, along
with her favorite finger foods. Seems she has been waiting
there awhile, and hunger lures her for a nibble on foie gras.
The cracker just reaches her lips when the room tilts and
throws her off balance. The bar vanishes, and the nearest wall
turns out not to be attached to the floor. It separates into an
ever-widening gap, revealing the room is thousands of feet off

the ground, and just then, she is jettisoned into space.

The omen interprets all too easily. A great rise before an even greater fall is in the cards.

Panic sets in. Desperation requires a creative response. A good psychic, or someone to hypnotize her, or perhaps break a hex of low confidence and negative thinking that may have been put on her by the last decade.

Parris breathlessly goes through his Team Margeaux spiel, and she realizes her career's second act has become as much about what he stands to gain, where he wants to be, as about her own welfare and well-being. Margeaux suspects she has vested too much power in his gold-digger hands, and decides to loop him out of her private, psychological drama.

Drexel responds to her S.O.S., posthaste. And with Drexel, Margeaux does not have to worry about future treachery, as she does with Parris: For instance, the selling of gossip about her life to the *National Enquirer* or equivalent rag.

"I have a friend who swears by his psychic. Aurora is her name — I always want to say Borealis is her surname, but no, it's Perkins, if you can imagine that. Anyway, she's big with the stars but stays way below the radar, and she apparently helps the police solve murders and abductions and predicts earthquakes. He's been seeing her for at least a decade. No kidding, he barely takes a dump without consulting her first. I'm sure it's like having a second mortgage, which he writes off on his taxes as a medical expense. But he insists he would continue anyway, she's worth every penny. I saw a photo of her and she kind of looks like a dolphin. Personally I think he's a little nuts — she tells him stuff, add a brighter color to the line. I'm like, really! Give him props, he's got the Midas touch and owns a pretty successful ready-to-wear line that's everywhere you'd want to be. As for myself, I'm a little curious, but she's a little outside my reach at $1,000 a session."

While Drexel collects info, Margeaux wonders if a better option would be the slow slog to revelation through expensive therapy. Grief therapy had only marginally helped with her father's and Griffin's deaths. There is no time, and a quick fix — a peek into the future — might indeed show the way to tomorrow, whatever it brings.

Later, Drexel messages the particulars, warning that Aurora only sees first-time clients face to face, and she is booked forever, so likely it won't happen any time soon. But call, mention you're a friend of Paolo, and that you're the newly widowed mother of four children . . . Paolo says she loves kids and mothers and may give you a discount."

A pack-a-day voice answers the phone. "Dearie, you're in luck. Aurora has an appointment at 10 a.m. Wednesday."

Without calculating how she will pull a Manhattan session off on such notice, she agrees.

Upon hearing her news, Drexel jokes: "Perhaps I'm stating the obvious, but today is Monday, you realize?"

"I do. I'll get the Wednesday red-eye up and be back by the end of the day, or the next morning."

"Allowing for a quick run through Bendel's, right?"

She explains the non-refundable scheduling fee of $750, which she'll forfeit if she has to cancel with less than 24 hours' notice or decides not to have an appointment. "No way. The fewer traces of my visit to New York, the better. Plus, I'm going to tell that Bible-thumping heifer controlling the purse strings that I'm going to D.C. to check on my husband's house."

"Good luck, I hope you get what you need."

Therosine!

She heads to the downtown office. A bribe of chocolates is intended to sweeten Griffin's sourpuss cousin, perhaps lightening the effect of the bad news. Besides the properties to be put up for sale and paying America, she has had to add two new line items that will not go over well: a wardrobe allowance for interviews and possible upcoming television work, and a substantial raise for Jorge and the new video equipment, which Therosine refused to approve over the phone.

There, after the dispensing of pleasantries, Margeaux explains her reason for coming. The gospel-inspired check-writer turns defensive as if to shield herself from evil-lite incarnate, claiming to appreciate the reason behind "your irrational, desperate outburst the last time you were here, but

I don't have time for that, so if this is round two…" Margeaux assures her she has come to her senses, and then Therosine reminds her, yet again, that Griffin had been holding on to the properties not just as an investment for his children but because all the tenants would be turned out to the streets. Never mind the fact that the buildings were run down and the government pays GJS Enterprises to keep them "as is" — "Most everybody has hot water, and those that don't probably are bad tenants, behind on their rent, and believe me, there are a lot of them." To diffuse the situation, Margeaux pretends sympathy and claims to understand Therosine's exacting nature. The term she later uses to describe her to Mutti is niggardly. Mutti cautions against ever using that word publicly or in front of the children, for obvious reasons.

"Therosine, as you yourself are a career woman, you can appreciate that I'm determined to get back to work. It's not only because my money is tied up, it's for my own sake. I miss work."

"That's nice," says Therosine. "When you're actually earning income, you could offset these additional expenses."

"I don't know when exactly I'll have work."

"You'll just need to delay hiring the girl until you do."

"She's already working for us. We owe her $2,000, which I've paid out of the house fund."

"Mrs. Saunders, I could use an assistant, too, but I don't just go out and hire someone."

"You are not fifty-six years old, and not grossly overweight and not chasing after four very energetic young children."

"Neither are you."

"Me?" Keep your cool, Margeaux tells herself.

"Maybe you should replace your mother?" Her pop eyes hover over the rims of her glasses. Then, with a faint trace of smile, she adds, "Or you should do more yourself, step up to the plate. Mr. Saunders would like that. He always said you placed the burden of raising the children on your poor old mother. The late Mr. Saunders would like you to be more practical."

Margeaux repels the assault like a good Burberry trench does rain. Perhaps if she offers makeup advice, it will smooth over this coarse relationship? Therosine would be so much more attractive if she would just stop dressing as if for a baptism in a water tank. Margeaux does not understand the fashion of piety, any more than the point of it.

"And I'm sure given your taste for fancy clothes, you have plenty in your wardrobe for any work you might get. And the gardener, I think it's a luxury you can't afford. Mr. Saunders had the gardener once a week or every two weeks, if I remember correctly."

Margeaux decides against correcting her on Jorge's schedule, but points out the gardener, simply by being there, provides security and is re-landscaping. "It'll add to the value of the house in case I sell it. And he does all the work of taking care of things."

"Then what's the camera for? Look, Mrs. Saunders, you have no budget for new landscaping or the gardener."

Margeaux smiles, snapping her Fendi baguette clutch shut, refusing to discuss it further and steering the conversation to what matters most.

"Therosine, I'm here to discuss the house in Washington; it's sitting there empty, as you know. I strongly feel it should be sold."

"I agree."

"I took the liberty of contacting an agent. Have you ever been to Washington, D.C.?"

"No, and I have no interest in going. Look at what it did to Mr. Saunders; turned a good man into a sad one. Going there is what killed him."

The comment startles Margeaux. Before she can stop herself, she asks, "Why do you think he stayed there?"

"His brother and the business . . . I guess he had something to prove. I don't really know."

"Do you think he didn't want to come home?"

"Oh no, Mrs. Saunders. More than anything, that's what he wanted. He used to tell me all the time how much he missed home."

Turning away, embarrassed and suddenly newly heartbroken: "I don't know what to think. . ."

"Well, it is all confusing. Just the other day, I was talking to Irving Finkelstein — you know, Mr. Saunders' attorney — I called him about the D.C. house, just to make sure it wasn't in some kind of legal knots that I didn't know about. And he said the strangest thing to me. He asked me if Jewells' father ever came clean. I didn't know what he was talking about, so then he told me that Mr. Saunders told him that Jewells wasn't his son. I was shocked."

"What?"

"That's what he said. He also that Mr. Saunders being in Washington might have something to do with that, that he was trying to fix something."

"Who is Jewells' father?"

"Mr. Saunders didn't mention that. Mr. Finkelstein said he kinda blurted out his thoughts and then seemed to think better before saying more. No mother, no father, no wonder Jewells was such a handful. Guess it don't matter no how. But Mr. Saunders sure did love that boy."

"Yes, he did."

"Well, at least the real-estate part of the D.C. mess can be fixed." Therosine adds, "Mr. Finkelstein give me the green light. We can sell it now. It's the one property I put on the list you asked for."

"You know, I haven't even seen it."

"Looks like a pretty house from the pictures. Delta has fares $69 each way."

"Oh really," says Margeaux.

"Yes. I checked."

"So thorough, Therosine. Griffin always admired that in you," Margeaux says, adding that this is the perfect time for a quick trip. Therosine wishes her luck.

Sadness-tinged happiness, yes, but Margeaux also feels an odd sense of relief-tinged gratitude.

Later, an outrageously inconvenient travel itinerary tenses Margeaux's shoulders and sinuses. As thoughtful as skillful, Jorge knows just where to apply pressure.

Not since *Today in Cincinnati* has Margeaux had to suffer the be-up-and-running 4:30 a.m. schedule. Doing so now inspires unpleasant memories of exhaustion, and the wearing of dark, obscuring sunglasses.

The livery car races her to the airport for the 6 a.m. flight, to leave one ugly airport only to arrive at another, before touching down in New York at 9:15 a.m. A taxi carries her to the psychic, and Margeaux chats by cell with Drexel, who warns the doyenne of the spirit worlds is frighteningly attuned, and to get the greatest benefit from the session, Margeaux should focus solely on her reasons for being there, and little else, lest the revelations head in a terrible direction. "What do you mean?" "You'll find out."

Shortly, on the fifth floor of a West Village apartment

building, she is greeted by Aurora, an elfin-size woman with a prizefighter nose, set off by a slash of red lips and a drape of pearls encircling a black buttony tweed jacket. Margeaux knows Karl Lagerfeld's Chloé when she sees it, but then is thinking, at $1,000 a session, a nose job should not be a hardship.

"It's good to have a trademark, one's own beauty mark, isn't it?" the woman offers, apparently mind-reading Margeaux's harsh critique.

Margeaux is too mortified to apologize, and takes the seat she is being steered toward.

"What brings you here today?" the woman asks.

"I'm trying to relaunch my career. And it's happening, and I'm terrified. I want to know how it's going to go, if I shouldn't get my hopes up. What should I do?"

"Oh, I see. Yes, it's all a little confusing, the fits and starts, the humiliating past experience that's scarred your confidence, shaken your faith in yourself. Picking yourself up is never easy, even when you are about to, once again, enter the spotlight, where you belong." With a flicker and bat of the eyes, she then circles the bull's eye: "Your husband would be over the moon for you . . . Griffin, isn't it? . . . such a noble name, one I imagine very difficult to live up to."

Exactly one and a half hours later, Margeaux steps out into the afternoon sun as if into a new day.

The whirlwind deposits her at the airport just as her

flight is about to close. Margeaux makes a call to Mutti, learning the children are fine and Therosine has just left a message about "cheapy" accommodations in the Washington area, among them near-the-bus-station motels and of course the Holiday Inn, in case Margeaux is too spooked to stay at the house. She texts her nemesis she will be arriving in the nation's capitol in one hour and will report back later in the day after meeting the realtor. To Drexel, just before the plane departs, she offers only, "Ready for takeoff on a direct flight to the future."

At Reagan National Airport, Margeaux is collecting her suitcase and heading toward ground transportation, when she notices a man motioning toward her. "I didn't order a car," she says, just realizing she should have.

"Ma'am, please follow me, Secretary Black is waiting for you."

Hoping to slip in and out of town, she has not imagined she would see him and is thoroughly, even unpleasantly, surprised. She has never forgiven him for publicly blaming Griffin for sloppy records and poor management of their company, in an effort to deflect accusations against himself.

"Well, well, well, Margeaux."

"I don't believe in coincidence, and yet." She leans in for a cheek-kiss.

"I'm just another Oompa-Loompa in the Clinton Chocolate Factory, so most times you'll find me here, coming or going. Just now I'm coming . . . have mercy, if you aren't a breath of fresh, gorgeous air."

"Really, Chief."

"I saw you collecting your luggage as I was going out." His expression, however unreadable, is perfected to compel, with glowing skin a cognac color (an acid peel?) Margeaux finds appealing.

"What brings you to Clintonland on this fine and fair day, and why didn't you call?"

"I'm here to deal with the house. We're going to sell it. You may remember telling me to come get his things."

"That was about a year ago! I hope the house is still there, crime being crime."

"It is. I'm in touch with the realtor you recommended."

"Let me take you . . . "

"No."

"I insist . . . We need to catch up."

Coincidence, indeed.

"Well, if you insist."

Almost immediately the Town Car is in a fuss of traffic. Tempers and the snarl dissipate not far from the airport.

"And where did you say you were arriving from?"

"I didn't say. But Chicago. I'm on way to the BET studios for an interview. The Clinton shit. And, well, you."

"Me?"

"Yes, you. Seems you're the talk of the town.

Surprised?"

"Well . . ."

"I was just about to amuse myself with a little entertainment. *60 Minutes* sent over a CD of an interview about me, asking me to comment. The interview is with you. So I asked myself: What could Mrs. Griffin Jewells Saunders II have to say about me — a man she doesn't know shit about? Let's see."

"That's interesting, they wouldn't even give me an advance copy."

"You aren't a cabinet member of the Clinton administration."

This moment was bound to occur, so no reason to feign innocence or ignorance.

Once the interview starts, almost immediately Margeaux is pained to see Griffin, alive in the digital hereafter. She listens to the voiceover and when she herself comes on, she thinks Parris got it right — burnished beauty that's been through a grave phase — and the dress, the Bill Blass, truly amazing, if only the viewing audience could see her standing, rather than sitting, a position creating a slightly frumpy effect. It then occurs to her that she may not have returned the dress, and the new charges, of about $6,000, will accrue.

"Of course it's nice to hear how well you're coping with the loss of Griffin and Jewells, but here's the part that interests me":

"Many in Washington and Cincinnati expressed

concern about what your husband knew and would
be willing to talk about in terms of his brother, Samuel
Tecumseh Black II, the Secretary of Commerce, a star
of the Clinton administration and a Democratic Party
apparatchik. Almost immediately after your husband's
death, questions of bribery and influence-peddling
swirled around both him and the secretary, and now
there is the grand jury and a special prosecutor. Charges
are expected to be filed any day now. What was your
husband's involvement in the secretary's alleged
schemes?"

"First, it has been devastating to me to have
my husband's name dragged through the mud in
this unseemly way. Chief, as we call the secretary, is
a wonderful man, and it is especially painful to see
his family suffering as they do. As far as I know, the
charges are baseless, part of a witchhunt."

"You feel these allegations are politically
motivated?"

"I do. Many of the accusations against
the secretary and his business relationship with
my husband come directly from the Republican
attack machine, the target of which is the Clinton
administration. There is nothing these hysterics
wouldn't do, including repeating lies that have
already been proven to be just that. As an example, my

husband and I purchased a house in Washington, D.C. That acquisition had nothing to with the Secretary of Commerce, and yet repeatedly the allegation that the property was jointly owned by the secretary and my husband is cited as an example of how the secretary's name and position were used to gain advantage. It's a deliberate lie intended to smear their reputations."

"Tell me about your husband and the secretary. Were they close brothers or like Cain and Abel?"

"Close, absolutely — it's an understatement, really. Their father was Samuel Tecumseh Black, a prominent figure in D.C. politics, as you've already mentioned. Griffin was the illegitimate son, never acknowledged or even seen by his father. This was a blessing — it drove my husband to excel — and a curse — he never felt good enough, I believe. He grew up poor in Cincinnati, Ohio, the son of a housekeeper to wealthy white families, while the secretary grew up in New York and Washington, with all that his father's wealth, power and position had to offer. The brothers first met at their father's funeral, when Griffin, on a whim, drove to New York from Chicago. The brothers both say that they instantly recognized each other, and I have always thought that their bond was even stronger because they — long-lost brothers — were only children at the time of the funeral."

"Mrs. Saunders, your husband and the secretary were two of the most successful cable technology entrepreneurs in the country, owning ten cable stations, a radio station."

"Which of course Secretary Black relinquished his rights to when he became a cabinet member of the Clinton administration."

"One of the controversies around your late husband concerns Premier International Inc., the company jointly owned by the brothers. One strain of the investigations into the secretary's finances focuses on hundreds of thousands of dollars your husband paid Secretary Black for his interest in business transactions that had cost him nothing. Essentially, it's a deal where you don't make any investment and then a few years later you make a profit.

"I don't know anything about their financial arrangements, except that the secretary relinquished his half of the business when he joined the Clinton Administration, as I've pointed out and is on the record."

"Your husband was involved in negotiations to sell cable technology to several Asian businessmen. Two of those businessmen have accused the secretary of extortion, and there appears to be a pattern here, where the secretary made the contacts, and your husband executed the plans and collected the monies."

"I know nothing about the workings of my husband's cable business. He was a businessman, and he had contacts all the over the world."

"The accusation against your husband was that he attempted to sell cable encryption technology to sworn adversaries of the United States, an act which is not only illegal — it carries the weight of treason. And the secretary —"

"My husband obviously isn't here to defend himself, and the secretary has denied any involvement."

"Many believe that your husband knew enough to not only send his brother to jail but to possibly bring the Clinton Administration down. Mrs. Saunders, do you believe your husband was assassinated?"

"I have heard others say such things, including that the secretary himself did it. Imagine that, when in fact he was in Eastern Europe at the time. Having done a short stint as a reporter, and as a former television show host, I know the harm of speculation in the absence of the facts, and I won't engage in it."

"One fact is not in dispute. With your husband's death, a material witness has conveniently been removed."

"I can only say the secretary is a great man who has served his country, and if the President of the

United States is confident in the secretary, who are we to doubt it?"

Margeaux is thrilled with her performance — not a cue missed, nor a false, ugly expression, nor spill of tears, just an appealing, sincere if calculated sadness with glittering lashes — until Chief jabs the monitor off and claps his attention to pull on her.

"Very entertaining, I'm impressed, and I can see you are too. You handled that like a goddamn pro. My problem is, what in the fuck are you doing an interview about me for in the first goddamn place? Margeaux, I'm so pissed off, I ought to push your pretty ass right out this fuckin' speeding car . . . right now."

Margeaux cannot tell if he is joking and reaches into her purse to grab a nail file.

"Goddamn deus ex machina couldn't help me right now, so throwing you out of this car wouldn't affect the outcome one way or the other!"

"You wouldn't, would you?"

"Yes, I sure the fuck would. Either you're an idiot or you think I am — goddammit, you could have at least let me know."

"I don't need your permission."

"A courtesy, I am your brother-in-law." He bangs his hand on the side of the door.

"For whatever that's worth."

"You blindside me, I blindside you. Consider yourself pushed out of a mutherfuckin' speeding car."

He holds up an envelope. Before Margeaux's mind spins and spirals, and eyes fill and flood, he spills the contents on her lap.

"Really, pornography!" Margeaux pushes the images to the floor. "I'm your brother's widow, remember?"

"Take a look. Your husband did. I imagine he was looking at these goddamn tantalizing pictures as he strangled Jewells just before they smashed into the bridge. Thank God he didn't see the video — quite fuckin' entertaining if you're into men sucking each other off and screwing."

She focuses on one of the images of two naked men kissing.

"Recognize anyone?"

"No."

"Look again."

"No, I won't."

"It's your fuckin' stepson!"

Margeaux scans several more photos until she arrives at one with a clearer face shot. "Oh my God! That's Jewells."

"You have to see it to believe it."

"Where did these photos come from?"

"From the FBI. The Cincinnati police were investigating some child pornographers, and voilà, Jewells the gay hustler."

"Hustler?"

"That's the word for pay and play. Here's another: Prostitution! No wonder Griffin lost his head."

"That's not funny," Margeaux says, crumbling into the seat, the photos cascading to the car floor. "Poor Griffin, my poor Griffin." Margeaux can now see Griffin's panic. Aurora the psychic said as much — "Perhaps in a fit, he lost all sense of reason and hope."

"It's pretty goddamn sickening," Chief adds. "That kid had trouble in his blood, just like his fucking mother."

The messy, eruptive kind of crying she scorns prevails. Rather than be seen in such a state, she buries herself in Chief's arms.

"There, there, Margeaux," he says, caressing her shoulder, proving he is capable of compassion. "I know this has been hard on you. I know you must suffer without my brother. You were the crown jewel to him, I hope you know that. He loved you more than anything."

She pulls herself away, first squeegeeing her cheeks and then staring into Chief's veiny eyes. "It was a suicide then, wasn't it?"

"Maybe, but it could have been a homicide . . . a crime of passion? Personally, I think Griffin had another one of those panic attacks."

Margeaux stares out at the hive of traffic on the expressway, hardly able to follow the direction of her ever-changing thoughts.

"Tell you the truth, I think my brother was cracking up. Griffin hated this town. Absolutely hated it. He didn't move way outside the goddamn Beltway for nothing, he did it to get as far away from these muthafuckas as he could. It was supposed to be for investment, not for him to hide in. He was more engaged when he was regularly commuting. He should have just stayed with you and the kids."

Margeaux politely pulls herself away from him. She says she is surprised because Griffin always claimed Washington was the place to be.

"He might have had his run of the chessboard in Cincinnati, but here, he rolled over and played pussy. It was fuckin' embarrassing, and I wasn't about to let him ruin everything we worked for, and was trying to keep the business on course . . . but you know how it goes, shit happens. The shit had a name: porn-star Jewells. And that's how we get a fuckin' pancaked Bentley and corpses. Those pictures. I would have done it too. I would have killed that fucked-up kid too. Idiot!"

Margeaux retrieves the photos from the floor. The other male is LoQuan. She nearly mentions she knows him, when Chief raises his voice loud: "Maybe now you see why you can't do anymore of these goddamn interviews?"

"As you know," Margeaux says calmly, in a low voice and turning toward him: "Griffin left everything to Jewells ..."

"Dumb, dumb, dumb . . . the fool never got around to it. It was an oversight that should have been fixed when Jewells was like fuckin' five years old. That's what I mean. He was just coming apart."

"The result is that I now have to go back to work, since I have been left with nothing but all the responsibility without the available resources to survive, except for Therosine's monthly allowance, which I run out of in a week. Probate could go on forever, and I still might end up destitute."

"Got it. Okay, I was hoping to talk out everything once I knew how this goddamn investigation will go down. Griffin and I agreed a long time ago, before you stepped into the picture, that whoever dies first gives his half of the company to the surviving brother, in this case me, with the understanding that the family would be provided for, in this case you and the children. The problem is, I'm in no position, in my current situation, to do anything about it, until this grand jury nightmare is over. But it's mine . . . and yours. You'll be set."

"Won't the government seize it?"

"No, they can't. Because legally, we are a Bermuda-based company. Something we did right before I accepted this goddamn job, and I'll give credit where it's due, it was Griffin's idea. I gotta say, it's insane to me that he would remember to take care of every little detail about Premier International, but then forget to take his personal assets out of Jewells' name and fuck up everything we had going on in D.C. Go figure!"

"What's happening with Premier International now?"

"Not a goddamn thing. It's in stasis, just like my fuckin' life is until this investigation is over."

"Are there bank accounts in Bermuda?"

"Yep, and in the Caymans. Government can't touch them either."

"Is there a lot?"

"Let's just say we were busy gettin' while the cotton was high. But let's get back to the business at hand. I understand your dilemma, so do what you've got to do, go back to your television career or whatever . . . but here's the thing, Margeaux. You can't use me as your goddamn launchpad."

"I didn't go to them . . ."

"Whatever, you understand what I'm saying, don't you?"

"Yes."

"Good."

The silence between them is filled with the sound of tires on gravel, as they turn up the driveway to Griffin's infamous house.

"How long are you here?"

"Just till the morning."

"You're in luck, there's an opportunity to see and be seen. I have a party — nothing formal, but there'll be heavyweights there, senators and ambassadors. Johnson of BET will be there — he's a good friend — and you pull out your bag of tricks, launch your pretty ass in the Black Entertainment Network universe."

"I don't have any more tricks. I'm just a has-been trying to make a comeback."

"Pity doesn't become you, Margeaux."

"Thanks, I'll remember that the next time I'm begging Therosine for a pittance."

"Good old Therosine — sounds like the name of a cough syrup."

"Did the human expectorant tell you I was coming to town?"

"That's funny . . . why wouldn't she?"

"Yes, Chief, why wouldn't she?"

Silence is his answer.

Then he says, "I take it you don't plan on staying here while you're in town?"

"Well, I didn't bring linens with me, and of course I don't know what condition the place is in."

"And the ghosts . . . that's reason enough."

Margeaux waves as Chief's car retreats down the driveway and out of sight, and she phones Mutti to let her know she has arrived and cousin Mitchell to urge him to call her back ASAP. He does, and she spins out the tale or her understanding of what Chief has told her, to which Mitchell replies, "I remember the porn ring business. Granted the FBI has its ways, and the secretary is a well-connected, powerful man and I guess maybe he could have made Jewells disappear from the story. Although Griffin's not knowing about it just seems unbelievable."

"It does, doesn't it? I don't know what to think about this man. He's capable of anything."

Margeaux puts it all out of her mind, the business at hand is more than enough.

The mess of the yard. The peeling paint. The chewed doorframes. A broken window.

Chief's assessment of the house rings immediately true. It is a beautiful, if sad, empty place. The décor consists of a bed and dresser, an air mattress where Jewells apparently slept, a relic of a desk and a couple used-looking office chairs, an Ikea-like table and chairs in the kitchen, and a box of plastic cutlery. After a year of living here, Griffin had been little more than a transient, like a college student requiring no comforts. Margeaux's impression had always been that he was eagerly awaiting her imprint to make a home of it with beautiful things. Just now, in the dining room, she finds the family portrait propped on the floor. The packaging had been shed, and strangely, its picture side leaning against the wall, as if he had decided against displaying it — which suggests he wished not to be reminded of what was left behind, as if it were unbearable. The image of Jewells calms her — how right she was about him, what a misery he was, no matter what

Griffin did to save him. Amazing how, somehow, some way, this terrible twist in the story of their lives held the unworthy son at the center. In a symbolic act of closure, she unfastens the portrait from its frame, then rolls the print up. She then unfurls and rips it into small pieces for the trash.

Standing in a slant of sunshine on the porch, a surprise calm comes over her. A comforting breeze rustles the trees and a crimson cardinal swoops into the branches of a nearby spruce. A year of turmoil of doubt and guilt finally lift like the dust on the gravel drive, then settles in its new place, to be boxed and archived as memories of the past.

The Mayflower Hotel in downtown D.C. has no available reservations, but she finds accommodations at the Willard. On Griffin's desk, she discovers a card for a driver, one Horace. She arranges a pickup for two hours later.

The Century 21 realtor arrives on schedule. Most of the preliminary work was done by phone before Margeaux left Cincinnati, and in the meeting they now discuss a listing price of $1.2 million. Margeaux is pleased.

"You should take whatever you want before you leave, Mrs. Saunders. Our landscapers and housekeeping will be here as soon as the contract is signed."

"I have, thank you. Donate or discard whatever you want."

Chief has cleared the house of important, business-related files, etc. He then mailed Margeaux the contents of

Griffin's jewelry box and other things he thought she should have.

Margeaux and the realtor walk out onto the porch together.

"I'll have my attorney and the executor of the estate look this over and be in touch. Thank you."

Shortly, Horace the Town Car driver comes to the porch to fetch her suitcase and they are soon on the road back toward the nation's capital.

"I was so sorry to hear about Mr. Saunders," he says, hurling his words to the backseat. "Last time I saw him I drove him over to look at the Bentley. He sure did like that make of car. The Brooklands R. Mulliner it was."

"Why do you think he was so fond of the Bentley?" Margeaux says, suddenly curious.

"He told me he had done business in one in the Cayman Islands and it blew him away."

"That's interesting."

"Something to do with the security — some *Mission Impossible* kind of alarms. Mr. Saunders was acting real strange. He kind of freaked out a little. Really paranoid."

"Why?"

"I don't know. Guess it had to do with the news, huh?"

"Maybe."

"I made a mistake, I told his brother where we was at, and he didn't like it one bit. He fired me . . . so that's how that went."

"Where were you that he didn't want his brother to know?"

"We were at the Bentley showroom. He was buying the car that . . ."

"He crashed."

"Yeah, well . . . It wadn't the car he was upset about, he was just upset . . . real paranoid. Obsessed with security cameras."

"He was under a lot of pressure."

"Well, he sure did like Bentley. You ask me, I think he liked this car so much because he was real gentleman. He wasn't too keen on ordinary cars, but you know what, this is a town of cars where everybody in a suit all look the same because the folks in them all be the same. Everybody's got that look in their eyes, and they all in a kill state and they just don't give a damn about anything accept holding up or taking down the Clintons or whoever be in charge. That's D.C. for ya."

"My husband was a gentleman."

"This place was a bad fit for him."

The bellhop carries her bag inside.

The last time she visited in D.C. was three years ago, for Clinton's swearing-in for his second term as President of the United States of America. She, Griffin, Jewells, Percy and Mutti stayed in a large suite at the Mayflower Hotel. It was bitter winter cold, and during the ceremony Margeaux snuggled in a chinchilla-lined cashmere coat and hat with the collar turned high against her cheek, her gloved hands clapped onto Jewells' while Griffin propelled the stroller bearing snowsuit-clad, two-year-old Percy. Cherish the memory, for the only other time her own happiness included Jewells, with her embracing him in any way, was her wedding day.

A bit of good luck strikes, her hotel window opens onto an uninterrupted, unparalleled view of the White House. At the Clinton inauguration, Chief failed to get invitations for the Saunderses to celebrate with the First Family. Unlike Margeaux, Griffin was unbothered — perhaps the true first sign of his later revulsion for D.C. life — for he had previously met the presidency-bound couple when Chief was head of the Democratic Party. Then, her estimation of her brother-in-law's influence was low, elevated only after he was named Secretary of Commerce, by which point she was less awestruck by the seeming glamour of national politics, seeing it as the filthy mud wrestling match it was. National media was where the action was, not among flinty bureaucrats, including those with the vitality of youth.

She wanders out to the wide busy street, hires a cab to DuPont Circle, stopping for a cappuccino and to speak with each of her children to say how much Mommy misses them and that she will be home soon. The girls babble, Fletcher prattles on about driving off the wrong highway exit, and

Percy cries that Jorge snatched away one of his Barbie dolls. Percy's story is confirmed by Mutti, who also says that she herself had a disagreement with Jorge over chopping down the wisteria vine. "He said you gave him permission." "To take out the flowers and dig up the hibiscus," Margeaux replies. Afterward, she texts Jorge, "Leave Percy and wisteria vine alone!"

She sends Chief a message saying she is staying at the Willard. He texts her that she should meet him at his Georgetown house at seven, and she texts back to meet her at the hotel bar. Warding off her womanizing brother-in-law is no way to spend an evening. She has complained of Chief's flirtation before.

"He's a foxy guy, and can't help it," Griffin had said, to which Margeaux had replied the analogy was more accurately to a wolf.

"He can't help himself. Maybe if you weren't my wife you'd have something to worry about. He's a fool for a pretty woman."

"Do you flirt with his wife?"

"Of course not. I'm not like him. And, to be honest, she's not exactly a pretty woman; handsome, yes, pretty, no. Once upon a time, she definitely was."

"You ever flirt with any man's wife?"

"No . . . and as if I would tell you if I did!"

"Any other women?"

"Mrs. Saunders, you're all I've ever wanted or needed in a woman, so why would I?"

Aurora the psychic had put it this way: "Your husband believed himself fated to you, and that there was no other woman for him."

Why had it been so hard to believe in his fidelity, even after a rock-solid eight years of marriage? Perhaps because of the stability — that's usually when a good man strays. Women, too.

The best to be said about Chief: At least he was honest about his lechery.

She leaves word with double-agent Therosine about the meeting with the broker, offering the figure the agent believes the house should fetch. She then walks in the direction of Georgetown, stopping at several boutiques and taking five-grand revenge on the turncoat.

A few hours later, her hand is in Chief's, about to be kissed: "Mrs. Saunders, a moment worth waiting for."

Sometimes, compliments are just tiresome, despite the worthiness of her new citrus-hued Celine sheath and Hermès lizard heels that send her towering over her shortish brother-in-law, putting at least six inches between them. She plucks a dust sprite from the top of his low haircut, and hooks her arm into his . . . bracing for what exactly?

By chauffeured car, they soon arrive in a sprawling Watergate apartment, where the best of African-American D.C. enthralls. Margeaux postures at Chief's side, activating her public persona like freshly applied parfum. Having been so long outside any spotlight, and being new to the glare of this scene, Margeaux is nevertheless at elegant ease at his side as they work the room. Pulled into her orbit is the B.E.T. mogul, a straight-staring, saturnine man impeccably dressed. She lets Chief do all the work of promoting her resume, even feigning embarrassment over his doing so and relief when he turns away for side conversation.

"My brother-in-law feels the need to both promote and protect me, and only manages to make me feel as if I need him to, when I don't."

"Of course you don't," says Mr. Johnson. "I saw your *60 Minutes* interview."

"I suppose you would have. Everyone seems to have seen it."

"You handled yourself like pro. You managed to be accessible and above it all at the same time."

"That's kind of you to say. I was very reluctant to do it, but I also felt compelled . . . just as I do now to be here with my brother-in-law . . . as the conspiracy wheels turn."

"In my experience, the foundation of politics has absurdity built into it. Imagine our Founding Fathers using the language of liberty and rights even as they hunted, bought, traded and bred their slaves as livestock."

"Yes, you're right, of course . . . which leads us to a silly girl under a desk."

"Yes, it does indeed, Mrs. Saunders. The truth is often unknowable in this town."

Chief, stepping back into the conversation, adds, "Truth is a lying muthafucka."

Mr. Johnson laughs and Margeaux pretends to, and soon the orbit widens as they drift in and out of more introductions and sharp party banter. It is extraordinary that, of all the Griffin condolences, not one comes from anyone who actually knew him. Until, finally, she shakes the hand of Carter-John 'CJ' Workman, the man whose who's-who barbecue Griffin had attended days before the crash.

"Griffin made a strong connection with my uncle. My uncle is a lawyer-diplomat who works on the Rwanda Truth-Reconciliation Commission in Arusha. I saw him maybe three or four days ago, and he asked about your husband. He didn't know, and of course he was shocked and saddened, like all of us were. But he told me something interesting. He saw Griffin a few days after my barbecue. Griffin evidently called him up late one night, sounding a little desperate. Now, my uncle is a gentle, caring, fatherly figure, which is why he's so perfect for Hutu and Tutsi genocide tribunals. My uncle said Griffin had a small breakdown, tears and all; and that he was very anxious and a little frightened of something — 'haunted' was the word my uncle used. Goodness, I was surprised to hear all this, because that wasn't my impression of Griffin, at all, Margeaux. But then again, it's hard to see behind the game face."

Just then, her own game face feels as if about to crack. Her perfected *60 Minutes* poise comes to her rescue.

Near midnight, they leave. On the way to dropping her off at the hotel, Chief lets fly compliments of every kind, from "captivating" to "You scaled Mount Johnson like nobody's business." But the comment that registered was: "I should have had you here to help build the Premier International brand."

"Griffin built that company before you signed on," Margeaux corrects, her tone unmistakably indignant.

"True, but what we needed was somebody smooth and slick — somebody to be me — and that Griffin couldn't do."

"You're suggesting I could be you . . . you're kidding?"

"Easily. You're a killer packaged like a Victoria's Secret model."

"And you're just a killer?"

"In a manner of speaking." He laughs at this, reaching for Margeaux's hand, kissing it.

Margeaux pretends coyness to hide her revulsion. To gain an advantage here, control herself she must.

"I've never wanted any woman more than I have you, and you belonged to my brother."

"Belonged?" Margeaux says. "I married your brother."

"And now you're free."

"I was always free. But I was and am still very devoted."

"I know that about you."

Margeaux changes the subject, chatting about Griffin's D.C. circle of acquaintances, and now wanting more than ever all the details she was devastated to hear in the immediate aftermath of her husband's death. "You mind if we walk? It's spectacular tonight, with that moon. I heard on the news it's called a supermoon, because it's orbiting so close to Earth. "

"Super romantic, too."

Margeaux smiles yes.

They promenade east along Constitution Avenue. From this vantage, all the magnificence of power is captured in the arrangement of monuments and buildings along its length, with the White House at center, all agleam, and the glowing moon high.

"Chief, can we be honest with each other?"

"Of course we can."

"I wonder. Quote: 'Truth is a lying mutherfucka.' How I am to believe anything you say?"

"Truth *is* a lying mutherfucka. But that doesn't mean it isn't truth."

"A truth relativist?"

They walk in silence, he bracelets his arm to hers, and Margeaux feels herself pulled to cross purposes. Flirting could prove risky, given the stakes. But shy of screwing him, even basic honesty is unlikely to come without the promise of more. Yet, there are so many questions — did Griffin commit a crime?; was he set up?; was he going to jail?; was he having an affair? — it seems impossible to highlight the magic one that could singularly unlock the painful others.

And now, looming mysteriously in the narrative, is Jewells. It then seems to Margeaux that her stepson may in fact matter less to Chief in this sad narrative, and she goes out on a limb. "Let's see just how honest you are, and I'll know you're lying and whether I can trust you."

"I'm all suspense."

"Who was Jewells?"

"What?" he laughs. "Cat and mouse, huh? Trick question, huh? Your stepson, Griffin's son."

"Oh, Chief . . . and I had such high hopes."

"He's not your stepson?"

Thinking fast, Margeaux says: "I'll get to the point. What did you promise Griffin to raise your son? That's the part I don't get."

"Margeaux, you know, maybe best to let sleeping dogs lay, especially when they're pitbulls."

"The dogs are dead — and that's your metaphor."

"Yeah, well . . . I didn't promise him anything. I mean, it's not that hard to imagine, Margeaux. Griffin and I, we were young, dumb and full of cum — we were fucking the same chick, some little ho we met in New York, and she got knocked up. And, basically, he did the right thing."

"It only proves just how wonderful and kind my husband was."

"A noble kind of guy." He laughs. "But, Miss Ohio Margeaux, it's hard to be noble, really hard. Never trust a noble man, because his loyalties are always a little fucked up."

"What does that mean?"

"Well . . . guess you asked the wrong question?"

Margeaux plays coy. "Barbara Walters I'm not."

"Good, that's the last thing TV needs. Now, I want to ask you something. Mine is an easy one. Before I ask, though, I want to tell you a few things first. When you started seeing my brother, I had you checked out. I knew about the ballplayers, your moguls and rich Frenchies, and I've seen the pictures from fashion magazines — so why my boring-ass brother? I just don't get that, at all."

"Of all the things you might have asked . . ."

"Your question didn't exactly stop my world?"

They head in the direction of the Washington Monument. The streets are nearly empty. The moon bigger, brighter.

"Is it safe?"

"It is if you've got a Glock, which I do. Don't worry . . . it's all properly registered."

"You are a very dangerous man." Margeaux stops,

facing him. "I should be afraid of you?"

"You asking or just sayin'"?"

"Says the Godfather."

"Says the Chief. Margeaux, you're family, I've got your back, because family is everything. Now answer my question."

"Cliche as it sounds, it's true. A girl wants someone she knows is rock-solid. Before coming to this city, he was a great father to our children and a husband to me. I shouldn't have signed on to the whole D.C. plan. I regret that . . ."

"Interesting that you didn't mention good ole love."

"No, you're wrong, I just defined the love Griffin and I shared."

"You're as boring as he is."

"Yes, I suppose I am."

The White House is now behind them, obscured by the flank and bulk of the IRS, but the full length of the Washington Mall can be appreciated, from the Capitol to the Lincoln Memorial, in the silver-lined moonlight. They cross over to the mall.

"You can't help but feel a stirring in your soul when you look at all this, this . . . well, this vision. It starts with Lincoln's dream for the free nation and ends with legislation of its laws to protect. There's a whole lot left out, but it's pretty simple."

"I hadn't thought of it that way."

"It's Democracy for Dummies."

"This is the most beautiful part of this city, I feel."

"It's like a heady Plato's Retreat . . . the tit of the Capitol building, the cock of the Washington Monument, the pubic hair of the mall. The power and the glory and exaltation. I get a little teary thinking about this incredible experiment, so perfect in its ideas and yet so flawed in its practice."

"You're certainly swept away by it all."

"I am. But that's another conversation for another time, Margeaux. I'm more interested in right now . . . where we left off. Honesty, I believe. On that subject, it's funny that you didn't mention Griffin's connections."

Meaning you? she nearly says, realizing they are alone, there is no one around. No one except George Washington's symbolic representation. Perhaps a failure of imagination, but to Margeaux the monument seems less phallic than a stake in the heart. She says, "That may be because I didn't need his connections. But perhaps you have other connections in mind? Yourself, for instance?"

"That's right. You can have his main connection now … you know that, right?" He takes her arm, pulling her toward him. "The only one that was ever worth something to you."

"Chief, please." She pushes herself away. "It's too late. Really too late. I'm tired. Let's head back, please."

He stops on the spot, jamming his hands into his trouser front pockets.

Fine. Margeaux goes on about the long day and early

departure, and he is unmoved, more aggressive, until she decides she has neither the will nor the energy to tussle with him. "Good night, Chief, thanks for the delightful evening. I'll be in touch, promise."

"Promise? Promise?"

In not waiting for a reply, and in turning away from him, Margeaux knows she is jeopardizing whatever gains this encounter has offered. Yet she does not care, because she knows he will not back down, not let it go . . . ever let her go, just as he likely would not let Griffin go.

Her pace quickens as she heads back toward the hotel. There are twenty-five feet or so between them, when she hears: "I don't know, Margeaux, maybe you're some kind of femme fatale."

Sensing he is following, she pretends to ignore him. Parked cars line both sides of the dark, wide street, making her less visible to passing drivers. She could step into traffic easily enough, if necessary. Where is the press when you need them?

He shouts just loud enough for her to hear him: "You know what that is, don't you?"

Then: "Killer of men."

Then: "All you beauty-queen bitches know how to fuck a man up, make him homicidal or suicidal or just fucking insane. But you, you . . there's a real murderous trend with you. I understand your daddy killed himself too. Guess you must get the killer gene from your Nazi grandparents? Yeah, I know all about it."

Margeaux stops.

"Touch a nerve, huh? Was your daddy a loser, and your momma a killer, pushing him to the brink? Yeah, I know your types. You want to be worshipped — you bitch goddesses — but you chose the weak ones. And you end up having to devour them."

Margeaux turns. Burns. Stares. And when he is standing in front of her, snaps at the top of her voice: "It just kills you to know that I would choose your bastard brother over you — you, the most powerful black man in the United States of America — any day! You would never have been in the running. Ever."

As if suddenly he is aware the world could be listening, he goes silent but catches up with her just as she steps off the sidewalk into the street in time to snag a cab. When it rolls to a stop, Chief opens the door with parting words for her: "You're right about one thing, Mrs. Saunders. I am the first and maybe the last most powerful black man in these United States for a long mutherfuckin' time. God bless America."

Later, in her hotel room, a sleepless Margeaux stands in the window looking toward the White House, atop which looms the moon so enormous it seems on a collision course. The intense brightness electrifies her engagement and wedding rings, the nimbus of diamond brilliance dancing over her hand, making light of this urgent feeling to flee.

The 6:30 a.m. return flight cannot come soon enough.

9

The invitation to meet with the management of WKRQ in Cincinnati comes much sooner than Margeaux has expected.

Parris is unsurprised: "Besides the fact those people in TV land loved you and gave you high approval ratings on *The Magda Show*, everybody who's anybody knows about the *60 Minutes* interview."

"The dull *60 Minutes* interview, according to you."

"No, the primetime-with-America *60 Minutes* interview that hasn't even aired yet. The word is out, you're fabulous again, only better now, after motherhood and the afterglow of triumphing over tragedy and scandal. Hon, what you need to do is think up a great idea to base a show on."

"But I thought what they wanted to discuss was my return to the talk show format, as a co-host. I thought it was for *Today in Cincinnati* or *This Week in Cincinnati* — I don't remember which program is theirs."

"My guess is as good as yours — and please get it right, it's *This Week in Cincinnati*, TWIC, which is worse than TIC. No matter what they want, you should walk in the meeting armed with ideas . . . that way you'll get more out of the opportunity."

"But my own show? I don't know what I'd do for an hour."

"What do you love?"

"What I love and what I'm good at are different things."

"Really? Hon, remember, no depth."

"I don't have depth. I have debt. I'm deep in debt."

"Think fluff and fun, and hey, throw in some smart financial stuff, too."

"Remember those beauty segments I did after I had Percy? What if we turned those into half-hour shows? One week it's about peels, and another about eyebrow and lipline tattooing, and another it's high heels, from fashion to foot problems. We could make it reportage, talking to the estheticians and makeup artists and fashion designers and boutique owners and doctors and scientists, really get behind the scenes. We could interview celebrity women, do makeovers. Features on fashion for children and beauty for girls. Weddings, bar mitzvahs. Beauty-at-large."

"Margeaux-at-Large. Love it! It's perfect. And you've got the cred to do it. International runway model, your face in all the chicest fashion magazines, your storybook marriage that went to hell, your family in high places and even soon in federal prison. You could talk about all that. Make it really personal. I mean, my God . . . you've got it all!"

"How personal is really personal?"

"Well, you don't need to talk about your menstrual

cycle. Actually . . . look, women didn't like you before because you were like the ice princess. Now you're just fabulous, like every other woman with a messy life, only you're nothing like every other woman with a messy life."

Later, in her journal, Margeaux scribbles in Oprah-esque fashion: "We should always reach for bliss. It's there waiting to be grabbed. Just be careful to know your bliss, so you don't grab the wrong thing."

After dinner, she lap-straddles the twins while Percy practices spelling. He has a knack for remembering the letters of his favorite accessories: hose, heels, clutches, rings, reds, all variety of minks. Fletcher reads aloud from *Funny Bunny*, while America folds laundry. Margeaux hates for her to do this in the family room, lest the children aspire to menial labor.

Mutti slumbers in the easy chair, in a round of presleep before turning in for the night. Compassion fills Margeaux. Hiring America was the least she could have done. She has only ever imagined herself as her Mutti's opposite. Yet, with the theme of husband-dead-by-suicide between them and now two generations strong, and the intense feelings that Chief brought out, the similarities are there to see. Similarities having nothing to do with the femme fatale nonsense, but a genetic fate of tragedy in the bloodline. Cinematic memories of her father are becoming more myth than factual, filled as they are with song and smiles and kisses, and not the stuff of real life. How sad that her own children were really too young to have strong memories of Griffin. The girls rarely point to his photo exclaiming "Daddy." The boys hardly mention his name at all. The one who lingers in their thoughts is Jewells . . . son of Chief! It is the sort of truth that will remain an untruth. Margeaux promises herself to be vigilant of her husband's memory.

Once the children are put to bed, she begins to outline how an episode of Margeaux-at-Large might look. The phone rings. LoQuan. Margeaux lets him go into message and shortly hears: "Mrs. Saunders, I ain't heard from you yet. I hope that don't mean you changed your mind. If it do, I got something else for you. Let's call it the offer you can't refuse."

Margeaux waits long enough to summon the necessary outrage and disgust to set up what must be a photo-finish to this criminal tale. Then, pushing the button to record the conversation, she calls him back: "Sorry, I had to go away. And I'm also sorry to tell you, I'm not interested in your offers. I'm flattered that you think so highly of me, but the answer is no. Now, if you don't tell me where to return the boots, I'll be getting rid of them."

"What, you don't like Gucci?"

"No, I actually don't . . ." It occurs to Margeaux that, in this instance, loss of poise and calm might be a good thing " . . . and if you really knew my taste, you'd know that . . . wouldn't you? I'm not talking about the clothes."

"I do know your taste. And you should like them. They'd look great on you."

"I'm talking about your ill-gotten gains."

"My what?"

"Never mind, I have to go. Get the address to me and I'll make sure you get the boots back."

She disconnects the call, knowing he is relentless and a P.S. is on the way. Sure enough, he leaves the following message: "You know, Mrs. Saunders, I thought you and me could do business. So I'm gonna tell you what I'm gonna do. You might have noticed the pictures of me and Jewells never got out in the news. It's because we was minors. Well, just like you, I got my own copy of the video — that's where the pictures come from. Before the police come in on it, me and Jewells beat those white faggots up when we figured out what they was up to and we stole their camera. So, guess what I'm gonna do?"

Still recording, Margeaux calls him back. "What are you going to do?"

"You should have worked with me. I mean, Mrs. Saunders, all you had to do was like buy the damn shit."

"What are you going to do with the video?"

"You'll find out, won't you?"

"You'd humiliate yourself like that? Pornography. Gay pornography?"

"No, I'd humiliate you like that."

"You're blackmailing me?"

"Look at this way, I'm sparing you from folks talking behind your back and laughing at you. Wouldn't want to fuck up your future career."

Margeaux breathes in calm and allows it to rise to her outer self. "And if I do buy the boots and the Ralph Lauren, you'll give me the video?"

"Yeah, but the price has gone up. The sale is over. Don't worry, you still get them for a fuckin' steal . . .ha, ha, ha, ain't that funny?"

"How much?"

"Ten grand?"

"I don't have that kind of money."

"Yes, you do. I know all about y'all Griffin Jewells Saunders. I know Jewells owns houses and apartment buildings. I told dumb-assed Jewells, but no . . . "

"Know what?"

"Jewells was a fuckin' chump . . . and you hated him, so don't even ack like you offended and shit. I'm the one that figured his daddy's scam out. And that's why I know you can get the money. Call me back in an hour and tell me you got it or I'm fuckin' calling up a new friend of mines in the media."

What scam? Pacing around her bedroom, suddenly frightened of where this could be going. Whatever it is, there is nothing to be done about it now but see it through. At worst, the children would be tarnished, fighting against rumor, gossip and jokes for the rest of their lives.

Safety concerns jump ahead of all others. Jorge proves that his devotion is without limits and is on his way over, no questions asked. He has a wife and children; America has mentioned that the wife is nice but that Jorge is more American than she is. Margeaux is unclear what this means but imagines it has to do with his infatuation with her.

Next, on a call with cousin Mitchell, she describes LoQuan's blackmail and then listens as he offers a summary of his research, from porn ring to high-fashion-accessories theft ring. In her mind, LoQuan need only be arrested immediately, minimizing the consequences.

"But Margeaux, the conversation you recorded isn't proof that he committed a crime. He could be pulling a fast one, to get money. Far as we know, he could have found the boots."

"In my size? He's fencing the merchandise, if not stealing them outright. I'll buy them and get them and you'll have your evidence."

"I doubt he's doing the stealing, it's not like boots like those go missing without being noticed. You didn't actually see him deliver them?"

"No, but I have a security video that's showing him. Also, wouldn't the boots have his fingerprints?"

"Yes, but that's also a problem. A lot of people's fingerprints are probably on them, doesn't mean he took them. After all, you did say he works in the stockroom. On the other hand, the blackmail is maybe good enough, given the other recordings. Those we can use."

The hour is late, and Mitchell promises that first thing in the morning, he will get in touch with the police and let them take it from here. Margeaux promises to send the audio of the blackmail and the boots he left at her house. She also promises not to call LoQuan again, and to phone the police immediately should he return. Mitchell is weak, she concludes — no drive, no moral core, just a tiresome cautiousness. If left to him, she could be killed.

Way outside her comfort zone, Margeaux is toying with her phone, trying to forward the recordings to Mitchell and to figure out what all this means, where her life at this bizarre moment is going — when it occurs to her that if this truly is the launchpad, she had better figure out a way to get herself in position. How to make the most of it.

She calls LoQuan. Summoning her best shaken voice: "Mr. LoQuan, hear me out. Because I like you, I'll do what I can to help. I don't want you to get into any kind of trouble. I'd like for you to get to wherever you're going."

"You can do $10,000 cash."

"You know I can't."

"No, you can . . . and you will . . . by tomorrow night."

"The bank is closed Sundays."

"Then Monday morning. Use the ATMs now and it

won't look so suspicious when you get the rest."

"How do you know I won't contact the police?"

"Because you know this whole sorry city will be laughing at you."

"Okay, LoQuan, you do know me . . . I'll admit it. But I also know you: You're so much better than this. You should be a stylist or a personal shopper at the very least, you're that good."

"I know I'm good, and you're right, I am better than this, but a nigga's gotta do what he's gotta do."

"What if I can't get it all?"

"Monday morning."

"And you'll bring the Ralph Lauren tuxedo, the Chanel clutch. . . and you're right, I love the Marc Jacobs too; definitely bring the handbag."

"I know you like a book, Mrs. Saunders. And yeah, I'll have it all."

To Mitchell again: "He'll be here Monday morning. Have your guys here at dawn, to play it safe."

"Margeaux? I told you not to speak with him."

"He'll disappear if we don't do something now."

"Cousin, I really want to help. I want to tell you no problem, I can show up with an undercover team, but there are always problems. I'll do what I can. Worse comes to worse, you could get the police once LoQuan's there with the stolen goods. As a fallback, get yourself a couple of security guards, just in case."

Disconnecting, Margeaux notices light in the carriage house. There's a text from Jorge.

Her precious Percy knocks on the door. She assures him she will be with him shortly, she has just one more call to make.

Bringing Parris in the loop is risky, if with a payoff.

"It's even better than *60 Minutes*," he screams, near giddy while listing the possibilities.

Leaving out the fact that a police presence is uncertain, Margeaux says, "I want you to get a couple of cameramen. We'll rig the carriage house so it's all caught on tape. We have to do this before the police get here. Make it one tomorrow afternoon. Can you handle it?"

"Hon, I've just had my first orgasm in months. It's so exciting."

"Not for me. I've got crow's feet."

"We'll just have to do a little makeup — let's call it your ambush look!"

Margeaux texts Jorge that she will come to him in thirty minutes. Percy and Fletcher are waiting their turn. Margeaux scatters her kisses wide, and tries to read a bedtime story. She marvels at this interlude of normalcy.

Her next move is inspired, popping into her head. She phones Chief. "Please call me, it's important."

Shortly, his voice fills her ear. He is in Houston, he

claims.

"I want to talk about what happened in D.C., but not now. Now, we've got a big problem."

"We?"

"In the photos you showed me of Jewells . . ."

"Stills from a video. . ."

". . . you didn't say anything about the Asian man he's in the photos with. His name's LoQuan Johnson, and he's about to blackmail me."

"Jesus-goddamn-Mary-Joseph."

"He recognized me at Saks, and now he's harassing me. He wants ten thousand dollars. I've contacted my cousin at the District Attorney's office, but I need your help. Could you get your FBI men to come around here ASAP. LoQuan is coming by here Monday morning for the money. I'm afraid he might hurt us."

"I'll take care of it. I'll get the goddamn Navy Seals if I have to. Till they get there, I know Griffin keeps a gun around there. But don't do anything stupid!"

Margeaux believes the gun is gone, but rummages through Griffin's closet anyway, without success.

Her final move of the night gets Jorge's full attention. Pillow talk includes a redacted confession about the danger around them. He worries that he and America could get in trouble with the police.

"We don't want to get deported."

"You won't be. It's nothing to do with you. The police will come to arrest LoQuan. They have nothing to do with immigration."

"No way. I go. I come back when police and TV people go."

Margeaux's emotion is not an act.

"You promise?"

"I promise, Señora Saunders."

As a parting gift, he will make arrangements for two legal friends to work as her security guards — "They gonna act like gardeners."

Come Christmas, she will be ever so generous.

10

Margeaux's rapid rise to TV show host had a rough start. Her first career break had been a brief stint as a TV news reporter in Chicago. Her beat was the stuff of crime novels. "Not at all a pretty job for such a pretty woman," offered one of a pair of flirty, annoying tech crewmen daily crisscrossing the city with her to cover the endless robberies, shootings, stabbings, homicides, blazes, burnings and breakdowns of one kind or other.

Clearly, the true reason she had been hired, quite literally, was to make attractive even the ugliest stories, to put a pretty face on bloodshed and carnage. Her predecessors had been beauties who had arrived dreaming of Peabody Awards and fled grateful to be alive — many completely changing their careers, according to the same crewman. The job required nerves of steel, but also laser focus, both traits Margeaux had in abundance thanks to pageant training. No matter the horror, her main concern had been striking the right on-camera tone: a seriousness somewhere between the grave and the glib. She quickly learned to hunker down into the fact-finding and shaping of her script for the smooth live delivery, the final punctuation of which was a twinkle of mischief. That most murders and shootings were covered after the fact kept her a safe distance from danger. She would arrive on the scene, conduct interviews and give a full 30-to-60-second report, while the injured were triaged and ambulanced away and the deceased drained of blood where they lay. She described it to Mutti as "standing on the shore at the end of a cyclone," claiming missing the action never bothered her in the least, since she was biding her time until she could finagle an on-set situation.

The lone exception — a violent crime in progress — also marked the end of her beat patrol. Her team had gone to investigate a shooting and hostage. The location was not Cabrini, the dreaded public housing project so often the backdrop for many of her most horrific broadcasts.

A harsh northwesterly wind had hurled across Lake Michigan, bringing Arctic cold and bone-penetrating dampness. Margeaux shivered in her parka as she and the crew rushed toward Humboldt Park. A crowd stood behind the police barricade at North Washtenaw Avenue, pointing to a freestanding dilapidated three-story rust-colored house, where a domestic dispute had resulted in a homicide. Margeaux proceeded as usual, gathering information. The suspect was a crazy brute: "He ain't right in the head, always beating up on her, and every coupla months, they go at it, a lot of yelling and cursing but mostly the police don't be called ''cause everybody know that just how it be with them, but this time, the screaming came and then pop!" said one of women Margeaux interviewed. "This time be different because she got her another man, that who dead up in the yard, and I believe he done kilt her too. Guess they three kids be his hostages now," said the woman's friend.

Margeaux went live, completely unaware that she would soon be in the national spotlight. She was on camera no more than four seconds, when she turned to indicate the building behind her, and both she and the viewing audience saw a very small naked brown body smash through the upstairs window and fall to the ground. Gunfire from the same window quickly followed, spraying the street. Margeaux heard whizzing sounds, and ducked down just as Dirk, the cameraman, moaned "oh, fuck" before dropping the video recorder mounted on his shoulder and falling to the ground. The camera equipment struck Margeaux on the head, knocked her unconscious. The EMT revived her just in time to glimpse the fatal mess of Dirk's neck.

In the hospital, Margeaux admitted to Mutti, "I wasn't ever afraid out there. I felt uncomfortable around those projects, who wouldn't? And I think the thing that helped me control myself had nothing to do with the fact that my job was on the line, it was that I knew I would never be in those people's shoes, I haven't, I don't and I will never have a life like theirs, and I have the choice to not ever set foot there again, because I could always quit a job and get another one."

Just now, down the rabbit hole of a dream, those words chase Margeaux as she runs through cosmetics at Saks, with LoQuan on her heels? "I'm gonna fuck you up."

If it is a sign of what is to come, she will either live to see another day in every possible way, or the end is near. Having the life Margeaux has had, with its theme of privilege adding coherence to even significant breaks in storyline, she knows that all will be well, and that she dwells in the realm of the positive, for in her future is the breakout breakthrough, the birth of the Margeaux brand. Not just the national headlines, but book deals, movie options, a makeup line: Margeaux Cosmetics.

Sunday morning, the children especially are displeased that America will not be coming back today. Percy shrieks with anger and Fletcher sulks, butting the heads of his army men in combat. The girls scream because it is what they do, and Mutti complains as is her wont: "I hope you're planning to stick around. For the thousandth time, I can't handle the children without help."

Margeaux holds back on what is going on — just as she downplayed the dangers of her Chicago crime beat — for fear of the reaction. But the possibility of the family in danger is real enough that she phones the security firm recommended by Mitchell. Mid-call, she imagines a standoff with the FBI and LoQuan, and decides to also book a hotel room for Mutti and the children for the next two days. She then calls America.

America has no babysitter for her own brood, and Margeaux suggests she bring her tots with her to the hotel for a holiday.

Mutti is not buying the reasons for these abrupt new plans, and a showdown tests her grace under fire.

"I'll tell you everything, but you have to promise me you won't try to change my mind."

"Margeaux, if we're in some kind of danger . . ."

"We are."

"Out with it."

The specifics about photos and the video starring Jewells and LoQuan the hustlers come out easily, as does the stolen merchandise, blackmail and bait for a trap. She gives false emphasis to the FBI as instigator of the effort, and explains why she is helping them, and how the sordid story is going to go public inevitably, because the Chief connection will set off a news-cycle storm.

Mutti easily zooms in on the Griffin dilemma, which Margeaux counters with Chief's hellish interpretation of the last moments of Griffin and Jewells.

"My goodness, I don't even know what to say."

"I do. The sooner LoQuan is caught, the better. So please don't quarrel with me. It's something I have to do. For Griffin's sake . . . my poor Griffin! Just help me get the children together."

"My heart just breaks for Jewells. It's very sad, the poor kid, to have gotten into such a hole."

"Why do you always come to his defense? He was horrible, rude, disrespectful, willful, destructive. This *shit* is all because of him. *Him*, not anyone else."

"Knowing what you know, and yet you have no sympathy. He wasn't a bad kid, any more than little Percy is bad . . . and any more that you were bad in your early teens. And I'm not just talking about the business with Thornton Childs. I'm talking about you making my life a living hell after your poor father passed away, but I don't guess you remember that? Why would you? Well, let me tell you, Margeaux, you were not much different than Jewells with the acting out. The difference is that you had beauty pageants and a mother who never let you out of her sights. The one thing that mattered to Jewells was his father."

"Oh, now you're saying it was all Griffin's fault?"

"No, I'm not saying that it's anybody's fault. I'm saying that Jewells was a confused kid. That's all."

"Please stop."

"I don't understand. It's too much."

"I don't understand either. Why all this had to happen? Well, there's enough blame to go around, but like it or not, I have to own it. My children, my house and the mess my husband and my porn-star stepson left me to clean up when they intentionally smashed into a bridge! Now, we can talk about how lost he was and horribly selfish I am after this monster is in jail, but at this moment, Mutti, what I need from you is a hand, not your lip."

"Fine."

Anger, even controlled, ill-suits Margeaux, though the venting releases held-back pressure, however misplaced. She takes a pause in the bathroom to collect herself. By the time the stress of current events is resolved, she knows the few gray hairs will have proliferated, forcing a reckoning with a complete hair-coloring, an act of surrender she has steadfastly resisted instead opting for a targeted approach. There's a procession of worrisome blackheads marching along the left brow-bone, an insurgency that can only be countered by an emergency acidic skin-peel. All to be dealt with soon enough, for the future is bright and beautiful, despite the problematic present.

Just breathe . . . inhale . . . exhale.

Her calm restored, she still does not apologize and is unmoved as mumbling Mutti packs for the children for the next few days. Bringing the boys onboard means promising Percy they will go by the downtown Saks to see the fall collections, and Fletcher will get an authentic Bengals helmet to wear to a live game. Mutti gets a kiss and hug and watery-eyed thanks. Finally, her gang pile up into the Suburban and Margeaux swears she will see them first thing in the morning. Tearfully, she remains waving in the driveway even after the car is out of sight.

Alone, she takes in this place she has happily called

home the last eight years, with its enviable architecture and curated landscaping. She wonders whether the generations of Wurlitzers who built it as their primary residence were a screwed-up lot. The property values suggest such dwellings are seldom home to prominent people with troubled lives, and she imagines a drumbeat among the neighbors to run the Saunderses out before real estate values plummet. From the moment she first saw it, the house's existence seemed destined to intersect with her own, but now it feels neither fabulous nor fateful but star-crossed. It is just another expensive house, one of many in an exclusive part of town.

"Don't go to pieces now," she warns herself, popping into the house for a tinkle and tweak. A new nude lipgloss with the prettiest shimmer of copper brings her slightly around, inspiring her into action rather than pity.

After checking the security cameras and alarms, she is on her way out, when she makes a fateful decision. Instead of the Audi keys, she grabs the ones to Griffin's Jaguar. She holds them up, looks out toward the garage, finding the car is in its usual place. Soon, sitting behind the wheel, she crumples, shaking the steering wheel, in a snotty, teary, chest-wracking cry. Suddenly, Griffin is there, standing near the lawn equipment, whole from head to toe. But for the miracle of Dior mascara with breakthrough emotion-resistant polymers, she would not have so clearly witnessed the moment. Husband and wife behold each other, with clear-eyed

Margeaux refusing to blink him away. But go away he must, although not before apparently inspiring her to reach under the seat, where she stumbles upon a pistol, a Saturday night special not much bigger than a cocktail napkin and its shape reminiscent of a fragrance bottle she has seen before. In stark terms, it suggests a terrible ending. Holding it is arresting … breathtaking. Excitement and fear compete to win her state of mind, with no clear victor as she anxiously places it on the floor under the seat on the passenger side.

Nevertheless, the world is righted between Mr. and Mrs. Saunders.

Mitchell agrees to meet her at the office, and at noon Margeaux brings the designer-fashion-made evidence to him at City Hall. She has not yet figured out how to transmit the recordings of her incriminating conversations with LoQuan. He suggests she leave her phone behind to let his technical team figure it out.

"Can't you just program another phone with my information?"

"We'd need a court order for that. That's effectively wiretapping. I'm sure you don't want us listening in on all your calls."

"Not indefinitely, just for the next couple of days. I'm giving you permission to eavesdrop. Why don't you just do it?"

"It's not up to me. We have to get a court order; otherwise, it would be inadmissible evidence. That's the law,

Margeaux. We don't fight crime by committing crime. And we don't have time, but I can try to speed things up. "

"How long will it take with your technical people?"

"Depends on whether anyone is here." He gets on the phone. Then: "Well, our tech guy isn't in his office. Can't you hang out awhile?"

"Can't you at least record the messages into your voicemail?"

He agrees, perhaps mainly to keep Margeaux from screaming.

Each readies their phone, and soon the audio LoQuan comes to life. It is simplistic to believe Jewells had deliberately cast this grim pall over the family. She cannot imagine what LoQuan did to persuade him into such depraved behavior.

Even Mitchell seems surprised. He holds up a thick file marked Juvenile Records. "This came yesterday."

"It certainly took long enough."

"Juvenile records are sealed for a reason. Anyway, LoQuan is a hustler in more ways than one. His is not your typical tale. He was actually born in the Philippines, not in California as he claimed. The father dumped the boy and the mother when he was a child. It seems his mother came to the States to find the father. He was in Oakland, California, amassing a long rap sheet, and she left LoQuan there. Now the father, a native of Cincinnati, came back to hide among his family, and he and the boy were living in Over-the-Rhine, when the father was murdered in a gun battle. It was drug-related. The family took the boy in, but he was apparently sexually molested and removed from the home and at eight ended up a ward of foster care. Stays at juvenile detention followed. He stabbed a man nearly to death, but apparently in a sexual assault situation."

"Why would Jewells get entangled with someone like him?"

"You yourself have said LoQuan's charismatic — very good looking and clearly somebody who knows how to get his way. Jewells was pretty vulnerable and troubled, which likely made him susceptible. It happens to a lot of young kids, even those with doting parents and privilege, they just get caught up with the wrong people. We see a lot of that in my business. One of the many hazards of children."

"He can't not have known what sort of person he was dealing with."

"Indeed, Margeaux — that's why I'm saying you should be very careful. You don't know what this character is capable of."

Margeaux leaves the Gucci boots with Mitchell, who all but promises to have the police on the scene to stake out the place. To her question of whether she should cancel the security, he says no. She decides against mentioning her call to Chief. The more law enforcement the better.

On the way home, Parris reassures her that he and his crew of one will be there; of course some three hours later than the time she requested. Team Margeaux is indebted to him, but no question he is not the person to depend upon, push come to shove.

Pedicures are so relaxing, but she is too wound up to submit. Instead, she decides to stop at the teller machine, withdrawing the maximum she can from all her accounts, totaling $3,000, just in case there's no law enforcement and the amount can hopefully lure LoQuan away.

Finally, she pulls into the garage, and there again, standing in the same place as before, is Griffin — suddenly more present in death than in life. Margeaux feels the love of her husband as in the beginning . . . a guardian angel. An urge to cry shudders through her, but a chance glance in the sideview mirror reveals LoQuan, strutting up the driveway with several shopping bags. Griffin's car has an emergency 911 button that is linked to GPS, one of many measures taken in his state of paranoia as a property owner in high crime areas of the city.

"Help, I'm about to be robbed." She whispers her address to the operator and disconnects, while fumbling for the gun under the seat, without luck. She then turns on the recorder and then slips her cellphone in her purse, visibly shaking . . .

Just breathe . . . inhale . . . exhale.

Then, she emerges from the car, and with her eyes focused on him, stops in the sightline of the zoom video camera, looping her purse over her shoulder.

"LoQuan, what happened to Monday?"

"Hey, like, I was on Madison Road, waiting for you to drive by."

"Well, you came for nothing. I don't have the money yet."

"Yeah, well, I figured that, but I also know you. Whatever you don't got, you can pay in other ways."

"What other ways?"

"That depends on what you've got."

"Not much — $3,000."

"That's cool." He puts the shopping bags down. "I know you must be like real excited to get the Chanel bag and shit."

"Thrilled. I could hardly sleep last night thinking about it."

"You a clothes ho. I knew that the first time I seent you."

"And when was that exactly?"

"Fuck, first time I come over to Jewells' place. Me and him was just hanging out, and I seent you coming out of the house. You was just wearing a tight red dress and sandals, but it was the way you was wearing it . . . and I was like, wow, this is one fine woman."

"What a charmer you are." She giggles. "It's hard for me to make you out. On the one hand, selling stolen retail, and the other, a personal shopper who really gets it."

"I'm just a businessman trying to make his way in the world. I see an opportunity, I go for it. How much cash you got?"

"Only three thousand . . . I just came from the bank."

"Give it to me."

The curse of the junkyard purse strikes. Margeaux has to remove it and set it on the car hood to extract the money.

The veranda camera should spy the extortion exchange. While he is counting, she peeks to see if her cell is still recording; it is, though what it will actually pick up is anyone's guess.

"I was hoping for a $1,000 bill. You ever seent one?"

"I don't think so."

Catching her off guard, LoQuan snatches the purse, stepping away from her. "Like I was saying . . . President Grover Cleveland on it. Pretty cool. President James Madison is on the $5,000 bill. I never heard of those mufuckers."

He stuffs the money inside.

"Take what you want, I just need my keys, my wallet and I'd like the purse too."

"No. I know a Birkin bag when I see one, and I got a cousin who would love this shit, so what if it's used."

"Okay," Margeaux says, trying to sound as if having fun. "What do I care, I'm getting some of the must-haves I must have." Steadying both breathing and nerves, she goes for the shopping bags. She takes the Chanel clutch from its box, acting annoyed that she will soil the ghostly white satin, damage the paillettes dripping with pearls. Almost against her will, she is moved . . . shaken by beauty, before reality stares her down.

"Tell me I don't know your taste?"

"No one knows me better, LoQuan . . . I'm so amazed by your genius."

"Word?"

Clueless as to a response, she goes "tite."

He seems to find this hilarious. Margeaux ignores him, holds the bag, trying to pose as "advertising" as possible for LoQuan but really for the camera. She then summons equal pretend-concern for the state of the other items, slowly going through each box, noticing that not all of the inventory is present.

"LoQuan, where's the Ralph Lauren tuxedo?"

"Sorry, Mrs. Saunders. You snoozed . . . I unloaded it on this other TV lady. Candy Cane, you know her?"

"I do."

"She knows you too. She wants the Marc Jacobs, but I got it for you."

Margeaux, scooped? Not if she can help it.

"I can't believe she bought stolen merchandise from you."

"Why not? You just did."

"Well, given the fact that you're blackmailing me."

"You had your chance. You forced me to it. You could have had a lot more with me." He winks. "But these fuckin' games, yes, no, maybe."

"I thought you were gay."

"Can I call you Mar*GO* . . . Mar*GO*, you shouldn't get the wrong idea about the pictures. I ain't like that. It was for the money. I do shit for money, like a whole lot of straight-up niggas doing gay porn. Hole is hole. To be honest, I like an old girl like you, I got just what you need . . . yeah, baby."

Old girl!

"And mines is better than your Mexican lawnboy's."

An emotion rises in Margeaux that can only be described as violent. Mindful of the video camera and hopeful of the imminent arrival of the police, she puts herself in a facial-massage state of mind, his voice little more than white noise. Short of tackling him first, the purse is beyond getting, and the only option seems to drag the scene out till the police show, edging ever closer to the lawn tools. She steps to the right of him, but in a way that pivots them both for perfect on-camera close-ups.

"You're so handsome, a face model, an original look . . . Tyson Beckford has nothing on you. So, you know this old girl is tempted, but if you don't mind, I've got to go to my children, and I have a million things to do. Can I have the pictures?"

"I was lying, I ain't got no pictures or no video. The police got that shit. I had to get your attention."

"You tricked me?"

"Yeah, guess I did."

"Well, then, I guess we're done."

"Now, you know I ain't leaving here without those diamonds. Rings and the Cartier earrings, please. I know that's what they are, 'cause I saw them in your jewelry box."

"You've got to be kidding me."

"Kidding? Me? MarGO, I know what's up. I came all surprise and shit, 'cause I know you were going to try to set me up. Y'all some cold-blooded muthafuckas. Jewells schooled me good about you, and like I know you hated him and his sorry, lying daddy, none of y'all gave a shit. Y'all rich African Americans supposed to be better than niggas, but y'all ain't shit. Now, bitch, give it up before I stuff that Chanel down your fuckin' throat."

Before she figures her next move she has already made it: raising her ring-free hand and clawing him in the face. The tumult lasts only a few seconds, in which she feels hands seize her throat, squeezing back her screams, and then, suddenly, the jammed air freed as her body rams the lawn tools, the hoes, rakes and hedgers clattering loudly. In the struggle, she hits the ground, his weight fully topping her. His hand finds a new hold on her neck, while hers grabs the sharp side of shears. The gasps are her own, lasting only until the first sprinkle of blood. The glint of the dripping blade in his shoulder briefly hovers above her face. "Ouch, that hurt," LoQuan smirks as if having fun. Popping bullets bring about a stop, his lips landing close enough to her cheek for a goodbye kiss.

It is a tabloid denouement that, after the unedited video

and cellphone audio of the entire exchange are leaked to both
the press and the internet, Margeaux will explain ad nauseam
to TV and radio shows audiences, print journalists and,
finally, in a one-on-one interview, to the queen of daytime talk
shows, Oprah:

"Even before the police came and saved me, I felt the
spirit of my husband was protecting me. Up until the moment
I lost control of the situation, I was focused on playing along,
letting LoQuan say all that would be needed to put him
behind bars. But the horrible things about my family — no
one will ever know just how fine a man my Griffin was, what
he went through, how he suffered, suffered for the sake of
family, for Jewells, a confused, easily misguided kid not
unlike many of the children we hear about all the time these
days — America's lost children. And to have my Griffin
trashed in this deeply personal way, with such ugly, vicious
lies, and with such venom — it's a good thing I didn't have
the gun. To look at LoQuan you would never imagine such
a criminal mind, but it just goes to show you should never
judge a book by its cover."

THE END.

To

Albert Newman Gentry II,

my fatherly uncle
most cherished and missed.

ACKNOWLEDGEMENTS

My ever-gratitude to the dear ones who gave both their support and expert points of view.

Inspired readers:

Tanya Gure, Sasha Dees and the ladies of South Beach: Carolyn A., Carolyn B. and Vanessa Gentry.

Brilliant editors:

Renate Elisabeth Nosarios, Claude-Albert Saucier and Molly Frances.

Fabulously quirky designers:

Tzu-Wen To and Fiona Ip.

Champion's champion:

my tireless publicist, marketer and partner in all things books: Michele Karlsberg.

Disclaimer: This is a work of fiction. Names, characters, businesses, places, events and incidents are either the products of the author's imagination or used in a fictitious manner. Any resemblance to actual persons, living or dead, or actual events is purely coincidental.

Also by the author:

Finlater
Toss and Whirl and Pass

Discover more about the author's work,
upcoming readings and future publications at

shawnstewartruff.com